THE HOLY LAND

THE HOLY LAND

ROBERT ZUBRIN
POLARIS BOOKS
LAKEWOOD, COLORADO

241606

Doctor Berger's bewilderment was equaled only by his outrage. "Now see here, officer," he said to the leader of the FBI agents who had just broken into his comfortable Seattle home. "There is no need for this. In this family we all support the war effort against the Minervans, of course, but there is no need for us to live like refugees. Melissa and I both have jobs here in Seattle, and a house, and the boys are doing well in an excellent school. It would be crazy for us to leave here to go and live in a tent camp."

"You have no choice. You are Kennewickians, and can only live in Kennewick." Agent Wilkes pointed to the door. "Now stop arguing and get in the van. We have other refugees to pick up."

Melissa was desperate. "You want us to leave right now? Can't we at least pack some possessions?"

Agent Wilkes shook his head. "No, certainly not. Possession of property by refugees is counter-productive. We need you to be as miserable as possible, so as to elicit the maximum amount of pity from Galactic observers."

The Bergers were aghast.

Wilkes turned to the couple's three boys, aged 8, 10, and 12. "Hi boys, ready to fight the Minervans?"

Tommy, age 8, held up his hand with his fingers shaped to suggest a six-shooter. "You bet mister. Bang! Bang!"

The agent smiled. "That's the spirit son, you'll make a wonderful martyr."

Melissa quickly snatched her smallest son away from the government man. "What are you talking about, martyr? He's just a child. If you want to fight the Minervans, send soldiers, grown men."

Wilkes shook his head. "We tried that. It didn't work. We're sending children now, because it makes the Minervans look really bad when they kill them. But don't worry, as soon as each of your boys is martyred, the government will send you a handsome cash bonus, guaranteed, within 10 business days of the event."

Melissa stared at the agent in silent horror. Then she felt a shove from behind, as strong arms pushed her and her family out of their door.

The Holy Land

Polaris Books
11111 W. 8th Ave, unit A
Lakewood, CO 80215

www.polarisbooks.net

Manufactured in the United States of America

First Polaris Books Edition 2003

Cover image of Earth provided by ORBIMAGE. © Oribital Imaging
Corporation and processing by NASA Goddard Space Flight Center
Book and cover design by Bill Floyd of Fidlar Doubleday

ISBN 0-9741443-0-4
Library of Congress Control Number 2003093079

To my father, Sergeant Charles Zubrin,
who, standing on the deck of his troopship leaving San Francisco Harbor
in December 1943, realized that it was as good a time as any to sing.

Chapter 1

The President stared at his Science Advisor in disbelief. "So, what you are telling me is that Kennewick, Washington, has been taken over by a bunch of space aliens."

"Minervans, sir," Dr. Beasley said, peering through his bifocals. "They call themselves Minervans."

"And who are these Minervans, and what do they want?"

"They claim to be refugees from oppression in the Central Galactic Empire. They say they need a place of their own, and since Kennewick is their ancient homeland, they've come to reclaim it."

The President shook his head. "That's got to be pure hokum." He turned to his CIA Director. "Fred, what do we really know about these guys?"

Fred Collins was ready with his report. "OK, here's what we've got. They're human, of generally Caucasian appearance, but of a somewhat peculiar type, being all of slightly above average height, with medium build, gray eyes, brown hair, and high cheekbones."

Beasley interrupted. "DNA analysis from hair fragments shows significant resemblances to sequences found among Hungarians, Finns and Basques. We've also identified some linguistic cognates to the same groups."

The President was appalled. "A mixture of Finns, Hungarians, and Basques. How disgusting."

Collins nodded. "Indeed. In any case, they landed about two months ago, and immediately started to buy all the property they could in Kennewick."

The President made a stop signal with his hand. "Hold it, Fred. I'm not following you. Landed? How? Buy? With what?"

"Apparently, they were delivered by starships of the Western Galactic

Empire. They made their purchases with greenbacks."

"Counterfeit?"

"No. Federal reserve notes. Legal tender."

Phil Brasher, the Attorney General, broke in. "Legal, my foot. Their cash may be good, but those people did not go through immigration. They are illegal aliens, and their presence here is an intolerable, criminal, violation of American sovereignty!"

"Obviously." Collins frowned, annoyed by Brasher's emotional interruption. "But to continue, as soon as they got some land, they knocked down all the old houses and replaced them with 300-story high skyscrapers built out a kind of superstrong plexiglass. They then filled them with fish farms, orange groves, robot factories, and housing. We estimate that they have about a million people living in there."

A stunned silence filled the room. Collins continued.

"Their customs are odd, to say the least. They despise contemporary American music. Instead they like to sing in groups resembling coeducational barbershop quartets. They travel around on a sort of motorized roller skates that can move them at close to 100 miles an hour over flat or rough terrain, and they like to fast-dance in their skates too. Their society is egalitarian, but with divided spheres. The men own the property and run their businesses, the women control the government and religion."

This sparked the President's curiosity. He was a very religious man. "Are they Christians?"

"Hardly. They worship the goddess Minerva."

The President was horrified. "Pagans! On our sacred land!"

Collins nodded. "Yes. And they get really nasty if anyone does anything to hurt an owl."

The President set his mouth in a grim line. "Nasty, I'll show them who is nasty." He turned to Jack "The Ripper" Ripley, his Secretary of Defense. "Jack, mobilize the armed forces. I want those pagans exterminated by Sunday."

Ripley smiled a wolfish grin. "Yes sir. With pleasure."

Dr. Beasley seemed distraught. "Maybe we're moving too fast. Certainly the Minervans are weird, but they offer a lot of benefits. In just two months they've restocked all the rivers in the Pacific Northwest with salmon and restored all the destroyed old-growth forests. They've sent their doctors to San Francisco and Seattle and cured hundreds of people of AIDS and cancer. They've deciphered Linear A. Their materials science is incredible and they are willing to share some of it with us. Their technology could improve our industrial productivity and raise living standards. Their knowledge of physics, chemistry, and biology is phenomenal. We could learn so much from them."

The President was decisive. "No. The only thing Americans need to know is how to be Americans, and they are not going to get that from a bunch of pagan foreigners from outer space. We're going to wipe them out."

General Smith, the Chairman of the Joint Chiefs of Staff, raised his hand. "Sir, what do we know about their military capabilities? If they have starships, an assault could be unwise."

Collins cut in. "You needn't worry about that, General. They have no ships. They're just a bunch of refugees, dumped here by the Western Galactic Empire. As far as we can see, they have no weapons at all. Losses of your precious troops should be minimal."

Smith seemed reassured. "Very well. In that case, I'll order a simultaneous land and air attack for the first of May. One hundred squadrons and ten divisions should do the trick. We better warn the local American population to get out of town, because we are going to blast the place to…Smithereens."

Everyone was delighted with the General's brilliant pun.

The President smiled. "You know, I think I see the hand of Providence in all of this. For the past several years, the American people have been depressed by the poor state of our national economy. Radicals have been spreading the lie that our hyperinflation has been caused by official corruption, denying its true cause, the failure of some of our people to follow the laws of the Bible. Now we have a chance to do God's work, killing pagans. This will bring us all together, and make us a happy, united, and devoted people again."

Everyone applauded.

"Speaking of hyperinflation," the President continued, "I suppose we're all due for another raise." He turned to Myra Chase, the Secretary of the Treasury. "Myra, have you brought the checks?"

"Yes sir, here they are," Myra said, passing the checks around the room. "Ten billion dollars for each member of the cabinet, and twenty billion for you, our beloved and infallible leader."

The President closed his eyes and pressed his hands together in prayer. "Let us give thanks to God, who has chosen to set our tables with this wonderful bounty."

"Amen," the Cabinet members intoned.

Collins spoke up. "By the way, Chief, the House Minority Leader is threatening to publicly expose these bonuses."

The President raised a crafty eyebrow. "Oh? How much does he want?"

"An equal cut."

The President was outraged. "Out of the question. Have him assassinated. And kill his wife and children too. We can't suffer this sort of extortion."

Collins nodded. "Right. How should we have the press report it?"

The President turned to Lisa White, his Public Relations Director. "Well, Lisa, you're always good at this."

Lisa strummed her fingers on the table thoughtfully for a few seconds, then looked up. "I think we should have them say they killed each other. Dysfunctional family, that sort of thing. Make it really disgusting. That way no one will remember them fondly after they're gone."

"Excellent!" the President exclaimed. He turned to Attorney General Brasher. "Phil, have the Justice Department draft the stories for the different media outlets to run, with the usual minor variations from left to right, highbrow to lowbrow, and so on."

"No problem."

The President stood up. "Well, this has certainly been a productive meeting. I'm really looking forward to watching the massacre on TV this weekend. If any of you need to reach me, the First Lady and I will be vacationing at Camp David starting Friday." He paused. "Oh, that reminds me, we want this to be a fun weekend. Lisa, could you arrange for some of the White House interns to join us?"

"Sure, what types?"

"Well, as you know, the First Lady goes for blacks, preferably spicy ones with some musical talent. I think I'd like to try out some classic blondes, private school types, you know, the kind that come in those cute little uniforms."

"I'll get right on it."

May 1.

Sergeant Andrew Hamilton lay motionless beneath the bush, his expertly camouflaged clothing making him nearly invisible. Slowly, silently, he unlatched the safety of his M-16.

The planes and helicopters hadn't had a chance. As soon as they had come over the horizon, the Minervans had held up little gold balls that glowed for a second and then unleashed a barrage of lighting bolts, knocking everything that flew right out of the sky. The Army's tanks had been wiped out the same way. But apparently the Minervan detection system only worked against machinery. Operating on foot, Hamilton's Rangers had worked their way in, and were now within firing range.

It was going to be a difficult shot. The Minervans were always moving around quickly on those roller skates of theirs, and their clothes were bullet proof. The only way to get one was to shoot for the head. But Hamilton's platoon were all expert marksmen, and they had a score to settle. Tens of thousands of American soldiers and airmen were dead. At least a few Minervans would pay the price.

A Minervan patrol approached, men and women dressed in black, moving fast through the valley. There were about a dozen of them; in numbers he had them three to one. M-16's weren't much of a match for Minervan lightning balls, but surprise was on his side. His men had been briefed. No one would fire until he did.

One hundred yards, fifty yards, now! Hamilton fired, and a split second later the whole platoon opened up. Blood sprouted from the heads of three or four of the Minervans, and they fell. The men cheered and kept firing. But then lightning bolts started coming back, exploding the guns in the soldier's hands in rapid succession, right up the line. Hamilton let go of his just in time and rolled free, but the shock when his rifle exploded six feet away knocked him unconscious.

When he awoke he found his hands bound behind his back. A young Minervan priestess approached, holding tight the gold owl pendant that hung from her neck. "Why are you doing this?" she shouted. "You killed six of our people!"

Dazed, Hamilton looked to his side. The bodies of what looked like his entire platoon had been dragged out of the bushes and lay exposed on the grassy embankment.

He turned again to face the priestess. "Are there any other survivors from my unit?"

"Of course not. Now what do you have to say for yourself?"

He stared back at her in defiance. "Well, at least we nailed six of you."

The Minervan shook her head in disgust. "You're crazy, you know that. You're absolutely out of your mind."

The next day, the Cabinet met again.

General Smith gave his report. "The Minervans have counterattacked, and moved out to a perimeter of 50 miles around Kennewick. They're holding in place there, and are offering a cease-fire. I recommend we accept."

The President frowned. "Why? Why should we quit just when they're losing their stomach for the fight?"

"Sir, we've lost over 1000 aircraft, 5000 vehicles, and 40,000 men. Our intelligence from Americans inside the Minervan occupied zone indicates that we have probably inflicted between three and four hundred casualties on the enemy. We are not winning this war."

White House Chaplain Reverend John Meade interrupted. "I find that statement very objectionable, General. Of course we are winning the war. We are Christians, and therefore good. They are pagans, and therefore evil. Good must always triumph over evil. Therefore, we must always triumph over them. I would have thought that a man of your piety would understand that."

Secretary of Defense Ripley nodded. "I quite agree. We've lost 40,000, but they've lost 400. That's one of theirs for every 100 of ours. We can afford that easily. There are 300 million Americans and only 1 million Minervans. At this rate, we will defeat them by simple attrition. No wonder they are begging for a cease fire."

The President bowed is head in prayer. "Let us all give thanks to God for this glorious victory."

Everyone prayed, stopping only when the President did. Finally, the President turned to General Smith.

"So General, you were saying?"

"Well sir, what I meant was that since in the achievement of the glorious victory, we lost all of our best troops, including the Green Berets, the Rangers, the 101st and 82nd Airborne Divisions, and the Marine Corps,..."

"They are not lost. They are martyred," the Reverend Meade corrected.

"Yes, but they were the only units that managed to score at all against the enemy, and we don't have them anymore. So if we are going to continue winning further victories, we need to regroup. The Joint Chiefs are all in agreement that a strategic pause right now would be in our interests."

The President was incensed. "I can't believe what I'm hearing. Forty thousand Americans have just given their lives in a holy cause, total victory is practically in our grasp, and you want to stop fighting?"

CIA Director Fred Collins coughed to gain attention. "Sir, my people have been working through Secretary Ripley's numbers, and I believe we have detected a flaw in his logic."

Ripley glared at the CIA Director. The pseudo intellectual sissies in the CIA were always trying to act superior to the Defense Department. "What flaws? We lose 100 to 1, but we outnumber them 300 to 1. We win. It's that simple."

Collins smiled his condescending Ivy League smile. "Actually it's not quite that simple. Certainly, we could win that way, but in doing so, we would lose 100 million Americans. That could significantly damage the administration's public support."

Ripley waved his hand dismissively. "Nonsense. We'll just tell the press not to cover our casualties. Aside from a few heroic martyrs that we can play for our benefit, no one will know we've lost anyone."

Collins shook his head. "I'm sorry. But it is the assessment of the Agency that with 100 million casualties, word would leak out. The result would be scandal that would be used to great advantage by the radical opposition. You see, it's an elementary problem in Threshold Theory..."

The President did not understand Threshold Theory, but his gut political instincts told him Collins was right. They could certainly cover up 1 million casualties, or 10 million, but 100 million was just too much. Even with a completely loyal media assisting him, word would indeed get out. The result could be a revolution that would force him to flee the country. While he had over 80 billion dollars socked away in Switzerland, that could all be made worthless if his successor continued his inflationary policies. For the good of his family, it was essential that he remain in office. He stopped Collins' lecture with a timeout sign.

"So, Fred, what do you recommend that we do?"

This was the question Collins had been waiting for. "We need to use a more subtle approach. The Minervans only appear formidable because they have technology and weaponry given them by the Western Galactic Empire."

The President's eyes lit up. "That's right! And didn't you say that there was a Central Galactic Empire that hates the Minervans, and tried to wipe them out? We could go to them for support!"

"Unfortunately, that's not possible. You see, a number of years ago, the Western and Eastern Galactic Empires allied and overran the Central Galactic Empire in a war. In the process, they rescued what was left of the Minervans. Now, while they didn't like the Minervans much better than the Centrals did, the allies, especially the Western Galactics, had made much of the oppression of Minervans in their war propaganda. So after the war was over, they were forced to do something to help them out."

"So where does that leave us?"

"Well, now that the Centrals are gone, the Western and Eastern Empires have become adversaries."

The President snapped his fingers. "I get it. Since the Westerners support the Minervans, we go to the Easterners!"

Collins shook his head. "We could, but that's probably not the best plan. The Westerners are more powerful than the Easterners, and if we brought in Eastern help that would absolutely cement Western support for the Minervans. They would bring in fleets of starships and armies of space marines. We'd never get rid of them."

"Then what can we do?"

"We need to undermine Western Galactic Empire support for the Minervans."

"How?"

Collins smiled. "Well, you see, Western Galactic backing for the Minervans is based upon the WGE's claim to be the defenders of the oppressed."

"So?"

"So we show them how in reality it is the Minervans who are oppressing us!"

"How do we show that?"

"They're invaders. We'll show the Western Galactics the millions of people they've made homeless."

"But they haven't made anyone homeless. Most of the Americans who were living in the Kennewick area before the Minervans arrived are still there, and those that moved out are now living in Seattle or Chicago or someplace like that."

"Well, they shouldn't be. We don't have room for them anywhere but Kennewick. We should round up everyone who has left, and put them in refugee camps right on the border of the Minervan occupied zone. And we should try to get as many of the local residents who are still living in the zone to move out, so we can put them in the camps too. There is no reason why Americans should have to live under Minervan occupation. It's completely unjust."

The President nodded sagely. "I see. So then we invite in the Western Galactics and show them what is going on. How the Minervans have caused millions of our people to live in misery." He thought for a moment. "For maximum effect, we should try to make the refugee camps as squalid as possible. No health care, no sanitation, no schools, no trash pick-up, no law enforcement, that sort of thing."

Lisa White, the Public Relations Director, now spoke up. "And we should keep any private charitable help to a minimum. Have them present, so everyone will know that the refugees are charity cases, but keep the amount of help small, so it doesn't undermine the image we need to project. If we handle it that way, we'll have the whole galaxy on our side in no time. The Minervans will never stand a chance."

The President smiled. "Excellent. Let's do it."

Attorney General Brasher stood up. "I'll have the FBI start rounding up the refugees immediately."

Chapter 2

Dr. Howard Berger, his wife Melissa, and their three small boys were spending a quiet evening in their comfortable Seattle home, when the FBI agents broke in.

"Dr. Howard Berger?" agent Wilkes asked.

"Yes."

"You and your family are under arrest. You must come with us right now."

"But why? We haven't done anything wrong."

"You're from Kennewick, aren't you?"

"Yes," the doctor explained. "But when the Minervans showed up, I thought it might be best to leave. I had a job offer here at the University Hospital, and Melissa had an offer from the Seattle Public Schools, so what with the probability of trouble and three boys to think of, we thought…"

"That's enough. You are a Kennewickian, and must be transported back to Kennewick at once."

Melissa cut in. "But I thought the Minervans are not letting any Americans back into Kennewick."

Wilkes nodded. "That's right, they're not."

Melissa's face showed her alarm. "But then, where do we go?"

"Until the aliens are driven out, you and your family will be housed in a refugee camp on the border of the Minervan occupied zone."

"But it could take years before they are made to leave," Melissa cried. "It could take forever."

The agent was unsympathetic. "It will take as long as it takes. The cause of Holy Kennewick must not be given up."

The doctor's bewilderment was equaled only by his outrage. "Now see here, officer, there is no need for this. In this family we all support the war effort against the Minervans, of course, but there is no need for us to live like refugees. Melissa and I both have jobs here in Seattle, and a house, and the boys are doing well in an excellent school. It would be crazy for us to leave here to go and live in a tent camp."

"You have no choice. You are Kennewickians, and can only live in Kennewick." Wilkes pointed to the door. "Now stop arguing and get in the van. We have other refugees to pick up."

Melissa was desperate. "You want us to leave right now? Can't we at least pack some possessions?"

Agent Wilkes shook his head. "No, certainly not. Possession of property by refugees is counter-productive. We need you to be as miserable as possible, so as to elicit the maximum amount of pity from Galactic observers."

The Bergers were aghast.

Wilkes turned to the couple's three boys, aged 8, 10, and 12. "Hi boys, ready to fight the Minervans?"

Tommy, aged 8, held up his hand with his fingers shaped to suggest a six-shooter. "You bet mister. Bang! Bang!"

The agent smiled. "That's the spirit son, you'll make a wonderful martyr."

Melissa quickly snatched her smallest son way from the government man. "What are you talking about, martyr? He's just a child. If you want to fight the Minervans, send soldiers, grown men."

Wilkes shook his head. "We tried that. It didn't work. We're sending children now, because it makes the Minervans look really bad when they kill them. But don't worry, as soon as each of your boys is martyred, the government will send you a handsome cash bonus, guaranteed, within 10 business days of the event."

Melissa stared at the agent in silent horror. Then she felt a shove from behind, as strong arms pushed her and her family out of their door.

Hamilton looked around his prison cell. He had to admit to himself that for a prison it was very nice, far nicer in fact than any home he had ever lived in. The room was large and airy, with bright sunlight shining in through the bullet-proof windows. There was plenty of comfortable furniture to sit on, a fountain in the middle of the room, music, movies, and books were available through touch-screen computers on demand, and the food was great. Still, a jail was a jail. He longed for freedom.

A knock on the door provided the briefest of warnings, and then it opened, revealing his captress, Priestess 4th-class Aurora, who had now apparently become his case-officer.

Aurora was pretty, as most Minervan women were, in an outdoorsy, girl-next-door kind of way. She was also quite witty and could be charming when she wanted to. Under other circumstances. Hamilton would have found her company quite enjoyable.

She favored him with twinkling eyes, as if somehow she found his appearance amusing. "Ready for your walk, Sergeant Hamilton?"

He nodded. Anything to get outside. She turned, and he followed her. For the briefest of seconds the thought crossed his mind that he could tackle her and make a break for freedom, but he discarded it, having observed the powerful electric shock Minervan clothing could give to any terrestrial assailant.

Suddenly Aurora stopped and looked at him. "Smart boy," she said, with a hint of a laugh. "Maybe you can learn something." Then she turned and continued forward into the garden.

For a moment, Hamilton froze. Could she read his mind? It was very disconcerting. But there was nothing for it. Picking up his pace, he was soon walking by her side.

The garden was filled with strange beautiful plants from faraway planets, with different ones every day. How the Minervans accomplished this was a mystery. Aurora was happy to talk about the garden, but while her discussions of the plants themselves were fascinating, her explanations of Minervan gardening technique were simply incomprehensible.

Whether through telepathy, or more conventional observation, Aurora clearly knew she had lost him. Without warning, she changed the subject to more serious matters.

"You know, Hamilton, you can leave here any time you want. All you have to do is admit what you did was wrong."

"You're asking me to make a public denunciation of my country? I'll never do that."

Aurora smiled. "Don't be ridiculous. I don't need you to make a public broadcast. All you need to do is tell me that you know you were wrong."

"That's it? Just tell you I was wrong, and you'll let me go?"

"That's it. Say it right now and you're a free man."

Hamilton found the offer astonishing, but he was not about to turn it down. "OK. I was wrong. Can I go now?"

Aurora frowned in disgust. "Don't be ridiculous."

"What do you mean ridiculous? I said what you asked me to."

Aurora folded her arms and looked at him severely. "But you didn't mean it."

Hamilton shook his head. "Look, I said exactly what you wanted."

Aurora's eyes went dark with fury. "But you lied. Admit it. You still think you were right in murdering six peaceful Minervans who were out in the country for a picnic."

Now Hamilton was offended. "I didn't murder anyone. I was a soldier, doing my duty by following orders, engaging armed combatants in the open field in wartime."

"So you believe that the fact that someone ordered you to kill Minervans absolves you of all responsibility to use your conscience?"

"Those Minervans were armed…"

"Only defensively. And what would you expect, with thousands of crazy savages like you running around trying to kill people?"

"But you killed thirty-six of my men."

"We certainly did not. All we did was destroy their weapons."

"Killing my men in the process."

Aurora shrugged. "It was their choice. If they had been willing to use their minds, they would have let go of their instruments of murder, and none of them would have been hurt."

Hamilton suppressed his rejoinder. It was obvious that the Minervan's view of things was totally one-sided.

Aurora continued; "You let go of your gun, which shows that you possess at least a small spark of Reason. That is quite interesting given your otherwise psychotic belief structure. Of course, if you are going to ever go free, you are going to have to use your mind to overthrow much more of your programming. None of my friends think you can do it. But I find your attempts fascinating."

Hamilton was struck by a sinking feeling. "Aurora, just what is my status here? Aren't I a prisoner of war? And won't I be released when hostilities end?"

Aurora laughed. "Now look who's having delusions of grandeur. Prisoner of war, indeed. Hamilton, you are so silly."

"But if I'm not a prisoner of war, why is the Minervan government keeping me?"

"The Minervan High Council has no interest in you."

"Then who is holding me?"

"I am, of course. I collected you, so naturally I own you."

Hamilton was astonished. Aurora went on; "And you're certainly not 'Prisoner of War.' That's the most preposterous thing I ever heard. You're a…"

"I'm a what?"

Aurora closed her eyes and put out her hand, waving it over his forehead, as if she was searching his mind for the right term. Evidently she did, for after a moment she opened her eyes and looked at Hamilton with an amused smile.

"You're a lab specimen."

Observing the crushed look on Hamilton's face, Aurora said; "Now don't pout. You're being treated well, aren't you?"

Hamilton said nothing, but gave the 4th-class priestess a sulky look.

Aurora nodded. "I'll take that as a yes. And you can take pride in the fact that you are contributing to the advance of Minervan science. You know, I was just told this morning by a representative of the Lower Council, that as a result of my studies of your outer mind programming, I will be promoted to Priestess 3rd class at the next full Moon."

She beamed at him proudly.

"Well, aren't you going to congratulate me?"

Not knowing what to say, Hamilton just said, "Congratulations."

Aurora looked at him keenly. "You know, Hamilton, if you were willing to let me into your inner mind, I could find out so much more. Priestess 2nd class would not be out of the question."

"What's in it for me?"

"Well for one thing, as Priestess 2nd class I would have many more resources at my disposal. I could take care of you much better."

Hamilton was unimpressed. "My existing cell is nice enough."

"I don't just mean more creature comforts. I'm talking about scientific resources. And with those, plus full access to your inner mind, I could remove your mental programming blockages. You could become fully human."

Aurora didn't notice the insulted look on Hamilton's face. Her eyes were ablaze with enthusiasm at the boldness of her thought. "Think of it, Hamilton, human!"

"I am human."

Taken aback by this defiance, Aurora put her hands on her hips. "Potentially, yes. But don't you see, that is what we need to prove!"

"I don't need to prove I'm human to anyone. I know it."

Aurora snickered. "You know it? If you could only hear how ridiculous you sound. Look at you, with your stupid insane thoughts reeking out of your outer mind, annoying everyone in sight, and your horrible skin and teeth, and your stinky grotesque clothing." She shook her head.

Hamilton was taken aback by this sudden tirade. He knew the Minervan did not think much of his beliefs, and he was willing to accept that Minervans, who all had perfect health, might find tooth fillings and minor scars disgusting, but his clothes? The Minervans had given him clean cotton slacks and golf shirts to replace his ripped and bloody army fatigues, and as far as he could see, he was quite presentable.

"What's wrong with my clothes?"

Aurora looked at him and shuddered, then threw up her hands. "Oh, forget it."

At that moment they left the garden to enter the square lodged between the four skyscrapers that comprised the Minervan 6th subsettlement. Despite the fact that the buildings were 300 stories tall and completely surrounded the square, sunlight illuminated everything. In the center of the square, a small phalanx of male and female Minervans was singing a rapid moving harmony, providing music to several hundred fast dancers scooting about the square on Minervan levitation skates. A group of small American boys moved among the Minervans on ordinary roller skates, serving snacks to the dancers.

"What's going on?" Hamilton asked.

"It is the celebration of the birth of the Great Owl." Aurora smiled. "Do you want to dance?"

Hamilton was amazed at the offer. "Can I?"

"Sure." The priestess drew two golden plates from her vestment pocket. "Just put these under your shoes and follow my lead."

Hamilton took the plates. They had no adhesive, but when he touched one to his right shoe, it stuck firmly in place. "How did it do that?"

Aurora fondled her golden owl pendant and winked. "Don't worry about it. Just put the other plate on and let's dance."

Hamilton touched the other plate to his left shoe. Instantly, Aurora took his hand and started whirling him around. She laughed a mischievous laugh. "Are you dizzy?"

"Yes."

"Good! Let's go!"

And with that, she took off with him in tow, pirouetting at about ten revolutions per minute while scooting in all directions across the dance floor at speeds greater than 60 miles per hour. At first Hamilton found it terrifying, but after a few minutes he started to get a feel for the skate dynamics, and was able to exercise some control. Soon the dance became exhilarating.

"Are we having fun yet?" Aurora laughed.

He nodded. In the distance, he saw a male Minervan jump in the air, taking his female partner up with him into a flying whirl that changed axes into a backflip that landed them both on their feet. The move seemed impossible, but somehow Hamilton felt he could do it. He resolved to try, and without bothering to warn Aurora, took off with as strong a jump as he could manage. The effect was dramatic. Soaring above the other dancers, they whirled halfway across the square, before doing a double backflip and landing on their skates.

The music stopped, ending the dance. Aurora's eyes were bright with delight. "Hey! Not bad for an Earthling. We'll make a dancer out of you yet. Now as soon as the next dance begins, let me show you…"

At that moment, Hamilton noticed something behind Aurora. One of the Earthling waiter boys was pulling an object out from under his shirt. It was a six-shooter, and he was raising it to point at the back of the priestess's head.

Without thinking, Hamilton whirled her around, and sticking out his leg, kicked the gun out of the boy's hand. But at the same instant, all the boys had their pistols in the open, and were blazing away at whatever Minervan was closest to hand.

The fight didn't last long. In the blink of an eye, Minervan lightning bolts were flying in every direction across the square, causing all the pistols to explode.

When it was over, one Minervan was dead from a pistol shot through his brain, and another was injured with a neck wound. Three of the boys were also dead, while eight others had their arms blown off and were screaming in agony. The only uninjured boy was the one Hamilton had disarmed.

The boy looked up at the former Ranger. "Traitor!" he yelled.

The Minervans all clustered around their dead and injured, ignoring the bleeding boys.

Hamilton turned to Aurora. "Someone has got to help those boys!" he shouted.

Aurora looked at him curiously. "Why?" she asked.

Chapter 3

The Ambassador and Commercial Consul of the Western Galactic Empire were ushered into the White House meeting room and greeted by the President and his cabinet.

The President was dwarfed by the Commercial Consul, but nevertheless aggressively approached him and shook his hand.

"Mr. Ambassador," the President said to the Consul warmly, "I'm so glad to finally meet you."

The Consul allowed his hand to be touched briefly, but then withdrew it nervously. "West Imperial Commercial Consul Fedris, at your service sir. Allow me to introduce our ambassador, the Reverend Priestess Junea."

Taken aback by his mistake, the President turned to Junea with some apparent embarrassment. "Oh, I'm sorry, Madame Ambassador. I hope you'll excuse my misunderstanding." He held out his hand.

The Ambassador Reverend Priestess Junea stared down at the President, hiding her disgust with the Mask of Serenity taught to all the acolytes of the triune Goddess. The President was a little man, with horrible skin and disgusting silver metal slugs in his teeth. His clothes, cut in the absurd Earthling style, stunk of sweat and chemical cleansers, and the skin of some dead animal adorned his feet. Horrible thoughts boiled forth uncontrollably from his outer mind, filling the room like a noxious cloud. There were traces of human feces on his hand; apparently the ribald stories claiming that Earthlings used their hands to wipe themselves after defecation were actually true! Briefly willing her eyes to high magnification, she could see that his hand was in fact covered with microbes of every description, including numerous obvious pathogens. She exchanged a quick thought with the Consul, commending him telepathically for having the will power to touch the savage, but declined to follow suit. Instead, she raised her hands in a gesture of blessing, and smiled. "Greetings," she said.

The Consul cleared his throat. "The Ambassador is very busy, and has a large number of planets to visit in this sector over the next few days. So if you would get right down to business and tell us the reason for your urgent call, we would greatly appreciate it."

"You don't want to dine with us first? We have had a special buffet prepared in your honor." The President indicated a nearby table, which was covered with fragments of dead animals and plants, cut and mutilated beyond recognition.

Junea shuddered. "No thank you. Please proceed with your presentation."

"Well alright," the President said. "As you know, several months ago our planet was invaded by Minervans. They have taken over our holy city of Kennewick, and desecrated it with their horrible pagan rituals. They have inflicted hideous crimes on the local population, and thrown our entire world into misery. We are a peaceful people, and have tried to convince them to leave, but they won't listen to us. So we ask the help of the Western Galactic Empire to free us of these monsters."

Junea smiled. "Ah yes, Minervans. They never seem to be popular, do they? Clever people in their way, but their single-minded fanatical attachment to Minerva always gets them into trouble."

The President nodded vigorously. "So, you understand our problem, having heretical pagans thrust among us, and taking over our holiest of cities."

Junea sighed. "Indeed. Of course, none of us denies that Minerva is a great goddess, but to deny, as the Minervans do, the divinity of the other Goddesses of the triune sisterhood, is the greatest of errors."

At this remark, shock emanated from the President's mind. Curious as to how her obviously truthful platitude could have elicited such a reaction, Junea peered into his mental cloud and saw that the savage had been programmed in some kind of local crackpot monotheism called Christianity. She shrugged.

The President said, "The Western Galactic Empire brought them here. We ask that you remove them."

Junea shook her head. "I'm afraid that's not possible."

"Why not?"

"Well for one thing, the Minervans are from here. They originated here, 20,000 years ago, in the place you call Kennewick. It's rightfully theirs."

The President slammed his pathetic little fist down on a desk. "That's crazy! Twenty thousand years ago? How does anyone know where they were then?"

Junea said, "It's in all the holy books, both the Minervans' and ours. In any case, there is really no point arguing about it. After the recent war, during which so many Minervans suffered at the hands of the Central Empire, Galactic public opinion demanded that the Minervans be given a home, and the Empress of the West committed herself to that goal. So a home is what they will have."

A spectacled man, whose thoughts seemed somewhat more ordered than the President's, but whose appearance and smell were even more grotesque, broke into the conversation. "But why didn't you just let them settle in your own empire? You have over a hundred million planets. Even if they did once come from Earth, it is clear that today they are culturally much more like you than us."

The President sneered. "I think Doctor Beasley has a point. The fact of the matter is that you don't like them either. Why don't you just join forces with us? Together we can wipe them out."

Junea raised her eyebrows. "We have quite enough Minervans living in the Western Empire already. The fact that we do not want more should in no way suggest that we support violence against them. The Western Empire is committed to defending the rights of all peoples, whatever their flaws. That is why people throughout the galaxy look to us for their protection."

The one the President called Doctor Beasley broke in again. "But then look what they are doing to us!" He looked for assurance to the President, who then sent him a very crude proto-telepathic affirmative. Beasley closed an electric circuit, and a cathode-ray video monitor emitting uncomfortable levels of beta ray radiation came to life. Juneau took a few steps back just to be safe.

An image appeared of Minervans engaged in an Owl Festival Dance. During a pause in the Festival, violence erupted between some small ragged and ugly Earthling boys armed with hand-wielded chemical projectile weapons and Minervans using reflective disarmers. Some of the boys were killed, but most just had their limbs blown off. The image panned again and again to the little screaming savages with dismembered limbs.

"See," the President said. "They are murdering our children. Poor little boys, with only six-shooters to protect themselves, being slaughtered by trained Minervan killers using advanced Galactic weaponry."

Consul Fedris was bemused. "Why did you have your children attack them? And with such obsolete weapons? Surely the result was not unexpected?"

"The children were just defending their country and their faith, using the traditional weapons of our forefathers," the President moaned, as melodramatic tears streamed from the rest of his retinue. "Who would have expected the Minervans to be so cruel!"

Junea stifled a yawn. "Well, I think I need to be going now."

The President said, "Wait, you haven't seen it all. Look at the horrible conditions our people made homeless by the Minervans are being forced to live in. Beasley, show them the second tape."

Beasley switched cassettes in the video machine, and now the screen showed a vast sprawling camp of crude canvas structures. Diseased and malnourished children in ragged clothing wandered listlessly about, searching through piles of garbage for something of value among the filth that surrounded them. The picture zoomed in to focus on two naked infants lying on the ground, whose distended stomachs and prominent ribs indicated advanced stages of starvation. Their mother sat nearby in a similar condition, staring hopelessly into space.

"You see," the President said. "They have no place to live and nothing to eat. They're starving!"

"Why don't you just let them move to one of your other cities?" the Consul suggested helpfully. "Our data shows that you have a nationwide labor shortage. If they moved away they could get jobs and buy whatever they need."

The President turned to the Consul. "You don't understand. They are Kennewickians. They can't live anywhere but Kennewick."

"Then why don't you ship them some food. You have a large grain surplus."

The President seemed momentarily at a loss. Apparently he hadn't expected this suggestion. Then he said; "No, the only solution is for them to be given back their native land."

Junea cleared her throat. "Fascinating. Well it was nice meeting you, but I have several more planets to visit." She turned to leave.

Her motion was interrupted by the Consul. "Excuse me, Your Reverence, but we have some business to conduct here before we leave."

Junea nodded. She had quite forgotten. "Ah, yes," she said.

The President, who an instant before had seemed depressed by the emissaries' apparent lack of interest in the plight of the Kennewickians, was now alert. "Business?" he said.

"Yes," answered Fedris. "While we can't help you in your conflict with the Minervans, we are prepared to offer you some business deals that I think you will find rewarding."

The President steepled his hands. "Please continue," he said.

Fedris smiled. "Well, I've just been informed by one of the scientists who happens to be traveling along with our party, that your country is sitting on top of a large reserve of helicity."

The President was puzzled. "What does that mean?"

"It means that this is your lucky day. Helicity is of no use to you, but it happens to be a great interest to some commercial organizations that I represent, and they are prepared to pay handsomely for it."

"What is helicity?" Beasley asked.

Fedris waved his hands dismissively. "I'm afraid that's rather complicated, and quite beyond your understanding. However, the main point is that you have it, and we want it, and I'm sure you'll be delighted with the kinds of things we are prepared to give you in exchange."

The President raised an eyebrow. "What is helicity used for?"

Fedris looked uncomfortable. "Well, it's an energy source for a number of handy devices, levitation skates, for example."

The President smiled. "And lightning balls? And starships?"

"Well, yes."

The President laughed. "My, my. It seems we have something to sell indeed. Well if you want it, you'll have to give us what we want. No sale unless you kick out the Minervans."

Junea interrupted. "I'm afraid that's not possible. And you will sell."

"Or?"

Fedris grinned a wolfish grin. "I'm sure that we don't need to explain that in detail to a man of your intelligence."

The President frowned. "I see. So why do you want to buy from us? Why not from some other country?"

"Because you have the most," Fedris said. "Also, as the most powerful of the local tribal despots, the example of your cooperation will help insure reasonable behavior from the others."

This was actually meant as a compliment, but the President took it otherwise. "I, sir, am not a local tribal despot. I am the lawfully elected President of the greatest nation on God's green Earth."

"Whatever," Fedris said.

The President sulked for a few seconds, then said; "So you are prepared to take it, but you prefer to buy it. You want to keep this a smooth deal."

"Exactly."

"And what exactly do we get if we agree to sell?"

Fedris brightened. "Oh, many fine things. For example we have technologies that could double your crop yields, triple your industrial productivity, and cure many of the diseases afflicting your population."

The President shrugged. "Boring."

Fedris said, "I see." He exchanged a quick thought with Junea, then proceeded. "In that case, how about this?"

The Consul removed a small cube from his pocket and placed it on the table. "Observe," he said as he touched it lightly on one side.

Immediately the room was filled with holograms of beautiful naked men and women engaged in sexual acts of every description to the accompaniment of intensely erotic music.

As Junea expected, the President and the other savages in the room were immediately overwhelmed and were riveted to the display, panting and rubbing themselves as they watched. Fedris let this go on for about a minute, and then touched the cube again to stop the show.

"Wow!" the President said. "That was great. You mean to say we can keep the cube if we sell you some of that helicity stuff?"

Fedris smiled. "Certainly. This one is only a sample. As soon as we conclude an arrangement, I'll arrange for shipments of new ones for each of you, every year. I assure you that you will never lack for the finest in joycubes for the rest of your lives. In addition, we will supply you with millions of mass market editions, that you can resell to your population at great profit, and help keep them happy too."

The President nodded thoughtfully. "Well, I must say that this deal is beginning to look more promising."

But Beasley had a question. "If you don't mind my asking, Mr. Consul, at the rate you propose to export it, how long will our helicity last?"

"At least sixty years," Fedris answered. "Possibly as long as seventy."

"Just sixty years?" Beasley looked at the President in dismay. "Mr. President, I'm not sure this deal is wise. Our helicity reserve would appear to be a non-renewable resource of great value. We can't let them take it for nothing but these little pleasure cubes."

Junea telepathed to Fedris. "This Beasley character, with his traces of rationality, could cause a problem." Fedris answered in kind. "Don't worry, I'm on top of it."

Fedris faced the President. "Oh, I didn't mean to imply that joycubes were all we would give you. We are also willing to supply you with large quantities of these."

With that he drew a small silver prism shape from his pocket and placed it on the table. "Observe," he said, and stroked it gently along the top edge.

Immediately, Beasley screamed and went into convulsions on the floor.

"Now," Fedris continued. "Let's say you have a subject like that one who questions your judgment or authority. All you need to do is bring them into the presence of one of these and..." Here he pressed down harder on the prism edge. Beasley screamed again as every part of his body twisted in pain.

The President watched, fascinated. "Can I try it?" he asked.

"Certainly," Fedris said, and pushed the prism over to the President's side of the table.

The President gave the top of the prism a light tap, and Beasley cried out in unendurable agony. He tapped again, and Beasley screamed again. He laughed with delight. "Hey, Jack, Lisa. Come here and try this. This is fun."

The other members of the President's cabinet gathered around, and all had a turn torturing Beasley. As the party continued, Fedris drew the President aside.

"And in addition, with the amount of helicity you've got to offer, we can give you a healthy supply of these." He drew from his pocket a small pile of glowing iridescent blue plastic triangles, each with the picture of a rather beautiful woman wearing some kind of crown at its center.

"What are those?" The President asked.

"Western Galactic bluebacks," Fedris said. "Cold cash, accepted everywhere. Don't leave home without it."

Looking around to make sure that the rest of the cabinet was sufficiently preoccupied, the President quickly pocketed the triangles.

"So you see, Mr. President, in exchange for something that you didn't even know you had, we offer copious supplies of joycubes, painprisms, and good old-fashioned moolah. Joycubes for you and your loyal subjects, painprisms for your police to apply to the disloyal ones, and enough bluebacks for all the fun the galaxy has to offer. Everything you need to maintain happiness and keep order in your country."

The President observed Beasley writhing on the floor to the merry ministrations of his cabinet. "Partner," he said, "You've got a deal." He stuck out his hand.

Fedris shook the hand without apparent disgust. Junea offered her blessing.

Hamilton sat with Aurora in the open-air cafe sipping raffa. The delightful Minervan drink filled the body with mild exhilaration, while imposing none of the numbing effects of alcohol. As the young priestess chatted on, he couldn't avoid reflecting upon how pretty she looked, and how sweetly musical her voice sounded.

"I want you to know, Hamilton, that I'm not ungrateful to you for your action in disarming that assassin yesterday."

"Oh? How do you know I wasn't just trying to save the boy?"

She smiled an amused smile. "Hamilton, haven't you learned yet? I know what you are thinking."

"Oh, yeah." He should have thought about that.

Her grin became broader. "And I know how you feel about me."

That one caught him by surprise. He looked at her sharply. "Now wait just a minute, your worship, you may be telepathic but..."

"You are in love with me."

"No, I'm..."

"Hopelessly, helplessly, utterly, totally in love with me."

With a shock of recognition, Hamilton realized it was true. He sat back in his chair, unable to speak. How had it happened? Had it been the exhilaration of the dance? Or had she used her telepathic powers to cast some kind of spell on him? It didn't matter. The situation was terrible. He was in love with a woman who viewed him as a clinical specimen.

"Poor thing," she said.

He looked at her in misery. "What can we do about it?"

"Why should I want to do anything about it? I think it's sweet."

"It's not fair!"

She chuckled. "What's that expression you Earthlings use? 'Life's not fair?'"

"How can you be so cruel?"

"Cruel?" she raised an eyebrow. "You murder six fine people without provocation, and won't even apologize for it, and I'm supposed to pity you for your emotional desperation?"

"But can't you see that..."

She interrupted him. "Enough. As I said, I am not ungrateful for what you did yesterday. So here is what I am willing to do. If you will give me your word of honor that you will not try to escape, or undertake any harmful actions against any Minervans, I will give you freedom of the city. You'll be able to go outside whenever you wish, walk around, visit people, even," she smiled, "go dancing. Just so long as you agree not to try to leave Minervan territory and come whenever I call you so we can continue our talks."

Hamilton thought the offer over. He knew there was no point trying to lie to her, so if he was to make the pledge, he would also have to decide to keep it. Giving up his right to attempt escape would be giving up his stand that he was a prisoner of war, which would reduce his dignity yet another notch. On the other hand, if he did not accept the offer, Aurora would keep him confined to his cell except when under her direct supervision, in which case escape would be impossible anyway. Yet his situation here was so humiliating. But then he thought: Wait, Aurora may think of me as a laboratory specimen, but I'm not. I am a man, and I remain a man no matter what she thinks. And if I stay here, and talk with her, and tell her all about me, just as she wants, maybe I can convince her that I am fully human. And if I can convince her, then maybe we together can convince the other Minervans that Earthlings are really human beings just like them, so we can all live together in peace. And maybe, if I can do all that, I can win her love.

Aurora's eyes went wide. "What a noble thought!" she said. "And so romantic! So you'll do it?"

"Yes. You have my word."

"Great! Wait till I tell my friends." Turning, she called out in Minervan to a group of young priestesses who were walking nearby. As they gathered around the table, she spoke to them rapidly in the musical Minervan tongue. Then they all turned to stare at Hamilton and started to giggle.

Aurora faced the soldier. "So, Hamilton," she said with an ironic smile, "you're not a laboratory specimen after all. You're a Man with a Mission."

"Yeah, that's right."

All the priestesses burst out laughing.

Hamilton reddened with embarrassment. I guess I have my work cut out for me, he thought to himself.

"Yes," Aurora said, struggling to contain her laughter. "You certainly do."

In the basement of the First Methodist Church of Kennewick, Minister Aaron Vardt looked at his little charges. "Now boys and girls, who wants to go to heaven?"

All the little children raised their hands.

The Minister smiled. "Very good. Now who here knows what you need to do to go to heaven?"

Many of the children raised their hands, and waved them anxiously, hoping to be the one called on. The Minister chose one little girl who he knew to be very bright. "Yes, Nancy."

Nancy said; "The way to go to heaven is to kill a Minervan."

Minister Vardt beamed his approval. "That's right, Nancy, Jesus wants us all to kill Minervans. And what is the best way to kill a Minervan?" He looked around for another bright child to call on. "Yes, Alan?"

Alan, age 9, knew the right answer. "The right way to kill Minervans is with a six-gun!" He made a gun out of his fingers and blazed away at the posters depicting the enemy that adorned the wall. "Bang! bang!"

"That's right, children, Alan is exactly right. The six-gun is our holy weapon. It represents our spirit and traditional values. Jesus will love us best of all if we use the six-gun. It is the divine tool that can allow each of you to achieve martyrdom."

On cue, Emily, age 13, spoke up. "But Reverend, we have no six-guns."

"Then let us turn the lights out and pray. Perhaps Christ will show us a way."

Emily threw a switch and the cellar went dark. All the children prayed in unison. "Our father, that art in heaven, please show us the way to kill the Minervans, the hateful enemies of all that is holy. Show us how to smite them, to shoot them, to poison them, to burn them, or slit their throats. Show us the way to inflict pain and misery on them here on Earth, as you will do to them in Hell everlasting…"

As the pious prayer went on, the Minister could hear the sound of a large crate being dragged into the room. Then the prayer ended. The Minister said, "Emily, you may turn on the lights now."

The lights came on. There in the center of the room was a magnificent man. Beside him was an open crate filled with Colt-45 revolvers. The man said, "Behold! Jesus has answered your prayers. Here are loaded six-guns for each of you. Go forth and slay the Minervans!"

With glee, the children ran up and seized their weapons. As they headed joyously towards the door, the Minister stopped them for a final review. "Remember children, it is important that others bear witness to your martyrdom. Don't try to shoot a Minervan until there is a TV crew nearby. And once they blow your hand off, you can cry all you want, but remember to stay in frame. And what is our priority order for TV coverage?"

The children all chimed in. "Galactic, interstellar, international, national, state and local."

The Minister nodded. "Very good. Now go forth and do God's work. I will meet you all in Heaven."

The children ran out the door.

When they were all gone, the Minister approached the Secret Service agent who had brought in the guns. "So Lou, how's tricks?"

"Not bad, Aaron. We've already rounded up enough new families of Kennewickian refugees to replace the martyrs you've expended three times over. Say, I heard the last lot of kids did pretty good."

Minister Vardt shrugged. "They did OK, I guess, killing one Minervan and wounding another before they were scragged. They could have gotten another if not for that traitor."

"What traitor?"

"Hamilton, the Ranger they took prisoner during the May 1 fighting. One of my boys would have nailed a Priestess if not for him."

The Agent stared at the Minister. "You can't let him get away with that."

"I don't intend to."

Chapter 4

It was the night of the full Moon, and Aurora was to be promoted. Hamilton read her note inviting him to the ceremony.

"Hamilton, you are to come to the Temple of Minerva tonight. Be there at 10 o'clock exactly, and enter through the service entrance at the back. But right before you go, take three showers using the enclosed soap, and then put on the enclosed clothes. Under no circumstances should you defecate between the time you shower and the time you come to the Temple. It is essential that you obey these instructions precisely.

Aurora."

Hamilton had done as he was instructed. The soap was very strong, but did not sting much after the first use. The clothes were made of an unusual fabric, and while within terrestrial norms were colored and cut in an indefinable way that somehow made him look a bit like a Minervan.

When he reached the Temple, he was admitted without a word through the service entrance and then seated behind a curtain off to the side of the main hall. From this position he could see the main podium but not the audience.

Without warning, the hall erupted in song as hundreds of female voices joined in singing the hymn to Minerva. Then as Hamilton watched, the twelve priestesses second class of the Minervan High Council advanced onto the stage holding torches. An older woman followed them. With shock, Hamilton realized it was the High Priestess Nendra herself. Then, wearing a white robe, with a shining golden laurel wreath wrapped around her hair, Aurora advanced onto the stage. Hamilton had never seen her so radiant. She knelt before the High Priestess, her eyes modestly downcast, but with a hint of a smile upon her face.

The music stopped, and the High Priestess spoke. "Sisters of Minerva," she intoned. "We are gathered here today on a most joyous occasion, to welcome into the ranks of the Holy Third Circle one who has in every way earned the love of the Goddess. Aurora, daughter of Melodia, daughter of Iris, daughter of Thetis, daughter of Atalanta, daughter of Artemisia: stand forth and face your sisters!"

Aurora rose to face the audience, and the hall erupted into joyous song. Light shone brilliantly from her laurel leaves, and her smile was even brighter. When the song stopped, the audience broke into applause.

The High Priestess let the clamor go on for about half a minute, and then raised her hands for silence. "Aurora," she said. "Welcome to the Holy Sisterhood of the Third Circle. Speak to us of your discoveries."

As Aurora mounted the podium, there were tears of happiness in her eyes. She faced the crowd. "Sisters," she said. "I give thanks to all on this glorious day. I thank my teachers, my mother, my grandmother, and my great grandmother. I thank our twelve great ones of the High Council, and you, divine High Priestess. Most of all, I give thanks to the Goddess Minerva herself, for all she has done for me and for all of us. Just think, ten years ago, we were wandering in darkness and in fear. Yet today, here we are, in the rebuilt Temple of the Goddess herself, living as free women in the holy land of our ancestors!"

The hall erupted into applause. When it subsided, Aurora continued: "As it was in the beginning, as it has been through the ages, we the Sisters of Minerva, have always been the guardians of Divine Reason, that faculty which alone distinguishes humans from beasts. Thus it is our custom, today as throughout the ages, that upon attaining the holy order of the Third Circle, one of our Sisterhood should present to all others a précis of the work by which she has advanced the cause of Reason. And thus, as did my mother, grandmother, and great grandmother, in their time, so I shall do tonight. This is the object of my study."

She paused, and suddenly Hamilton felt her thoughts inside his head. "Hamilton, walk onto the stage right now!"

Taken by surprise, Hamilton did nothing. Then Aurora touched her owl pendant and Hamilton felt a mild but startling electric shock in his genitals. "I said NOW!" her thought shouted again.

This time Hamilton moved. As he entered the dais, her thoughts came again. "Now stand with your feet on the two silver stars, and hold your arms spread wide."

The two stars were about a meter apart. Hamilton stood on them and stretched his arms. He looked out into the audience. Hundreds of female faces were staring at him with amused looks. He felt so embarrassed by their examination that, electric shock or no, he decided he'd had enough. But when he tried to leave, he discovered he could not move a muscle. He was paralyzed!

At this thought, the whole audience broke out into giggles. Aurora looked at him and smiled a mischievous smile. The she faced her audience.

"This is the specimen, Sergeant Andrew Hamilton, collected by me while he was in the act of murdering a group of Minervans out picnicking in the country. I had him wash properly today, and as you can ascertain, his smell is now within acceptable bounds. To me, this indicates that the hideous stench of Earthlings is not genetic, but, in at least some cases, could be ameliorated by instruction in proper sanitary habits."

A murmur of surprise rippled through the audience.

"You will also notice, Sisters, that despite various unsightly mutilations, his physical characteristics, while markedly below Minervan standards, are not freakishly so." With that, she touched her owl again, and Hamilton's clothes disappeared leaving him totally naked in front of the crowd. As he blushed in humiliation, the women all burst into laughter.

Aurora waited for the merriment to subside, then continued. "In fact, my measurements show that in composite relevant physical indices, the specimen falls roughly within the 5th percentile of Minervan males. My research also indicates that, however, he places within about the 95th percentile of Earthling males. So, the point is that he is no more than two standard deviations below the Minervan mean, and two standard deviations above the Earthling mean. Thus there is, in fact, an overlap between Minervan and Earthling male physiological characteristics, and the statistical difference is not more than four standard deviations apart."

There was a stunned silence in the hall. Then one of the Second Class priestesses on the dais spoke. "But that is only physical characteristics. Surely you don't mean to imply that there is an intellectual overlap?"

Aurora bowed to the Second Class Priestess. "No, Your Eminence. Certainly not. Intelligence tests show true mental abilities nearly entirely lacking."

That comment got Hamilton mad. He couldn't open his mouth to talk, but he thought as loudly as he could. "That's not fair, Aurora. You know I have a brain!"

A titter of laughter surged across the hall, as everyone overheard Hamilton's defiant thought. Aurora looked at him and smiled, and then continued her speech to the Sisters, saying, "As I shall now demonstrate."

She turned to Hamilton again. "Now Hamilton. Here is an elementary intelligence test. I'll ask you three very simple questions. If you can get any of them right, I'll set you free. So try as hard as you can. OK?"

Hamilton suddenly found his mouth was free to move. "OK," he said.

"Very good. Question number one. "Who played 7th base for the Pegasus Thunderbolts in the Galactic championship of 19,372?"

"What?"

Aurora snickered. "You mean you don't know?"

"Of course not…"

Aurora turned to the audience. "He doesn't know!" Everyone laughed.

She turned back to Hamilton, "OK, question number two. On what planet was the twelfth of the Holy Owls born?"

"Earth?" Hamilton guessed. Everyone laughed again.

Aurora shook her head. "Well Hamilton, here is your last chance. If a man and woman enter the Temple of Minerva, what must the woman say before the man is allowed to speak?"

Hamilton thought hard. The Minervan religion was obviously matriarchal. The women were intermediaries between the males and the Goddess. He ventured a try. "She has to say, 'Oh Great Goddess Minerva, condescend to grant this poor pathetic male the right to speak in your presence.'"

There was hushed silence in the hall for several seconds. Aurora raised an eyebrow. "Not bad, Hamilton. It's not the right answer, but it's got potential."

She turned back to her audience. "And that is my final point, potential. The specimen has almost no actual intelligence, but he exhibits significant potential intelligence. I would even go further. You will have observed, Sisters, the persistent heated thought in the specimen's mind: 'This is not fair.' I have examined this concept of 'fair' and as near as I can determine, it is a crude approximation of the Minervan concept of 'just.' It must thus be considered a proto-rational thought."

The same Second Class Priestess who had spoken before spoke again. "My dear, don't you think you are going a bit far with this speculation?"

Aurora looked respectfully at her senior, and said, "I know it may seem incredible, but may it please Your Eminence, I have done my research with diligence and this is my night to speak."

The High Priestess said, "Aurora, this is your night to speak, but this is also your time to conclude."

Aurora bowed. "Yes, divine one." She turned to face the audience for the last time. "So, to conclude, my research indicates that Earthlings may, and I underscore may, be potentially human. And while this hypothesis can only be considered tentative and will require a great deal of further work to substantiate, I believe that it indicates that, when it would not otherwise result in inconvenience or loss of amusement, we should seek to minimize the pain and suffering that our actions might cause among them."

A shocked silence filled the room. Then the High Priestess said: "Ah, the refreshing idealism of the young. In time it will be followed by wisdom. Let us rejoice."

All the women began to sing a final soaring hymn.

After it was all over, Aurora gave Hamilton another set of clothes and walked him home.

"So you see, Hamilton, I spoke up for you and your people before the entire Sisterhood. What do you think about that?"

"Oh, yeah. You were a regular Martin Luther King."

She peered at him, annoyed. "So now you're sulking again. Just what is your problem?"

Hamilton turned to her enraged. "Aurora, you just humiliated me in front of every priestess in the city!"

"Oh, poor baby."

"But..."

She held up her hand. "Hush, creature. You have no right to complain. I did everything possible to make you look good. I had you wash properly so you wouldn't smell. I gave you decent clothes so you wouldn't look ridiculous. I showed everyone your almost-normal physique so they would know that not all Earthlings are completely grotesque. I translated every word of the ceremony for you, so you would know what was going on. I chose the three easiest questions I could think of for your intelligence test, and even gave you a hint so you could score a few points. I removed your shell of arrogance, so everyone could see how cute your little psyche is."

"You mean you subjected me to ridicule in front of 600 Minervan women."

"So? Everyone had a great time. They all thought you were very funny, you know."

Hamilton drew himself up straight. "Aurora, I have to have my dignity."

Aurora looked at Hamilton, puzzled. "Why?"

"Because I am a human being."

The priestess smiled indulgently. "There you go again, making completely unsupported assertions. You're not advancing your case with such nonsense."

"But I thought you told the gathering that…"

"I told them there was some evidence indicating you were potentially human. Don't let that go to your head. There is a big difference between being potentially human and actually human. There is no evidence for the latter."

"How can you say that? Look at our cities. Look at our civilization!"

Aurora put a hand on Hamilton's shoulder and looked at him with pity in her eyes. "Hamilton, you are so proud of your cities. But you should understand that, compared to how civilized people live throughout the galaxy, your habitations are just a collection of smelly hovels. Now it is true that your poverty of intellectual, artistic, architectural and technological accomplishments, while offering no evidence for your putative humanity, does not necessarily prove the opposite. But look at your behavior, how barbaric it is; not only in your futile and insane attacks upon us, but even in your treatment of your fellow Earthlings. Why just yesterday, your own government machine-gunned twenty of your people who were trying to escape the Kennewickian refugee camps to return to America to find work."

Hamilton's eyes were downcast. "Yes, I know. That was wrong."

"So why should anyone believe that you are human?"

The soft sympathy in her voice made her indictment even more crushing. Hamilton wanted to cry. But he stifled the impulse and walked on for several minutes in silence. Then he was struck by a thought. He turned to the priestess.

"Aurora, this evening I heard you say that ten years ago you and your people were living in fear. Fear of who?"

Instantly, the look of sympathetic superiority vanished from the priestess' face. In its place there appeared an expression of desperate terror.

"The evil ones. They tried to kill us all. They killed my parents, my sisters, and my brothers. I saw them do it! I was only a little girl at the time, but I still remember it. They tried to kill me too!"

She started to shake. Hamilton held her to comfort her. "How did you escape?"

She sniffled. "They were doing horrible things to my older sisters, and weren't watching me. So I jumped out the window and hid in a barrel. I could hear them searching for me, but I was so small they couldn't find me. I hid in the barrel for two days and two nights, listening to the screams as they photolysized hundreds of Minervans. Then space marines from the WGE hit the planet and I was rescued."

"What's the WGE?"

"The Western Galactic Empire. They saved us. And then they brought us here."

"But who were these evil ones? And why did they want to kill you?"

"The evil ones. The Central Galactics. Worshippers of the false goddess Aphrodite."

Hamilton was puzzled. "Aphrodite? The goddess of Love?"

Aurora became hysterical. "Don't believe it, Hamilton! Don't believe it! It is not Love she stands for, but Passion, irrational passion. That is why she hates the true Goddess Minerva, the Goddess of Reason, and all of her people. That is why she had her followers try to kill us all!"

"But she is real then? You called her a false goddess."

"Oh, she is real alright. But she is not a goddess. She is…" Aurora held her hand over Hamilton's head to extract a word. "She is satanic. And so are all her followers." She looked into the Ranger's eyes with desperate sincerity. "Hamilton, worship your Christ or whatever other local totems you like. I'll understand. But promise me this, that you will never join the cult of Aphrodite."

She seemed so vulnerable that Hamilton was deeply moved. "I promise," he said softly.

Aurora put her head on his shoulder and sobbed. He held her for a while, but then could not resist delivering his follow through.

"So, these Central Galactics, they were civilized humans then, with beautiful buildings and impressive technologies? Not primitives like us?"

Aurora backed away, and looked at Hamilton, her eyes tearful, yet determined. "Those who willingly abandon their humanity are much more to be despised than those who have never had it."

It took Hamilton a few seconds to absorb the meaning of this comment. Then he said: "So then, being civilized is not everything?"

Aurora shook her head. "No, I suppose not." She paused for a few seconds, and then managed to muster a weak smile. "Touché," she said.

They walked back the rest of the way to Hamilton's cell in silence.

Chapter 5

The President stared at Attorney General Brasher in amazement. "You're saying that the radicals are blaming us for the moral decay of the country? Us? The true keepers of the faith?"

Brasher nodded. "Yes, they say we are flooding the country with pornographic joycubes that are destroying the minds and moral fiber of our citizens."

Beasley said, "I told you we shouldn't have taken those…"

The President cut the Science Advisor short with a light tap on his silver prism. "There was no choice. It was sell on their terms, or have the stuff taken."

"But they also offered agricultural technologies," Beasley whimpered. "We could have…"

This time the President pressed down hard on the prism, achieving much more satisfactory results. "That's enough of that. Those joycubes are bringing in vital revenue to this administration." He paused, then turned to his Treasury Secretary. "Myra, that reminds me, do you have the checks?"

"Right here, Mr. President. Ten billion for each of us, and twenty billion for you."

"Well done. As I was saying, the joycubes are helping to balance the budget and have contributed greatly to social peace. It's not our fault they are pornographic. It's the WGE who makes them, not us."

Lisa White was on the case. "Precisely, Mr. President," the Public Relations Director said. "What we have here is an elementary problem in public relations. We simply need to shift the blame where it is due. The Weegees are the ones behind the Minervans, and they are the ones behind the joycubes. They are the real enemy that is trying to destroy our country."

The President nodded. "That's right, that's right."

Lisa became enthusiastic. "Mr. President, this is nothing less than a godsend in disguise. The Minervans were too local a threat to really motivate our people. But the Western Galactic Empire is a Great Devil against whose enormous menace we can unite our nation in eternal holy struggle."

"Excellent," the President said. "Mobilize the press, the ministries, and the educational system. Our nation must speak with one voice, think with one mind, and have but one thought in that one mind. Death to Pagans! Death to the Minervans! Death to the Western Galactic Empire!"

"That's three thoughts," Beasley tried to interject, before the President cut him off with a tap on the prism.

White House Chaplain Reverend John Meade intoned, "Surely Christ will bless us in this holy cause."

General Smith, the Chairman of the Joint Chiefs of Staff, raised his head sheepishly. "Excuse me sir, but our intelligence indicates that the Western Galactic Empire includes over a hundred million planets, and has a fleet of over a hundred billion interstellar battleships and a hundred trillion space marines. I'm not sure our armed forces can handle them."

The President stared at his General, shocked by his comment. "What! Are you scared?" He turned to his Secretary of Defense for an alternative opinion. "What do you think, Jack?"

Defense Secretary Jack Ripley thought carefully. "Well, I think we'll need a significant increase in the defense budget."

That was unacceptable. Money was needed for more important things. But all his political instincts told him that a holy war would be the best possible thing for the administration. What to do? He looked to CIA Director Fred Collins for advice.

On cue, Collins spoke up. "Gentlemen, I think you underestimate the genius of our glorious leader. Of course we will not assault the WGE in open warfare. That would be idiotic. Only military simpletons would consider such an idea." He looked at Smith and Ripley with disdain. "All we need to do is mount a hate campaign against them. That will serve our purpose of uniting the nation. The Weegees will probably not even find out about it, and if they do, they won't care so long as we keep the helicity flowing. Politics is politics and business is business, and the Weegees understand that as well as we do."

Now it was the Minister's turn to be shocked. "I cannot believe what I am hearing. You mean to say that our holy war against the Weegee pagans will be a sham? I cannot condone such a course."

The President was taken aback. Meade's legions of the faithful were central to his political base. He hastened to interject: "No, Reverend, it will not be a sham by any means. We will mobilize the faithful at every turn to hate and smite the pagans. But, except for our continued battle against the Minervans, we will not attack them as a government. That would give the Weegees too big a target to hit back at. Instead we will leave it to the faithful themselves, under your guidance and that of your shepherds, to strike the holy blows. It will not be the Army of the United States that brings the Western Galactic Empire to its knees, but the Army of Christ, with you as its vicar."

Reverend Meade reflected. The offer was tempting. With government support, he could lead the battle against the galactic pagan foe, without interference from defeatists like Smith and Ripley. Furthermore, the hate campaign would greatly expand his own political base, and thus his private funding sources. And yes, it was true that the US armed forces would be of little avail against the fleets of the WGE. More subtle techniques were called for to strike effective blows, and these could be implemented far better by his own faithful followers than by Smith's uniformed cannon fodder. He nodded, "Very well. But I'll need arms, funds, and a base of operations to train my elite cadres."

"It can't be inside the United States," said Collins.

"How about Peru?" the President offered.

Meade smiled. Peru would do nicely. "Christ will bless you for this."

Hamilton watched the video screen in disbelief. Yankee Stadium was completely filled with people of every age and condition screaming at the top of their lungs.

"Death! Death! Death!"

The camera then switched to an image of the White House Chaplain, Reverend John Meade.

"And what does Jesus command us to bring to the Western Galactic Empire?" the preacher asked the crowd.

"Death! Death! Death!" the multitudes responded.

"Death to the pagans!" called the preacher.

"Death to the pagans!" responded the crowd.

"Death to the Minervans!" the preacher yelled.

"Death to the Minervans !" shouted the crowd.

"Death to the Western Galactic Empire!" Meade screamed.

"Death to the Western Galactic Empire!" screamed the utterly transported crowd.

Then cheerleaders deployed throughout the stadium began leading the several hundred thousand attendees in a furious chant.

"Death to the Weegees! Death to the Weegees! Death to the Weegees!"

As the mob chanted on, hundreds of floats depicting the Milky Way Galaxy were paraded into the playing field of the stadium. Then, on a pre-arranged signal, thousands of the Reverend's flock jumped over the bleacher walls to storm the field. Surrounding each effigy galaxy, the rioters pulled down their pants and started urinating on its western spiral arm.

The crowd cheered them on lustily.

"Death to the Weegees! Death to the Weegees! Death to the Weegees!"

Hamilton heard a sound behind him. It was Aurora, watching the video over his shoulder.

"You Earthlings are quite insane," she said.

In view of the display on the TV, this was a difficult charge to dispute, but Hamilton had to try.

"We're not all like that."

Aurora arched an eyebrow. "Oh no? Are you claiming to be different? You who submerged your own conscience to murder six people?"

The charge of murder rankled. "It was not murder," he protested. "It was combat. What I did was entirely honorable. If you hadn't captured me, I would be a hero now."

Aurora smiled ironically. "My point exactly. You can't say your behavior was right, because it wasn't. So instead you say it was honorable, which translates to mean 'approved by the herd mind.' And indeed, you are correct. If I hadn't collected you, that mob of psychotics would be cheering you this very moment. Does that make you proud?"

The priestess had cut him to the quick. The crowd was crazy. He could see that. Would he have been their hero if he had gotten away after scoring on the Minervans? Certainly. Did that mean that everything he had done was just the act of a psychotic with a few more combat skills than the rest? Was there no courage, no honor, in his platoon's heroic sacrifice? Did he have nothing to be proud of at all? He could not admit it. He would not. Yet the mob's frenzy was a horrible mirror. Did he look that grotesque to Aurora?

"Poor Hamilton," she cooed, deepening his humiliation with sympathy.

Now a large statue of an extremely beautiful woman was paraded out on the playing field. She wore a blue robe with a golden triangle pendant, and her spectacular auburn hair, elegantly coifed, was topped by a jeweled crown. A golden owl sat on her right shoulder, and in her right hand was a small golden staff topped by a double-headed ax. In her left hand was another staff, around which two snakes coiled in a double helix.

"Who is that?" Hamilton asked.

"It is the Empress Phila Minaphera, the 243rd, supreme ruler of the Western Galactic Empire."

Observing the golden owl, Hamilton commented, "Looks like she believes in Minerva too."

"Yes," Aurora answered. "All the Weegees do. But note also the snakes of Aphrodite and the double ax of Hera. Their belief is not pure."

"So you mean they believe in all three Goddesses?"

"They believe in three Goddesses, and in one triune goddess with three manifestations. Three in one, one in three, as they put it. That's what the triangle symbolizes."

Hamilton was bewildered. "Three or one? I don't get it."

Aurora shrugged. "Neither do we."

Suddenly flames erupted around the statue. As the flames grew, the cheerleaders led the crowd in a roaring chant.

"Death to the Empress! Death to the Empress! Death to the Empress!"

Soon there was nothing but cinders. As the ashes collapsed in a heap, the crowd shouted its applause.

Hamilton turned to Aurora. "I take it the Weegees are not going to appreciate that little display."

Aurora shook her head. "No they won't. But they probably won't react so long as your people don't actually do anything and the helicity keeps flowing."

Hamilton already had a rough idea of what helicity was, and so didn't ask for more details. A more serious question was troubling him. A mass frenzy of the sort exhibited in the stadium could lead to war, even if that was not the government's intention. "If it comes to a fight, what are our chances?"

Aurora giggled. "Less than zero." Apparently she thought the question preposterous. This offended Hamilton's military pride.

"What do you mean 'less than zero?' What do they have?"

"Well for starters, the Western Galactic Empire includes over a hundred million planets, and has a fleet of over a hundred billion interstellar battleships and a hundred trillion space marines."

"For starters?"

"Yes, that's just their active duty forces. Counting their reserves, they have a hundred times that many."

"Oh," Hamilton said. "But numbers aren't everything. What's their military technology like? Not as good as yours, I suppose?"

"Much, much better. And we'd be on their side, remember?"

Hamilton was awed. "So they would just crush us like ants."

Aurora laughed. "There you go again, with your delusions of grandeur."

Hamilton looked back at the TV. In light of the ridiculous imbalance of forces, the irrational frenzy of the rally seemed even more disgusting. He turned the monitor off.

"Would you like to go for a walk?" Aurora asked.

"Sure." He needed some fresh air.

Chapter 6

As they strolled out through the amazing Minervan garden, Hamilton turned to the priestess. "Aurora, tell me about the galaxy. Is the Western Galactic Empire the only major power? Or is there also an Eastern Empire?"

"So you want to know about Galactic geopolitics?"

"Yes."

"Very well, I'll gratify your curiosity. There certainly is an Eastern Galactic Empire, and it is almost as powerful as the Western Galactic Empire. The Eegees worship only Hera, the Goddess of might and justice, which makes them quite obnoxious. But they allied with the Weegees to crush the Central Empire during the recent war. It seems like a strange alliance, but the Eegees had no choice. The Centrals had them slated for extermination as soon as they finished with us."

"So what happened to the Central Empire?"

"They have been reorganized as the neutral and disarmed Central Union. They say they've seen the error of their past ways, and now preach nothing but love."

"But you don't buy it."

Aurora rolled her eyes.

Hamilton continued, "Are there any other powers?"

Aurora nodded. "There is the Confederation of Northern Princesspalities. Individually, the Princesspalities are quite weak, with less than a million planets each. But there are thirty of them federated together, so collectively they are about a third as powerful as either of the two major empires. "

"And what is their religion?"

"They worship both Minerva and Aphrodite, each singly and as facets of a diune Goddess. Yes, I know, quite incomprehensible. But it gives them a lot more in common with the Weegees than the Eegees. The Centrals too, look to the Weegees for protection, since at least they include Aphrodite in their pantheon, whereas the Eeegees do not. So long as they both continue to lean that way, the Western Galactic Empire will have the edge."

"So long as? Why would they change?"

"They could change if they felt the WGE was getting too powerful. That's why the Weegees are careful not to throw their weight around too openly. So for example, that is the reason they prefer to pay for your planet's helicity supply rather than just take it."

"I see. Well we've covered the Center, the North, the East and the West. What is in the South?"

"The south is a region of primitive barbaric planets, generally considered too insignificant to be worth seizing by any civilized power."

Hamilton had a good idea what was coming. "Don't tell me. The Earth is in the south?"

Aurora smiled. "The deep south."

As she said this, the two of them emerged from the garden into the settlement's central plaza. Numerous outdoor cafes had been set up on the left hand side of the square, and a large number of Minervans of both genders were enjoying an afternoon of raffa sipping and conversation. On the right hand side of the square, a multitude of Earthling children aged between 5 and 10 were milling around. Not playing, just milling around, as if they were waiting for something. There were also television crews in the square, some with very odd-looking equipment, pointing variously at the café crowd and at the children.

Hamilton felt his stomach tighten. It was obvious that something dreadful was about to happen.

Aurora read his mind. She said, "Yes, we know. They are about to attack and will all have their hands blown off."

Hamilton turned to her. "You know? Then why don't you do something? They're just children, for Christ's sake!"

Aurora held up her finger. "No heresy, please. I am a 3rd circle Priestess of the one true Goddess Minerva, you know."

Hamilton looked at her with pleading eyes. "Aurora, they are just children. Show some compassion."

Aurora stared at him hotly. "Compassion? We are showing compassion! They have their guns hidden under their shirts. If we disarmed them now, their stomachs would be blown apart and they would all be killed outright. So instead, we are waiting for them to draw their weapons. In consequence, they may even get off a few shots and some innocent

Minervans could be hurt, or possibly killed, by these crazy little assassins."

At this point one of the unusual video teams approached. It consisted of a woman reporter and a man. The woman was a sensuous brassy blonde about six foot three, allowing her to tower a bit over the 5'11" Hamilton and the 5'9" Aurora. The cameraman was even taller, and his incredibly well-muscled body showed clearly through his skin-tight shirt. Both were clothed in red, and had golden double-helix snake lapel pins. As the woman approached, Hamilton felt a wave of erotic power emanating from her, causing his lower parts to stiffen.

The woman looked at him up and down, and apparently pleased with her effect on him, smiled a Mona Lisa smile. "Excuse me Sir," she said, "You are an Earthling living here in Minervan-occupied Kennewick, are you not?"

"Yes." Hamilton managed to reply.

Her smiled broadened. "Very good. I'm Kolta Bruna, with the Galactic News Service. I'd love to interview you to get your views of life under the Minervan occupation."

Aurora interrupted. "Did you say your name was Kolta Bruna? Any relation to Kalta Bruna, the former Governess of Pegasus 3?"

Kolta Bruna seemed pleased. "Why, yes. She is my mother. I'm delighted that you've heard of her, even in this far-off place. I'm sure you'll be pleased to hear that she has now resumed her political career, and was recently appointed Mistress of Culture for the Central Unions' 62nd Province."

Aurora's stare turned hard. "Your mother had my family murdered."

Kolta Bruna waved the accusation off with a shrug. "Oh, really, that was a long time ago. Can't you people just let by gones be by gones?"

Aurora began to shake. She held up her hand and pointed at the reporter. "May Minerva damn you to Tartarus, you, and your daughters, and your daughters' daughters, for 1000 generations," she intoned.

Kolta Bruna winked at Hamilton. "And they pretend to be oh-so-rational. So, my little Earthling, are you ready for your interview?"

Hamilton nodded. But before Kolta Bruna had time to respond with her first question, all hell broke loose in the square. The children drew their guns, but only a handful had time to get off a shot before the Minervan lightning balls did their work.

Seconds later it was all over. One Minervan and eight children were dead, three other Minervans had non-lethal bullet wounds, and over fifty children were screaming in pain as their life's blood drained out through the stumps of their mutilated arms.

As at the dance, the Minervans crowded around their own wounded, ignoring the dying children. Kolta Bruna and her cameraman, along with hordes of other TV crews went to focus in on the children in agony, but did nothing to help them. Hamilton stood still, paralyzed by the sheer misery of the sight. Why wouldn't anyone do anything to help the children?

Suddenly someone did. A late-middle-aged Earthling man carrying a small black bag charged out into the carnage of the square. Ripping the children's clothing to get material, he rapidly tied makeshift tourniquets around the bleeding stump of one child after another. Hamilton felt his spirits rise. At last, here was something he could do. He ran into the square to help.

But as Hamilton neared the doctor, the man was surrounded by a group of three Earthling toughs. The tallest pulled the older man up, bodily separating him from a little girl he was trying to help.

"Hey bud, what's the big idea?" the tough said.

The doctor struggled and shouted in desperation. "Leave me alone! I'm trying to save them!"

"They don't need you to save them," the tough replied. "They're here to be martyrs."

"Let him go," Hamilton said sternly.

The fattest of the three toughs turned to face the new arrival. "Oh, so if it isn't the traitor," he snickered.

That was the limit. Hamilton's Ranger training went into gear. In one swift motion he lashed out with his foot, smashing in the face of the fat man. The tall man let go of the doctor, and threw a punch at Hamilton, but the soldier blocked it, and stepping in, decked the man with an upward punch to the jaw. Then grabbing the limp man, he whirled, and used the tough's body to block the blow from a crowbar that the third creep had aimed for his head. Hamilton then threw the body at the man, who dropped his crowbar and fled in terror.

Hamilton watched the tough run for a few seconds to make sure he was gone, and then turned to look for the doctor. The man was already back on the ground, and having finished tournequeting the little girl, was now working on a nine-year-old boy. The older man wasted no time in pleasantries.

"You there. Start doing what I'm doing."

Hamilton nodded. "Right," he said, and went swiftly to work.

He had staunched the bleeding of about a dozen of the children, when he sensed a familiar presence standing above him. It was Aurora.

"Why are you doing this?" she asked. "These are assassins. If you save them, they will try to kill again."

Hamilton looked up, tears in his eyes. "Aurora, how can you be so heartless? Can't you see they are just children?"

Just then Kolta Bruna arrived with her cameraman. "Priestess," she said, "I must protest this outrage. These two Earthlings are ruining our footage. On behalf of the Galactic News Service, I demand that they be removed so that the story can be photographed as planned."

Aurora regarded the reporter dourly. "They're ruining your footage, are they?"

"Yes," Kolta Bruna replied. "And I remind you that the GNS has spent a good deal of bluebacks to send us here, and will not be pleased at all if we are interfered with."

"I see," Aurora said. The priestess held up her left arm and snapped her fingers three times.

"Thank you, Priestess," said Kolta Bruna.

A few seconds later, three well-built Minervan men arrived in response to Aurora's summons. From his position on the ground where he was still trying to complete a final tourniquet, Hamilton looked up at them. He could see they were all in prime physical condition. Even without their electroshock clothing, there was no chance he could take them. "Please, Aurora," he begged, but the priestess silenced him with a thought. She then turned to her men.

"Do you see these two Earthlings?" she asked, indicating Hamilton and the doctor.

"Yes, Priestess 3rd Class Aurora," the apparent leader of the squad replied.

"See that no one interferes with them."

The look of satisfaction on Kolta Bruna's face turned to one of outrage. "You'll never get away with this!" she cried.

Aurora smiled a thin smile. "Carry on, Hamilton," she said, and strolled off.

The presence of the three Minervan protectors emboldened several other Kennewickian adults to join Hamilton and the doctor in the rescue effort. Working fast, the enlarged team managed to stop over forty of the children from bleeding to death. But they were still in dreadful pain and in danger of infection.

Dr. Berger stood up and tried ineffectually to rub the blood from his hands. "We need to get these kids to my clinic, fast," he said.

Hamilton addressed the Kennewickian volunteers. "We'll need transportation. Do any of you have trucks?"

One of the men raised his hand. "Charlie and I have our semis just across the river, but…" he looked over at the Minervan guards. Earthling vehicles were banned from the Minervan settlement.

Hamilton spoke to the squad leader. "We need to bring trucks in here if we are to save these children. Will you let us?"

The man shook his head. "Sorry, Earthling, but that is against the rules, and you know it."

Hamilton was incensed. "The priestess told you not to let anyone interfere with us."

The squad leader smiled. "That's right. But she just meant that you should be allowed to bandage the little assassins. She didn't say anything about letting you savages bring your machines in here."

The man was probably right. But Hamilton had to try. He said, "Ask her." Then he thought as hard as he could, hoping that Aurora was listening. "Aurora, please let us save the children."

The squad leader was silent for several seconds, then he lifted his eyebrows. "She says it's OK. But we inspect the trucks first, and they only come in as far as the middle perimeter."

The middle perimeter was only a quarter mile away. They could move the kids there by hand. Hamilton sent Aurora a thought of thanks. Then he addressed the team. "Right. Charlie and Al, the two of you hoof it for the river and get your trucks. The rest of you, start carrying these children to the old firehouse on Main. That's right on the middle perimeter." He pointed to one of the volunteers, Susan Peterson, a Registered Nurse. "Susan and one of the guards can watch the kids that are there, while Dr. Berger stays behind until the last of them are moved out of here. OK people, let's move."

Chapter 7

By four o'clock, the thirty-nine surviving children were lying in cots in Dr. Berger's makeshift clinic in the Columbia-Kennewick refugee camp. A few were sleeping, but most were still writhing in pain.

Hamilton looked around. The place was a squalid mess. Except for bandages, iodine, and aspirin, no medical resources were in sight. The doctor, his wife, Susan, and some other volunteer helpers moved from cot to cot doing what they could. But the prospects for the little patients were not promising.

Finally, the doctor and his wife approached Hamilton. "We want to thank you," the doctor said.

Hamilton shrugged. "There is no need for thanks. I did what any man would do."

The doctor's wife smiled. "I don't think Howard made himself clear. We want to thank you for saving our son." She held out her hand. "I'm Melissa Berger, by the way."

Hamilton was confused. He pointed to the wounded children. "You mean one of these is…?

Melissa shook her head. "No, not one of these. It was our youngest son Tommy that you saved two weeks ago at the dance." Tears began to form in her eyes. "He's all we have left, since his two older brothers were…martyred."

Hamilton's mind raced back to that event. The little boy with the pistol, aiming for the back of Aurora's head. His instinctive kick that had saved both the priestess and the boy. "You mean your son was the little boy who was going to kill Aurora?"

Melissa nodded, and said "yes." Then she froze, staring over Hamilton's shoulder in terror. Hamilton turned. In the entrance of the tent stood the priestess Aurora.

"Do go on," she said. "This is a very interesting conversation."

Hamilton pleaded. "Aurora, please. These are good people. They mean you no harm. Look into their minds. You'll see what I'm saying is true."

Aurora folded her hands across her chest. "Oh, I already have. And you are quite right. These two," here she indicated the doctor and his wife, "are remarkable. I have no quarrel with them. It's their son I am after."

Melissa Berger fell on her knees before Aurora. "Please priestess, don't take Tommy," she cried. "Don't take my last little boy away from me."

Aurora's voice was calm and level. "So his two older brothers were assassins, too?"

Howard Berger's eyes were wet. "You must understand. It's not their fault."

The priestess raided her eyebrows. "Not their fault? How can the action of any being not be considered their fault? Are you saying that Earthlings lack free will?"

"No, what I mean is that they are just children, and easily deluded. They get recruited by…"

Aurora raised her hand. "Enough. Bring me the boy. Now." She touched her owl, threateningly. "Or do I need to make him come here myself?"

The Bergers didn't move. Aurora said, "very well," and touched her owl again. Then she stood in silence, as if waiting.

A few moments later a small boy in a nightshirt came running into the tent. "Mommy!" he exclaimed, "I just had the scariest dream!" he ran into his mother's arms, who held him, sobbing. "Mommy, what's wrong?" he asked. "I'm the one who had the scary dream." Then he looked up and saw the black-robed priestess standing above him, and froze in sheer terror.

Aurora stretched out her hand, and held it above the head of the boy for several seconds. Then she looked at Dr. Berger.

"Dr. Berger, your son is totally psychotic, and will kill the next chance he gets. I need to prevent that."

Berger managed to look her in the eye. "What do you intend to do?"

"Well, he tried to kill me, so I'm entitled to his life. But I am not a vengeful person. The minimum penalty prescribed by law is that he lose his right hand. That will suffice."

The doctor was horrified. "You mean you are going to cut off Tommy's hand?"

Aurora nodded. "Yes, we can do it surgically with no risk of infection back at the settlement."

Hamilton intervened. "Aurora, this is wrong."

She looked at him. "I'm sorry Hamilton. It may be unpleasant, but it's not wrong. It's the law."

Melissa sobbed. "Have mercy, priestess, have mercy."

Aurora said softly. "I'll see that he suffers no undue pain. Now if you'll just be good enough to give him to me…"

She reached down, but at that moment Tommy bolted from his mother's arms and scooted under the tent flap to escape outside. Aurora ran outside after him, and Hamilton followed. There were two Minervan men standing guard outside.

"Where did he go?" she asked.

The guard answered, "He ran that way. I think he is over there, hiding in one of those barrels."

Aurora closed her eyes for several seconds, then she nodded. "Yes, he is. Follow me."

Aurora walked directly towards a group of trashcans, one of which was lying on its side. The two Minervans, Hamilton, and the Bergers followed her. She halted just in front of the toppled can. It was obvious she knew Tommy was inside.

"Shall we remove him?" one of the guards asked.

Aurora said nothing.

Hamilton guessed what she was thinking. "A child hiding in a barrel," he said suggestively.

Tears formed in the priestess' eyes. "It's not the same," she said adamantly. "I wasn't an assassin. I hadn't broken any laws. It's not the same, Hamilton, it's just not the same."

"Then prove it's not the same," Hamilton pressed his advantage. "We know what the Centrals would have done in a situation like this. What are you going to do?"

Aurora stared up into the sky, in the direction of the constellation Pegasus. "Goddess help me," she whispered. Then she turned to the Bergers, with authority in her voice. "Doctor and Mrs. Berger. Your son is a menace. I cannot let him go free. But if you will pledge me your words to keep him confined to the immediate vicinity of your home, I will spare him."

"Oh, yes, thank you, priestess," Melissa said. "Thank you."

"We'll do anything you say," the doctor confirmed. "I'd love to keep him confined to camp."

Aurora pursed her lips. "Very well, here is what you must do. Tie him up tonight so he can't escape. I'll send Hamilton out tomorrow with an unbreakable ankle ring that will give him a severe electric shock if he ever travels more than 100 meters from a microcontrol unit which you will inject into Mrs. Berger. Once that is done, you can untie him. He will be bound to stay within 100 meters of you until I deactivate the ring. Are those terms acceptable?"

The Bergers nodded.

"Then it's done." Aurora signaled to her men. "Remove the boy." Then she turned to the Ranger. "I'm walking back to the settlement. Hamilton, you come with me."

They walked in silence for several minutes through the pale moonlight. Then Aurora spoke.

"So, Hamilton, I see you're feeling pretty proud of yourself right now."

There was no point lying, so he admitted it frankly. "Yes, Aurora, I am."

"You're pretty arrogant, you know that? To think, a subhuman Earthling male having the gall to think he can teach morality to a 3rd circle Minervan priestess."

Hamilton smiled. "Well, did you learn anything?"

"Oh, would you please stop it with your silly arrogance. I'm really mad at you. You took advantage of me tonight."

Hamilton was flummoxed. "I? I took advantage of you? How?"

"I confided in you. I told you my deepest feelings, my darkest memory. So you knew how horrified I would be to find myself resembling the Centrals in any way. You made a false mirror and threatened to have it show me as some kind of aphrodemonic monster. You knew I could never face that, and you exploited my vulnerability."

"I wasn't exploiting your vulnerability. I was employing your receptivity to teach you something really important."

Aurora put her hands on her hips. "And exactly what did you, a smelly savage, think you were entitled to teach me?"

"I thought you said I didn't stink anymore."

"I said 'smelly,' not 'stinky.' Now answer the question. Just what did you presume to teach me?"

"That you were being cruel."

"That does it!" Aurora threw up her hands and walked several steps, then turned to face Hamilton. "So I was being cruel, was I? You Earthlings are always saying that we Minervans are sooooo cruel. We buy back our ancient homeland and offer to help you in innumerable ways. You refuse our help. So we are cruel. You send armies to kill us. We beat you off, but do not pursue. So we are cruel. You brainwash your children to expend their lives in hopeless attempts to kill us. We stop them. So we are cruel. Today I let you rescue dozens of the assassins, and I even came to the hospital to see how they were. But then I find one, just one, who hasn't received his lawful punishment and is planning to try to kill again. Not only that, but he's the very same one who tried to kill me. But even if you don't care about my life, or that of any other Minervans..."

"I do care about your life, Aurora."

"Oh shut up. Even if you don't care about anyone but your little assassin friend, ask yourself this question: What would happen to him as soon as he made his next attempt?"

Hamilton looked down at the ground. There was only one answer. Aurora waited for him to say it, and not just think it. "He would have his arm blown off."

Aurora nodded. "Exactly. So instead of letting that happen, I act to enforce the law, and have his hand removed in a clean, safe, and painless procedure. But you call me cruel. And not just cruel, but morally equal to the most evil beings who ever polluted the universe. You can't imagine how low that made me feel." She started to sob. "It was not I who was cruel tonight, Hamilton. It was you."

For a few moments, the invincible priestess was just a distraught girl, and Hamilton held her to comfort her. "But don't you feel good about being kind to that poor little boy?"

She sniffled and backed away a step. "How can I feel good about bending the law for no logical reason? Tell me, Hamilton, what rational basis is there to be kind to people who are so despicably cruel that they send their own children to be mutilated and killed for the sole purpose of displaying their pitifulness on Galactic TV? In the entire known universe, there is no other race that sinks so low. Tell me Hamilton, why should we be kind to such utterly contemptible creatures?"

The accusation was damning. Hamilton could think of no words of his own to answer her, but from the depths of his memory came lines he had acquired while participating in a high-school play. He recited:

"The quality of mercy is not strain'd.
It droppeth as the gentle rain from heaven
Upon the place beneath: it is twice bless'd;
It blesseth him that gives and him that takes:
'Tis mightiest in the mightiest; it becomes
The throned monarch better than his crown;
His scepter shows the force of temporal power,
The attribute of awe and majesty,

Wherein doth sit the dread and fear of kings,
And earthly power doth then show like God's
When mercy seasons justice."

Aurora stopped sniffling and looked at the Ranger with curiosity. "Hamilton, that's very good poetry. Did you write that?"

Before Hamilton could respond in words, she read his mind. "Oh, Shakespeare. Who was that?"

"He was our greatest poet. He was born in England about 400 years ago."

She started to walk again in the direction of the settlement. "Rather unlikely. From the quality of his verse form it seems far more probable that he was a Minervan living in exile."

"But could a Minervan have written its content?"

The comment stopped the priestess in her tracks. She regarded the soldier silently for several seconds. Then she said; "You are a very interesting study subject, Hamilton."

Hamilton returned Aurora's eye contact without flinching. Was she just trying to cut him down to size? He decided to put a positive spin on her remark. "Interesting study subject? Well I suppose that is a step up from laboratory specimen."

"It certainly is. Just don't let it go to your head." Aurora looked at Hamilton intently. "You know Hamilton, I really do think you have a lot of admirable qualities. You may be a savage, but you are a noble savage." She smiled. "I really want to get to know more about you. Why don't you let me enter your inner mind? I could learn so much."

Hamilton was curious about the pleading nature of the request. "I don't understand. You hold all the cards. Why are you asking my permission?"

"You mean that since you are mentally helpless anyway, why don't I just barge in and do as I like?"

"That's the general idea."

"Because that would be wrong."

Hamilton was baffled.

Aurora laughed. "I see, you don't understand. You're wondering why I, who am always making you do this or that, should suddenly require voluntary cooperation in this matter. Look Hamilton, the things I make you do are all strictly external, and, I might add, clearly for your own good. But were I to enter your inner mind, all of your thought processes, and your very soul itself, would lie naked and helpless before me. To assume such a power over any sentient being, even a primitive protohuman like yourself, without his voluntary consent would be a fundamental violation of the Goddess Minerva's first commandment."

"And what is that?"

"Respect the Mind."

Hamilton thought for a moment. "Well, in that case, I really want to thank you for your consideration. With all due respect, Aurora, I think you have quite enough power over me as it is. Please don't take it personally, but my answer is 'no.'"

Aurora looked upset. "Oh come on. I won't make any permanent changes. I just want to go in and have a look. "

"No."

"Just a peek?"

"No."

The priestess stamped her foot. "Why not? It would mean so much for science, and for me. Don't you care about me?"

"You know that I do."

"Then why not? Come on, be a sport."

"Well, it seems to me from what you say, that even if you don't make any changes, that after you've seen my inner mind, you'll know how all my thought processes work. Is that right?"

"Yes, certainly."

"So in other words, you'll have read my playbook, and your power over me will be greatly and permanently increased."

Aurora looked sheepish. "Well… true. But…"

"So the answer is no." Hamilton walked on.

Aurora hurried after him. "OK, I'll tell you what. I'll promise to refrain from taking any unfair advantage."

"Unless such refraining would cause inconvenience or loss of amusement?"

"Right, exactly," Aurora nodded enthusiastically.

"Forget it."

"Meanie," the priestess pouted.

Chapter 8

The President and his cabinet watched the Galactic News Service broadcast with delight.

The newscaster was a gorgeous erotic blonde dressed in red, and her holoimage standing in the center of room was a sight to excite the relevant zones of not only the men in the cabinet, but some of the women too. The picture quality was perfect, depicting not only the newscaster but the area surrounding her to infinite depth, fully justifying the 3 million bluebacks that had been spent converting the Abraham Lincoln bedroom into a state of the art modern holotheater.

"This is Kolta Bruna, reporting from Earth for the Galactic News Service," the newscaster began.

"Quiet, everyone," the President said. "She is about to talk about us."

The newscaster continued. "I'm here in Minervan-occupied Kennewick. The scene here is one of brutality unmatched in recent times, as the Minervans inflict atrocity after atrocity on the poor defenseless natives of this primitive world."

The holoimage changed, and now the room was filled with three-dimensional reproductions of mangled children, screaming in pain as blood flowed from the stumps of their mutilated arms.

"These Earthling children had their arms blown off by the Minervans, right before my eyes this afternoon."

The picture changed back to the reporter.

"I am sorry that I cannot show you more of this massacre. But the Minervans, apparently wishing to hide their actions from Galactic scrutiny, prevented us from filming the children's expiration."

"GNS's investigative team has since discovered that the massacre was committed using surplus weapons supplied to the Minervan High Council by the Imperial Western Galactic Naval Reserve."

"With me now to discuss today's horrifying events is Minister Aaron Vardt, pastor of the First Methodist Church of Kennewick. Reverend Vardt, I understand that you were Minister to many of the children who were killed here today."

"Yes," the Minister sobbed. "The poor innocent little children, murdered just as their lives were about to begin. How could the Minervans be so cruel?"

"Indeed, that is the question the whole galaxy is asking right now. But tell me Reverend, what will you Kennewickians do now?"

The minister stopped sobbing, and firmed his features in an expression of manly determination. "We will fight. We were born in Kennewick. We have lived in Kennewick. We can only live in Kennewick. Kennewick is our holy city. It is sacred to Jesus Christ, our lord and savior. We cannot live unless it is free of pagan intruders. Our children have shown us the way. We are all prepared to become martyrs in the holy crusade to liberate Kennewick."

"Of course," Kolta Bruna nodded. "And what do you think of the Western Galactic Empire, which gave the Minervans the weapons they used to commit the massacre?"

"In the past, I, and I think most Kennewickians, admired the Western Galactic Empire, and I have always hoped for peace between our two great nations. But the Weegees must understand that by supporting the Minervan crimes, they themselves are committing crimes. They are sowing hate, and the day will come when they shall reap what they sow."

Kolta Bruna smiled to her Galactic audience. "'They shall reap what they sow.' Something to think about. Perhaps the Universal League should take a look into what is going on here before the violence gets out of control and people on civilized planets are forced to endure the consequences. From the primitive Earth, this is Kolta Bruna, for the GNS."

The President switched off the holotheater. "Ladies and Gentlemen of the Cabinet," he grinned, "I think we are beginning to make some progress."

CIA Director Collins nodded. "Yes, but we are running out of children in Kennewick to martyr."

Attorney General Brasher answered him. "That's no problem, I'll have the FBI round up a few hundred more in Seattle and Portland and we'll ship them right over. It'll be easy. Actually, with the success of the Reverend Meade's hate campaign, it should be possible to collect as many as we need as volunteers."

Public Relations Director Lisa White cut in. "That's good as far as it goes. We certainly need to keep the child-martyr blood flowing. But if we leave it there, the story is going to get stale. We've got momentum now, but we need to take the story to the next level."

The President looked at her curiously. "What do you mean 'next level?'"

The PR director spread her hands. "Look, this 'pity our misery' stuff is nice, and it has some traction because the lesser powers are all hyper-sensitive about Weegee power politics, and the Weegees need to be concerned about that because they need to keep the minor players in their camp. Fine. But nobody is going to do anything unless we make what is happening here a matter of more immediate concern to the galaxy at large."

The President steepled his fingers thoughtfully. "You mean, make people on civilized planets endure some consequences." He turned to the White House Chaplain.

"So, Reverend Meade, how are things coming along in Peru?"

The Chaplain had been waiting for this question. "We're almost ready, Mr. President."

The President smiled. "Excellent. Well, I think the events of the past twenty-four hours are sufficient cause for celebration. Myra, do you have the checks?"

As Hamilton and Aurora left the garden and entered the café plaza, the Ranger could see two tall strangely-dressed young women standing next to a vacant table at Aurora's favorite hangout. One had auburn hair and wore a blue robe, while the other's hair was flaming red and she wore a robe of green. Upon seeing them, a big smile appeared on Aurora's face. Without a word to Hamilton, she ran forward and exchanged joyous hugs and kisses with each of the newcomers.

Hamilton approached the three at a walk, and stood for several minutes while they chatted away merrily in some melodious alien tongue, ignoring him completely. Finally, the three disengaged and looked at him.

"Hamilton," Aurora said, "I'd like to introduce you to two of my oldest friends. This," she indicated the auburn-haired woman in blue, "is Danae. She is the daughter of the commander of the WGE expedition that liberated Pegasus 3. I stayed with her on her father's ship during the last year of the war. And this," Aurora pointed to the red-headed woman in green, "is Freya. Her mother was the governess of Cassiopeia 2, in the

Northern Princesspality of Thespia, where we were given refuge during the period between the end of the war and relocation."

The women were both quite beautiful, and standing a few inches over six feet tall, more than a bit intimidating. They looked at Hamilton and smiled the kind of smile an Earth woman might have for a little boy or a puppy. Somehow Hamilton mustered the mental will to say "Hi."

Danae said; "Yes, We're here with the Universal League mission to make sure that the Minervans aren't being too harsh on the natives. So if you feel Aurora is treating you badly, you can just come straight to us." The three women giggled conspiratorially.

Freya turned to Aurora. "Aurora, you didn't tell us your Earthling was so cute. He's not at all as grotesque as we had imagined."

Aurora grinned. "Yes, I really lucked out there. I don't know how I would have managed spending days with a typical specimen."

Danae chimed in. "And he hardly smells at all. Was he like this when you collected him?"

"No, that took some training. But it wasn't too hard. He's remarkably clever for an Earthling. Let's sit down and have some raffa and I'll show you his mind."

"Aurora, please..." Hamilton began.

The priestess cut him short. "Hush, Hamilton. There's no need to be frightened. These are my best friends. Can't you see that they like you? Now be a good boy and sit down at the table so they can get to know you better."

There was no use arguing, so Hamilton obeyed, and soon found himself sitting at one edge of a five-sided table with Danae on his left, Aurora on his right, and Freya facing him catty-corner from the chair beyond Aurora. Danae ordered drinks for all.

"He's really quite remarkable," Aurora began. "He actually demonstrates a small capability for proto-rational thought. And watch this." She turned to Hamilton. "Hamilton, recite your poem."

Hamilton did as he was bid, and the women watched him intently. When he was done, Aurora said, "He actually believes that it was written by an Earthling." She laughed merrily, and the other women joined in.

When their laughing had subsided, Aurora continued. "But the point is, that he seems to understand, however dimly, how impressive it would be if an Earthling really had written such a piece. That suggests that he may have some limited ability to apprehend beauty."

Danae and Freya looked amazed. Aurora continued, "Now let me show you his outer mind. As you can see, it's very chaotic, but there are all sorts of interesting fragments floating about."

As she said this, Hamilton could feel three presences roaming around in his mind, gently touching and triggering different thoughts.

"What an amusing collection of neuroses," Danae commented.

"Yes," Aurora agreed. "They're incredible. I've catalogued over forty."

"What's behind there?" Freya asked.

"That's his psyche. It's very cute, but he keeps it hidden behind a shell of arrogance. Would you gals like to see it?"

"Oh yes," Danae said. Freya nodded enthusiastically.

"OK," Aurora said. "It will take me just a minute to remove his shell."

Hamilton knew what was coming. Aurora was going to humiliate him in front of her friends. He tried to stand up to leave, but his muscles refused to answer his command.

"Now, Hamilton," Aurora began, "let's go back to the time when you were five years old and..."

It took only a minute for Aurora to summon up a string of embarrassing memories from Hamilton's early childhood, and then he was stripped. Inside his mind, his psyche stood naked, a little boy staring upward at three beautiful smiling women.

"Awww, how cute!" Freya and Danae said in unison.

At this moment Kolta Bruna appeared. "Hello ladies," she said. "Having some fun with an Earthling, I see. And you have his psyche stripped already. How delicious. Well, what are we waiting for? Let's tickle him a bit and expose his inner mind." She slid into the vacant chair at the table, and simultaneously Hamilton felt a fourth presence enter his mind.

Aurora grabbed Hamilton's hand and held it tightly in hers. He felt her voice speaking firmly inside of his mind. "Hamilton, you are not five years old, you are an adult. You are a soldier in the United States Army. More than that, a Ranger, a Sergeant in the Rangers. The best of the best. Stand tall. Stand proud!"

Suddenly Hamilton's psyche was half-grown and had clothes. Two of the feminine presences slipped out his mind, leaving only Aurora and the newcomer. Now Aurora's voice said: "Here, take this." Inside his mind Aurora's presence seemed to give something to his psyche, something that somehow resembled a small round shield. "Good," Aurora's voice said. "Now hit her with it. I'll help you." He felt a force inside him lift the shield, and it smashed into the newcomer with a violent blow. The newcomer fled. Aurora gave his psyche an affectionate pat on the head, and then, leaving him with the shield, followed the intruder out.

Kolta Bruna rubbed her forehead. She looked angrily at Aurora. "That was rude!"

Aurora stared at the reporter coldly. "Stay out of my property," she said.

Kolta Bruna shook here head. "You people. When will you learn that the war is over?"

"Is it?"

There was several seconds of uncomfortable silence at the table. Then Freya reached out and touched Aurora's hand gently.

"Aurora dear, we know how much you have been through, but you've got to let your hatred go. The war is over. It's time to forgive. Kolta Bruna is a wonderful and kind person. We went to college together and hit it off from the first day. Danae is friends with her too. I know you would like her if you would just give her a chance. She's so savvy and sophisticated, and has so much insight into relationships. The four of us could be such good friends, if you could just put the past behind you."

Aurora didn't answer, but tears formed in her eyes.

Danae spoke with sympathy. "Listen, Aurora, you know how I feel about the Central Empire. My father won three gold triangles and was commended by the Empress herself for his role in helping to defeat them. After the Central's raid into Sagittarius, our home planet was considered too risky to stay on, and I spent the second half of the war growing up in a battlecruiser. I saw their cruelty in action in their sneak attack in the Orion Cluster, and in the Pegasus campaign, and every battle right up to the end. But it did end. Their empire is disarmed, their Empress has abdicated, and apologies have been given and accepted. It's all ancient history now."

Aurora shook her head. "Fifteen years ago is not ancient history."

Kolta Bruna scoffed. "There's no point talking with her. She cannot forgive because she cannot love."

"That's an age-old anti-Minervan slander," Aurora said.

"It's simply the truth," Kolta Bruna smiled. "You deny Aphrodite, ergo, you cannot love. Everyone knows it."

Aurora looked to her friends for support, but to her dismay, they just stared down at the table. Infuriated, she launched a counterattack.

"Oh, and I suppose it was love that you were demonstrating on Pegasus 3?"

Kolta Bruna was dismissive. "There you go again. Always fixated on the past."

Aurora crossed her arms. "Is it the past? Your broadcast yesterday would seem to indicate otherwise."

"So you object my bringing to Galactic attention your oppression of the natives?"

"I object to the fact that you are running a campaign whose purpose is to mobilize Galactic opinion to pressure the WGE to stop supplying us with tools we desperately need to defend ourselves."

"Well I hardly think the WGE would have given you your advanced weaponry if they had known you would use them to massacre children."

Danae broke in. "The arms in question were surplus class-8 reflective disarmers. They hardly could be termed 'advanced weaponry.' In our opinion, they are the minimum required to provide the Minervan settlement with security from the local savages."

"But wouldn't peace be a better path?" Freya asked. "Why can't we learn from the past? No good ever comes of violence."

"Freya," Aurora said, "we offered the natives all sorts of benefits, but they just want to kill us. We tried peace. Believe me, we tried."

Kolta Bruna smiled. "But if you didn't have your WGE-supplied weapons, perhaps you might have tried a little harder."

Aurora looked at the reporter coldly. "You haven't changed a bit. You're just trying to get us all killed."

Freya said, "Aurora, its really very unfair of you to link prior Central Empire anti-Minervan excesses with their current opinions. The Centrals have repented of their old militaristic ways, and are trying to be the opposite of what they once were. That is why they are so upset now, when they see the oppression going on here."

Aurora was adamant. "It's not oppression. It's self-defense."

"When the strong do violence to the weak," Kolta Bruna said, "that is oppression. And all people with love in their hearts must oppose it."

"Why don't you take your loving heart back to Pegasus 3 and jump into a photolysis chamber. I'm sure there are still plenty of people back there who can operate it for you."

"Aurora, that was a horrible thing to say." Freya's eyes were tearful. "You know, Aurora, how special you are to me. We were like sisters when we were girls. It pains me so much to see you like this. Why can't you embrace the Goddess of Love, alongside the Goddess of Reason? Can't you see that there is a whole side of reality, a wonderful side, that you are missing out on? I wish so much that you would open your heart to Aphrodite. You'll feel so blessed when you do."

Aurora looked at her girlhood friend. "Freya, your people were kind to me, to all of us, and every Minervan will always be grateful for the help you gave us in our time of need. But don't ask us to change our religion. The torch of Reason is an ancient trust, which we have used to bring light to the Galaxy. We will never betray it. We will never dilute it. We will never," she looked briefly at Kolta Bruna, "pollute it. We are what we are. We are proud of what we are, and we will not change. And certainly I, a Priestess of the Third Circle, as was my mother, and my mother's mothers for five generations, certainly I will never abandon our faith."

"But," Freya pleaded, "love is such a wonderful thing. Why can't you…"

"We do love, just as you do."

Freya was bewildered. "I don't see how that is possible."

Danae cut in. "Freya, give the girl some space. Minervans have a right to keep to their ancient ways."

"Such as oppressing the helpless natives of a primitive planet," Kolta Bruna chided.

"We are not oppressing anybody!" Aurora shouted.

"Oh really?" Kolta Bruna arched an eyebrow and smiled. "Why don't we find out? We have an Earthling right here at the table. Let's ask him." She turned to Hamilton. "Earthling, how do you feel about the Minervan occupation? And how…oh, I see, well this is very interesting indeed." She paused and smiled at the other women. "How do you feel about your personal captivity to our brainy little friend here?"

All four women turned and looked at Hamilton, who found himself completely confused. The question had thrown his thoughts in a jumble. He wanted to be fair. Aurora sometimes could be very cruel, but she was also sometimes quite kind. He had fired on her first, and she had taken him prisoner in open combat. He couldn't fault her for that, and certainly in all material respects she treated him far better than the US Army treated its POWs. On the other hand, she seemed to be completely oblivious to his need for dignity—it had been only minutes since she had last humiliated him for her friends' amusement. But then she had protected him from some kind of mind-rape from this very woman who was now trying to get him to denounce her. And then there was the business with the wounded children the previous week. Aurora had let him save them; this other woman had tried to stop him so she could film them dying on camera.

He looked at Kolta Bruna and said: "I think you are full of shit."

Kolta Bruna was enraged. She looked around the table and said, "Ladies, are we going to tolerate such insolence from a savage?"

Aurora laughed, "Out of the mouths of savages—the primitive truth! Hamilton, you really are a poet!" She laughed again.

Danae said, "His words may have been rude, but I think we all caught his thought-stream. Rather incoherent perhaps, but eloquent nevertheless."

Kolta Bruna shook her head. "It just proves my point. She has him totally confused." She turned to Hamilton. "Look, creature. Don't you realize that she just let you haul off those pups in order to avoid bad PR? If you had just let them die in the plaza, as they themselves wanted, our footage could have helped liberate your planet. Doesn't that mean anything to you?"

Hamilton bristled. "Doesn't it mean anything to you that the children were dying? Whatever her motives, I'm glad she let me save them. You would have had them die, just to spice up your TV show."

"I was thinking of the greater good for your people."

"Oh, yeah. You're so concerned about Earthlings that five minutes ago you were going to mind-rape me."

"I'm concerned about the plight of Earthlings as a whole, not particular Earthlings." Kolta Bruna smiled. "As a woman, I need to have some fun now and then. The kind of pleasure I could have derived by playing around with your inner mind a little bit would have refreshed me, giving me new energy for my campaign to help your people. Of course you don't think about that. You just think about yourself." She turned to the others. "Really. What can one expect from a savage?"

Aurora intoned: "Entering the inner mind of any thinking creature, even that of a savage, without its voluntary consent, represents a fundamental violation of…"

Kolta Bruna cut her off. "Your religion, little priestess, not mine."

"What you tried to do was a sin," Aurora insisted. In response, Kolta Bruna just shrugged.

Freya said, "Really Aurora, you can't expect Kolta Bruna to be bound by the commandments of a Goddess she does not believe in. Now why can't we all just be friends?"

At that moment, a Minervan man ran into the plaza holding a very large dead and discolored salmon. "They've poisoned the fish!" he wailed.

Aurora's eyes opened wide with horror. "Oh no," she said. "Not the fish farms."

As the group at Hamilton's table watched, a large crowd of Minervan men quickly surrounded the fish farmer. From the opposite end of the plaza, the Temple gates opened, and out stepped the High Priestess Nendra, followed by the twelve members of the Minervan High Council. A man with two large owls adorning his shoulders stepped out from the crowd and, holding the dead fish in both hands, faced the advancing officials. "High Priestess," he said. "The men of New Minervapolis demand action."

The High Priestess looked at the dead salmon and nodded solemnly.

Aurora spoke urgently to Hamilton. "Hamilton, run home and stay in your quarters until I tell you it's safe to come out. All Tartarus is about to break loose."

Kolta Bruna grinned. "Well, it looks like it's not going to be a slow news day after all. If you'll excuse me ladies, I've got work to do."

Aurora didn't bother to answer. She looked at Hamilton, who was just getting up out of his chair. "I said run, Hamilton. I meant it. Run, now!"

He just made it out of the square when the riot began.

Chapter 9

That evening, Hamilton watched the broadcast with dismay.

"This is Kolta Bruna, reporting from Earth for the Galactic News Service."

"The Minervan occupation of the Earthling city of Kennewick reached new levels of horror and brutality today with the unleashing of the full force of the owl worshippers' militia on the helpless natives."

The camera showed images of rampaging groups of perfectly fit Minervan men beating up Kennewickians of all ages and sexes. One Earthling man trying to fight back threw a punch, and had his arm fried by electroshock when it touched the Minervan's clothing. Another American pulled a knife, only to have it blow up in his hand. Resistance was obviously impossible.

"The purpose of these latest systematic atrocities appears to be to drive the last remaining Kennewickians from their homes."

As Hamilton watched, the terrified Earthling population stampeded towards the border. Behind them as they fled, their homes were squashed flat by invisible forces stamping down on them like giant elephant feet.

"The evicted Kennewickians are all being forced to live in wretched refugee camps on the edge of the Minervan occupied zone. There they will starve or die of disease in droves, except for those who the Minervans allow to enter the city by day to slave in their greenhouses and fish farms. But even these will be forced to undergo the most brutal and humiliating treatment seen anywhere in the Galaxy today."

"Specifically, all Earthlings not under the direct supervision of a Minervan mind reader are banned completely from the inner city, all the way out to the inner perimeter. Between the inner perimeter and the middle perimeter, Earthlings may work, but must undergo automated outer mind scans once every four hours. Between middle perimeter and the pre-

May 1 border, all Earthlings slaving for the Minervans must subject themselves to outer mind scans every twenty-four hours. Earthlings living
beyond the pre-May 1 border have been allowed to keep their homes, but
all those remaining between the old border and the new outer perimeter
must now undergo mind scans every ninety-six hours. Between the outer
perimeter and the American front line is the zone of the camps, which the
Minervans now state they will invade 'as required,' or in other words,
according to whim, to subject the poor starving folk there to these gratu-
itous cruelties."

"As I saw these brutal actions today, my heart broke with pity for the
poor helpless and innocent Earthlings, forced to live under the iron heel
of a people without love."

"The Universal League Charter calls for freedom from oppression for
all peoples everywhere. Some say the Earth is a trivial planet of no importance. Perhaps in itself it is. But is this not a test case for the UL Charter?
Will the owl worshippers be able to turn it into a meaningless scrap of
osmopropylene? And what will be the cost to all of us if they do?"

"From the primitive planet Earth, this is Kolta Bruna, reporting live
for the GNS."

There was a knock on the door. Hamilton switched off the video and
went to answer it. But before he could reach the entrance, the door opened
and Aurora walked in.

The priestess looked at the Ranger. "I see you've been watching
Kolta Bruna's broadcast."

Hamilton nodded. "Was it as bad as she said?"

"No, but it was bad enough." Aurora walked to the center of the room
and stared at the fountain. "Over a third of the fish farms were destroyed.
Under the circumstances there was no holding them back."

"Holding who back? You mean the Minervan men?"

"Yes. And as you can see, they are not as gentle as we are."

Hamilton joined the priestess at the fountain. "I thought in your society the women ran the show."

Aurora looked amazed. "What? That's absurd. We have hardly any
power at all. All we control is religion, government, science, education,
and life inside the home. The men run nearly everything else."

"Meaning what?"

"They control the military and the economy."

"So the men in your society own all the wealth?"

"Not exactly. The men own all the factories and fish farms and have
all the jobs in them." Aurora put a finger in her hair and gently twirled a
lock. "Of course, since we control the government we can balance the

scales a little by taxing their excess income."

"How much of it do you tax?"

"Only 90 percent. However, when a Minervan woman chooses a man for a husband, she assumes ownership of 90 percent of his income. Thus together, these two measures set the male share of national income at 1 percent, which is bearable, although we hope to trim it considerably and obtain a more reasonable split in the future."

"Ninety-nine to one isn't reasonable enough for you?"

"Of course not. What do men need money for? It's only their control of the means of production that allows them to take such an unfair share." Aurora sighed. "It's pretty much the same way all over the galaxy, except on primitive planets like this one where it is even worse. But the cause of women's rights is advancing, and I think that some day we will obtain equality."

"So by male control of the economy, what you really mean is that the men do all the work?"

"Exactly."

"But the women get all the money."

"Alas, no. Only 99 percent."

"Right," Hamilton nodded, "only 99 percent. And in civilized Galactic societies, does male control of the military work the same way?"

"Yes, they staff every position in every ship and regiment. All we get to do is decide on war or peace, and then tell them who to attack, when to attack, when to retreat, and what weapons and tactics they can use. All the rest is entirely under their control. It's completely unfair."

"So today…"

"Some Earthling tank-scrubbers dumped poison into the central plumbing systems of five of our largest fish farms. Over a billion blue-backs worth of capital was destroyed. Naturally, the men were enraged by the loss of their property. Furthermore, unless something was done, the sabotage could be repeated and our food supply seriously endangered. So the High Priestess gave Colonel Iskander permission to mobilize his militia to clear the whole inner city of Earthlings. Naturally, to minimize bloodshed she forbade them to use any weapons except disarmers and thumpers. The former only came into play a few times since most of the Earthlings knew better than to draw arms, and the latter aren't used until the Earthlings have been warned to evacuate their buildings. It was pretty messy, but overall I would have to say that Iskander's men acted professionally, and only thirty or forty Earthlings were killed by our forces."

"Professionally? I saw your men do some rather brutal stuff during Kolta Bruna's broadcast. How can you excuse that?"

"By necessity. But how can you excuse what your comrades in arms did today?"

"My comrades? The US Army? Why? What did they do?"

"They gunned down several hundred of the Kennewickians who tried to push through the refugee camp area to enter the United States."

Hamilton hung his head in shame.

"Yes, just a little detail that Kolta Bruna neglected to include in her galaxy-wide broadcast." Aurora walked across the room and activated a view screen to provide a view of the fish farm area. "But the thing I don't get, is how did five Earthlings manage to enter our fish farm buildings with sabotage plans in their minds, without someone catching them. They had to walk right by any number of Minervans. Their thoughts should have given them away instantly."

Hamilton shrugged. "Maybe some Earthlings are naturally resistant to mind reading."

Aurora shook her head. "Not possible. It takes several years of telepathic education in a civilized school before someone can learn how to deny access to their outer mind. No Earthling has ever had such an education, or could make use of it if it were given to her. And the only other way to mask someone's thoughts is with an anti-telepathic brain implant, but that is far beyond your technology."

Aurora's last statement provoked a thought in Hamilton's brain, which he instantly tried to hide. It was no use.

The priestess looked at him in disbelief. "You mean you think that the US Government is buying advanced technology from some Galactic power and supplying it to the Kennewickian underground? Holy Minerva! What else do you know?" Her look turned into a stare, and Hamilton felt her presence enter his mind and start a systematic examination of all of his thoughts.

It wasn't fair. He hadn't meant to give the Kennewickian's secret away, and actually he didn't really know anything. It was just a guess. But it was probably the right guess, and he had come up with it by reflex in the presence of a Minervan priestess who instantly realized that it had to be true. Aurora had tricked him into becoming a traitor! And now here she was, foraging around his outer mind, examining his every thought in minute detail. But his psyche still had the little round shield. He charged her with it, hoping to expel her intruding presence from his brain.

It didn't work. In one swift mind-shattering blow, Aurora's presence slapped the shield out of his hands, and Hamilton's half-grown psyche found itself sprawled on his mind's floor disarmed, and looking up in helpless terror at the angry face of a vengeful and mighty priestess.

"Don't you dare ever try that again," Aurora said, in the real world.

Hamilton was shaking violently, and could not speak. Aurora regarded him silently for several seconds, and then took pity on him. She led him to a couch, and made him sit down, and then sat down herself right next to him.

"It's OK," she said softly, patting him gently on the head. "I won't hurt you. Don't be frightened. I won't hurt you."

Gradually, Hamilton's terror eased, and he found himself able to speak. "What happened?" he asked.

"You did a very foolish thing," Aurora kept her voice soft, almost sympathetic.

Hamilton was still dazed, so Aurora continued. "Hamilton, I gave you that little shield so you would have some way to defend yourself against mind-violators like Kolta Bruna. It won't work against anyone with even a basic Minervan education, and in trying to use it against me, a Priestess of the Third Circle, you were like a small boy with a toy disarmer ball charging a land battleship."

"I guess you proved that well enough."

Aurora stroked his head gently. "Yes, and you could have gotten seriously hurt. Now I'm willing to give you the shield back, but you must promise never to abuse it again. Will you promise that?"

Hamilton nodded. "Yeah. OK."

"So that means that you can never try to use it against any Minervan, and certainly not me or Danae or Freya. It's very rude. I saved your life, you know, so..."

"Huh? You saved my life?"

"Sure. Who do you think it was who gave you the idea to drop your weapon before it exploded?"

"I thought of that myself!"

"No, that was me. You just accepted my suggestion."

"Then why didn't you save the others?"

Aurora shrugged. "I tried. But none of them would listen."

Hamilton was flabbergasted. At the very moment he had been trying to kill her, Aurora had been trying to save his life!

"That's right," the priestess said. "And then I collected you fair and square. So I'm more than entitled to all of the thoughts in your outer mind. You need to accept that, otherwise I can't give you your shield back."

Hamilton almost wanted to cry. The situation was so degrading. Yet Aurora's denial to him of any privacy in his outer mind was nothing compared to what he might be subjected to from Kolta Bruna or others of her kind if he didn't have the shield.

"OK," he said. "I accept your rules."

Aurora smiled. "That's a good boy. Here you go."

An instant later he felt the return of the shield. Even though he now knew it wouldn't work against Aurora, having it back made him feel less defenseless, and it steadied his still-shaky nerves.

"Feel better now?" Aurora asked.

"Yes. Thank you."

Aurora stood up and started walking around the room. "You know you shouldn't feel guilty about giving away the Kennewickians' secret. After all, you never really knew it."

Hamilton just shrugged.

"But what I don't get," the priestess went on, "is why you don't see that whoever gave them that stuff certainly didn't have their best interests in mind. The action was designed as a provocation to force us to do things that would make the Kennewickians' condition even more miserable than it already was."

Hamilton hung his head in his hands. "What are you trying to do to me, Aurora? Turn me into a traitor?"

"Some of your compatriots already call you that."

"But I'm not."

Aurora nodded. "So you can defy the herd opinion. Very good."

"But you would make it true."

"I'm just trying to get you to see Reason."

Hamilton mustered defiance. "No. I don't agree. This wasn't like the child-martyr stuff. This was a serious act of resistance."

"To what purpose?"

"Why to fight back, of course. To try to throw you out by wrecking your food supply."

"And why is it necessary for them to throw us out?"

"Because you are their enemy. You've taken their town away from them."

"So, we are their oppressors because we deny them access to their town?"

"Yes."

Aurora arched her eyebrow. "Really? And what then are those who deny them access to their world?"

Hamilton stood up. "Are you saying that the real enemy of the Kennewickians is the United States Government?"

Aurora smiled. "Well, duhhh."

Hamilton folded his arms. "I can't accept that. There may have been some mistakes, but…"

The priestess cut him off. "Hamilton, these denials are pointless. I can see that you know the truth. For the sake of your sanity, you need to face it and admit it."

Hamilton said nothing, but just stared at the Minervan with sad and helpless eyes. She was asking him to accept that the cause he had dedicated his life to uphold, the cause for which the members of his platoon had sacrificed themselves, was a complete fraud. He couldn't do it. If he did, what would he have left?

"You would have your mind," Aurora said softly. "Respect your mind."

Chapter 10

The Western Galactic Imperial Spaceliner Esperion entered the Draco system and took a standard orbit around Draco 4.

Dave Christianson gazed out the porthole at the spectacular view of the nightside of the planet. Draco 4 was the capital of the 714th district of the 99th or "Cepheus" province, the center of a miniature empire which itself consisted of some 1,000 worlds. The planet's 43 billion people lived well, and the lights from their innumerable cities shone like a vast assembly of iridescent jewels. Christianson smiled. There would soon be a gnashing of teeth among the unfaithful.

He had obtained passage aboard the Esperion as a student, with plans to enroll in the Department of Joycube Design in one of Draco's lower academies. His bluebacks were sufficient for a ticket purchase, and no unacceptable thoughts were detected in his mind by the Weegee pagan priestess who served as ship's Chaplain. So blueblacks being bluebacks, he had been accepted as a passenger riding in the ships fourth class steerage section.

So far everything had gone according to plan. The Weegees were so arrogant. They never suspected that mere Earthlings were smart enough to obtain modern anti-telepathy technology. But, as promised, the implant had worked like a charm. He was as immune to mind-searches as a Minervan High Priestess.

The ship had been in orbit now for several hours, and all passengers and most of the crew had debarked. Christianson moved quietly through the empty ship's passageways, heading for the Engineering Section. His training had been thorough. He would know exactly what to do.

The door to Engineering was unlocked. Christianson slipped through the entrance and was gratified to see that the only people present were the Chief Engineer and Chaplain Calliope, who were engaged in intimate talk with each other. How delightful, Christianson thought, a pagan tryst. Hopefully the two lovebirds would be sufficiently distracted by each other not to detect him. Trying not to make a sound, Christianson headed directly toward the Hyper Drive controls.

"Excuse me, sir," the Chief Engineer said, "but the engineering section is off limits to passengers."

The Chief Engineer was about 6'7" tall, and built like a heavyweight prizefighter. He headed towards Christianson in a series of rapid long strides. The thought flashed through the Earthling's mind that if it came to hand-to-hand, the Engineer probably could easily break him in half. But there would be no hand-to-hand. Christianson reached into his pocket and squeezed as hard as he could on a small prism. The Engineer yelled in agony as the involuntary contraction of his powerful muscles ripped apart his nervous system, and dropped to the floor dead, his eyes bulging from his horribly contorted face.

"What have you done?" the Chaplain screamed. Christianson looked at her and squeezed his prism again. But either because the range was greater, her muscles were weaker, or because he had exhausted most of the prism's charge on the Engineer, the Chaplain did not die, but only fell to her knees, writhing with pain.

So much the better, Christianson thought. Let her watch.

He turned to the controls and started to activate the Hyper Drive.

From under the weight of a thosand tons of pain, the priestess tried to plead with him.

"No, not the Hyper Drive! If you start it this close to a planet…"

Christianson interrupted her. "It will suck the whole pagan world into the ship's singularity. Praise Jesus."

Calliope grabbed her golden triangle pendant, closed her eyes, and gritted her teeth, as if she was praying really hard.

Suddenly alarm klaxons rang throughout the ship and knockout gas hissed from the ventilators.

"Too late," Christianson snickered, and closed the arming switch. "Jesus is Love," he intoned, touching the start button.

An instant later Draco 4 entered the Hyper Drive's singularity, and the ship flashed into a nova.

The Esperion nova consumed not only Draco 4, but Draco 1,2,3,5,6, and 7 as well. But the Western Galactic Imperial Navy Battlecruiser Defiant on patrol near Draco 8 detected Calliope's distress call, relayed by the Esperion's superluminal transmitter during the last seconds of its existence. In consequence, Defiant's captain was able to get his ship's shields up before the blast wave hit, and the ship and the small WGIN base on Draco 8 were both saved.

A few hours after the disaster, the Captain and his ship's Chaplain met on Draco 8 with the Base Commander and High Priestess. He handed a small rod to the Commander, who inserted it in a holoplayer. The image of a small grotesque primitive humanoid in ill-fitting modern clothing appeared, playing at a set of merchant ship Hyper Drive controls.

Calliope's voice filled the room with her agony. "A savage of some kind has broken into the Engineering Section. He's starting the Hyper Drive. The ship will go nova in seconds. Activate shields! Activate shields!"

Then the savage said: "Jesus is Love," and the transmission went blank.

The Captain turned to the base High Priestess. "Who is this 'Jesus,'" he asked.

The High Priestess exchanged somber looks with the Defiant's Chaplain. "We'll find out soon enough," she said.

The Western Galactic Imperial Navy's 99th Fleet was its southern-most command, responsible for protecting a frontier province which bordered on the galaxy's most barbaric region. Admiral Phillipus and all the veteran staff at Fleet HQ on Cepheus 6 were used to trouble. But the news today was grim indeed.

He looked around the meeting room table nervously. Seated at the table were not only his own Squadron Commodores and Chaplains, but Pallacina, the Provincial High Priestess, and Marissa, Imperial Governess of 1,000 planets of the First District. All sat in silence, waiting for the even more important attendee who was expected shortly.

A thought from the High Priestess informed the Admiral that the moment was at hand. "All rise," he said.

The door of the meeting room opened, and as the walls played the WGE Imperial anthem, Princess Minaphera 245th, ruler of the million planets of Cepheus Province and 2nd in line to the Imperial throne, made her stately entrance, followed by her train of advisors and courtiers. The Princess was a young woman in her twenties, and beautiful beyond description. She wore an enchanting blue robe of the latest style, a glowing tiara crown, and a magnificent iridescent triangle pendant adorned her perfect neck. A throne was brought in, and with infinite grace and poise, she sat down in it and crossed her legs.

All present raised their right hand with three fingers extended. "For Reason, Love, and Justice; Everywhere and Forever!" they chanted in unison.

The Princess smiled a radiant smile. "Loyal subjects, please be seated."

The officers and officials at the table all sat down in their chairs. The Princess' retinue all sat on the floor at her feet.

The Admiral nervously cleared his throat and faced the Princess. "Your Divine Majesty," he said. "If you would like chairs or floor cushions brought in for your advisors we can…"

The Princess stopped him with a wave of her hand. "That won't be necessary." At her nod, one of her courtiers removed her sandals and began placing them on a small velvet pedestal. However, apparently through nervousness, he let one of the shoes slip from his fingers and it fell off the pedestal to the floor. The Princess frowned and touched her pendant, and instantly the offending courtier disappeared in a photolysis flash. One of the other courtiers dashed forward to complete the job of enshrining the sandals.

The Princess sighed. "Poor thing, that was the second time he did that." She then flexed her toes, causing the Admiral's heart to miss a beat.

The Princess directed her imperial visage back to the naval officer. "Why don't you proceed with your briefing, Admiral. Exactly what has happened?"

Admiral Phillipus swallowed his fear and began to talk in as professional a manner as he could manage. "Yes, Your Divine Majesty. Today, at approximately 0900 hours Universal Time, the merchant ship Esperion in orbit around the 714th District Capital Draco 4 suddenly activated its Hyper Drive, causing destruction of that system. Between then and 0930, the same thing happened in two more systems in the 714th district. At 1020 a Hyper Drive startup alarm went off on a merchanter orbiting Hydra 2, in the 713th. By then however, we had a fleet alert out, and we were able to blast the ship before its engines activated. Since that time there have been no further incidents."

The Princess looked somber, but not surprised. Apparently she had been told this much already. "Yes, those are the basic facts," she said. "But what have you adduced about the cause of these events?"

"May it please Your Divine Majesty, we have traced the course of all four ships involved. It seems that whether by coincidence or other causes, all of them were recently in the Procyon District of the Southern Sector."

"I've never heard of that District."

"Understandably, Your Divine Majesty. It is very small, primitive, and deservedly obscure. However there is one planet in that District that has been in the news a bit recently. It's called Earth."

The Princess nodded. "Ah yes. The jungle planet where the Minervans were resettled. But do we know anything else?"

"Only this," the Admiral said. "This is a fragment of an emergency broadcast transmitted by the Esperion right before she blew. One of our warships managed to pick it up."

The room darkened, and for the next 30 seconds was filled with the holo of Calliope's last distress call. After it ended, there was several seconds of shocked silence.

Finally, the Princess managed to collect herself. "So all this destruction was done by savages? How can that be possible? Surely the ships' Chaplains would have picked up the malevolent thoughts of any pre-telepathy subhumans." She turned to the High Priestess. "Priestess, do you have any indication of the development of telepathic humans in that District?"

"No, Your Divine Majesty," Pallacina answered. "All of the planets in that district are extremely primitive. None show any trace of genuine mental development. Some even have male-led governments."

The Princess' look darkened. "Eminence, I may be only 22 years old, but I assure you I am not one to be trifled with. Male-led governments, indeed. I'm not a child anymore, you know."

The High Priestess looked nervous. "Your Divine Majesty, I was only speaking the truth. Some of them, for example Earth, really do have governments largely led by men. It's a phenomenon we sometimes find among deviant primitive planets deep in the Southern Sector."

The Princess looked astonished. "But that's absurd! How could they possibly survive?"

Pallacina shrugged. "Apparently, not very well."

The Princess turned back to the Admiral. "Well if they are too primitive for telepathy, could they have been given antitelepathy technology by someone? Eegees for example?"

The Admiral shook his head. "We've looked into that. So far we've been able to find no evidence for any EGE activity in that region. However Earth has significant reserves of helicity, and consequently a large income stream. A number of the local despotisms have acquired a hefty supply of bluebacks. It seems unlikely that they would be sophisticated enough to do so, but in principle it's possible that they could have used some of their cash to buy anti-telepathy gear on the open market."

The province's Chief Commercial Consul Frondrippus broke in. "Excuse me, Your Divine Majesty, but I think the Admiral is speculating outside his area of expertise. We must not let these attacks make us become so paranoid that we lose essential opportunities for trade with the undeveloped sector. Just because someone has bluebacks doesn't mean they will use them to attack us."

The Princess put a finger in her hair and thoughtfully twirled a lock. "No, but this little 'Earth' place seems to be popping up repeatedly in this discussion. What do we know about it?"

The High Priestess answered. "Not much more than what has been said here. It's an ultra-primitive planet ruled by a patchwork of perverse male-dominated despotisms. It has very large sources of helicity, which our commercial organizations are currently extracting from orbit and selling on the interstellar market. The planet's surface was visited several months ago by Ambassador Junea and consul Fedris, who negotiated the required deal and left immediately afterwards. Their report gives the local despotisms an NTIRA rating."

"NTIRA?" the Princess inquired, a bit puzzled by the colonial trade administration acronym.

"No Threat. Incapable of Rational Action," the High Priestess explained. "The only civilization on the planet is a single Minervan settlement, New Minervapolis, which has had no difficulty defending itself against the local savages using little more than obsolescent class-8 hand-held security devices."

"Which supports my point," Frondrippus added. "If the natives of Earth cannot prevail against a few Minervan settlers, they can hardly be considered a threat to us."

"Perhaps," the Princess said. "But somebody has incinerated three of The Empress' planetary systems, and outside of Earth, we don't seem to have even a theoretical possibility. Surely someone must know more about that planet than what we've heard so far." She turned to Pallacina. "Eminence, have your people search the Imperial Library Archive for any monographs that anyone may have written about Earth or its inhabitants."

"At once, Your Divine Majesty." Pallacina leaned back in her chair and closed her eyes for several seconds. Then she opened them. "It seems there is one registered text, a Scholar's Thesis by a Minervan 3rd Class Priestess named Aurora, who is living in New Minervapolis. It's mostly a psychological work, based on her detailed study of the outer mind of an Earthling male. Would you like me to retrieve the full text?"

"No. I want to speak to the priestess herself. Admiral, would you be good enough to patch in a superluminal holo transmission to this Aurora?"

Admiral Phillipus was thunderstruck. "But Your Divine Majesty, a superluminal holotrans from here to Earth would cost over a million bluebacks a second!"

"I'm sure the Fleet Budget can cover it. Now if you would be so kind…" The Princess fingered her pendant string.

The Admiral was quick to respond. "Of course, Your Divine Majesty. Right away, Your Divine Majesty."

The calling bell on Aurora's holophone beeped persistently in the darkness. Lying on her sleeping mat, the young priestess tried to ignore it by hiding her head under a pillow, but the bell would not be ignored. Finally Aurora gave in and, wearing only her night shift, stumbled out of bed to answer the phone.

She looked at her bedside chronometer. It was 3 o'clock in the morning. "Now who could be calling me at this hour?" she wondered, and touched the receive key.

An image of a young woman with auburn hair wearing a blue robe appeared in her living room. The image appeared hazy. Aurora rubbed her bleary eyes, trying to make it become clear. Still, there was only one person on the planet who looked like that.

"Hi, Danae," Aurora said. "What's with the late-night call?"

"Greetings, Aurora. I am the Princess Minaphera the 245th," the image said.

"Oh, yeah," Aurora yawned, "and I am Penelope the Wise, the First High Priestess of All the Minervans."

"You are being very disrespectful," the image said in an imperious tone.

"Right. Look Danae, I don't know what this is about, but give me a second. I need to get some water to clear my eyes." She turned and walked toward her altar fountain.

"Halt, priestess. Turn and face me," the image voice said.

Aurora stopped in her tracks. Something was wrong. The voice had a Weegee accent like Danae's, but it wasn't Danae's voice.

Aurora turned and saw that the woman in blue was wearing a glowing tiara crown, and that standing behind her now was a very high-ranking WGE Naval Officer and a Weegee Provincial High Priestess. Finally realizing the truth, Aurora threw herself on her knees.

"Oh, Your Divine Majesty, please forgive me. I meant no disrespect. I didn't know it was you. How could I? Who would believe a Divine personage like your glorious majesty would ever call on a humble being like me? Please, I beg your forgiveness. I beg. I beg."

The image's voice took on a softer tone. "Rise, Aurora. We understand. You are forgiven."

Aurora struggled tearfully to her feet and faced the Princess. "How may I be of service to Your Divine Majesty?"

"Are you the Aurora, Priestess Third Class, who wrote the Scholar's thesis, 'An examination of the outer mind of a male Earthling protohuman?'"

"Yes, Your Divine Majesty."

"Then it will please us if you answer our questions."

"Well, certainly I will, Divine Majesty. But wouldn't you prefer to speak with our High Priestess Nendra? I am only…"

"No. It is you with whom we wish to speak."

"Very well, Your Divine Majesty. I am at your service." Feeling a little ridiculous in her nightshift, Aurora curtseyed.

"Aurora," the Princess began, "in your study of your Earthling's mind, did you examine his religion?"

"Yes, Divine Majesty."

"Please describe it."

"It is called Christianity. It centers on a God who…"

"A God? You mean a male Goddess?"

"Yes."

The Princess turned to the High Priestess. "This is preposterous," she said. The High Priestess shrugged. The Princess turned back to Aurora. "Very well, continue."

"Yes, Your Divine Majesty. And I quite agree, their religion is completely absurd. However, as I was saying, according to their mythology, this male God sent his only son Jesus down to Earth to…"

The High Priestess interrupted. "Excuse me. What did you say was the name of their God's only son?"

"Jesus," Aurora answered.

The Princess, the Admiral, and the High Priestess exchanged significant looks.

"And what does the expression 'Jesus is Love' mean?" the High Priestess continued.

"It is a victory chant, comparable to the 'Love Conquers All' slogan of the Centrals during the last war. It is frequently pronounced by their zealots right before they launch a suicide attack."

The three Weegees turned to face each other.

Aurora asked, "Shall I continue to describe their religion?"

"No, just stay as you are," the High Priestess replied. Aurora waited patiently. It was clear they were engaged in telepathic conversation about something important, but mind impulses did not carry across superluminal transmitters.

Finally, the Admiral turned to face her. "Aurora, do you love and revere the Empress Minaphera and the Western Galactic Empire?"

"Yes sir, I do."

"Why?" the Princess asked. "You are not one of our subjects"

"Divine Majesty," Aurora replied, "the WGE saved my life and those of my people. If you need my help," she held up three fingers. "For Reason, Love, and Justice," she pledged. "Everywhere and Forever."

The Admiral returned her salute by raising three of his own fingers, and nodded his approval. "Very well," he said. "We need military information. What military technology do the Earthlings have?"

Aurora shrugged. "Just primitive things. Projectile weapons, poison gas, biotoxins, chemical and nuclear explosives. Nothing much."

The High Priestess asked, "Do they have any telepathic abilities?"

"Absolutely none. Mentally speaking, they are all as helpless as infants."

"But do they have any antitelepathy technology?" the Admiral inquired.

"Certainly none of their own," Aurora said. "But an incident that occurred here yesterday leads me to suspect that they may have gotten their hands on some."

"Explain," the Admiral said.

"Five of the savages managed to walk right past our people and poisoned nearly half our fish farms. There was at least a 6th class Priestess in every farm. I don't see how that's possible unless…" Aurora stopped talking. While telepathy did not function through the superluminal transmitter, she had long ago developed a keen eye for observing the facial expressions that went along with various thoughts. It was clear that her information had made a dramatic impact. But certainly the Weegee worthies were not upset about the Minervan fish farms. Something much more important must have occurred.

"What has happened?" she asked.

There was a moment of silence from the other end. Then the Princess spoke.

"It would seem that the followers of Jesus have evaded our security screeners as well. Three star systems have been destroyed. Two hundred billion people are dead."

Aurora's eyes went wide with horror. "Holy Minerva!" she exclaimed.

The Princess continued. "The situation on Earth is obviously completely out of control. Accordingly, the Western Galactic Empire will now undertake rectification measures. A squadron will be dispatched to Earth. It will arrive in about a week. Priestess Aurora, since you have pledged loyalty to the Empire, I expect you to assist us in our inquest. Please prepare to transport up to our flagship upon its arrival. Bring your Earthling specimen with you. That is all."

The transmission ended and the holoimages disappeared.

Aurora looked at the statue of the gray-eyed Goddess of Reason and Wisdom that was the central adornment of her living room. "Minerva help us," she whispered. "Help us."

Chapter 11

"This is Kolta Bruna for the Galactic News Service."

Hamilton sat with Aurora, Danae, and Freya in the open air café watching a holotheater broadcast of the latest from the GNS. He looked around the café plaza. No other Earthlings were in evidence, as under the new laws they were banned from this area. However, as long as he was under Aurora's direct supervision, his presence was tolerated.

The broadcast continued.

"I'm here in Washington DC, the capital of the United States of America. The USA is the principal chiefdom of the Earth, and the one which has suffered the most from the Minervan invasion."

"I'm looking out upon a large public area set amid the principal shrines of the city."

The holo showed a huge crowd partying on the Capital Mall.

"The people here have turned out in vast numbers to celebrate the destruction of Draco 4 and two other Weegee provincial star systems."

The image now panned among the crowd, showing images of people defecating on effigies of the Western Galactic Arm, and then dancing on their manure, trampling it into the face of portraits of the Empress Minaphera, which were laid on the ground for this purpose. The people in the crowd wore tee shirts and hats bearing the slogans "Jesus is Love," and "Death to the WGE!" A rock band blared out a celebratory beat, and everyone danced in time with its tune chanting;

"Kill the Weegees!
Kill the Weegees!
Death to the West Galactic Empire!
Kill Minervans!
Kill Minaphera!
Death to the West Galactic Empire!"

The image returned to that of Kolta Bruna. "The feeling of exhilaration in this crowd is overwhelming, as they rejoice in the fact that after so many months of one-sided oppression, someone has struck back at those who are supporting their Minervan oppressors."

"No doubt some will use these images to place the blame on the poor Earthlings for the recent tragedies in the WGE's Draco District. But let us ask ourselves, who really is to blame? Can anyone believe that the Earthlings would have become so enraged as to attempt such desperate measures if they had not first been subjected to the torture of Minervan occupation? And who can believe that the WGE would have become a target for their frustration if it had not maintained a consistent one-sided policy of support for the Minervans, whatever their crimes? So who can blame these poor people, in using the only effective means at hand to call the attention of the Galaxy to their plight?"

"In the wake of the August 11th tragedies, there will be those who advocate the easy path of punishing the Earthlings. But is it not obvious that these poor benighted primitives are the victims in all this? Isn't it clear that in responding to the August 11th tragedy, the civilized nations of the galaxy need to take a broader view of the affair than that represented by the crude impulse to exact revenge against these underprivileged creatures whose lives are so hard already? Rather than strike back against these simple beings for what we perceive as their misdeeds, should we not consider punishing those who caused their desperation, those who should have known better, and whose brutal violation of all the codes of civilization were the ultimate cause of this disaster?"

"And if we do not address the cause of the Earthlings' misery, rather than its symptoms, will we not only have ourselves to blame, should such tragic events be repeated?"

"This is Kolta Bruna reporting for the GNS."

As the broadcast ended, Danae turned to the others at the table.

"There may be complex causes," she said, "but those who committed this evil deed will be punished." She looked at Hamilton. "So, what do you have to say for your people now, Sergeant Hamilton?"

Hamilton gulped. The auburn-haired Western Galactic junior diplomat appeared to be as merciless as she was beautiful. "Please, Danae. Tell your people that we are not all to blame. Punish the guilty, yes. But spare the innocent."

Danae's smile was crushing. "The Empress is always just."

Hamilton was desperate. A group of Earthlings had committed a terrible crime against a power that could snuff out the whole planet with a touch of a button. Danae was merely a minor functionary in the Weegee power structure, but she was the only access he had. If he could get through to her, at least there might be a chance to influence the Weegees to be merciful.

Aurora was his best hope. He turned to her. "Aurora, you know my mind. You know I would never do anything like that. Most Earthlings are like me, not like those maniacs. Please tell Danae that. The whole planet should not be punished for the sins of a few criminals."

The others looked to Aurora, who hesitated for a few seconds and then spoke. "Hamilton, it is true that while you are a killer you have elements of proto-rationality that would almost certainly prevent you from committing such horrible crimes as occurred yesterday. But aside from you and few others, such as the Bergers, I have detected little evidence of potential for sanity among Earthlings. Nevertheless, you need not fear that the WGE will exterminate you without cause. What Danae said is true. The Weegees are a fair and just people."

Hamilton detected a note of uncertainty in Aurora's voice. He turned back to Danae for reassurance. "Is that right? You're not planning to exterminate us?"

Danae looked at her fingernails. "Not without cause."

Hamilton persisted, "But…"

Freya cut him off. "So Aurora, is it really true that the Princess of Cepheus called you by holophone last night?"

Aurora blushed. "Yes," she said, and giggled.

"What's so funny?" Danae asked.

"Well, Danae, she woke me in the middle of the night, and between the haziness of the image and the bleariness of my eyes, I thought she was you."

"You're kidding!"

"No, but I thought you were. So when she told me she was Minaphera the 245th, I told her I was Penelope the Wise!"

"Oh no," Danae gagged.

"What was the Princess wearing?" Freya asked.

"Oh she had a splendid tiara, and a magnificent blue robe, but you should have seen me. I was wearing my night shift!"

All the women laughed uproariously.

"Did she tell you when the fleet would arrive?" Danae asked.

"In about a week," Aurora said. "They want me to transport up to their flagship and bring my specimen."

Hamilton was thunderstruck. He was going to be taken away into outer space!

Aurora continued. "Danae, I'd really appreciate it if you came with me. You Weegees have always been good to me, but I'd feel so alone up there among all those foreigners without a friend."

Danae smiled a sympathetic smile. "I'm sorry, Aurora, but I don't think that will be possible. It is a military expedition, after all. But I'll put a call through and tell someone I know aboard the flagship to be sure to take special care of our little Aurora."

"Thanks Danae," Aurora said.

Freya said, "But after the military action is over, there is sure to be a diplomatic reception. As part of the Universal League mission here, we'll certainly be invited. We can all get together again then."

Danae nodded. "That's right. Won't it be great? The three of us together on an Imperial Flagship. We'll get to watch the Princess cast sentence on the captives, and then dance the night away at a Grand Victory Ball!"

"With all those dashing young officers, who'll all be so eager to show off for us after they've crushed the Earthlings." Freya winked and put her arm over Aurora's shoulder. "Of course Aurora here will already have had her pick. You'll leave a few for us, won't you, Aurrie?"

Aurora managed a weak smile. "OK, I'll try."

Hamilton was terrified. I'm being kidnapped by aliens, he thought.

Four days later the news broke that the fleet would arrive the next morning.

Hamilton was more frightened than he had ever been in his life.

Earth's peril was imminent. Danae had said the Weegees would not exterminate the planet "without cause." Unfortunately, a group of Earthlings had conspired successfully to murder 200 billion Weegees. In most places Hamilton was acquainted with, that would suffice for "cause."

And the fools weren't even making any attempt to hide their guilt. Instead the open-air celebrations of the Weegees' disaster continued in every American city, with obvious government consent. Did they have any idea what kind of reaction they were setting in motion? Hamilton did. He had seen it in Danae's eyes, in her hard, calm, and merciless expression as she watched the crowd trampling crap on the face of her Empress.

But in a way his own plight was even more hopeless. The Earthlings would at least all die together. But he was about to be taken away from the only world he knew, to be the lonely and pitiful laboratory specimen of a race of galactic superbeings.

Aurora had called him her lab specimen, yes. But at least while under her control he had been living on Earth, where most things were still familiar and where there were plenty of other native-born Americans around. But now he was about to become a helpless freak in a bizarre · world completely defined by a race of people who were so superior they made even the Minervans seem insignificant.

Aurora was a powerful telepath who had spent a year growing up as a Weegee Navy brat. Her nation was a Weegee ally and her best friend was a Weegee minor functionary. But it didn't take telepathic abilities for Hamilton to see that she was scared shitless at the prospect of being taken aboard a Weegee ship, to be the sole representative of her people among these titans. What then should Hamilton feel? He was a mental deaf mute, and a member of a tribe of savages who had committed the most horrible crimes imaginable against his new captors. To the Weegees he would be utterly beneath contempt.

Hamilton's character was not one inclined towards considering suicide. Yet it was plain to see that, as soon as he was transported aboard the Weegee ship, his life would be effectively over.

Yet he still had one night on Earth left to him. One night in which he would still have the capacity to do something meaningful. He decided to visit the Bergers. Maybe he could help out in their field hospital. It might not be much, but at least it was something. For a few final hours he could feel like a man.

He was right about the hospital providing an opportunity to do something useful. Even as he approached, he saw a group of Kennewickians bringing in about two dozen dismembered children on stretchers.

Hamilton was quick to lend a hand. He didn't bother to ask what had happened. The bloody stumps terminating the right arms of the wounded children made that all too obvious.

There weren't enough beds or cots available, but Melissa Berger had thrown down mats of straw and covered them with blankets to create a line of make-do mattresses.

"Here, put them here," the doctor's wife urged.

As the volunteers laid the children down, Dr. Berger moved quickly among the wounded, checking their tourniquets and applying antibiotics.

The children were screaming in agony.

"Do you have any painkillers?" Hamilton asked Melissa.

The doctor's wife, who was attempting to cradle and comfort one hysterical little girl, looked bleak. "No. We ran out of morphine last week, and the last of the aspirin went yesterday. At the rate things are going, we'll be out of antibiotics in three days, and then..." She shook her head. There were tears in her eyes.

"Why can't you get more? I thought the Minervans were still allowing medical relief shipments."

"They are. But the US government and the major Christian charities have all stopped sending any. I can't understand it. They bewail our plight endlessly on TV, but they won't do a thing to help. It's like they want us to suffer, just for show."

Hamilton nodded, but said nothing.

Just then a bugle rang out. Hamilton could not recognize the call, as it was not one of the standard military tunes. Melissa looked dismayed. "Oh, no," she said. " Not now."

"What is it?" Hamilton asked.

"It's the call to prayer. Under the new law, all loyal Americans must face Washington five times a day and pray to Jesus to destroy the Minervans and the Western Galactic Empire." She cast a worried look at her husband. "Howard has already gotten into trouble for refusing to stop treating new patients during prayer time. If the Faith Police should come by now..."

At that moment, Susan Peterson, the Kennewickian nurse, dashed into the tent. "They're coming!" she said breathlessly, and fell to her knees.

"Quick, kneel!" Melissa said, and pulled Hamilton down with her. The two then copied Susan, pressing their hands together in an attitude of prayer. But Doctor Berger just kept on working.

Then a tall husky man in minister's clothing and three other thugs wearing large crosses entered the hospital tent.

The minister took in the scene with a glance. "Dr. Howard Berger," he said. "I am Reverend Captain Witherspoon, commander of the 4th Kennewickian District Faith Police. You are in violation of the Faith Preservation Act. You will come with us immediately."

Melissa scrambled to her feet. "No. You can't just take him!"

The Reverend Captain Witherspoon looked at the doctor's wife. "I'm sorry, Mrs. Berger, but your husband was warned. He chose to ignore the law of the land, and must now pay the price."

By this time Hamilton was also on his feet. "What's the penalty?"

The minister-captain was disdainful. "There can be no greater crime than sacrilege. The penalty is death."

Hamilton was outraged. Dr. Berger was the noblest man he had ever met, and these thugs were going to kill him. The former Ranger thought he might be able to take out the four goons, enabling the doctor and his family to escape, but where would they be able to go afterwards? And what would happen to the hospital after they ran? No, resisting arrest by force wouldn't work. He decided upon another tactic.

"You can't just kill a man without a trial," Hamilton said.

"Oh, you needn't worry about that," the minister-captain scoffed. "He'll have a fair trial in City Court before we execute him."

"When?" Hamilton demanded.

"Why tonight, of course, immediately after prayers." Witherspoon smiled. "Justice delayed is justice denied. Come on, it's time to go."

As two of the thugs kept their eyes on Hamilton, the third grabbed Dr. Berger and pulled him bodily from the child he was tending. Melissa took a step forward as if to interfere, but the minister blocked her path.

"Take care of the children," the doctor gasped as he was hauled from the tent. Then he, the minister, and the three thugs were all gone.

Hamilton turned to the two women, who were both in tears. "We've got to move fast. Susan, take Charlie and Joe and all the other hospital volunteers, and have them go through the camp and turn out the parents of every child Dr. Berger has saved. Tell them to come down to City Court right away. We're going to need all the help we can get."

Chapter 12

City Court was packed.

A tall man wearing a police uniform emblazoned with a large cross stood up and addressed the crowd.

"Hear ye, hear ye, hear ye! All rise for our most holy Judge, Reverend Aaron Vardt."

A distinguished looking man with silver hair entered the room and took a raised seat upon a dais. He wore a minister's collar with a finely tailored suit. A large golden cross adorned his neck, and there were gold or jeweled rings on every finger. While not truly fat, it was clear that, unlike most Kennewickians, Minister Vardt was eating well.

Vardt motioned with his hand, and the bailiff spoke. "You may all be seated."

Everyone sat down.

Judge Vardt smiled. "I'm delighted to see that such a large crowd of faithful citizens has turned out tonight to witness the punishment of an unbeliever." He turned to the guard. "Well bailiff, let's not keep the folks waiting. Bring in the prisoner."

The bailiff walked to a side door to the left of the dais and opened it. A few seconds later, two guards entered, followed by Dr. Berger, and then more guards. Berger wore a hideous orange prison jumpsuit and had his arms shackled behind his back. The guards manipulated him to a position in front of and beneath the judge, and forced him to his knees.

Vardt looked down on Berger. "Dr. Howard Berger," the Minister intoned. "You have been observed to have committed aggravated violation of the Faith Preservation Act. Do you have any last words before this court passes sentence?"

Dr. Berger looked up at the Minister with defiance. "I certainly do. This is not a legal court. You're not a judge, Vardt. I demand a real trial with a real judge. This is City Court. Old Judge Stone should be sitting on that bench, not you. Where is Judge Stone?"

Berger struggled to his feet and faced the crowd. "Where's Judge Stone? Where is Mayor Wagner? What has happened to them?"

One of the guards grabbed Berger and shoved him back to his knees, simultaneously choking off his words with a powerful grip around the doctor's throat. An angry murmur rippled through the crowd.

The judge banged his gavel. "Silence! Order in the court! Since the prisoner has nothing to say in his defense, the court will now pass sentence..."

It was now or never. Hamilton stood up. "Wait! You can't pass sentence. What Dr. Berger said is true. You're not a judge. Under US law, no one can be sentenced to death without a fair trial with a real judge and a jury of his peers."

For several seconds, dead silence filled the room. Then Minister Vardt said icily, "Excuse me, but aren't you the traitor who foiled our attack on the pagan festival June 6th? Apparently birds of a feather flock together."

Hamilton locked eyes on the Minister. "You have no right to call me a traitor. I've risked my life fighting the Minervans in direct combat. Have you?"

Vardt seemed at a loss for words, but the bailiff intervened. "Your question is ridiculous. Minister Vardt is much too important to risk in combat."

"Oh, yeah," Hamilton sneered, "but he still needs to answer what I said. The doctor deserves a fair trial, and the lot of you are breaking the law by not giving him one."

The Minister became enraged. "Enough!" he shouted, and banged his gavel. "The prisoner has committed crimes against the faith. Civil statutes and procedures do not apply. Therefore, in accord with the authority vested in me by God, Jesus, and the Holy Bible, I sentence the unbeliever Howard Berger to death by stoning."

Susan Peterson stood up. "But you can't do that, your honor. Dr. Berger is the only physician left in Kennewick. Without him all the injured children will die."

The judge frowned. "If it is the will of Jesus that the children should die, then they must die. They are all martyrs, and if not for the sacrilegious interference of the prisoner, would be enjoying eternal happiness in paradise already."

Mary Ellen Thomas, the mother of one of the maimed children stood up. "But I don't want my little girl to be a dead martyr. I want her to live.

Dr. Berger is keeping her alive."

"At great peril to her immortal soul!" the Minister rebutted.

Mary Ellen tried to plead, "But..."

Vardt cut her off. "Silence, woman. Stop your infernal whining. You have nothing to complain about. When your daughter finally achieves martyrdom, you will get a handsome compensation payment from the US government, minus, of course, a small commission deducted by our church to cover our expenses in indoctrinating her."

This last comment provoked rage from Hamilton. "So, you're the one who has been brainwashing the children and then sending them to be butchered!"

The judge looked at Hamilton curiously. "Of course. What's your point?"

Hamilton was stunned. "But, but... they're children!"

Vardt smiled, "and therefore make the purest of martyrs. Does not the Bible say, 'and the children shall lead them?' It is through the blood of our child martyrs that Holy Kennewick shall be redeemed. And I'm proud to say that today we graduated another class of blessed martyrs who shall go forth tomorrow to achieve eternal salvation through holy sacrifice. Their inspiring actions will glorify Jesus, enrich their parents, provide our church with much needed commissions, and possibly kill a few Minervans too."

The judge's words provoked angry murmurs from many of the parents seated around Hamilton, but cheers of approval from the guards and members of the choir, who were also present in the Court in large numbers.

Hamilton faced the crowd. "You're cheering? Don't you see how crazy this is? Your children are being maimed and killed, and all it is accomplishing is convincing the Minervans that we are insane subhumans who need to be crushed."

"We are not concerned with the opinions of pagans," the judge said.

Hamilton shook his head. "You should be concerned, when they're the ones with the superior firepower."

A tall man, a member of the choir stood up. "What would you have us do, soldier boy, give up the fight?"

"No," Hamilton said, "but we have to fight back using tactics that can win. The Minervans have us outgunned. So we can't use violence."

"There is no other way," Vardt said.

"Yes there is!" Susan Peterson stood up on her chair. "We can use passive resistance, like Martin Luther King and Mahatma Gandhi."

"That's right," Hamilton said. "We need to use the leverage we have.

The Minervans need us to do all kinds of scut jobs in their greenhouses and fish farms. If we threaten to stop work, they'll have to negotiate."

"Yeah," said Charlie, the truck-driving hospital volunteer. "We should do like we used to in the Teamsters. Organize and strike. Strike for our rights!"

For a second time, Doctor Berger broke free of his guard. He ran a few feet and then turned and faced the audience. "Charlie's right!" he shouted. "Let's stop this mindless bloodshed and do something effective. Let's act like civilized people, and win ourselves equal rights with a general strike. No more bloodshed, General Strike!" He started to chant, "No more bloodshed, General Strike! No more bloodshed, General Strike!"

The volunteers and parents around Hamilton joined the chant. "No more bloodshed, General Strike!" It started to spread to other citizens, and then even to parts of the choir. "No more bloodshed, General Strike!" Hamilton felt his spirits lift, as he chanted with gusto. Reason was triumphing over madness! "No more bloodshed, General Strike! No more bloodshed, General Strike!"

Suddenly a shot rang out, and the hall fell silent. The bailiff's gun was smoking, and Doctor Berger lay dead on the ground.

The Reverend Aaron Vardt surveyed the crowd. "There will be no general strike," he said coldly. "We do not wish for equal rights with the Minervans, we wish to destroy them. That can only be done through holy violence. Those who give their lives in this crusade will be rewarded by Jesus with eternity in Paradise. Those who shirk their duty to kill pagans will be punished with eternal damnation." He pointed to the body of Doctor Berger. "An unbeliever has met his deserved doom. Let us all give thanks to Jesus for his divine justice. Let us devote ourselves to his holy cause, of killing all pagans everywhere, until all worship only the one true God, the lord of Love, Jesus Christ, Amen."

Hamilton tried to fight back his tears. "You're mad! The Western Galactic Navy is arriving here tomorrow. They have billions of starships. They can wipe us out without blinking. Your crusade against pagans is going to get every man, woman, and child on this planet killed!"

Vardt smiled. "Oh ye of little faith. All the starships in the universe are but chaff on the wind compared to the power of Jesus. In coming here, the pagans are but hastening their own doom. For so it is written. Let us therefore rejoice; the hour of our deliverance is at hand. Choir, hymn number forty-nine."

The choir began to sing:
"Jesus loves me
This I know

To kill the pagans
We will go..."

Armed bailiff or not, Hamilton was so furious he wanted to make a run at the judge, but a soft hand on his left arm held him back. It was Susan Peterson. "Come on Hamilton, there's nothing more we can do here. Melissa will need us."

Hamilton nodded and swallowed his rage. He turned to the truck driver standing on his right. "Charlie, would you give me a hand with Dr. Berger's body?"

Charlie wiped away a tear. "Sure," he said.

Later that night, Hamilton stood by helplessly as Melissa Berger cried and cried over the body of her husband. Around him, and up and down the long hospital tent, wounded children on cots and straw mattresses were crying, too. A few of them were crying for the lost doctor; most, uncomprehending, simply cried to express their own pain.

Nurse Susan Peterson moved among the wailing children, offering ice packs to some, attempts at reassurance to others. But there was really very little she could do.

"Oh, you brave, noble, foolish man," Melissa whispered, rocking the corpse's head at her breast. "What am I going to do without you? What am I going to do?"

There was a rustle of sound at the tent flap. Hamilton turned. It was Aurora.

The priestess was dressed in her finest black robe, and her gold owl pendant shimmered like the Moon. "Come, Hamilton," she said. "The fleet has arrived."

Hamilton looked at her with sad eyes. "Must we go right now? Something terrible has happened."

Aurora's eyes widened with horror, and she stared first at Hamilton, than Susan, and finally Melissa, obviously reading their minds. "Oh, no," she said. "Not Doctor Berger."

She ran to the center of the tent where Melissa sat on the ground, cradling the body of her husband. She looked in silence for several seconds at the grieving wife, and then said simply, "I'm sorry. He was a good being."

Melissa said nothing. All around them the maimed children screamed their agony. Aurora shook her head and started to leave but then did an about-face and walked back to where the doctor's wife was sitting.

"What is it now?" Melissa said. "What do you want from us now?"

Aurora did not answer. Instead she closed her eyes and clutched her owl in her right hand, while holding her left out before her at full length. As she did so, a little girl who was lying on a cot in front of her stopped crying, closed her eyes, and slipped into a peaceful sleep. Then, as Hamilton, Melissa, and Susan watched in amazement, the priestess slowly turned around, and as she did so, all the children fell asleep.

She then walked rapidly back to Hamilton. "Now we must go," she said, in a voice that brooked no argument.

But before she passed him, Hamilton saw that there were tears in her eyes.

WGE Ambassador Junea looked at the President and his Cabinet with disgust. All their purchases of advanced technology had not altered their subhuman appearance, or done much to suppress their hideous smell. Oddly, however, their minds were not leaking thoughts in the obnoxious but useful manner they had in their first meeting. Apparently the Minervan suspicions were true. The savages had acquired antitelepathy technology. She exchanged that thought with Fedris, and he concurred. The guilt for the demise of Draco 4 was now all too clear.

"The fleet is here," Junea said. "The hour of punishment is at hand. We require you to transport up to the flagship to face Princess Minaphera."

The President smiled, revealing his horribly mutilated teeth. "Well I certainly appreciate your invitation to meet the Princess, but my schedule is full for the next several days. Perhaps next week, after she has finished punishing the planet-assassins, we can all get together for a social occasion."

Junea was shocked. The creature's impertinence was astonishing. "So," Junea said, "you are not even going to attempt to beg for mercy before the Princess renders judgment?"

The President twinkled his blood-shot eyes. "Why should we beg for mercy? We're not guilty of anything."

Even with her mind-reading abilities blocked, Junea could see that the subhuman chieftain was lying. "I don't think the Princess is inclined to believe that," she said thinly.

"No, not currently, of course. But once she hears our side of the story, that will all change."

Junea had to smile. One could only imagine the impression this hideous thing would make presenting his case to the Princess. The idea was so funny she had to suggest it. "Then why don't you go and explain yourself to her?"

Fedris exchanged a thought with her. Inside he was laughing as hard as she was.

"No," the President said. "What with all the anti-Earthling prejudice recent events seem to have aroused, we feel it would be better to retain professional representation."

That was a surprise. "Who?" Junea asked.

The President leaned forward, causing Junea to back away a step to avoid his awful smell. "You," he said, and then turning to Fedris continued, "and you."

Junea was flabbergasted. "You can't be serious."

"Of course I am."

"I'm afraid that is not possible."

"Why not? You seem quite qualified."

This was amazing. The insignificant creature actually thought her refusal to serve him was based on modesty! Junea decided to spell the situation out for him. "Indeed, Consul Fedris and I are certainly qualified to represent your hopeless case, but we choose not to because we have no interest in doing so."

"Oh, but you do," the President grinned. "You most certainly do."

Something about the President's grin made Junea uncomfortable. He seemed too confident. "I don't know what you're talking about," she said.

The President walked around the room and took a seat in a big chair covered with dead animal material, and then put his feet up on a large desk made out of a murdered tree. "Fred," he said grandly, "why don't you explain to our ambassador friends why their interests and ours now coincide."

An Earthling only a bit less hideous-looking than the President now stepped forward. Although his teeth weren't quite as sickening as the President's, his smile was almost as disgusting and his smell was almost as bad.

The thing bowed to Junea and nodded to Fedris. "Ambassador, Consul. Allow me to introduce myself. I'm Dr. Fred Collins, Director of the Central Intelligence Agency."

"And he is intelligent too," the President called out gaily. "Fred went to Harvard. It's about time you met him. I'm sure the three of you are really going to hit it off."

"Yes," Collins said. "We have a lot of common interests. Information and money, for example. I find those subjects fascinating. Don't you?"

Fedris sent Junea a thought of alarm. Did this creature know something he shouldn't?

"You know," Collins continued, "I really want to thank you two for arranging the deals that have given us so many of your wonderful bluebacks. Everything you said about them is true. They really are good everywhere, and you really can buy practically anything with them."

Collins rambled on. "One of my favorite things to buy is antitelepathy implants. It's so nice to have some mental privacy again. Don't you agree? I really want to thank you for making such a wonderful thing available to the people of Earth. We understand, of course, that you made a lot of money yourself on that sale, but you earned it, both of you."

Here Collins stopped, and simply broadened his hideous smile.

Junea could only stare at the horrible creature.

The President spoke up. "You two look upset that everyone here seems to know all about your trading activities. I hope none of the items you sold were used in the planet-murders. I hear the Princess isn't the forgiving type."

Junea received an urgent thought from Fedris. "Ambassador, they are threatening to implicate us as complicit in their planet assassination!" Junea thought back, "I know that, you fool. What are we going to do about it?"

Fedris ventured. "Getting us into trouble with the Princess won't do you any good."

The President laughed. "Oh, no, Fedris my boy, you have us all wrong. No one wants to get you or the lovely ambassador into any trouble. We're just saying that we all need to work together to make sure the blame for the recent unfortunate incidents falls only on the guilty."

Junea said coldly, "And who do you claim that is?"

"Why the Minervans, of course," the President replied. "It is their brutality that provoked such an anguished response."

Junea shook her head. "I'm afraid that won't fly. It wasn't Minervans who exploded those star systems, it was Earthlings. Whatever their provocation, they are the ones who did it, and it is those who did the deed who must be punished for it."

The President shrugged. "Well then, in that case, the guilty party is Peru."

Junea was bewildered. "What is Peru?"

"Oh, I'm sorry," the President said. "I shouldn't have expected you to know such a minor detail about the Earth. Peru is a country. It's located here."

The President pointed to a green-colored patch on the lower part of a globe that adorned his desk. "All the planet assassins came from Peru. So clearly, if any nation of Earth is to blame, it is Peru, not the United States of America."

Junea raised an eyebrow. If that were true, there might be some hope. All their anti-telepathy sales were to the USA. She exchanged a thought to that effect with Fedris. He answered telepathically. "Unfortunately our evidence indicates they were Americans." Probably so, but perhaps the Earthlings had a counter. She decided to find out.

"Fedris," she said. "What were the names and birth places of the four planet assassins?"

Fedris looked at his helicpad. "David Crockett Christianson, born Provo Utah, USA; George Washington Jones, born Newark, New Jersey, USA; Mickey Mantle Ostrowski, born Yonkers, New York, USA; and Thomas Jefferson Clark, born Norfolk, Virginia, USA."

"They all sound like Americans," Junea said.

Collins waved his hand dismissively. "No, former Americans. It's true they were all born in our country with those names, but that was decades ago. Since then, they all moved to Peru, and become Peruvian citizens. They used US passports to get onboard your ships, but those passports were old. In fact, our records show some time ago, all four changed their names as well as their citizenships. Their real names were David Crockett Christianson de Peru, George Washington Jones de Peru, Mickey Mantle Ostrowski de Peru, and Thomas Jefferson Clark de Peru. You see, all Peruvian citizens with good traditional Peruvian names."

A nice cover story, but Junea knew it wouldn't be enough. "If we are to convince the Princess, we'll need more evidence than that."

"Certainly, certainly," Collins said. "You'll have all the evidence you need. Here are photographs taken by our reconnaissance airplanes showing the planet-assassin training camps in the Peruvian mountains." He handed Junea some slimy pieces of paper with images on them. As they smelled vaguely toxic, Junea quickly passed them on Fedris.

A moment later Fedris transmitted a thought. "May the Triune Goddess be praised. The images really do show training camps. I'll have one of our ships take better images for confirmation." He then punched a few buttons on his helicpad.

Junea looked at the President. "Remarkable," she said.

"You see," the President said, "not only are we not involved in planet-assassination, but we are your staunch allies in the struggle against such crimes. Without us, you might never have discovered the Peruvian conspiracy."

Junea said, "But what about the mass demonstrations in your cities calling for death to the Western Galactic Empire?"

The President shrugged. "What of it? In the United States we have freedom of speech. If the people want to vent their frustrations with Minervan oppression with public demonstrations, they are free to do so. It doesn't harm anyone. The point is that no part of the US government played any role in the recent planet-assassin attacks on the WGE. Far from it. We are willing to help you with intelligence and even deploy our armed forces to assist you in the war against Peru."

Fedris said, "Alright, so you have some counter-evidence. How are we supposed to make anyone believe it? There are just two of us and a whole court filled with advisors who are much too sophisticated to be readily convinced by this sort of stuff. The Princess will never believe us if all of them are arguing the more obvious case against you. How are we to prevail against such numbers?"

The President pursed his lips. "You can't."

Junea and Fedris looked at each other crestfallen.

"But," continued the President, "you don't need to. All you have to do is win them over to your side."

"How can we do that?" Fedris asked.

"It's really very simple," the President said. "Just use some of these."

With that, the savage chieftain opened a case made of dead animal skin revealing bundles of hundred-thousand blueback chips.

Junea's eyes widened. "You're giving those to us to assist in transforming the views of the court advisors?"

"Sure," the President smiled. "Thanks to you, there's a lot more where that came from. We certainly wouldn't want to leave our friends in the lurch at a time like this."

Junea and Fedris exchanged a thought. There was more than enough in the case to do the job. About twice as much, in fact.

Junea said, "Well, in that case, I think we would be remiss if we did not do everything we could to convince the Princess of your innocence."

"Good," the President exclaimed. "I'll send Lisa with you. She's our Public Relations Director, and can fill you in on all the other details you need to bring the Princess around."

A diminutive and ugly Earthling woman stepped forward. She had obviously made an attempt to cover her Earthling smell with an even more powerful odorant. The net effect was to give her a stench beyond creation. "I look forward to working with you, ambassador," she said.

Offended by the creature's awful smell, both Junea and Fedris took an involuntary step backwards. Unfortunately, this allowed the female Earthling to seize the case of bluebacks and snap it shut.

Junea sighed and made the sign of the triune blessing.

Chapter 13

Encased in a small Minervan travel sphere, Hamilton and Aurora sped through the night crossing Washington State from Kennewick to Seattle.

It had been several hours since the incident in the Bergers' hospital, and Aurora had recovered from the emotion she had expressed there.

"So, a general strike to demand equal rights," she mused. "You know, Hamilton, it never would have worked."

"Why not?" Hamilton was irritated with Aurora. She had shown real compassion in the hospital, but now she was suppressing her feelings, and was back to her usual haughty hyper-rational self. "You need us to do your scut work. Is trampling on us so much fun that you are willing to scrub fishtanks for the privilege? I don't think so."

Aurora crossed her arms. "Now there you go again, accusing us of sadistic cruelty. The reason why we don't give Earthlings equal rights is because, one, being non-rational you don't deserve them, and two, if we ever gave you them, you would use such privileges to kill us. Can you deny my logic?"

Hamilton frowned. "I deny your first point. We are rational creatures."

Aurora was dismissive. "So, killing Dr. Berger was rational? He was the last Earthling physician left in Kennewick. Without him most of the wounded assassin children will die. Yet your Minister, the very man who recruited the assassins, had him killed, and most of the Kennewickians supported him."

"Most, maybe, but not all. Our side had a lot of support."

"Most is too many. While I would be the first to insist that there are genuine examples of limited proto rationality among Earthlings—such as Dr. Berger, certainly, or even, to a much lesser extent, you—the dominant mental condition is clearly insanity."

"But don't you see, Aurora? If you treated us better, a lot more people would see things Berger's way and less would follow Vardt."

Aurora raised an eyebrow. "Hamilton, the anti-Earthling ordinances that you detest so much were only imposed after the assassin attacks began. Earthlings had equal rights, or something close to them, in New Minervapolis before the trouble started."

"Close to equal is not equal."

Aurora laughed. "Hamilton, get real. They had a lot more rights than they would have under any Earthling government."

"Maybe," Hamilton admitted. "But they were still treated as inferior beings."

"They were treated as inferior because they are inferior. They are uneducated, dirty, smelly, and totally irrational. Genetically Earthlings have a physiology that is nearly human. Yet you reject the greatest gift of the Goddess Minerva, the human capacity for individual reason. It is not we who deny your humanity, it is you."

"But still…"

Aurora cut him off. "Look Hamilton, no one enjoys being mean to Earthlings. But the fact of the matter is that, until Earthlings decide to use their minds and become rational beings, they are going to have to be treated like the very dangerous animals that they are. It's perfectly clear that if we do not control the travel and possessions of Earthlings within New Minervapolis, they would exploit their lack of control to murder us. So if we have to clean the fish tanks ourselves, we will. But don't ask us for equal rights, because you can't have them until you change."

As the travel sphere passed over the Cascades, Hamilton sat in silence for several minutes, thinking about what Aurora had said. Then he spoke up again.

"So you wouldn't have yielded to our strike. Still, I think we could have won something by trying it."

"Oh, what is that?"

"Respect. The respect due to rational humans who fight for their rights using respectable means."

Aurora smiled. "That's quite a mouthful, Hamilton."

Hamilton decided to use another tactic. "Aurora, back in the hospital —why did you cry?"

"I didn't cry."

"Yes you did. I saw the tears in your eyes as you walked past me."

"OK, so I felt some emotion. The situation was so horrible."

"Were you sorry for the wounded children?"

Aurora looked out through the transparent wall at the countryside, which was beginning to show its grand stands of trees in the early dawn light. "No, not really. As assassins they were past pity."

"Then why did you remove their pain?"

"Out of respect for Dr. Berger. It's what he would have tried to do had he still been alive."

"So you felt sorry for the Bergers?"

Aurora turned to face Hamilton, all mirth gone from her expression. "Yes, certainly I felt sad for Mrs. Berger. But that was not what brought on my tears."

"Then what did?"

"It was seeing the triumph of evil over good. Dr. Berger, and you of his faction represented the smallest flicker of incipient reason trying to assert itself among Earthlings. You were like ants trying with all your might to lift the foot of a huge beast. But instead the beast just put a little extra weight on its foot and you were all crushed. I like you, Hamilton, I really do. You have only the tiniest spark of proto-rationality, and you constantly make yourself ridiculous by pretending to have more. Nevertheless, what you do have is there, and your attempts to manifest it, however silly, show a core of nobility in your soul. But you are so weak, Hamilton, and the dark forces holding you down are so strong. I fear there is no hope for you."

Hamilton was shocked. "So you felt sorry for me?"

Aurora nodded. "For you, and the entire race of Earthlings. Without reason you are all doomed."

At this moment the sphere slowed to a stop on the runway of Seattle-Tacoma International Airport. A hundred yards away, its delta wings glowing in changing iridescent colors, stood the space transport. They had arrived.

Hamilton was surprised to discover that they had to wait a long time before boarding the transport. There were only about ten other passengers, and a kind of security checkpoint had been set up, manned by WGE Flight Inspectors. As Hamilton and Aurora stood in line, an elderly Weegee woman and her granddaughter, a pretty girl with an apparent age of 9 or 10, were meticulously searched.

First the suspects' possessions were taken, unpacked, and each and every object examined with a microscope, x-rayed, and subjected to an array of scanning devices.

"Why so many different types of scanners?" Hamilton asked Aurora.

"They are trying to be thorough." Aurora explained. "Each scanner operates on a different principle. The first is gravitic, then electromagnetic, nucleonic, helicic, bionic, cyberic, and finally psionic. Thus each object is searched individually for any potentially-threatening source of physical or metaphysical energy, self-replicants whether biological or otherwise, and stored thoughts or pseudo thoughts."

"I see," Hamilton said, only partially understanding. As he watched, the woman and her granddaughter were stripped naked, and their clothes were searched in the same way. Then the two were placed on tables and every inch of their bodies scanned several times with each of the security instruments. The process took over an hour.

"Are they going to search all the passengers this way?" Hamilton inquired of his traveling companion.

"No, that would take much too long," Aurora answered. "They're just doing spot checks."

Hamilton looked at the line in front of him. Behind the woman and girl currently being searched were two WGE Space Marine officers, apparently returning from a brief shore leave in Seattle. If the search was just a spot check system, these would certainly be waved on through. However following the Space Marines was a group of four young Earthling men in fairly good physical condition wearing soiled paramilitary clothing and blazing-cross medallions. The four had farmer's tans and scruffy beards, and were carrying bulky, heavy-looking boxes with the lettering "CNN" hand-scrawled on them. The men were clearly nervous and spoke to each other in whispers. TV reporters, apparently, but to Hamilton they seemed like suspicious characters. He wondered what thoughts Aurora was picking up from their minds.

"Nothing at all," the priestess said. "Those four must be wearing anti-telepathy implants." She continued, answering his unspoken thought. "And yes, I do find them very suspicious."

Hamilton nodded. It was obviously going to be a long wait. If the WGE Flight Inspectors were so thorough that they would take an hour searching two of their own civilians with such care and attention, then surely they would spend considerably longer examining much more dangerous-looking types like the four CNN men.

Finally, the scanning of the Weegee matron and girl was over. As expected, the WGE Flight Inspectors allowed the Space Marines to pass without a search. Now it was the putative reporters' turn at the checkpoint, and Hamilton mentally prepared himself to settle in for the duration. But to his amazement, the four men were simply asked to show their press credentials and then were permitted to proceed on board.

Apparently Aurora was equally astonished by this development. She approached one of the WGE Flight Inspectors. "Sir," she said in a respectful tone of voice. "May I suggest that it might be wise to search those four Earthlings that were just allowed to pass."

The Flight Inspector, whose typical Weegee height of 6'6" made him dwarf the 5'9" Aurora, put his hands on his hips and looked down on her indignantly. "So, are you trying to tell me how to do my job, little priestess?"

"No, certainly not," Aurora said mildly. "It's just that I've lived on this planet for almost a year now, and have studied the Earthlings thoroughly. And if any of them ever fit the profile of dangerous assassins, it was those four. I know that in New Minervapolis our security men would definitely have pulled them out for a scan."

The Flight Inspector laughed. "Well, little priestess, this may be a shock to you, but this is not New Minervapolis, and this is not a Minervan transport you are boarding. This is a ship of the Western Galactic Empire, and its boarding procedures are subject to the laws and regulations of the Western Galactic Empire. And in the Western Galactic Empire we believe in equal rights for all. So we do not search people simply because they have suspicious profiles. That would be suspicion-profiling, a practice which we find abhorrent, because it is unfair and could lead to costly lawsuits. Therefore rather than search those who are most suspicious, we only search those who are least suspicious."

Aurora tried to press her case. "I don't understand that. I spent some time on a Weegee warship when I was a girl, back during the war, and I know that in those days, Navy search procedures specified that..."

The inspector cut her off. "That may be how things were in the bad old days, but the war is over, little priestess, and we've progressed a lot since then. Now I understand that you are worried, but you needn't be. I assure you that I and my detail are experts in our field. In point of fact, prior to our enlistment into the Flight Inspection service, all five of us were part of the Dolphia security team. So you can be sure we know what we are doing. You are holding things up. Now, if you have no more issues, we'd appreciate it if you would take your study specimen and board the transport without further delay."

Aurora shrugged in resignation. "It's no use. OK, Hamilton, let's go." She then walked through the checkpoint towards the transport. The Inspectors gestured for Hamilton to follow, and he hurried after her.

When he reached her, he found her muttering. "WE know what we are doing. WE were part of the Dolphia security team. Unbelievable."

Hamilton looked at her. "What is the Dolphia security team? Is it the WGE Secret Service?"

Aurora gave an ironic laugh. "Hamilton, Dolphia is a network of centers for distribution of cheap consumer goods throughout the Cepheus sector."

"Kind of like the US Army PX system?"

"No," Aurora smiled. "If you would like an Earthling analog, I would say it is more like J.C. Penney's."

"Oh," Hamilton said dully.

They boarded the transport.

There were about forty seats in the transport, and only ten passengers, so both Aurora and Hamilton were able to get window seats, he on the port side of the eighth row, and she on the starboard. Then the door was dogged closed and the colors on the wings began to shimmer and change. As Hamilton watched, the rate of color change accelerated, until all parts of the wing glowed iridescent in all colors at once. Then without a sound, the craft took flight.

Hamilton felt no acceleration, but in fact their rate of both climb and speed increase must have been extremely fast. When he looked down and to the rear, Seattle was visible, but rapidly shrinking to insignificance. Then the sky turned black and the stars came out in brilliant profusion far beyond anything Hamilton had ever seen. They were in space.

They were not done climbing, however. This was clear to Hamilton as the Earth changed from a curved surface to a sphere, which shrank until it was only about the size of a full Moon as seen from Earth. Hamilton recalled from somewhere that the Earth's diameter is about four times that of the Moon. So if they looked the same size, that meant the Earth was four times as far away, or about a million miles.

Then among the stars, Hamilton started seeing softly-glowing spherical bubbles, first just a few, then dozens, hundreds, and thousands. He wondered what they could be.

"Weegee battleships," Aurora said, answering his unspoken question. "We're inside the squadron's picket perimeter now. We should be approaching the flagship shortly."

Sure enough, one of the spheres began to grow, and Hamilton could pick out numerous little domes and other artificial structures on its surface. A small orifice opened, and a tiny delta-winged object flew out in the direction of one of the other spheres. Then Hamilton realized that the tiny delta-winged object was a transport, similar to the 737-sized vessel in which he was riding. Comparing it to the flagship led to an astonishing conclusion: the flagship was at least several miles across.

"Jesus," Hamilton said, expressing his amazement.

From the aisle seat in the row in front of Aurora, one of the CNN reporters turned and smiled at him. "Fear not, brother," the reporter said. "For the Lord is with us."

Then the man stood up and walked forward towards the pilots' area.

One of the pilots turned and said: "Excuse me sir, but…" Then he went into convulsions, as did the other pilot and the two Space Marines seated near the front.

The man faced the rest of the passengers. "Brothers and Sisters," he said. "This is a blessed day! For today we give our lives for Jesus. We will take this transport, the tool of the devil, and use it to smite Satan's legions in the flagship of his pagan fleet!" He held out his hand, displaying a silver prism. "In the name of Jesus, I command thee, pagan pilots, accelerate thy vessel and smite the flagship of the Whore of Babylon!"

With that, his fingers tightened around the prism, and the two pilots went rigid. Then with a robot-like motion, one of them pushed a lever forward. Immediately the rate at which the flagship was growing in their view accelerated dramatically.

"Grandma, we're going to crash!" the little Weegee girl wailed.

Hamilton thought fast. The CNN man was performing an act of resistance, yes, but it was worse than pointless. Crashing the transport would kill all aboard, but probably would do little more than dent the flagship. Worse, it would convince the Weegees beyond all doubt that the Earthlings were mindless savages who needed to be crushed. As a soldier, Hamilton was prepared to give his life for his country, but not this way. The man needed to be stopped.

But how? If he tried to rush him, the man would use his prism and cut him down before he was halfway up the aisle. Suddenly, Hamilton had an idea. He reached down and pulled off his right shoe, and then in one quick motion stood up and hurled it straight at the hijacker's face.

Hamilton had once pitched Little League baseball, and his aim was still true. The throw was a direct hit. The hijacker was stunned, and loosened his grip on the prism for an instant. That was all it took. In the moment he lost control, one of the Space Marines pulled out a little wand,

and the CNN fanatic disappeared in a flash of light. The liberated pilots' hands scrambled for a bunch of buttons on their control boards, and the transport was saved.

Aurora said. "That was a very good throw, Hamilton. I'm glad I remembered that you had that skill."

Hamilton looked at her. "What do you mean, you remembered? I'm the one who remembered."

Aurora just smiled.

Chapter 14

The transport flew through an orifice opening in the flagship, then settled down into a large landing bay. Looking out his window, Hamilton could see that the bay was huge, and quite elegant, featuring decorative iridescent columns shimmering in geometrical arrays over a beautiful tiled mosaic floor. The door opened, and the passengers exited.

At the bottom of the ramp, Aurora was greeted by two WG Imperial Navy officers. One was a young man, perhaps a year or two younger than Aurora. The other, whose uniform sported a fair array of decorations and insignia indicating superior rank, was middle-aged.

The younger man approached Aurora. "Priestess Third Class Aurora?" he said.

"Yes."

The junior officer smiled and offered his hand. "Lieutenant Danatus, Imperial Navy, at your service."

Aurora's eyes went wide with pleasure. "Danatus! I didn't recognize you. You've grown!"

"So have you, Aurrie."

Aurora rushed forward and gave the young man an affectionate hug, and then turned and faced Hamilton. "Hamilton, this is Danatus, Danae's kid brother. I knew him when I was a refugee child aboard the Weegee fleet during the war." She smiled broadly. "He was a real pest, but we girls kept him in line."

Hamilton extended his hand. "Sergeant Andrew Hamilton, United States Army."

Surprised, the man stepped back, but at a look from Aurora he seemed to recover himself and gingerly took the Ranger's hand. "Pleased to meet you," he said politely.

The older officer cleared his throat, demanding attention. Danatus quickly disengaged from Hamilton. "Aurora," he said, "this is Commander Tiranus, with the Special Security Division. He's in charge of arrangements for the foreign guests that have been brought aboard the flagship for the inquest."

Aurora nodded to the senior officer. "Commander," she said.

"Priestess," Tiranus said, returning the nod. "Welcome to our flagship. At his own request, Lt. Danatus has been assigned to your guard detail. He will show you and your study specimen to your quarters."

Tiranus turned on his heel and headed off to speak with the newly-arrived Space Marines. As he moved away however, Aurora noticed the three remaining CNN reporters carrying their boxes and heading out the landing bay into the ship, with no Weegee escort at all. She quickly called after Tiranus.

"Commander Tiranus."

He turned to face her. "Yes, priestess?"

She pointed at the departing reporters. "Excuse me sir, but those Earthlings. Aren't you going to arrest them?"

The officer appeared puzzled. "No. Why should we?"

"Sir, they have all the appearances of classic assassins, and one of their group attempted to crash the transport into the flagship."

"Yes, and he was dealt with."

"But sir, the other three...."

Tiranus interrupted her. "Are innocent of any wrongdoing."

Aurora appeared flustered. "But sir, don't you think they are rather suspicious?"

Tiranus smiled a thin smile. "My dear young Minervan Priestess. I understand that your people live by a harsh, unloving, and unforgiving code. But in the Western Galactic Empire we believe in equal rights and equal love for all. We do not believe in guilt by suspicion, and we do not believe in guilt by association. That is part of the reason why we are loved and respected by people all over the galaxy. Perhaps if you Minervans took some of our example to heart, and learned to love, forgive, and think the best of everyone, you would not be so disliked, and the rest of the galaxy would not be forced to endure the consequences of the violent hatred which your attitudes so often provoke."

Tiranus tuned on his heel and stalked off. As Aurora watched him go, a tear formed in the corner of her eye. "I can't believe it," she sniffled. "It's been just ten years since the war, and now they're saying the same horrible things all over again."

Danatus put a soft hand on her shoulder. "Don't worry, Aurrie. Most people don't think that way. You'll find you have a lot of friends here."

The priestess turned her teary face towards the young officer with an expression that pleaded for reassurance. So he added, "I promise."

Aurora regarded the three CNN reporters, who were now disappearing down the long corridor that led out from the landing bay. "We're being placed under guard, while those assassins are being given the free run of the ship." She shook her head.

"They're reporters," Danatus said. "They need to be able to move freely to get their story."

"Aren't you at least going to search their boxes?"

"We can't. We don't search other reporters, and they are suspicious, so searching them would be suspicion profiling. That would be illegal."

Aurora shook her head again. "May Minerva awake you," she said.

Danatus smiled. "Thanks for the kind thought. Come on, Aurora, let me show you to your rooms."

The flagship was astonishing. Its corridors were the size of avenues, each side of which were decorated with exotic trees, iridescent sculptures, and glorious beds of fragrant alien flowers. The ceilings were illuminated with a vague blue light and so high that they seemed like a natural sky. Crowds of royal blue-clothed Weegee men and women moved around chatting or shopping, or sat in open-air bistros sipping drinks or playing board games. In several places the corridors opened into fair-sized plazas in which choruses sang and skate dancers danced. If Hamilton hadn't known he was inside a warship he would have thought he was outdoors in the center of a very unusual but quite pleasant town on a delightful planet. Apparently the Princess knew how to travel in style.

"I apologize for the rather crude appearance of everything in this part of the ship," Danatus commented. "This area is for the low-ranked enlisted men. But we'll be in officer country soon enough and things will become a lot nicer."

Indeed they did. As they moved forward into shipboard zones reserved for personnel of ever higher grade, the streets became wider, the trees taller, the flowers more luxuriant, statues more impressive, and the furnishings in every way more elegant. Finally they entered an enormous boulevard lined with transparent glowing crystal palaces that emanated wonderful fragrances and beautiful soaring music.

Aurora telepathed Hamilton a comment. "Yikes," she thought.

Aurora asked Danatus. "So, is this where the Princess lives?"

Danatus smiled. "No, these are the junior officer's quarters."

The priestess's eyes went wide. "Junior officers in these? On your father's ship…"

Danatus interrupted her. "Aurrie, really. My father's ship was an old-style light battlecruiser, optimized for speed and firepower. This is an Imperial Flagship. We need to keep up appearances." He stopped in front of one of the smaller palaces. "Ah," he said. "Here are your quarters. I'm sorry if it's a bit shabby. I tried to get you better, but this was all I could arrange."

Aurora eyed the magnificent structure in awe. "That's OK," she said. "We'll manage."

Danatus gave her a friendly slap on the back. "That's the spirit, Aurrie, you were always ready to rough it. But if you do need anything, there will be a Space Marine detail in the outer foyer who will be available to help you. Now go inside and get some rest. I'll be by at 0900 tomorrow morning to take you to the inquest, which will take place in the secondary administrative discipline shack," he indicated a fabulous building some distance down the boulevard, "starting at 1000 hours sharp."

A moment later, he was gone. Aurora stood staring at their crystal palace for some time.

Finally she turned to Hamilton. "Yikes," she said aloud.

"Yikes," he said in agreement.

Then they started climbing the 100-meter-long staircase that led to the palace door.

The palace interior was appropriately palatial, complete with numerous frescos, mosaics, gardens, sculptures, and other works of art. In the center of the main ballroom was an array of musical fountains spewing glowing multi-colored water in changing patterns depicting splendid visionary landscapes in the air. On a pedestal stage surveying the fountain were crystal statues of three beautiful goddesses. One had an owl perched on her shoulder; this Hamilton recognized as Minerva. The remaining two were strange, but as one carried a double-headed ax and the other a staff with two coiled snakes, Hamilton surmised readily enough that they must represent Hera and Aphrodite.

Aurora frowned when she saw the triune altar, and turned away from it, surveying the ballroom, as if looking for something. Her eyes lit upon two circular pads about fifteen feet in diameter which were covered with satiny sheets. Quickly she ran and pulled the covers off of one of the pads, and threw them over the statues of Hera and Aphrodite. Then she knelt down in front of the statue of Minerva and spent several minutes in quiet prayer.

Finally she stood up and faced the Ranger. "Hamilton, come here," she said. "I need to make a sacrifice to cleanse this altar."

Alarmed, Hamilton backed away. "Hold on, Aurora. Your religion is your business, but I have no intention of being anyone's sacrifice."

Aurora laughed. "Hamilton, you are so silly. I'm not going to kill you. I just need a few drops of your blood to offer to the Goddess as an apology for the sacrilege that has been done to her here. Now stop acting like a frightened child and come here so we can get the job done."

Hamilton stepped forward gingerly. He offered his left hand. "Can you take what you need from there?"

Aurora smiled and took his left in hers. "Yes, certainly." Then moving swiftly, she removed her owl pendant from her neck and slashed it across his left wrist causing it to bleed copiously. Hamilton tried to snatch his arm back, but found he couldn't move at all. Then Aurora held his arm so that his blood fell at the feet of Minerva. She looked at the statue and intoned. "Oh, great goddess Minerva, please accept this sacrifice and forgive the insult that has been given to thee in this place. Know that we, who are here now, worship thee and only thee." Then she slashed the owl in the opposite direction across Hamilton's wrist and the wound healed as if it had never been there at all. She released Hamilton's hand and he found he could move again.

"There," she said. "Now was that so bad?"

Hamilton rubbed his wrist. "I guess it was OK." He regarded the statue. "Aurora, you told the Goddess that 'we' worship only her. You know that I don't follow your religion."

Aurora shrugged. "Obviously. But Minerva is only interested in the thoughts of rational minds."

"So I don't count."

"I'm afraid not. But you know, if you would really like to become human, my offer still stands. Just let me into your inner mind with permission to rearrange things, and I'll fix you up. It would take a lot of work, since many of your psychotic complexes are rather deeply dug in, but if you really cooperate I think that in a few months you could be debugged and then reprogrammed to be nearly as human as any Minervan male. I'll do it at no charge. How about it?"

"No way."

"Phooey." Aurora sighed. "Oh well, I suppose it is unrealistic of me to expect a subrational being to comprehend its own mental inadequacy. But I like you anyway. It's just too bad that…"

"Sorry."

Aurora dropped the subject and surveyed the ballroom. "Well, Hamilton," she said. "We've got a lot of time to kill. Can you play cha-chostrat?" She pointed to a table with an inset quad nine squares long and seven squares wide, with two rows of playing pieces on each side.

"Is it like chess?" Hamilton asked. Hamilton was an expert chess player. He eyed the pieces with interest. Perhaps this was a game where he could show himself a match for Aurora.

They sat down at the table and Aurora explained the rules. As she did so, Hamilton could not help observing how the game mirrored Minervan and Weegee concepts of religion and society.

The rules were as follows. Each side had two rows of pieces. In the front row were the smaller pieces, similar to pawns in chess, but with each one representing a different specialty of space marine. These male pieces all had limited moves. In the second row were larger pieces denoted by figurines representing one Empress, two princesses, two countesses, and two priestesses. These all had more powerful moves. The male pieces were all limited in another way; the pieces they attacked were simply killed, and thus removed permanently from the board. The female pieces, on the other hand, did not kill, they captured, and the prisoners they took were then returned to the board on any vacant square as partisans of their new possessor. In the center of the board stood the Goddess, immobile but all-powerful. If a priestess could be moved next to her, the person who made the move could ask her to change the shape of the board, with various specified shape changes possible depending upon the square of approach or other circumstances. The idea of the game was to capture the opposing Empress. This could only be done with a female piece, as killing such a royal personage with a space marine was considered to be quite beyond the pale.

Thus while novel in many respects, the game was chesslike enough, and Hamilton happily accepted Aurora's challenge. In their first game, however, she crushed him in less than twenty moves. No matter, Hamilton thought, that was just his first try whereas Aurora had undoubtedly played the game for years. He asked for a rematch, and Aurora accepted, delaying only to get some raffa for them to sip during their second encounter. In this game she soundly beat Hamilton again, although it took her some twenty-five moves to do it. They got up to get a snack.

"Well Hamilton," Aurora said as they wandered among the huge buffet of bizarre delicacies offered to them in the palace's main banquet hall, "you seem to have some aptitude for chachostrat. I tell you what. Let me give you some odds and we'll see if we can have an even match."

Carrying their snacks back with them, they resumed their seats at the chachostrat table.

Aurora took two of her space marines, changed their color from purple to orange and placed them on Hamilton's side of the board. "Here," she said. "You can have two of my marines. That gives you nine in all against my five. Let's see if that will even things up."

It didn't. Within thirty moves Hamilton's forces were totally smashed and he had to resign.

"OK," Aurora said. "Perhaps we need to increase the odds. Take two more of my marines."

Now Hamilton had eleven marines—almost two solid rows—against Aurora's three, who were barely enough to form a limited redoubt in front of her Empress. Surely if he played methodically he could box her in and win.

Moving carefully to make sure that no pieces were left unprotected, Hamilton advanced his marines up row by row. Everything seemed to be going according to plan. But then Aurora removed her bootlets and stockings, and started to slowly rub her shapely girlish feet together. The action was distracting. Hamilton made a mistake and lost a marine. Then he made another error and his position was penetrated. A few moves later he found himself routed.

Aurora smiled. "I think we shall have to give you maximum odds. Take all of my marines."

Hamilton set his mouth in a grim line. He realized now that she was trying to humiliate him by beating him while offering great odds. Yet he couldn't refuse the challenge; to do so would be to admit defeat in advance. She was willing to play dirty—it was obvious to Hamilton now that her bit with her feet was a willful ploy to destroy his concentration. But he had two full rows of marines against her none, and was wise to her tricks. He would teach her a lesson.

The game began in similar fashion to the previous one, with Hamilton slowly advancing his phalanx. Aurora played with her feet, but the Ranger managed to keep his eyes mostly averted, and only made one mistake, losing a marine which, under the circumstances, he could afford. But then Aurora started combing her hair and humming to herself in the most enchanting way. This was hard to ignore, and Hamilton's concentration began to falter, causing him to lose two more marines. Aurora took her prisoners and dropped them into the central area to exchange them in a bloodbath which left the area around the Goddess temporarily unguarded. Hamilton had one move to save himself but, distracted by Aurora's siren act, he failed to see the danger. Taking advantage of the situation, Aurora moved up her Priestess and had the Goddess reverse the squares on Hamilton's side of the board. This threw his formation of Marines uselessly to his rear and exposed his Empress front and center, under direct attack by Aurora's mobile feminine forces, which had been preconcentrated for the occasion. Two moves later it was all over.

Hamilton was not one for whining, but he couldn't help thinking that Aurora had not played fair. Combing her hair to break his concentration was over-the-top. That was enough for the priestess.

"So, it's my fault that you can't control your own thought processes? I wouldn't have had any problem with you combing your hair."

"Aurora, really, you know it's not the same."

Aurora said, "Hamilton instead of blaming others for your failures, why don't you look at yourself?"

So, Hamilton thought, all this was some kind of lesson. "OK," he said. "What's your point? That you are a better chacostrat player than I am? I concede it. Or is it that you are smarter than me? I concede that too. So what?"

Aurora smiled. "Hamilton, you weren't just beaten at chacostrat, you were utterly and totally crushed. So what I am trying to get you to see is that your mind is completely inadequate."

"Oh, thanks Aurora, that makes me feel real good."

"You don't need to feel good. You need to change."

Hamilton scowled. "I tell you what, let's just change the subject. Can we get the news here? I'd like to find out what's happened since the fleet arrived."

Aurora nodded. "Good idea. I'm sure this place is equipped with an excellent holotheater. Now where are the controls?" She looked around, then said, "Oh there they are."

Apparently the controls were telepathic in nature, because even though Aurora did not touch anything, the ballroom suddenly became alive with holographic figures depicting the latest news events from Earth. First the ballroom was filled with images of Earthling assassin children having their hands blown off in New Minervapolis, with an accompanying breathless commentary by Kolta Bruna. Hamilton paid no attention to the reporter, as the scene of carnage itself commanded all his attention. Then on the far side of the ballroom he briefly saw what looked like images of Charlie and Susan trying to bind some of the children's wounds, only to be driven off by Kennewickian toughs. This got him so mad that he actually started across the ballroom to try to intervene, before he realized that he was only watching images.

Then the scene changed and he was on the Capitol Mall, in the midst of a mass rally of the Cosmic Christian Crusade. All around him were images of religious Christians pissing on effigies of the western arm of the Milky Way Galaxy, and chanting "Death to the Minervans! Death to the Empress! Death to the Weegees! Kill all pagans, kill, kill, kill!"

An image of White House Chaplain Rev. John Meade raised double victory signs as he faced the crowd from a holographic grandstand on the mall side of the Capitol building. "Jesus is coming! Victory is near!" he intoned as the crowd applauded madly. "Let us join in a holy crusade to exterminate all pagans throughout the universe. With Christ on our side, we are invincible!" Cheers roared from the crowd.

Hamilton turned away from the newscast in disgust. Mercifully, Aurora switched the holotheater off.

This is insane, Hamilton thought. Don't any of them realize what is about to happen? Why can't they see how crazy they're being?

"Why can't you?" Aurora said.

Chapter 15

True to his word, Danatus arrived to escort them to the inquest at precisely 0900. Unlike the previous day, however, when the main boulevard of the junior officers' quarters had been largely deserted, now the street was lined with spectators, and Aurora and Hamilton made their progress to the Secondary Administrative Discipline Shack under the scrutiny of hundreds of curious onlookers.

The SAD Shack was a fabulous structure made of iridescent crystal, about three times larger in scale than the palace in which Aurora and Hamilton had spent the previous night. Instead of a ballroom, it had a main plaza in the center of which was a glowing shaft. Danatus led the two foreigners to the base of the shaft, which then opened to reveal a luxuriously-appointed elevator car. The three entered the elevator, and the entrance disappeared. Aurora felt a mild vibration but no acceleration. Then the entrance reappeared and they exited the elevator into a modest sized lobby which was filled with chatting Weegee military officers and priestesses.

An elderly officer with lots of medals adorning his uniform approached the three. Aurora recognized the man as Phillipus, the Admiral who had been present in the holotransmission when the Princess had phoned her.

Danatus saluted sharply. "Lieutenant Danatus, sir! Reporting as ordered with the Minervan witness and her specimen, sir!"

The Admiral turned to Aurora. "Priestess third class Aurora, welcome. Thank you for assisting us at this inquest."

Aurora held up her hand, three fingers outstretched but pointed inward at a 45-degree angle. "I'm proud to be of assistance, Admiral."

Admiral Phillipus raised an eyebrow. "That's an old style Navy salute. I appreciate the sentiments you are apparently trying to express by it, but you should know that it is reserved for Navy combat veterans."

Danatus interjected. "Sir, if I can be so bold. The priestess Aurora is a Navy combat veteran."

The Admiral turned to the lieutenant. "How so?"

"Sir, during the war she was taken aboard my father's battlecruiser, the Warhawk, when we liberated Pegasus 3. Four months later, during the Andromeda battle, the ship was hit and a fire started in the children's quarters. Aurora rallied the children to put it out. She was awarded the Little Star of Young Valor."

The Admiral looked at Aurora and smiled. "Well, well, a Little Star. Why aren't you wearing your medal?"

Aurora blushed. "Sir, it wasn't much. All I did was put out a fire."

"On one of Her Divine Majesty's warships in the middle a major fleet action." The Admiral shook his head. "Priestess, you should not be so modest."

Aurora reached into the pocket of her robe and pulled out a small golden pin in the shape of a nine-pointed star with a glowing iridescent jewel at its center. With fumbling hands she pinned it on her robe in the spot above her heart. She looked at the Admiral bashfully. "I've always treasured it," she admitted, with a tear in her eye.

Phillipus nodded, "As well you should."

Aurora fought down a lump in her throat and mustered the will to ask a question. "Admiral, I'm worried. Some of the officials I've met aboard your ship seem to blame my people for what happened in the Draco sector. Surely you must know that we Minervans would never do anything to harm the Western Galactic Empire, and that the horrible things that were done to you were done by the same assassins who have been attacking us on Earth. We're on the same side, fighting the same enemy."

"Yes," the Admiral said. "But some people think that we wouldn't have the same enemy if we weren't on the same side."

Aurora was shocked. "How can they say that? The Empire has been attacked. Are there really people in positions of responsibility who would appease these savages by sacrificing us? That's not something that the Navy that I knew would ever do."

"Nor is it something that we will countenance now," Phillipus said, "if I have any say in the matter. Don't worry Priestess, there are many of us old Navy men who still remember the war. We remember that we never met a Minervan that wasn't our friend, who wouldn't welcome us, or help us, even at great risk to his or her own life. Yes, there are some in and around the court that would sell you out for convenient access to the savages' helicity, but the Navy remembers its friends. We won't let you down."

Aurora smiled. "Thanks sir. I feel a lot better now."

Three harmonic tones sounded. The Admiral said: "Come. It is time for us to enter the court."

They all filed into the courtroom. Weegee senior officers and priestesses all took seats in the central area. Aurora and Hamilton were shown to assigned seats in the front row of the left section, with two space marines positioned on either side. Looking across the front row, Aurora could see a Weegee senior diplomat in the first row of the right section, with a middle-aged Earthling woman seated next to her. The Earthling's skin was slightly pink, indicating that she had recently washed herself properly for the first time, and she wore an expensive Weegee gown of the latest and highest style. Aurora wondered who the Earthling woman could be. A quick reading of Hamilton's mind provided the answer. He recognized her. She was the White House Director of Public Relations.

Five harmonic tones sounded, and everyone in the courtroom stood up. Then the Princess entered, followed by her train of courtiers. The Princess assumed her seat on the throne raised on the dais in front of the courtroom, and the courtiers rushed to sit at her feet. One of the courtiers removed the Princess's shoes, and quickly, but with the greatest of care, placed them on top of a small velvet pedestal. Then the flagship's chaplain raised her hand with three fingers outstretched, and everyone chanted in unison; "For Reason, Love, and Justice; Everywhere and Forever!"

Aurora recited the pledge with gusto, and for good measure made Hamilton say it, too. It was true that the pledge could be taken as a hymn to the so-called Triune Goddess, and therefore heresy, but Aurora chose to interpret it as a secular oath of allegiance to the WGE. As such she could say it without hesitation. Any anti-Minervans in the Weegee court who wanted to cast doubt on Minervan loyalty would get no help from her.

The Princess smiled. "Loyal subjects, be seated."

Everyone sat down.

The Princess continued. "We are gathered here today to determine what our response should be to the recent acts of planet assassination performed by savages from planet Earth. We understand that the primary local chiefdom has obtained representation. Is the advocate for the savages present?"

The Weegee senior diplomat seated on the right flank of the court stood up. "Yes, Your Divine Majesty. I am Ambassador Junea, and I have been retained by the government of the United States of America to present its case before this court. I have here with me a representative of that government, Mrs. Lisa White."

The Princess looked at Junea, and then, with some curiosity, at Lisa White. "So that is an Earthling," the Princess said, and then wrinkled her nose. "Odd, but she does not stink at all. It appears that some of the reports about the inhabitants of this planet are inaccurate."

"Oh, quite so, Your Divine Majesty," Junea replied. "I think you will find that much of what you have been told about Earth and its citizens requires correction."

"We shall see," the Princess said. "Admiral Phillipus, present the indictment."

Admiral Phillipus stood up. "The evidence before this court is that on or about 0900 hours WGE Universal time, on the 122nd day of the 16,471th year since the revelation of the Triune Goddess, that four savages of the planet Earth acted in concert and conspiracy to illegally activate the hyper drive of four starships in the immediate vicinity of four inhabited planets. Three of the conspirators were successful and, as a result of their actions, three entire planetary systems belonging to Her Divine Majesty, Minaphera the 243rd were destroyed, together some 200 billion of Her Divine Majesty's subjects, as well as several million visiting subjects of monarchs friendly to Her Divine Majesty. In addition, some 12,300 WGE and 240 allied starships of various types were destroyed, as well as civilian and government property with an estimated total value of over 50 heptillion bluebacks. These actions were done without any provocations whatsoever. As the damage done was so immense, and the risk of further such activity is so apparent, it is the recommendation of the Imperial Department of Public Safety, Cepheus Sector, that the implicated tribes of savage humanoids inhabiting the planet Earth, generally known as Earthlings, be immediately and totally exterminated."

Aurora felt the scream of terror inside Hamilton's mind when he heard the recommendation. She tried to calm him, but it was all she could do to simply stop him from speaking.

The Princess nodded. "An excellent summary. Well, ambassador Junea, do you have anything to say before this court approves the DPS recommendation?"

Junea stood up. "Yes, Your Divine Majesty to Be. In the first place, there is no direct evidence linking the four incidents in question, and so the allegation of conspiracy is clearly groundless and must be dismissed."

Admiral Phillipus said; "Your Divine Majesty to Be,…"

The Princess said, "That's enough of that. Just call me 'Divine Princess.' This is a field trip to the galactic outback. There's no need for us to be so stuffy and formal."

"Yes, Divine Princess," the Admiral continued. "I object to the ambassador's assertion that there is no evidence linking the attacks. We have four attacks with an identical modus operandi occurring at the same time, with Earthlings involved in every one..."

"No," Junea interrupted. "We only know that someone who acted in such a way as to appear to be an Earthling was apparently involved in one of the attacks."

"There were Earthlings aboard the other three ships," the Admiral said.

"But there is no evidence whatsoever that any of them were involved in any wrongdoing," Junea said.

The Admiral appeared frustrated. "All four ships had visited Earth in the month before the attacks. Earth is the common thread that links them all."

"No," Junea corrected. "Earth is one potential common thread. But there are many others. For example there were citizens of the Cepheus sector on all four ships. The captains of all four ships were graduates of the Cepheus Merchant Marine Academy. All four vessels employed engines made by Draco Stardrive, which is suggestive that what some are calling a conspiracy of planet assassinations may be nothing else than a coincidence of mechanical malfunctions. The close relationship between the Cepheus Sector Naval Squadron and the Draco Stardrive Company is well known. I find it interesting that it is the Navy that is so adamant that the source of the disasters was an Earthling conspiracy. Can it be that in order to protect their comfortable corporate retirements, some of our valiant naval officers are engaged in a coverup, and are proposing to massacre billions of helpless savages to protect their bloated contractor friends in the shipbuilding industry? Perhaps that is what this court should be investigating."

Admiral Phillipus looked to his monarch. "Divine Princess, this is outrageous!"

"I quite agree," the Princess said. "On the basis of the evidence, this court is satisfied that all four incidents were the result of willful sabotage by Earthling savages. The Advocate for the Defendants will confine her arguments to those parameters."

"Very well," Junea nodded. "Then conceding that point in obedience to your divine wisdom, let us consider what might have caused four simple savages to perform such destructive acts. Let us look at the horrific oppression that all Earthlings have been subjected to by the Minervan occupation of their planet..."

The Admiral interrupted. "Divine Princess, that is absurd. The Minervans have occupied only one tiny locality called Kennewick, less than one millilightsecond in diameter. None of the planet assassins were from Kennewick. Ascribing Minervan culpability to their actions is completely far fetched."

"Not if we consider the psychological effect of seeing their fellow Earthlings from Kennewick humiliated every day by their brutal Minervan overlords," Junea said. "How can one possibly blame such poor simple savages for wanting to strike back in the only way they knew how?"

The Princess arched an eyebrow. "But they did not strike back against the Minervans, ambassador. They struck back at us."

"Yes, Divine Princess," ambassador Junea replied. "But can we be so blind as to not see what they see? Is it not obvious that the Minervans' ability to oppress and humiliate the poor innocent Earthlings is due entirely to the fact that our own Empire has transported this loveless people to their planet, that we have armed them, and continue to supply them with advanced technology that they use to brutally crush the legitimate aspirations for dignity and self determination of the planet's rightful inhabitants?"

This was too much for Aurora. She stood up. "Divine Princess," she said. "We Minervans are rightful inhabitants of the planet Earth. We originated there, in the region now called Kennewick 20,000 years ago. It is from there that we spread, to colonize the galaxy and give birth to all the great galactic civilizations. It is only one small part of the Earth, and the only part that we claim. But it is our homeland and ours by right. It is stated thus in all the most ancient holy books."

Junea waved her hand at Aurora dismissively. "Shall our Empire and its citizens be subject to ruin and massacre in the name of this sort of Minervan religious claptrap?"

A Weegee High Priestess seated in the front row of the courtroom's central sector stood up. Aurora recognized her as Pallacina, the High Priestess of the Cepheus Sector. "Ambassador, be warned. On these matters our holy books and those of the Minervans concur."

"Perhaps," Junea said. "But this is the modern age and we must be practical. The prophecies of Penelope the Wise may still serve as the great guide to life for the little priestess and her kind, but we have the interests of a hundred-million planet Empire to consider."

"Yes, we do," the Princess said. "And in that light I am particularly incensed that you appear to be implying that the party ultimately at fault in the recent planet assassinations was the government of Her Divine Majesty, Minaphera the 243rd. Is that what you are saying, Ambassador, that we are to blame? Are you saying that in choosing to support the claim of the Minervans to Kennewick, that Her Divine Majesty, Minaphera the 243rd, has made a mistake?"

A hushed silence filled the courtroom. The Princess fingered her triangle pendant and waited for the Ambassador's answer. Finally, Junea said, "no, Divine Princess. Of course not."

"Very well," the Princess said. "You may proceed with your defense."

"In that case, Divine Princess," Junea said, "let us consider if beings as primitive as the Earthlings can actually be blamed for anything. Earthlings are mindless savages, raised in a culture of violence. They are incapable of rational thought, and thus their actions must be considered as not matters of choice, but culturally conditioned reflexes. While in our culture, planet assassination is considered a crime, in theirs it is the natural, just and proper response to the sort of insults and humiliations the Minervans have imposed upon them. Retaliation of any kind against the Earthlings would thus be pointless, and in fact immoral, as there was no way the Earthlings who committed the act could comprehend its consequences in terms of how their actions might be considered by cultures external to their planet. Indeed, if we place the actions of the Earthlings within their own proper cultural context, it would appear that they did nothing wrong at all. The Minervans, on the other hand, believe as we do that planet assassination is immoral. Yet they willfully chose to act in such a way so as to provoke such behavior. Therefore the blood of 200 billion of Her Divine Majesty's subjects is on their hands, and theirs alone. I ask the court that my clients be absolved and the Minervans punished for this heinous crime."

"An interesting argument," the Princess said. "I think that this might be a good time for the court to bring forward its expert witness."

"Thank you, Divine Princess," the Admiral said. "May it please the court, we call Priestess 3rd Class Aurora to the witness stand. We also enter into evidence her Earthling specimen, Sergeant Andrew Hamilton, of the United States Army." He beckoned Aurora forward into the witness box.

Aurora advanced to the designated area, keeping a tight control on Hamilton, who was obstinately trying to resist his assigned role. It did him little good. Within a few seconds she had him standing on the specimen foot-stars.

"Divine Princess, I object!" Juneau seemed outraged. "The witness is a Minervan and has an obvious interest in defaming my clients."

"Objection noted, but overruled," the Princess said. "The witness' expertise is unique and indispensable to this court. We shall, however, be alert to any coloring of testimony to suit Minervan interests. Let the witness be warned that she is to expected to be strictly objective in her evaluations. The Court Chaplain may swear in the witness."

The Court Chaplain raised her right hand. "Priestess 3rd Class Aurora, in the name of the Triune Goddess, and her three attributes of Reason, Love, and Justice, do your swear to speak to this court Truth, all the Truth, and Only Truth?"

Aurora looked at the Chaplain and saw an evil glint in the woman's eye. It was clearly a trap. Aurora was being asked to take a heretical oath. If she did so, she would be dishonest and undoubtedly exposed as such. If she refused, her testimony would be discarded, with potentially catastrophic consequences for the Minervan settlers, as the proceedings would continue without their voice being heard. Still, there was nothing for it but honesty.

Aurora raised her hand. "In the name of the one true Goddess, Minerva, giver of Reason and Wisdom, I so swear."

Junea was on her feet in a flash. "Divine Princess! The witness has refused the oath. Can there be any greater proof of Minervan duplicity? She came to this court planning to lie. Her testimony cannot be accepted. Rather she and her specimen should be photolysized at once, as a lesson to all those who show such contempt for this court and everything it stands for."

There was scattered applause throughout the courtroom and among the courtiers. Aurora was terrified that Junea's recommendation might be approved. But then Admiral Phillipus spoke up. "Divine Princess, the witness was not showing contempt. It is unreasonable to ask a Minervan to swear by the Triune Goddess. She swore honestly, and should be respected for her integrity, all the more so since the incentive for her to pretend conformity to our faith was so high."

The Princess rubbed her pretty bare feet together thoughtfully. "I don't know," she mused. "She really should take the oath."

"Exactly," said Junea. "Divine Princess, your infinite wisdom is never wrong."

"But," continued the Princess, "as long as she is here we might as well hear her. After all, an oath is no guarantee of truth telling anyway."

"But…" said Junea.

The Admiral interrupted her. "The Divine Princess is never wrong. The witness may now testify."

Chapter 16

The Princess looked down on Aurora from her throne. "Priestess, you have devoted intensive study to the mental architecture of Earthlings, have you not?"

"Yes, Divine Princess, I have."

The Princess leaned forward, her green eyes intense. "And what then have your studies revealed relative to the question of the sanity of the Earthlings?"

Aurora steeled herself to stand up straight, and return the Princess's gaze with respect but with dignity. The question was a very dangerous one; if she made the slightest misstep in her reply, those of ill will will twist her meaning with devastating results. If the Earthlings were seen as utterly irrational, the blame for their actions would be placed on the proximate rational creatures stimulating their activity, i.e. the Minervans. But if the Earthlings were described as fully rational, then the Minervan treatment of them would be portrayed as criminal oppression. There was a fine line to be walked, with disaster waiting on either side. Silently, she sent a brief prayer to Minerva for help. Sing in me, Goddess, she thought. Then she began to speak.

"Divine Princess, members of the court. It is true that measured by civilized galactic standards the Earthlings are not sane. That much can be ascertained by one look at their bizarre male-dominated social structure, their absurd religions, or their disgusting behavior. You will observe for example, my study specimen here, Sergeant Andrew Hamilton, recently collected from the United States Army while attempting to murder Minervan picnickers. Note that he has no telepathic abilities or even any mental self-control, leaving his outer mind in a chaos dominated by various infantile neuroses. I'll pause a bit now so you can sample him for yourselves."

Here Aurora stopped speaking, giving the members of the court some time to explore Hamilton's outer mind. In a few moments the men present began to smile and the women began to giggle.

"Oh, my," the Princess exclaimed. "He's like a little baby pretending to be a man. How cute!"

Everyone in the court laughed, and Hamilton flushed red with embarrassment. Aurora smiled. "Yes, cute, except when they turn deadly. You will notice he has no thoughts of remorse for the six Minervans he murdered, or for that matter for dozens of Earthlings he killed earlier in his military career. Yet observe the thought that just emanated energetically from his inner mind."

The Princess looked quizzical. "'This is not fair,'" she paraphrased. "What is that supposed to mean?"

Aurora nodded. "'Not fair' is the creature's notion describing a condition whereby a party holding a certain advantage makes improper use of it to the detriment of a party not holding such an advantage. In other words, 'not fair' is a crude approximation of the human concept of Injustice, which necessarily implies some dim awareness of its converse, Justice."

A shocked silence filled the court. High Priestess Pallacina was the first to speak. "But my dear, as you, a third class priestess, must certainly know, Justice is a divine attribute flowing from the Goddess. This creature has no awareness of her whatsoever. How then can he possibly…"

Aurora shook her head. "I'm not sure. I need to go into his inner mind to find out, and so far he has resisted giving me permission. I'm keeping him in the hope that someday I can change his mind on that account, as the benefits to science could be immense. Yet for present purposes, the evidence before us suffices. He is capable of protorational thought on the subject of justice and injustice, and thus right or wrong. Now let us ask the creature a simple question. Hamilton, was the destruction of Draco 4 just or unjust? Was it right or was it wrong?"

Everyone turned to observe Hamilton, who seemed to be writhing in agony. Yet without any mental abilities, his thoughts came tumbling out uncontrollably. "Oh no, if I let them know I think it was wrong, they'll kill everyone on Earth. But they can read my mind. And I know it was wrong. It was wrong. It was horribly, horribly wrong."

The Admiral nodded. "Guilty as charged."

"No!" A telepathic scream practically deafened the courtroom.

Aurora looked at Hamilton in amazement. In his distress, the soldier had actually managed a coherent thought projection. It was a feat usually accomplished by Minervan children at the age of 3 or 4, but to her knowledge no Earthling had ever done it. She hadn't even thought it possible. That the Ranger was able to do it bespoke a potential for humanity that elicited her deepest feelings.

"We are not all guilty!" Hamilton's mind screamed again.

That was true, and though of secondary importance, it was a subtlety worth considering. But he would never make his point with childish telepathic screaming. Taking pity on the man, she said softly, "Hamilton, speak using words. I'll translate for you." With that, she remobilized his head and upper body, leaving only his feet rooted in place.

Hamilton flexed his fingers and rubbed his jaw, as if to restore circulation that had never been cut off. Then he faced the Princess.

"Your Majesty," he began, eliciting expressions of shock and outrage among the courtiers. The Princess frowned and briefly touched her pendant, but then shrugged and indicated for him to continue.

"It is true that the evidence points to involvement by Earthlings in the horrific acts against your empire, and I won't dispute it. But what I do dispute is that all Earthlings are of the same moral character as those who committed those crimes. Look into my mind. I know you can. You will see that not only did I not have anything to do with those actions, but that I have moral principles that would prevent me from ever doing anything so morally abhorrent."

The Princess peered at him, looking hard. "Very well, creature. I accept the fact that you personally did not participate in the planet assassinations, and also your claim that you view those actions with revulsion. So what?"

"Well, the fact of the matter is that most other Earthlings are equally innocent."

"It is clear that you believe that. However, we require facts." The Princess turned to Aurora. "Priestess, what is your evaluation of the accuracy of the savage's last comment?"

"It is only partially true. While obviously only a minority of Earthlings had any foreknowledge of or direct involvement in the planet assassination plot, many cheered its success afterwards. Still, as Hamilton says, there are also substantial numbers who view the actions with horror, although more for fear of the consequences than for grief for the murdered."

The Priestess regarded Hamilton. "Well savage, partial truth is conceded to your statement. What conclusions would you therefore have us draw from such premises?"

"Since some are guilty, but others are not, you should punish the guilty but spare the innocent."

The Princess raised an eyebrow. "I asked you for conclusions, not instructions. You presume much, savage, to tell a Princess of the Western Galactic Empire what she should or should not do."

Hamilton stood his ground. "I asked that you punish the guilty but spare the innocent. Is that not justice?"

The Princess smiled. "Of course it is, in cases applying to rational beings. But those categories hardly apply to violently insane subhumans." She laughed and looked at Aurora. "Priestess, your specimen is most amusing. He seems to actually believe he is human."

Aurora returned the monarch's grin. "Yes, Divine Princess. We have had many conversations on exactly that point. He simply doesn't understand. Still, on the basis of my research, I would have to say that he and a number of other Earthlings may be potentially human. Therefore, though justice does not require it, I believe that while destroying the United States government which masterminded the planet assassination, it would be desirable to spare as many of the non-guilty Earthlings as practicality allows. It would be…merciful." She looked at Hamilton and smiled. He deserved that much.

Junea stood up. "Oh listen to this, a Minervan talking about mercy. Next thing you know she will start talking to us about love." A titter of laughter rippled through the courtiers.

The Princess regarded Junea. "Ambassador, I am somewhat perplexed by your remark. Given the disposition of this court towards dealing forcefully with the Earthling menace, I thought her plea on their behalf was very generous."

"Divine Princess," Junea replied. "That's what she wanted you to think. But she was obviously being dishonest. Consider her use of the word 'mercy.' Minervans don't believe in mercy, since it is an attribute of Aphrodite, the manifestation of the Triune Goddess they detest the most. She talks of 'justice,' an attribute of Hera, a divine manifestation which Minervans also deny. The Minervans believe in neither mercy nor justice. They just want to preserve some of the Earthlings to be their slaves. She refused the oath, and as foretold, she has lied."

The Princess seemed thoughtful. "Her choice of words would appear to demonstrate some insincerity. But in what matter has she lied?"

Junea's voice took on a commanding tone. "She lied when she said the US government masterminded the planet assassinations. That is a gross slander of my clients, who are entirely innocent of any such heinous acts. The whole galaxy knows how horribly the Minervans have been oppressing the American people, whose only defender is the US government. Now, by lying to this court, the Minervan witness is trying to frame my esteemed clients, and by so doing, enlist the aid of the Western Galactic Empire in the owl worshippers' hideous campaign of persecution, oppression, enslavement, mutilation, and murder of the helpless natives of this poor planet."

Junea took a step towards the throne. "Divine Princess, do not let yourself be deceived. Do not the Triune Scriptures warn us to 'Beware the Minervans, they of fast words and sharp-edged thoughts. Beware those who pretend to Reason, without Love or Justice.'"

Aurora was incensed. "Divine Princess, I object! The ambassador is engaged in crude ancient anti-Minervan slander. We Minervans believe in Love and Justice as much as anyone."

High Priestess Pallacina looked skeptical. "But you deny their existence as independent divinities."

Aurora tried to speak calmly, for she knew her next words would not be well received. "They are derived attributes of Reason, and we celebrate them accordingly."

The High Priestess shook her head. "If only you would see the light, how much happier you would be."

Junea sneered. "Yes, if only they would, how much happier we would all be. We wouldn't have 200 billion dead citizens to mourn, if only the Minervans had been willing to treat the Earthlings with Love and Justice. And now, these cold, calculating, cruel but clever creatures are trying to enmesh us in their schemes of conquest. We must not let them succeed. Divine Princess, members of the court, we are responsible for the safety and well-being of the greatest empire in Galactic History, one which has brought the glorious benefits of a civilization based on Reason, Love, and Justice to the countless citizens of more than 100 million worlds. Our subjects adore us and our allies respect us because we use our great strength to defend the weak. But think of the consequences if the Minervans entrap us as their assistants in their campaign of ruthless brutality. What will be the effect on our allies in the Northern Confederation and the Central Union? What will be the effect on the inhabitants on the primitive but vital helicity-rich worlds of the Southern sector? Will not the effect be to push them all into the camp of our dangerous adversaries of the Eastern Galactic Empire? Your Divine Majesty to be, our empire is mighty indeed, but even we will not be able to stand for long if the entire galaxy is united against us. Yet that is precisely the objective towards which the Minervans are striving. This is how they repay us for saving them in the last war. Shall we lose our empire by falling again for the lying tricks of this tiny group of disloyal and ungrateful heretics? I say no!"

At this dramatic crescendo, most of the courtiers and the diplomatic personnel who comprised about half of the audience burst out in vigorous applause. Aurora blanched with terror, for she had not felt so much anti-Minervan thoughts since the horror of Pegasus 3. She looked up at the Princess, who returned her glance not with hatred, but with almost as unnerving cool suspicion.

Admiral Phillipus cleared his throat. "Divine Princess, the Ambassador has raised some serious concerns. Yet the validity of her argument rests entirely on her contention that the Minervans are lying when they say that the United States government was behind the planet assassinations. In fact, however, all of our intelligence indicates that the Minervan accusation is true."

Junea waved her hands dismissively. "Nonsense. All of your intelligence comes from the Minervans. Naturally it will support their deception."

"As a military man, I have to say that I have always found Minervan intelligence to be very accurate." Phillipus turned to face the audience. "Fellow officers of the Imperial Navy, how many of you owe your lives to the information supplied to us by Minervans during the last war?"

Aurora turned and watched, as several men, all middle-aged Navy officers of medium or high rank rose to their feet. Then more of their brethren did the same, along with several Fleet Chaplains, until nearly a quarter of the audience was standing.

"And look," Phillipus said, pointing at her medal. "The witness herself is a Little Star, earned in combat aboard the Battlecruiser Warhawk in the decisive battle of the Andromedan Clusters. She and her kind were our friends then, and they are our friends now!"

At this remark, one of the Fleet Chaplains started to applaud, slowly but loudly, and was quickly joined by the other standing officers. Aurora felt her throat tighten with gratitude as kind thoughts from several of the veterans entered her mind.

Junea waited for the applause to die down. "Thank you, Admiral, for that heartwarming display of sentimental esprit de corps. Yet it is clear why Minervan intelligence was often good during the last war; they were depending upon our victory for their very survival. But now, instead of helping us with our just war, they are attempting to drag us into their own unjust one. In consequence of their machinations, 200 billion of Her Divine Majesty's subjects are now dead. That is not what I call friendship." She turned to the throne. "Divine Princess, in view of its inherently untrustworthy origin, I ask that all intelligence supplied to this court by Minervan sources be stricken from the record."

The Princess rubbed her feet together as she considered this request for several moments. Then she said, "Ambassador, your points are well taken, yet I am not sure I will go so far as to grant your request. I think instead that what we should do is retain the Minervan evidence, but note the uncertain veracity of its source and require further substantiation prior to its acceptance as fact."

Junea bowed her head. "Divine Princess, your wisdom is exceeded only by your beauty."

Appearing frustrated, Admiral Phillipus again advanced to a position before the throne. "Divine Princess, this is all obfuscation. The evidence of US government guilt in the planet assassinations is clear and self-evident. It requires no uncritical belief in the Minervans. Rather, the facts speak for themselves."

The Princess leaned back in her throne. "Very well, Admiral. Present the facts."

"Yes, Divine Princess." The Admiral activated a psioswitch, and holograms of four Earthling males somewhat physically inferior to Hamilton appeared in the courtroom.

"In the first place we have the identity of the assassins themselves. Here they are: David Crockett Christianson, born Provo Utah, USA; George Washington Jones, born Newark, New Jersey, USA; Mickey Mantle Ostrowski, born Yonkers, New York, USA; and Thomas Jefferson Clark, born Norfolk, Virginia, USA." The Admiral pointed to Hamilton. "Members of the court. Observe the thoughts in the Earthling specimen's outer mind. He recognizes each of the perpetrators as an American."

Aurora looked into Hamilton's mind, and saw that he was trying to hide something. It would do him no good. In seconds everyone else saw it, too.

The Admiral smiled. "And observe the Earthling's own conclusion. He thinks they were sent by the US government, too." Hamilton reddened, but the Admiral just continued. "And note also his opinion of the actions. The deeds were so despicable that even a simple savage like this finds them contemptible."

Junea snickered. "Well if it isn't enough that the Admiral is using Minervan testimony to impugn my client, now he expects us to take seriously the chaotic thoughts of an ignorant savage, one whom, moreover, has been the subject of Minervan psychological manipulation for months."

"Nevertheless," said Phillipus, "say what you will. It is clear that all four assassins were born in the United States and each were named after American mythological cult fetishes. They therefore must be assumed to be loyal subjects acting on behalf of the tribal sachems of the United States government."

"Wrong," said Junea. "The real names of the assassins were David Crockett Christianson de Peru, George Washington Jones de Peru,, Mickey Mantle Ostrowski de Peru, and Thomas Jefferson Clark de Peru. These are not American names, they are Peruvian names. The alleged assassins were born in the United States, yes, but they had so little in common with the peaceful, civilized customs of the United States government and its policy of friendship for the Western Galactic Empire and respect for the Empress Minaphera the 243rd that they renounced their American citizenship and moved to Peru where they adopted Peruvian names, customs, and citizenship. The alleged assassins were not agents of the United States, they were traitors to the United States!"

The Princess seemed startled. "Ambassador, how did you learn this?"

"The information was given to me by the United States government itself. You see, Your Divine Majesty to Be, the US government, far from being a part of the assassin problem, is straining all of its resources to find out who is behind it. They are our friends and partners in the war against planet assassination."

The Admiral frowned. "Oh really, Ambassador? Then how do you explain this?"

Phillipus activated another psioswitch, and the holoimages of the assassins vanished. Instead the courtroom's apparent space expanded to a full holotheater projection of a crazed Earthling rally of the Cosmic Christian Crusade. The courtroom audience watched in horror as thousands of savages in a large physical stadium screamed "Death to the Western Galactic Empire" while committing obscenities to crude representations of the Empress and astronomical models of the WGE. "Observe," the Admiral said, as he zoomed in on the mystic who was leading the affair. "The sachem orchestrating the event is a leader of the US government."

A computer ID appeared under the mystic sachem, labeling him as Reverend John Meade, Chaplain of the Chief's House. Then mercifully, the Admiral cut the projection off. "Well," he said. "Ambassador, do you deny your client's involvement in what we have just seen?"

"No," Junea replied coolly. "Of course not. The United States government regularly organizes such demonstrations in order to allow its subjects to peacefully vent their rage against the perceived allies of the Minervans, without any negative consequences. Far from being directed against us, the purpose of the CCC rallies is to protect us."

The Princess seemed skeptical. "Ambassador, I have been doing a little research on my own. Does not the Earthling term 'crusade' mean holy war whose objective is to kill non-believers? And does not therefore a cosmic Christian crusade imply a holy war to kill all non-Christians throughout the cosmos?"

Junea smiled. "Your Divine Majesty to Be is well-read. However the sources you have been supplied with suffer from a common misconception. It is true that in the distant past the term 'crusade' sometimes referred to military combat in the name of good. However, on the modern Earth, 'crusade' is generally taken to mean inner struggle on behalf of the good that is within oneself. The term Christian may have once referred to members of a particular local cult, but today it simply means one who loves. Cosmos means universal. So far from being anything menacing, a cosmic Christian crusade is simply the joining together of many people in a shared inner struggle to love everyone everywhere."

Aurora gagged.

The Admiral looked sternly at Junea. "You claim the US government wishes to help us fight the planet assassins. Yet all I am hearing are excuses to try to get themselves off the hook. If they are really our allies, where is their help?"

"Right here," Junea said. "Lisa, would you be so kind?"

The pink-faced recently-washed Earthling woman stood up. "Your Divine Majesty to Be, I am Lisa White, Director of Public Communications for the United States Government."

Junea said, "The Divine Princess will note that Mrs. White is wearing an original Felgorgious gown."

A murmur of admiration rippled through the female courtiers. The Princess said, "Yes, I can see that. My sisters and I frequently buy from Felgorgious ourselves."

"Hardly the sort of place where a planet assassin would shop," Junea observed.

The Earthling drew a package of physical images from her carrying case. As she did so, Junea took several steps away, apparently because the images were covered with mild chemical toxins. Aurora wrinkled her nose. The things smelled bad, even for Earthling artifacts.

"These," Lisa White said, "are reconnaissance photographs that United States military aircraft have recently taken over Peru."

"What's an aircraft?" the Princess interrupted.

"It's like a spacecraft," the Admiral explained, "only it is limited to subluminal speeds and travel within the atmosphere of a single planet."

The Princess seemed amused. "Really? How quaint!" She turned back to Lisa White. "Do go on."

Lisa White pointed to her images. "As you can see, these are training camps for planet assassins."

Aurora willed her eyes into high magnification to pick out details from the crude images. As she did so, she was aware that nearly everyone else in the courtroom was doing the same. Yes, there was no doubt about it, the images represented common electromagnetic light reflected off of physical structures which were consistent with a training camp for planet assassins.

"Now," Lisa White continued. "These are images of the same camps taken one month ago."

Aurora zoomed in again on the images, and recoiled in shock. There was no doubt about it, three of the four planet assassins were clearly there. "Holy Minerva!" she said involuntarily.

Junea turned to her with a scowl. "Holy Minerva, indeed. You knew it all along. Yet you tried to frame my client for your own, evil, unjust purposes." She faced the throne. "Your Divine Majesty to Be, I ask that the lying Minervan witness receive her punishment!"

Aurora fell to he knees and looked up at the Princess with tears in her eyes. "Divine Princess, I didn't know, I couldn't have!" Then she picked up a fleeting involuntary thought from Hamilton, and paused, turning to face Junea. "In fact," Aurora said, "I still don't."

"What do you mean, Minervan?" Junea said spitefully. "The evidence is right there for all to see."

Aurora faced the Princess again, and spoke as calmly as she could. "Divine Princess, the evidence may be there but it doesn't make any sense. Why would the Peruvians, on their own accord, launch an attack on the Western Galactic Empire?"

Junea interrupted. "Why? I'll tell you why. Because they were so upset with the way you Minervans are treating the Kennewickians that they felt they had to do something about it. And since Peru is an impoverished country, they didn't have the benefit of the CCC rallies to deflect the anger of their people, which my client has wisely and fortunately been able to provide, and the inevitable result was violence."

Aurora crossed her arms. "I don't buy it. By Earthling standards of travel, Peru is far away from Kennewick, and the Earthlings there are poor beyond belief. I doubt if anyone in Peru would give half a cup of raffa rinds for Kennewick. I'll tell you what I think. I think that the American government sent their planet assassins down to Peru for training, so if they were caught, they could deflect the blame."

Junea huffed, "You have no proof for such outrageous accusations!"

"No, but I have Reason," Aurora glared.

The Princess appeared confused. "Reason without evidence verses evidence without reason. What are we to do?"

"We could eliminate both the United States government and Peru," the Admiral offered helpfully. "That would be the safest course."

The Princess nodded thoughtfully. "It might appear to be so."

A man in the uniform of a high-ranking member of Western Imperial Commercial Consular Service stood up. "Your Divine Majesty to Be shows great wisdom in applying the words 'might appear' to the purported safety of the course of action that the Admiral has suggested to you. His proposed course of action is indeed misconceived."

The Princess steepled her hands. "Continue," she said.

The man bowed. "Divine Princess, I am Fedris, Senior Imperial Commercial Consul for the Procyon Sector. As such, I was responsible for arranging the WGE monopoly concession on the Earth's helicity."

An elderly man in an even higher-ranking WG Imperial Consular uniform standing behind the Princess leaned over and whispered something into her ear. The Princess said, "Excellent work, Fedris. You should know that Cepheus Sector Chief Commercial Consul Frondrippus is very impressed with you."

"Indeed, I am," Frondrippus said. "The Empire owes a great deal to this man. I suggest we take his policy advice very seriously."

"Then by all means," the Princess said. "Let him proceed."

Fedris bowed again. "Thank you, Divine Princess. Following the Admiral's advice would be an enormous mistake. The Earth is one of the largest reserves of helicity in the entire Southern Sector, and the United States is the leading helicity source on the Earth. Were we to retaliate against the US government without definitive evidence that they were the ones behind the planet assassinations—a notion which I, based on my extensive contact with the highly sophisticated shoppers who comprise the American leadership, find extremely unlikely—it would be seen by all the helicity exporters of the Southern Sector as an attack on them. The result would be to open up hundreds of important helicity source planets to the EGE."

Frondrippus nodded sagely. "That is very true. Strategic helicity supplies would be endangered. Quadrillions of bluebacks worth of trade concessions could be lost."

The Princess waved her hand dismissively. "Those are secondary considerations. Our primary concern must be to ensure the security of Her Divine Majesty's subjects."

"But," continued Frondrippus in the gravest of tones, "with the loss of the trade concessions, huge amounts of Cepheus Sector and Imperial court tax revenues based on the Southern helicity commerce would also disappear."

The Princess sat silently for several seconds, as several suddenly agitated courtiers in rapid succession came up and whispered urgent advice to her. Then she said, "I see." She looked down from her throne. "Priestess Aurora, I believe you are sincere. The US government has, without question, been involved in organizing assassins against your settlement. But the evidence in this case is clear. The attack on the Western Galactic Empire came from Peru, and it against Peru that we shall retaliate. My judgment is final."

She extended her feet into her shoes, and everyone in the courtroom leaped to attention. "For Reason, Love, and Justice, Everywhere and Forever!" all chanted in unison.

The Princess stood up and favored the attendees with a radiant smile. "Thank you, loyal subjects." She turned to face the Admiral. "Admiral Phillipus, prepare the fleet for action."

Chapter 17

Hamilton looked across the plaza of his palace-cell to the altar, where Aurora had just finished praying to the statue of the Goddess Minerva. It had been three days since the trial, and nothing much had happened. The two of them had been kept confined to the junior-officers-quarters palace until today, when word had come that they would be taken out for dinner by Danatus. Upon receiving the invitation, Aurora had stopped their chachostrat game and told him to wash while she spent some time communing with her deity. Now they were both ready, and just in time. One of their Space Marine "attendants" entered and announced that Lieutenant Danatus and his company were awaiting them on the exterior plaza. They got up to leave. Perhaps now they would get some news.

When they reached the main entrance they looked down the grand stairway and could see that Danatus was not alone. With him was a party of half a dozen Weegee junior officers as well as several young Fleet Chaplains. As Hamilton and Aurora began to descend the long stairway, Hamilton could not help observing again how tall all the Weegees were. The men were all at least 6'6" and the women at least 6'2". On Earth, among his own kind, Hamilton's slightly above-average 5' 11" height and excellent physique had never left him feeling at a physical disadvantage in any company, and even among the Minervans he was close to normal. But here he was dwarfed, and somehow the fact that they now were going to mix socially with the Weegees made the physical disparity even more intimidating.

"Aurora," Hamilton asked, "why are the Weegees so tall? Is it genetic? Or nutritional?"

"No," replied the priestess. "It's a cumulative relativistic effect, resulting from extensive space travel."

Hamilton was confused. While not a scientist, he had read popular books on physics and astronomy. No height growth was predicted by Einstein's theories. "I don't get it. According to the theory of relativity that I've heard about, going fast makes your length contract, but only while you are doing it and only as observed by someone who is not moving with you. It certainly doesn't make you grow bigger."

Aurora smiled. "Your scientists have not thought through the implications of their own theories. It's really quite simple."

Hamilton stopped on a landing halfway down the staircase and faced the priestess. "How so? Please explain."

"Well," Aurora said, "as every child knows, the theory of relativity predicts that time slows down as you approach the speed of light. You do understand that much, don't you?"

Hamilton nodded. He didn't understand exactly why that was supposed to happen, but it concurred with what he had read. If one twin set out on a trip at a speed close to the speed of light, he would be younger than his brother when he returned home. Time went by slower for the fast traveler. "Yes. That's what our scientists say, too."

"And of course," Aurora continued, "we also know that everything in the universe is shrinking."

Hamilton was startled. He had never heard that before. "What? You say everything is shrinking? There's no evidence for that!"

Aurora looked amused. "Of course there is. What do you think causes the Red Shift?"

Hamilton did another double-take. He had heard of the Red Shift. It was discovered by the astronomer Edwin Hubble in the 1920s. Light from far away galaxies shifted towards the red, or long wavelength, end of the spectrum. "Now wait a second, I know all about the Red Shift. It's caused by the Doppler Effect. Far-away galaxies are moving away from us at great speed, and it stretches out the light from them into longer wavelengths, which makes them look redder. It's the proof that the universe is expanding."

Aurora laughed. "Don't be ridiculous. The universe isn't expanding. That's obviously physically impossible. It only appears to be expanding because everything in it is shrinking. What silly ideas you Earthlings have." She started walking down the staircase again.

"But wait," Hamilton said, hurrying after her. "How does the idea that everything is shrinking explain the Red Shift?"

Aurora looked at the Ranger with pity in her eyes. "Hamilton, really, even you should be able to think this through. You do understand, don't you, that the light we see today from far away objects was actually emitted in the distant past, and that we only see it today because it has been traveling at finite speed?"

"Yes." Far away light was old light. That was one of the few parts of modern astronomy that Hamilton actually did understand.

"Well," continued Aurora, "since the light from distant galaxies was emitted in ancient times when everything was bigger, naturally it has longer wavelengths than contemporary light, and therefore appears redder."

Hamilton stopped in his tracks. Aurora's theory seemed to hold together, yet he thought he detected a flaw in her logic. "But wait," he said. "If everything in the universe is shrinking, then so should the waves of old light. Their wavelengths should shrink with time just like everything else, and thus appear normal to us today."

Aurora frowned. "I thought you said you understood relativity, Hamilton. Time goes slower as you approach the speed of light. At the speed of light, time stops altogether. Now what speed does light travel at?" She looked at him as she would at a very dull child. "Well?"

"At the speed of light, I suppose" Hamilton managed to say.

"Right. And therefore how much time does the light experience while it is traveling?" Aurora looked at Hamilton with a penetrating gaze.

"None? So the lightwaves stay bigger because they experience no time?"

Aurora patted Hamilton on the head. "Very good," she smiled. "Perhaps there is hope for you yet." She resumed her walk down the staircase. "And as you can see," she said, pointing towards Danatus and his friends, "the same effect is evident with the Weegees. They do so much near-luminal, luminal, and super-luminal travel that their net time experience is much less than that of more stationary people. Therefore they have not shrunk as much, and accordingly appear larger to the rest of us."

"But you've spent a lot of your life in starships. How come you are not as tall as they are?"

"Hamilton, really. The shrinkage retardation that can occur within the lifetime of a single interstellar traveling human is minute. It is the cumulative effect that has developed over many generations that we can observe among the Weegees today."

It seemed incredible, but as they approached Danatus' group, there was no denying the facts. The thought crossed Hamilton's mind that it was good that Earthlings had finally gotten involved with the starfaring races of the galaxy. If they had remained an isolated immobile race for much longer, Earth's inhabitants would have been doomed to become midgets by comparison with everyone else. Perhaps now they had a chance to catch up, or at least hold their own.

Danatus extended his hand in warm greeting to the priestess. "Good to see you again, Aurrie. Allow me to introduce you to my friends."

Hamilton stood by while Aurora was introduced to each of Danatus' companions. Then he fell in walking with the group towards the restaurant district. They chatted with each other rapidly in Weegee as they strolled, making Hamilton feel very alone, as without Aurora's simultaneous telepathic translation the conversation was totally incomprehensible.

The restaurant district was as festive as it had been when Aurora and Hamilton had walked through it the first time, with music playing and people skate-dancing around the fountains that adorned the larger plazas. The only apparent difference was that glowing blue triangular pennants bearing the portrait of the Empress Minaphera were now flying in abundance from every building. As they passed through one of the fountain squares, the party was joined by a man and a woman with red hair wearing the green attire of the Northern Confederation. The man joined in the conversation with Aurora and the Weegees, but after a brief interaction with that group, the woman fell back to walk beside Hamilton.

The woman turned her intense green eyes on the Ranger and said something incomprehensible. Hamilton looked at her miserably. The woman was very attractive, and emanated a kind of carefree, friendly warmth, but he couldn't make out a word she was saying.

The woman's face took on an expression of concern. "I'm sorry," she said. "I didn't realize you needed mental assistance to understand human speech."

Relieved to have someone to talk with, Hamilton decided to take no offense at the implied insult. "Ordinarily, I don't," he said ruefully.

The woman smiled. "Now, now," she admonished gently. "There is no reason for you to be ashamed. You are what you are. It's not your fault that you can't think like a human. The Goddess loves you for what you are. You don't need to try to be something you are not."

Hamilton didn't know what to say.

She stuck out her hand. "Allow me to introduce myself. I'm Priestess 3rd Class Urania, of the Anthropo Institute, currently detailed to serve as Science Officer aboard the Northern Confederation Frigate Bold Rescue."

Hamilton took her hand. "Sergeant Andrew Hamilton, United States Army."

Urania grinned. "Yes, I know. You're Priestess Aurora's study specimen. I've read her report. Such excellent research, truly amazing given the primitive conditions she had to work in. You must be very proud of her."

"Yes, Aurora is …amazing," was all Hamilton could muster.

"You know," Urania continued breezily, "much more could be discovered if proper facilities were available. At the Anthropo Institute we have a complete array of the latest mind-probing technology and comprehensive backup with top-quality specialists available in all related sub-disciplines. Perhaps after this war is over you could help me prevail upon Aurora to take you back with us. With the equipment we have, we could map every thought, pseudo thought, and neurosis in your outer mind with unequalled precision, perhaps well enough to allow us to assist you in overcoming your instinctive defensiveness against an inner-mind survey. The gains for science could be so spectacular."

Hamilton gulped. "I'm not sure that would be such a good idea."

Urania detected his alarm. "There's nothing to worry about," she said reassuringly. "At the Anthropo Institute Aurora would be given full Co-Investigator status, with complete authority to direct the research. So there would be no loss of experimental continuity. And you would be kept in safe, sanitary facilities that are fully compliant with the Interstellar Committee on Scientific Practices in Anthropological Research regulations on the humane treatment of laboratory subjects."

Hamilton didn't like where the conversation was going. "Why do you need me for an investigative subject? There are six billion other Earthlings."

Urania shook her head. "Unfortunately they've all now been contaminated by uncontrolled contact with Weegee consumer technology. You were collected under pristine conditions, and Aurora has done an excellent job in documenting all of your interactions and mental changes since that time. So as a scientific specimen for studying Earthling psychology, you are absolutely unique. We really must have you."

The Ranger decided to change the subject. "So, you are from the Northern Confederation. What are you doing here with the Weegee fleet?"

Urania smiled. "We're here to help our sisters in the Western Galactic Empire in the war against the Peruvian planet assassins. The Empress Minaphera has called for an grand interstellar coalition to fight this menace, and the Universal League has endorsed her call. Accordingly, our squadron has been sent here to join in the liberation of Peru."

"I didn't realize the WGE needed any help in fighting Peru," Hamilton said. "I heard they had a thousand space battleships in this fleet, plus over ten thousand cruisers, destroyers, frigates, and patrol boats. How big is your squadron?"

"We have five frigates and a fast emergency repair vessel."

"That doesn't sound like it should change the strategic balance very much."

"In strictly military terms, no," Urania conceded. "However from a political point of view, it is essential that the galaxy stand united against such barbarism. So we have sent our reconnaissance squadron, the Eastern Galactics have sent a prison ship, and the Central Federation is sending a medical vessel. As soon as the latter gets here, the assault should begin."

"All for an attack on Peru." Hamilton shook his head. Even the US Army would have no trouble taking out Peru. His guess was that any one of the WGE warships would have been more than sufficient to do the job.

Urania read his mind. "Actually, our presence in the Interstellar Coalition Armada is not superfluous. While the planet assassins must be brought to account, it is essential that the archeological treasures and unique natural environment of Peru not be damaged in the process. As I'm sure you've noticed, the Weegees, while good-hearted people, lack refinement in certain areas. By participating in the expedition, we can help insure that the campaign is conducted with proper attention to esthetic considerations."

Hamilton was bewildered. "You are concerned about the fate of Peruvian archeological sites?"

"Yes indeed," Urania said. "Inca art represents a priceless storehouse of neoprotoarcheosymbolic representations, and is valued as such by connoisseurs across the galaxy. Many people in the Northern Confederation were quite skeptical about the merit of this expedition, but when we heard about the wanton damage that the Peruvian planet assassins were doing to Inca statues, we realized we had to act. At our initiative, the Cultural Committee of the Universal League has identified the preservation of Inca artifacts as a key priority to be incorporated into the rules of engagement for this war. We intend to make sure that those priorities are observed."

"That's nice," Hamilton mumbled.

Urania nodded. "I'm sure that, as an Earthling, you must be very proud of your Inca heritage."

"Well, actually..." Hamilton began.

Urania cut him off. "Have you been to Peru many times?" she asked suddenly.

"No, never," the soldier replied. "But I went to Mexico once. I think that the ancient Aztecs there had statues and buildings a lot like those of the Incas in Peru."

"No, no, not at all." Urania shook her head. "Amazing. You've lived your entire life on Earth and never once gone to Peru. But don't worry, we have an extensive collection of Inca art at the Anthropo Institute, which we should be able to augment significantly at the conclusion of this campaign. We can make duplicates of the best pieces, and put them in your living quarters. Wouldn't that be wonderful? You could spend the rest of your life in a naturalistic setting of scientifically-authenticated Inca décor."

Just then they reached the restaurant. The party was shown to a long table. Hamilton tried to maneuver to sit near Aurora, but was unsuccessful. Instead he found himself at the far end, with Urania as his sole conversational companion.

It was going to be a long night.

Chapter 18

Aurora looked across the table at Danatus. The man had tried to act amiable throughout the dinner, but it was clear that underneath there was something that was worrying him.

"Danatus, what wrong?"

The young lieutenant strummed the table nervously with his fingers.

"You can tell me, Danatus, we're old friends," Aurora urged

Danatus looked around for guidance to the other assembled WGE junior officers and Fleet Chaplains.

"I think it would be OK," said Kalia, who with an appearance suggesting an age in the mid thirties, was the most senior of the Chaplains present. "She's clearly loyal, and seems pretty sharp. Perhaps she might be able to help."

"Right," Danatus said. "That's what I was hoping you would say."

Aurora folded her hands together. "Well," she prodded. "What is it?"

Danatus looked at Aurora with deep concern. "Aurrie," he began, "something terrible has happened."

Aurora was alarmed. "What? What is it?"

"Someone has launched a series of attacks on our senior officers from inside the flagship. We fear much worse is to come."

"Someone? Who? Attacks from inside? How? Tell me."

Danatus spread his hands. "That's just it. We don't know who or how. All we know is that starting yesterday, a series of our most senior officers, including Admiral Phillipus, High Priestess Pallacina, and the Princess's own Captain of Bodyguards all became violently sick."

Aurora looked at the young officer amazed. "What do you mean, sick? You mean sick like an Earthling infested with microorganisms?"

"Yes," Danatus said.

Aurora was horrified. Civilized humans did not get sick. At least not naturally. "Reason help us! How could such a thing have happened?"

"We don't know," Kalia said. "The only real clue is that in each of the victim's quarters we found a small sheet of compounded tree-flesh, with each sheet carrying traces of what appear to be bioengineered spores of Pathocoli Cygnus."

Aurora stared in shock. Pathocoli Cygnus was a type of bacteria with interstellar distribution. Long ago it had killed billions, until starfaring humans had been genetically immunized. In modern times it persisted as a mere nuisance, known only to afflict the most primitive worlds of the Southern Sector. Now someone had weaponized the old scourge, and was releasing it inside the flagship. "How is the Admiral?" she asked breathlessly.

"Still alive. It looks like he'll recover. But Pallacina and the Captain of Bodyguards are dead. It seems that the largest doses were received by those closest to the Princess."

"Holy Minerva! It was an assassination attempt!"

"That's what we think," Danatus said. "The question is, an assassination attempt launched by who?"

Aurora had a pretty good idea of "who." She turned to Kalia. "Tell me, were there any markings on the sheets of tree flesh?"

Kalia nodded. "Yes, there were." She closed her eyes and projected in image of the markings into Aurora's outer mind.

Aurora recognized the markings immediately. They were American Earthling writing. The inscription read; "Jesus is Love! Death to the Western Galactic Empire!" She dropped her jaw. Surely the Weegees must recognize the nature and source of the message. She looked at Kalia. "It was clearly sent by Earthlings!" she exclaimed.

Kalia said, "Now don't jump to conclusions, dear. Anyone could have put that inscription on the tree-flesh sheets."

"Anyone, that is," interjected a thirtyish officer who had not spoken much during the dinner, "who had a good knowledge of Earthling."

Aurora looked at Danatus with alarm. "Danatus, what is this?"

Danatus looked sheepish. "I'm sorry, Aurrie, but I had orders. This is Lieutenant First Class Firanus, of the Special Security Division."

"Greetings," Firanus said with a sardonic smile. "Please don't be alarmed. We have not yet concluded that your are guilty. We have another suspect as well."

Aurora's eyes blazed. "How dare you accuse me of this crime? Admiral Phillipus is my friend. What motive could I have to try to kill him, or the Princess? And what means?"

Firanus laughed. "Oh, I think your potential motive is pretty clear.

You want to enrage the Empire into action against the American Earthlings, so you commit an atrocity against the royal household and sign it in their name. But you made a mistake. We are not naïve, you know. The notion that the Earthlings would be so foolish as to try to kill the Princess and then claim credit for the deed was too preposterous to believe."

"You are too preposterous to believe!" Aurora shouted. She calmed herself and turned to Kalia. The Chaplain had to be the one running this show. "Priestess Kalia. I am amazed that you have allowed yourself to be diverted from the obvious truth. My record of loyalty to the WGE is well documented. It goes back to my childhood."

"Yes," Kalia said. "But you are a Minervan first."

"I see no contradiction." Aurora's voice was firm. "And in any case, you've had me confined and under guard the entire time I've been on this ship. I've had no access to the internal matter distribution system. So there is no way I could have sent the contaminated tree-flesh to anyone."

Kalia nodded. "Those facts do pose certain difficulties for your accusers. However, as Lieutenant Firanus has stated, we do have an alternative suspect. Perhaps you can help clear yourself by providing some information."

"I'll tell you anything I know," Aurora said.

"Very well." Kalia gestured to Firanus. "Proceed, Lieutenant."

Firanus pressed his right forefinger to a ring on his left hand, and a recessed holoimage appeared on the table. "Priestess Aurora," he said. "Do you recognize these people?"

Aurora gasped. It was the elderly Weegee and her granddaughter, from the space transport. "You suspect them?" she asked, amazed.

"Yes, we certainly do." Firanus' voice was deadly serious. "That's Priestess 3rd Class Premora, the WGE medical-science attaché to the Universal League observation team on Earth. She warned us that the Earthlings might attempt a biopathogen attack on the Empire, but her reports were not deemed credible. By launching such an attack herself, she would not only redeem herself, but be made famous across the Empire for her unique foresight. Her promotion to Priestess Second Class would be virtually assured."

Danatus said, "So she had the motive, and with her knowledge of Earthling, her access to Earth's native pathogens, and her biological expertise she certainly had the means. That's why I've been telling them Aurrie, it has to be her."

Aurora sighed. While Danatus' pointing the finger away from her was no doubt well-intentioned, the idea that the Weegee matron was the guilty party seemed completely absurd. "I saw her come aboard the space transport. Both she and her granddaughter were scanned. It was a full spectrum job, biopaths included. There was no way should would have been able to transport pathocoli."

"The perfect alibi, wouldn't you agree?" Firanus said.

Aurora shook her head. "No. It was obviously Earthlings."

Firanus looked at Kalia. "It seems, Your Eminence, that the Minervan and Premora are singing the same tune. Perhaps they are working together."

Aurora's ears lifted. "Your Eminence" was an honorific reserved for Priestesses of the Second Class or higher. Chaplain Kalia was more than she appeared. Aurora zoomed her eyesight in on the Chaplain's skin. The traces of at least two rejuvenations were evident. Chaplain Kalia was older than she appeared, too.

Kalia faced Aurora. "My dear, you really need to be more forthcoming. Your attempt to pin the blame for this on your Earthling enemies is simply not credible."

"Your Eminence," Aurora pleaded. "The Earthlings have just assassinated three of your planets. They celebrate openly the 200 billion deaths they caused. They hold hate rallies demanding your destruction every day. The Goddess-forsaken notes carrying the diseases have their signatures right on them. For Reason's sake, why do you find it difficult to believe they sent them?"

Kalia was cool. "The modus operandi in this attack was totally different from that of the previous planet assassinations. Also, the technology used was clearly beyond Earthling means. While they certainly have access to Pathocoli Cygnus, they almost certainly wouldn't know how to weaponize it. Also, they have no means to deliver it aboard our ship. But you and Premora, on the other hand…"

Aurora thought fast. "No, Your Eminence. With all due respect, you are wrong. The Earthlings have piles of bluebacks. They've already shown they have the sophistication to buy antitelepathy technology on the open market. They could also have bought this."

"But aside from your study specimen," Kalia said, "there are no Earthlings aboard this ship."

"Not so," Aurora said. "There are at least three."

"That's right," Danatus chimed in helpfully. "I saw them come aboard myself."

Kalia turned to Firanus. "Lieutenant Firanus. You told me there were no Earthlings on board. Would you care to clarify this matter?"

Firanus gulped nervously. "I meant there were no credible Earthling combatants. The three individuals observed by Danatus were reporters for the Earthling news service CNN. They came here to report the news, not to create it."

"Oh, really?" Aurora sneered. "Well it just so happened that there were originally four of them, and one tried to crash the space transport into the flagship."

"And he was dealt with. The others were entirely innocent. You should know, Your Eminence, that this Minervan tried to implicate them as soon as they came aboard our ship. Commander Tiranus noted it himself. He predicted that she would attempt to transfer the pathogen attack blame to them as soon as she was confronted."

Kalia looked at Aurora sadly. "Really my dear, your constant attempts to direct us against the Earthlings do you very little credit."

"Your Eminence," Aurora interjected, practically in tears. "Surely you must see that…"

Kalia held up her hand with forbidding authority. Aurora stopped speaking instantly.

Kalia asked Firanus. "Lieutenant, where are these three Earthlings now?"

"They are all gone, Your Eminence."

Kalia arched an eyebrow. "Gone, how?"

"Two were inadvertently photolysized when they got into a barroom fracas with some Space Marines."

Kalia looked shocked. "Our Marines photolysized some civilians in a barroom brawl?"

Firanus nodded. "Yes, Your Eminence. They claim they were provoked by the Earthlings urinating on images of the Empress. It seems more likely the soldiers involved were just venting anti-Earthling prejudice. There's been a lot of that among the lower ranks since the Draco tragedy."

"And the other Earthling," Kalia enquired.

"He was deported back to Earth after he was caught trying to shoplift a portable anti-matter generator from the Dolphia Camping Supply Store on Deck 19."

Aurora broke in. "So you see, Your Eminence, there are your assassins. Fanatics who openly display their hatred for the Empress. Criminals who try to steal weapons."

"Weapons? What weapons?" Firanus said.

"The anti-matter generator. You said the Earthling tried to steal one."

Kalia spoke to Danatus. "Lieutenant Danatus. You are a weapons officer. Would you say that a portable anti-matter generator qualifies as a weapon?"

Danatus appeared miserable. "Sorry Aurrie, but I think you got a bit carried away with that remark. Anti-matter has some energy content, but it releases it in an omni-directional manner. Hardly the sort of thing one would want for a weapon."

Firanus shook his head. "Your blind hatred betrays you again, priestess."

Aurora protested. "No, don't you see? For a civilized person, an anti-matter explosive is too crude to consider for a weapon. But for an Earthling it would represent an almost Goddess-like power. Massive omni-directional destruction; they could not conceive of anything better."

Kalia said, "You expect us to believe that even savages like the Earthlings would be so insane as to send our leaders poisoned letters and sign them? You expect us to believe that there are creatures so demented as to create weapons that destroy in all directions at once, without any discrimination whatsoever? You really expect us to believe that?"

Aurora spread her hands. "What happened at Draco 4?"

There was silence at the table.

Chapter 19

The time for action had arrived.

Commodore Collinus stood at the flagship command post, watching the fleet deploy. With Admiral Phillipus incapacitated from his near-fatal bout with Pathocoli Cygnus, the Commodore was in operational command. As he gave his orders with apparent calm, however, Collinus was also keenly aware of the eyes of Princess Minaphera and her top courtiers boring into his back from 10 meters away. The eyes of the Empire—and the future Empress herself—were on him. If he handled himself well, his future would be assured.

The key thing was to be methodical, and avoid all risk of nasty surprises. The Earthlings might be technologically backward, but their command of large amounts of bluebacks gave them the ability to acquire dangerous weaponry. Moreover, their successful planet assassination attacks and their near-successful pathogen assault on the flagship—Collinus was not one of those whose suspicions were directed elsewhere—showed a fiendish ingenuity in using such capabilities as they had with deadly effect.

So there would be no sloppiness of improvisation. This attack would be done by the book, with frigates and destroyers positioned on the outside of the fleet, backed up by light and heavy cruisers, then the battlecruisers, with the massive firepower of the heavy battleships at the very center.

His Executive Communications Officer approached and saluted. "All units report in position and prepared for battle," the XCO said.

"Very well," Collinus replied. He turned to face the Princess.

"Your Divine Majesty to Be, we are ready to engage the enemy."

"It's about time," one of the male courtiers cracked, sending a cackle of laughter through the rest. The lot of them were silenced by a snap of the Princess's fingers.

"Very good, Commodore," she said. "Please proceed with your assault."

Collinus gave her his sharpest salute and turned to issue his orders.

"All ahead, 0.01 luminal."

"Yes sir," the XCO said. "0.01 luminal, dead ahead."

The fleet began to move. At 0.01 luminal it would take over 500 seconds for the fleet to cover the million miles of space separating its staging area from the planet assassins' Peruvian bases. But there was no reason to rush, and plenty of wisdom in not doing so. The coalition armada almost certainly had a huge advantage in firepower. The Earthling's best chance lay in pulling some kind of surprise. With his slow but methodical approach, Collinus would not give them that chance.

Tension mounted as the range closed. "500,000 miles." The XCO announced. "450,000 miles. 400,000 miles."

No movement was evident on the Earthling side. In fact, no Earthling ships were visible at all. The lack of a visible enemy was unnerving. Could the Earthlings have acquired cloaking technology? If so, their sudden appearance at close quarters could be devastating. It could be even worse if they had acquired autonomous helitorpedoes, or "heledos." Those could be kept cloaked until impact. A ship could be blown to hadrons before it even knew what hit it.

"300,000 miles," the XCO intoned. "250,000 miles."

Now the fleet had moved to inside the orbit of the Earth's large semiplanetary satellite. Having the Moon at his back made Collinus even more nervous. If this was a trap, his retreat could be cut off.

Then it happened. Just after the XCO announced they had passed the 200,000 miles mark, the officer suddenly raised his head in alarm. "Sir!" he cried. "We are picking up a series of electromagnetic impulses, being directed at us by transmitters in Peru!"

Collinus leapt to the nearest sensor console. "Show me the waveform!" he shouted.

The technician pushed a button, and the waveform showed on his screen. It was a series of rapid pulses. "Sir," the technician said. "It appears to be some kind of primitive range determination device."

Yes, thought Collinus. But range from where? It would make no sense to use electromagnetic radiation for range determination if the weapons associated with them were near the transmitters. That was obvious, since his superluminal warships could easily outrun the electromagnetic waves on their return bounce. The Earthlings had to know that. No, the only way such a ranging system made any military sense was if weapons it was being used to guide were already in direct proximity to their targets. Cloaked heledos! It was a trap. There was not a moment to be lost.

Collinus shouted his orders. "Evasive maneuvers! Raise all shields! Fire at will, point blank range!"

Instantly, the fleet broke formation, with ships veering in every direction at hyperluminal speeds. A light cruiser crashed into a heavy cruiser, causing a blast that incinerated a nearby frigate as well. Helicannons fired in every direction, tearing massive rents in the fabric of space-time and smashing in the hulls of any warship so unlucky as to be in the line of fire. On some ships the engines melted, overtaxed with the effort to provide full mobility, shielding, and firepower at the same time. On others they exploded. On every ship sirens wailed and casualties mounted, as undersized damage control parties desperately tried to cope with the havoc of battle.

Commodore Collinus stared at his war room holodisplay and tried to suppress a rising sense of panic. The battle was turning into a disaster, and he didn't know what to do.

The XCO spoke. "Commodore. There's been an overload explosion in our main helicannon battery. The gunners want to evacuate."

"Stand and fight!" Collinus yelled. "Stand and fight!"

In her palace-cell in the junior officers quarters area, Aurora heard the staccato crackle of the flagship's massive helicannon, and then the crashing detonation as the vessel took its first blow. Damage alert sirens wailed eerily, bringing back a nightmare memory from her childhood.

"Holy Minerva," she cried. "We're hit!"

Hamilton looked confused. "How is that possible? You know no one on Earth has anything that can strike this fleet."

Aurora didn't know. But another crashing explosion left no doubt about the reality of their predicament. "It must be Eegees," she cried. "The fleet has been ambushed! Come on, let's get to Damage Control. They'll need all the volunteers they can get."

Unimpeded by their vanished guard detail, Aurora and Hamilton ran from the palace to emerge onto a boulevard that was filled with smoke and panicked Weegees of every rank running in every direction.

"Which way?" Hamilton shouted.

Aurora looked up and down the boulevard. She had no idea where Damage Control was headquartered on this ship. But the ship had a medical center near the Secondary Administrative Discipline Shack; she had seen it on the day of the trial. She pointed in that direction. "To the hospital! We can help out there. Let's go!"

They took off at a run.

Admiral Phillipus staggered from his hospital bed. His body ravaged by the assault of Pathocoli Cygnus, the old officer barely had the strength to walk. But he had to get to the command bridge. The fleet was in danger.

The 5th class priestess who was serving as his nurse suddenly appeared in the doorway and blocked his path. "Now, Admiral," she said. "Where do you think you're going?"

"I've got to get back to my post."

She shook her head. "Sorry, sir, doctor's orders. You are to stay confined to your bed until you effect full recovery." She looked at her clipboard and added brightly, "Which should be in just three more days."

"But the fleet is under attack," he pleaded.

She shook her head. "Back to bed, sir."

He tried to push past her, but in his weakened condition he did not stand a chance. Then suddenly the ship shook from another detonation, and a huge piece of the ceiling came crashing down on the two of them. The Admiral was knocked to the ground, stunned.

When he rallied his senses he saw the nurse was lying on the ground next to him, stone cold dead. There was nothing he could do for her. He crawled from the room, finally managing to bring himself back to his feet once he made it to the hall.

The hospital corridor was filled with toxic fumes and rushing people. Trying to avoid eye contact with anyone who might recognize him, the Admiral made it to an auxiliary emergency stairwell. Leaning heavily on the banister, he stumbled down the stairs. There was an emergency exit in front of him. He pushed it open with all his might, but it didn't give. Then he pushed again and opened a gap. He squeezed through the opening and emerged onto the street.

The boulevard was a scene of chaos, mitigated only by the stretcher-bearers who, running into the hospital with their bloody loads, at least seemed to have a purpose to their activity. He looked up the boulevard towards the command section. The distance to the bridge was over a mile. He would never make it there unassisted. But any WGE officer he turned to for help would be bound to immediately return him to the hospital.

Then a sweet voice with a familiar Pegasus twang sounded behind him.

"Admiral Phillipus, is that you?"

He turned. It was the Minervan priestess with her study specimen.

"Help me," he croaked. "I've got to make it to the bridge."

The Princess was besieged on every side.

"Your Divine Majesty to Be, we must withdraw," Commodore Collinus said.

She shook her head. "Is there really no alternative?"

"Please, Divine Princess," Chief Commercial Consul Frondrippus urged. "There is no time to be lost. If we lose the fleet the whole Southern Sector will go up in flames, and all of Cepheus will be thrown open to attack."

She turned to Flagship Captain Renatus. The man had written the Empire's leading textbook on maneuvers and tactics. "Renatus?"

"I see little choice, Divine Princess. We must withdraw and regroup."

The Princess eyed the fleet holodisplay. Most of the squadron was engaged in chaotic evasive maneuvers, some had already begun to retreat. Only the flagship had stood its ground, protecting the cripples that were too damaged to move.

"Those are our people out there, we can't just abandon them," Fleet Chaplain Kalia protested.

"We must," insisted Collinus. "This position is too exposed."

The Princess gnashed her teeth in frustration. She did not want to abandon the wounded ships. Tens of thousands of subjects would be lost, but even worse, accepting defeat at the hands of the Earthlings could destabilize the entire Southern Sector. The credibility of the Empire was at stake. Yet all the responsible military opinion recommended withdrawal. Losing a battle would be bad. Losing the Fleet would be a disaster. She faced Commodore Collinus. "Very well," she said distastefully. "Do what you must."

Collinus turned to the XCO. "Order an immediate general retreat."

A voice sounded from the doorway. "Belay that order, Mister!"

The Princess gasped in surprise. Standing in the entrance to the Command Bridge was Admiral Phillipus. Wearing soiled hospital bed-clothes and supported on either side by the Minervan priestess and her Earthling, the Admiral's gaunt disease-ravaged figure was a sight to evoke pity.

"Admiral Phillipus," Frondrippus said. "What are you doing here? You should be in bed."

"No," the Admiral said decisively. "I should be here." He turned to face the Commodore. "Collinus, what's the situation?"

"Desperate, sir. We're surrounded by cloaked heledos. Ten percent of the fleet has been destroyed, and another twenty percent is heavily dam-aged. Gun batteries are dead on most of the rest. We need to withdraw at once."

"No. We need to attack. XCO, order a general advance."

"Belay that," Collinus snapped. "Admiral Phillipus, you are not well. I am in command."

The Princess smiled. "Not anymore you're not."

Frondrippus expressed shock. "But Your Divine Majesty to Be! Surely you must see that Admiral Phillipus is sick. His illness has addled his judgment. We must withdraw!"

The Princess ignored him. "It's your show, Admiral."

"Yes, Divine Princess. XCO, issue the order. 'All ships, advance at once.'"

"But sir," Collinus protested. "What about the heledos?"

The Admiral set his mouth in a grim line. "Damn the heledos. Full speed ahead."

The order went out, and those ships that were still combat capable started to move forward.

Admiral Phillipus eyed the 4-d fleet holodisplay. Damage had indeed been massive. Helicity reserves were way down. To save power they would have to go in much slower than he would like, and there would be no power for shields. If the enemy still had significant firepower in reserve, this could be a suicide mission. Without the protection of a helic-ity shield, only the massive flagship would stand any chance at all. As a man of honor, there was only one position he could take. He turned to the

Princess.

"Divine Princess, the flagship must lead the attack. The danger could be very great. I advise you to take the Imperial Yacht and relocate the court to a safer position."

"Very well," Frondrippus nodded, and he and most of the courtiers started to move rapidly towards to door.

"No," the Princess said calmly. "My subjects are facing peril for me. I will face peril for them. I will remain here."

The Admiral felt a surge of pride. The Princess was still young, but she had the blood of 244 Minapheras in her. She would make a fine Empress some day. He snapped her a Navy combat veteran salute.

He turned back to the holodisplay. Since the advance had resumed, the enemy had gone strangely quiet. No doubt they were holding their fire until the fleet approached psioray range, at which point they would cut loose with everything they had. None of the smaller ships would last a microsecond. He called out his new orders. "XCO, tell the rest of the squadron to hold back and guard our flanks. We're going in alone."

The XCO called out the closing distance. "Range 100,000 miles. 90,000 miles, 80,000 miles. 70,000 miles sir. We are within psioray effective range."

Still no sign of action from the Earthlings. No doubt they were engaged in multiplexing their helicannon-targeting quadratures on his pseudo-coordinates. That way, when they opened fire, the result would be instant annihilation. There was not much time. The flagship needed to fire first, and get out quick.

"All psioray batteries, open fire on Peru."

Nothing happened.

The Admiral stared in horror at the holodisplay. At most there could be seconds left. "XCO, get me the psioray battery. They need to fire at once."

"Yes, sir!" The XCO punched a button, and immediately the holoimage of a young Navy lieutenant hovered in the room. The man had taken severe burns, and his grime-soaked uniform was ripped in several places. Phillipus heard a gasp from the Minervan priestess beside him.

"Lieutenant Danatus, sir!" the man said.

"What's your status, Danatus?" The Admiral shouted. "We need a psioray firing on the double!"

"I know, sir! We've had an overload explosion that destroyed battery one. Battery two is out of power. We're trying to crosslink the reserve helicitpower from one to two."

The Admiral stared speechless. What the young officer was trying to do was incredibly dangerous.

The holoimage of a hand tapped Danatus on the shoulder, and his image turned to face its owner. Then he faced the Admiral again. "We've got it sir! Firing a three-second psioray burst, ...now!"

The ear-piercing whine of a psioray battery at full power shattered the air of the bridge for three seconds. Then it was over. "That's it," the Admiral shouted. "XCO, get this squadron out of here. All ships to withdraw to defensive formation around the damaged units. We'll take them in tow to a repair station near this system's ringed gas giant."

The Admiral watched the fleet holodisplay for several more seconds until he was sure all ships were out of danger. Then he turned to face his monarch.

The Princess was beaming.

Chapter 20

"This is Kolta Bruna reporting for the Galactic News Service."

The President watched the gorgeous blonde reporter with intense interest, and not only for her very sexy looks. He also wanted to know what she had to say too.

"I'm here in Peru at one of the base camps of the Earthling resistance fighters that the Western Galactic Empire has labeled 'planet assassins.' Just one hour ago, this camp, along with the rest of Peru, received a massive three-second psioray bombardment from the Weegee battlefleet. With no shielding to protect them, the natives were forced to take the full-intensity of the blast, resulting in the shrinkage of every inhabitant of this country to less than 1/100th of their normal size."

The President turned to CIA director Collins. "Holy smokes, Fred, they shrunk them!"

Collins just gaped at the holotheater image.

"But, despite that," Kolta Bruna continued, "the resistance soldiers here are still full of fight."

She leaned down to inspect a paramilitary Cosmic Christian Crusader uniform that was lying in a heap on the ground. "Give me a hand here Fotius," she mumbled. "I need to find one of the little buggers."

A tall blonde-haired alien—apparently her soundman—stepped into the picture and started helping her search the uniform.

"Be careful," she urged her companion. "It's important that no one step on him until we are done with the interview."

Suddenly she smiled in satisfaction. "Ah, there he is!" She gently pulled aside the uniform to reveal a tiny naked figure on the ground.

The President stared in amazement. The man was less than half an inch tall. Kolta Bruna leaned down to the man, and as she did so the camera zoomed in.

"We need a real tight shot here," she urged her unseen cameraman. "Do you have it? Great. OK, Fotius. Bring in a nanophone and up the gain to max. This little guy is going to need some help to be heard."

Fotius' hand came into frame holding the end of a toothpick-sized device near the miniature man.

"Sir," said the reporter, "I'm Kolta Bruna, with the Galactic News Service. Would you care to identify yourself for our interstellar holovision audience?"

The man replied in a tiny high-pitched voice. "I am Corporal John Wayne Atkins de Peru, of the 44th Battalion of the Cosmic Christian Crusaders."

Kolta Bruna leaned in closer to allow maximum magnification of her subject, while keeping her head and magnificent hair fully in-frame as well. "That would be the famous 'Fighting 44th,' would it not?"

"Yeah, you got that right, babe," the man squeaked.

"I am honored to make your acquaintance," Kolta Bruna said. "Sir, what is your view of the military situation, now that the Weegees have delivered the full weight of their attack?"

"Is that the best they can do?" Atkins chirped. "Bring them on! We'll show them what war is really like."

At this point a small lizard ran into the picture and started to munch the soldier between its tiny jaws.

"Help!" the little man cried.

"I'm sorry," Kolta Bruna said. "But as a reporter I can't interfere. It would be a violation of journalistic ethics. But do you have any final words for our interstellar audience?"

"Yes," Atkins screamed. "Death to the Minervans! Death to Minaphera! Death to the Western Galactic Empire!"

Kolta Bruna stood up and smiled for the camera. "So there you have it, ladies and gentlemen. True to their heroic Inca roots, the Peruvian freedom fighters have absorbed the full shock of the attack of the Western Galactic Imperial Navy, and are prepared to fight on until total victory is achieved. The question is, 'What happens now?' Our GNS survey shows that more than an hour after the Weegee assault, over 80 percent of the Peruvian Earthlings are still alive. At this rate, it could take days before they are all consumed by the local minifauna. So, has the much-vaunted Western Galactic Imperial Navy finally embroiled itself in a hopeless quagmire? Do the much-abused taxpayers of the WGE have the patience to endure the massive financial burdens of such a long war in pursuit of their ruler's continuing blind support of Minervan oppression? Will the cultured peoples of the galaxy, aware of the grave risk that Weegee military action poses to irreplaceable Inca artifacts, allow this war to continue?"

"From embattled Peru, this is Kolta Bruna reporting for the GNS."

The broadcast ended, the President switched off the holotheater. "So Fred, what's your assessment?"

"Peru is finished," Collins pronounced.

The Reverend Meade objected. "Are you sure? Our men down there are true Christians. They are not of the weak-faithed sort that gives up easily."

"Perhaps not," Collins said. "But it is the assessment of the Agency that in their current condition they are unlikely to prevail against the Western Galactic Empire."

"Then we'll need to set up another operation somewhere else," the Reverend said. "Immediately. We can't afford to let up our pressure on the pagans for even an instant."

"OK, where?" the President said.

"It would save a lot of time if we could conduct the training for our crusaders right here in the USA," Meade observed. "That way we wouldn't have to relocate all of our volunteers overseas."

"No," Collins objected. "It can't be inside the United States. You saw what they did to Peru."

"That's right," said Defense Secretary Ripley, in uncharacteristic agreement with the CIA Director.

"Oh, you of little faith," Meade said.

The President looked back and forth between his key advisors. Ripley and Collins knew more about strategy than Meade, but the Reverend controlled a critical political constituency. On the other hand, the President did not relish the idea of being eaten by a lizard. He decided to propose a middle course. "How about Mexico? It's close enough for fast set up, but foreign enough to keep us safe if the Weegees should get nasty again."

Meade looked thoughtful. "I suppose that Mexico would be acceptable."

"Perhaps," Collins said. "But how do we get the Mexicans to accept the risk? They're not as stu...I mean brave, as the Peruvians, you know."

Treasury Secretary Chase, who was just then in the process of handing out the Cabinet's weekly bonus checks, held up a brown envelope marked "Alfonso." "We could discuss possible adjustments in our foreign assistance. Positive," she dangled the envelope a little higher, "or negative." She pressed the envelope down on the table with her thumb and smiled.

"That'll work," the President said.

Even the skeptical Collins had to agree the President was probably correct. "Most likely."

Jack Ripley was more affirmative. "No doubt about it." But then he paused, as if wanting to say more.

The President noticed. "Something eating you, Jack?"

"Yes, Mr. President. What do you make of this report from Lisa White claiming that the Weegee fleet engaged in a heavy battle in space right before they attacked Peru? Do you think it is possible they were attacked by their enemies, the Eastern Galactics?"

"No," Collins interjected without hesitation. "We've already looked into that. The Eegees have joined the punitive expedition, and in fact their propaganda ministry is criticizing the Weegees for not dealing with us more harshly. They are repeating the Weegee claim of an engagement with the Peruvian fleet."

"Which we all know to be pure hokum," the President chuckled. "The Peruvians didn't even have a kite, let alone a fleet. No, the Weegees are just trying to make themselves sound brave by telling a fish story."

"Indeed, that is the evaluation of the agency as well," Collins said. "However we are concerned about the fact that Lisa White is playing these lies back to us."

The President raised a crafty eyebrow. "You think she may have gone over to the enemy, Fred?"

"There does not appear to be an alternative explanation."

The President was decisive. "Very well, have her killed as soon as she returns. There can be no forgiving anyone who betrays Christ to aid the cause of the pagan infidels. See to it, Phil. And take care of her husband and children as well. We really have to discourage this sort of thing."

Attorney General Phil Brasher nodded his assent. "Sure thing, boss. Can I mobilize the faithful to help hunt down their friends, too? We might uncover other co-conspirators."

The President thought briefly. Lisa White and her husband both came from prominent political families. An exemplary mass execution of those who might consider themselves above the law could prove very useful in reinforcing the loyalty of others. "Yeah, Phil. Roll em up."

Brasher smiled his wolfish smile. "I'll get right on it, Mr. President.

"Now I'm not so old that I don't know what you two lovebirds have probably been up to, but this is my house, and while you are here, you are going to have to live by my old-fashioned rules. Since you are not married, you need to sleep in separate beds. Andrew can sleep in his own room, and as for you, my dear…"

Sally spoke up quickly. "Alice can sleep with me."

The cot had been laid out in Sally's room, and when the social evening was over the two young women had retired to that location. Sally flopped down on her bed and looked at Alice, who was trying to snuggle under the blankets on the cot. Sally had spent the evening looking forward to this moment. They were going to be sisters, and finally they were alone. It was time to start exchanging secrets.

"You know, I really admire you," Sally began.

Alice opened her eyes. "Why?"

"For what you said. That you want to make peace with the Minervans. Even after all they have done to you, you are willing to forgive and forget. I could never be like that. When someone does something to me, I want to get them back. Even though they've never done anything to me, I still want to get even with the Minervans, for what they did to Andy."

Alice smiled. "They're really not that bad, you know."

That was an amazing comment. Sally stared at her new friend. "Are you a radical?" she finally whispered.

"What do you mean, a radical?" Alice asked, with an apparent innocence too total to be real.

That settled it. Everyone had heard of the radicals. Sally leaned over. "Don't worry, I won't give your secret away. I'm a bit of a radical too."

"You are?"

"Yes. You know what I think? I think the government and the Minervans are in cahoots."

Alice seemed startled. "Why do you think that?"

"It stands to reason. The Minervans want to make the Kennewickians their slaves, and the government is secretly helping them do it, so they can have an enemy they pretend to fight, double our taxes, and keep the money."

Alice said nothing, but Sally could see she was skeptical.

"Don't you see, it has to be true. That's why everybody in Kennewick is starving. Think about it." She pointed to a map on the wall. "Kennewick is just a tiny place compared to the rest of America. Looking at the map, my guess is that there are at least a thousand Americans living outside of Kennewick for every one that is inside. Would you say that is correct?"

"That seems about right," Alice said.

Sally nodded. "But they are making everyone give one tenth of their income to help the people of Kennewick. Now one-tenth of a thousand is a hundred, so if the Kennewickians were really getting the money, they would each have as much money as a hundred other people combined. They'd be rich! So its pretty obvious, the government is keeping all the money, except maybe for part which they split with the Minervans. And if anybody dares to oppose them, they arrest them and ship them off to Kennewick, where they sell them to the Minervans to keep as slaves. It's just a big hustle, and they're all in it together."

Alice blinked at Sally, wide-eyed. "That's an amazing theory, Sally. What does your father say about it?"

Sally sighed. "Oh, I would never dare say anything like that to Dad. He'd ground me for sure. He says it's our duty to speak respectfully about our national leaders. But deep down, I think he knows that they're not really patriots at all, and that if we are ever going to beat the Minervans, the American people are going to have to do it ourselves."

"But you were willing to tell me."

Sally smiled. "If we are going to be sisters, we have to be willing to tell each other our secrets. I've always wanted to have a sister. Do you have any sisters?"

Alice suddenly looked very sad. "I did, but they were killed."

"Those horrible Minervans!" Sally exclaimed.

Alice seemed like she was about to say something, but then stopped.

"What is it?" Sally asked.

Alice shook her head. "Nothing. I'm just tired. Sally, I've had a very exhausting day, and need to go to sleep now. We can talk more tomorrow, Okay?"

Sally nodded. "Sure." She turned off the lamp.

A few minutes later, Alice was deep in sleep. She must really have been exhausted, Sally thought. It was only ten o'clock.

Not tired enough to go to sleep herself, Sally got out her flashlight, and with a favorite novel in hand, started to read under the covers. She was able enjoy her book for about half an hour, when she heard a strange moaning sound from Alice's bed.

Sally stuck her head out from under her blanket and looked in the direction of Alice who was mumbling something in a disturbed sleep.

"Olekildi, Aladapa Minu," Alice seemed to say.

What could that mean?

Her disturbance growing apparently more forceful, Alice spoke again.

"Olekildi! Olekildi! Aladapa Minu! Aladapa Minu!"

Sally watched in amazement as Alice continued to rave. She tried to identify the language. A fan of foreign movies, she was acquainted with the sound of several tongues. But the language Alice was speaking in was unrecognizable. It wasn't French. It wasn't Spanish or Italian. It wasn't German or Russian. And it certainly wasn't how they talked in Wisconsin, the land of cheese.

Chapter 27

"But Your Divine Majesty to Be," Frondrippus pleaded. "This is a disaster. We must accede to their demands."

The Princess frowned.

"I say we give the savages a taste of helicannon," Admiral Phillipus interjected. "That ought to straighten them out."

Ambassador Junea moved quickly to squash that suggestion. "No. This is no time for such simplistic male folly. The use of brute force on our part against the Earthlings would send the entire Southern Sector into the Eegee camp."

"Indeed," said Kalia. "It would endanger relations with the Central Union and perhaps even the Norcs as well. Both the Eegee and old Aphrodemonic propaganda machines have gone into overdrive warning of Western Galactic Imperial arrogance."

"Even as the Eegee court itself privately pressures us to take sterner measures against the savages," the Princess muttered.

"Yes, because they intend to take full advantage of the galaxy-wide political fallout," Junea said. "Is our interest in the Minervans really substantial enough to justify risking such consequences?"

"I don't think so," Kalia said.

"And, then there is the matter of Urania," Junea added. "She is the third-cousin to a Norc countess, and one of the Universal League's leading experts on Inca artifacts. Galactic society would never forgive us if we were to put her, or the artifacts themselves, at risk through intemperate action."

"Quite true," said Fedris. "And we shouldn't forget that there is a great deal of money at stake too. Wouldn't it be simpler if we just gave the Earthlings what they want? Then we could rescue Urania, save the Inca artifacts, preserve good relations with our allies, and protect inter-

stellar trade from economic collapse. I'm sure the Divine Princess real-
izes that interstellar trade is the primary basis of court tax revenues. A
graceful concession to the Earthling's requests would meet all of our
needs."

"But we can't just sacrifice the Minervans on an altar of bluebacks,"
freshly-promoted Lieutenant Commander Danatus burst out.

The Princess smiled at her new favorite and touched his hand.

"Your Divine Majesty to Be," Junea said. "I'm sure your handsome
young friend has his uses, but this is a policy debate. We have serious
matters to discuss, that require the consideration of rational female minds,
with perhaps some input from mature males," here she indicated
Frondrippus and Fedris, "knowledgeable in certain areas. Emotional
beings with the limited outlook of Navy men really have no place here."

"I beg you pardon," Admiral Phillipus said.

Kalia seemed uncomfortable with Junea's remark. "I think the
Ambassador went a bit too far in her comment. Perhaps she just meant to
exclude young naval officers."

The Princess suddenly stood up. "I think she went way too far. This
monarchy owes its throne to Naval officers, young and old alike, and I
will not have the service demeaned in my presence."

"But, Your Divine Majesty to Be," Junea pleaded, "I was just pointing out that…"

The Princess cut her off. "I've heard quite enough. This monarchy
will not negotiate with assassins, and we will certainly not give in to their
demands. The credibility of the empire is at stake. The Empress
Minaphera the 243rd, my grandmother, has given her word to protect the
Minervans, and that word will be honored. Furthermore, we will not submit to economic extortion. We will break this savage helicity cartel. They
have declared a ten-fold price increase. That will hurt us, but we can
endure it. If I am not mistaken, such a price rise will drive down demand
to the point where helicity exports from the Procyon district are no longer
needed." She turned to the Trade Counselor. "Is that not true, Mr.
Frondrippus?"

"Yes," the official sputtered. "But…"

"In that case," the Princess continued, "I want this district completely blockaded. We'll pay ten-time the price if we must, but the other
Southern Sector districts will take all the gain. The Earthlings and their
neighbors will not get a blueback. We'll see how they like that."

She turned to her senior naval officer. "Admiral Phillipus. I don't
want a single micropiffle of helicity to be lifted from any planet in this
district. Deploy the fleet accordingly."

The Admiral smiled. "I'll do it with pride, Divine Princess." Then he snapped his hand up in the special salute reserved for honoring navy combat veterans. "For Reason, Love and Justice; Everywhere and Forever," he pronounced. Kalia saluted too.

Junea and Fedris looked at each other, totally aghast. If the blockade went on for any length of time, they would be ruined.

The Hamilton family heard the news of the announcement of the Weegee blockade from the radio while eating breakfast.

"I guess you were right," Harry Hamilton said to his son. "They didn't give an inch."

"Well, at least it might mean an end to the import of those horrible pornography cubes," Mrs. Hamilton commented.

"And those torture machines," Sally added.

"Rule Minaphera," Aurora sang to herself and took a tiny sip of the slightly toxic stimulant the natives called "coffee." For once, even the crude Earthling drink smelled good.

Harry Hamilton looked out the window. "Hey kids," he said. "Who cares about the news? It's a beautiful day. Let's go for a walk."

Aurora let Hamilton hold her hand as they walked along with his other family members through the neighborhood in which he had grown up. She had never let him do this before, but it appeared to be expected behavior for the role they were playing. Or she was playing. There was an obvious tactile proto-telepathic emanation from Hamilton's hand that told her that he wished this fantasy was real.

Hamilton's homeland was beautiful, albeit in a bizarre kind of way. Unlike Kennewick, where the plants had been green, the trees here had multi-colored leaves, with yellow, orange, and red colors predominating. She had elicited a puzzled response from Mrs. Hamilton when she had asked if they also had green-leafed trees.

Sally kicked a small pile of red leaves that were living on the ground separate from their mother tree. Then Hamilton did the same thing. Since this seemed to be an expected form of behavior, Aurora did it too. The sensation was pleasant.

So this is what it felt like to be an Earthling, Aurora thought. She had put away her black robe and borrowed blue pants and a red-checkered shirt from Sally. Both were made of a very rough fabric derived from vegetable material, and they smelled bad and scraped the skin. But aside from the obvious practical necessity of garbing completely in genuine Earthling attire if she was to preserve her disguise, Aurora relished the sense of discovery of experiencing savage life from the inside. No civilized human had ever put Earthling clothes on before, eaten complete meals made of their food, or slept in one of their houses, let alone one of their beds. It gave her a totally new perspective on her earlier studies of Hamilton's outer mind. When she got back to New Minervapolis, the publication of her observations would be sensational.

She looked at Sally, remembering their conversation of the previous night. Her report on her observations of Hamilton's younger sister's ideas would be most sensational of all. The girl's analysis was wildly flawed, of course, but the fact that she was capable of thinking so freely without regard to the conventional beliefs of the Earthling herd-mind showed that she was far more intelligent than her brother. Hamilton, of course, had evinced distinct proto-rational tendencies, and faint traces of such traits could be identified in his parents. So taken as a whole, the Hamilton family showed a clear pattern of advanced proto-rationality in youth, deteriorating monotonically with age.

The circumstances of the Hamiltons' life seemed quite ordinary among Earthlings. Their house was about the same size as the others in their neighborhood, so there was no reason to believe that the intellectual powers of the Hamiltons were significantly exceptional. If they were, one would have expected them to take advantage of their intellectual superiority to acquire a larger house and other superior possessions. Therefore, it was reasonable hypothesis that the mental characteristics of the Hamiltons were in fact typical of Earthlings as a whole.

Strongly proto-rational at youth; less so with age. Could it be that Earthlings were born, as true humans were, completely proto-rational, but instead of being educated in a way that developed their minds, had their embryonic mental powers stamped out by their social herd? If so, then maybe something could be done to save them.

They reached an open field where groups of young Earthling men and women were running around, throwing an ellipsoidal inflatable object made of dead animal skin from one to another. One of the young men came trotting up to the family.

"Hi Sal," he said. "Care for a little touch-football? We're playing Mahopac today, and we're short handed." He turned in the direction of Hamilton. "I see your big brother is home from the war. Hey Hamster, still know how to throw the old ball around?"

Hamilton smiled and emitted a crude proto-telepathic affirmative. "Sure. Good seeing you again, Tom."

Tom looked at Aurora, letting his gaze wander from her feet to her head. "And who might this be? Has there been some kind of mistake? Maybe I should join the army, too."

"Her name is Alice," Hamilton said.

"Whoa. Good going, Hamster. So, Alice, how are you at touch football?"

Aurora had no idea. She answered honestly. "I don't know. I've never tried."

The stranger gave a slight frown, but Hamilton said, "Don't worry, I'm sure she'll do fine."

The game was very frustrating. The Mahopaclings had a larger percentage of males on their team than the Peekskillings, and most of them were bigger and faster than Hamilton and his friends. Consequently, they were able to run with the spheroid across the field twice during a time span in which the Peekskillings were only able to accomplish the same feat once. On one occasion, Hamilton kicked the spheroid to the far end of the field, and while this accomplishment apparently had some value, it was of a lower order than a run-across. In apparent deference to her inexperience, the stranger on the Peekskilling team who always got the spheroid first never threw it to her, forcing her to spend most of the game running around without any ability to affect the proceedings. There was some kind of time limit to the game, and as it approached, the fact that the Mahopaclings had accomplished more caused all the Peekskillings to become very sad.

The Peekskillings gathered for a little group meeting away from the other team.

"OK, this is it," Tom said. "Fourth down, 50 yards to go. We're three points behind and up against the time-limit. This is our last chance. A first down would do us no good, but a field goal would at least tie the game. Hamster, do you think you can do it?"

Hamilton looked down the field in the direction they were supposed to travel. "I don't know," he said doubtfully. "It's pretty far."

"It's our only hope," Tom said decisively. "So here's the play. The Hamster will stand to my left. I'll lateral him the ball. Bill and Sam will stay on the scrimmage line in front of him to block, the rest of you run off to the right and divert them as best as you can."

They went back to line up facing the Mahopaclings. "Hup, hup, hup!" Tom said, and suddenly everyone was in motion.

Aurora ran off the right, as ordered, then looked back. Hamilton had the spheroid, and was preparing to kick it. However she could see that he did not believe he could project it all the way across the field, and a quick elementary calculation combining the four relevant variables of the strength of his muscles, the Earth's gravity, the mass and probable drag coefficient of the spheroid showed that he was right. However the area in the middle of the field directly in front of him was bereft of Mahopaclings. If he were to throw the ball there, she could run to meet it and achieve a run-across.

She telepathed him the relevant thought. "Hamilton, throw the spheroid, there!"

Hamilton did a double-take and looked at the empty spot and then at her. He stopped his pre-kicking motion. Aurora reversed her own direction of motion and ran towards the vacant spot. Suddenly, Hamilton hurled the spheroid, and it moved fast and level, spinning in the manner of the particles emitted by the Earthling projectile weapons on an interception course with Aurora. She jumped in the air to catch it.

As she landed she sensed a Mahopacling running up behind her, so she used her leg elastic capability to bounce off in a line perpendicular to her pursuer's line of motion. She whirled, to face another Mahopacling positioned directly in front of her required line of advance. She leaned quickly to the left and then the right, and noted that her adversary did the same, preparing to run in whatever direction she did. Scanning his outer mind, she could see through his eyes that another Mahopacling was coming up on her from behind. With no time to be lost, she leaned to the left again and threw him the conviction that she was about to run in that direction. Then she bolted to the right, escaping past him. Two more Mahopaclings appeared in front of her in succession, but she faked them out the same way.

Now she was running down the edge of field, and a group of Peekskilling game-watchers who had been sitting on a field-side set of tiered benches had jumped to their feet, and were shouting, "Go! Go! Go! Go!"

However there were still two remaining Mahopaclings, fast movers both, and they were running down the field on a course converging with hers. A quick calculation showed that she would not be able to evade them. But then she sensed Sally, moving just a bit behind them. If Sally would change her direction of motion to the left, Aurora would be able to swing sharply to the right, and by the time the two Mahopaclings reacted, Sally would be positioned as an effective obstacle in their path of pursuit.

As subtly as she could, Aurora slipped the suggestion for the required course of action into the periphery of Sally's outer mind. The response was instantaneous. "Alice, this way!" the girl shouted.

Aurora braked her motion, and then took off in the required new direction. The Mahopaclings turned swiftly too, but as if by lucky chance, they found Sally directly in their way. They were bigger than her, and bowled her over instantly, but one of them went down himself in the process, while the other stumbled for a moment, long enough for Aurora to get downfield of him. Now all she had to do was outrun him in a direct sprint for the run-across finish line.

"On Wisconsin!" Harry Hamilton bellowed from the side of the field.

Then she was across the finish line and her Peekskilling team-companions were hoisting her on their shoulders, yelling and cheering. They smelled awful, but their thoughts felt good.

To celebrate their victory, the team and their friends had all gone to a place where they were given canisters filled with either a hideous urine-colored brain-destroying toxic liquid with white foam on top or frozen cow-milk mixed with excessive quantities of sugar. Most of the Earthlings selected the urine simulant, but given the choice, Aurora took the sugared-cow-milk-ice without hesitation. Sally seemed to want the yellow fluid, but her parents made her take the frozen sugar cow-milk instead. They said it was better for her, but chose the stinking urine-like liquid for themselves.

After enjoying this questionable repast together, the team split up to retire to their respective hovels. While some traveled with the Hamiltons part of the way back to their home, these others eventually departed in their own directions, leaving the family walking alone.

Then the sound of a shrill siren filled the air.

Immediately, all members of the Hamilton family dropped to their knees, facing south. Dozens of Peekskillings poured out of their houses and fell to their knees as well. Bewildered, Aurora quickly mimicked them, kneeling down beside Sally.

"What's going on?" she asked the girl.

Sally looked at her with an amazed expression. "It's the Call to Prayer. You don't know what the Call to Prayer is?"

Aurora shook her head. "No. What do we do?"

Sally looked quickly to either side, and then whispered, "copy me. If you don't, you can get into a lot of trouble."

Aurora nodded her assent.

Then the Earthlings all stuck their faces close to the ground and began to chant in unison.

"Our father, who art in Washington.

Infallible leader, holiest of mortals,

True son of Jesus, our lord of love.

We love you. We shall live for you, and die for you,

As you lead us to salvation,

through extermination,

of the pagan spawn of Satan.

Death to pagans.

Death to pagans.

Death to pagans.

Death to…"

As this monotonous chant went on, Aurora could hear the crackling roar of snapping neurons in the brains of the nearby Earthlings. It was horrible. The Earthlings' exercise of group immersion/submission in the herd-mind was even more damaging to their mental constitutions than their toxic drinks.

Chapter 28

That afternoon, Sally got some time to herself. She locked herself in her room and logged on her computer to cruise the internet. There was something she wanted to find out.

She had listened carefully, and then written the mysterious words down. "Olekildi, Aladapa Minu." What language were they? And what did they mean?

She tried a large number of online search engines, encyclopedias, and dictionaries, but none of them turned up any positive results. Finally in frustration, she gave up looking herself and logged on to one of her favorite chatrooms. This one was frequented by a lot of foreign book fans. The people who hung out in it were very literate. Maybe one of them would know.

She typed in her nom-de-plume for this group. >Portia here. Who else is around?

Answers came back. As per the group's convention, they were all named after either famous authors or characters.

>Dante
>Clemens
>Esmerelda
>Natasha
>Pierre
>Saki

A good turnout. Sally pounded in her query. Her words appeared on her screen, followed by those of the others.

Portia > Does anyone here know what the words "Olekildi, Aladapa Minu mean? Or even recognize the language?"

Dante > It's not Italian, I can tell you that.

Esmerelda > Duhhhh.

Clemens > It sounds like Hawaiian.

Saki > Yes it does. But I am Hawaiian, and I can tell you it doesn't make any sense in any island dialect I know.

Esmerelda > I would say it was Hungarian.

Portia > No. I tried a Hungarian dictionary. It isn't Hungarian.

Pierre > Maybe it's Finnish.

Natasha > It does sound a little like Finnish. I'm from Saint Petersburg, and we meet Finns sometimes. Are you sure the first word is Olekildi?

Portia > Yes.

Natasha > Then it's not Finnish. Finns used the phrase Ole Kiltie to mean "Please." But it's two words, not one, and it's definitely a "t" sound, not a "d."

Pierre > True. Also I'm checking my online dictionary now. "Aladapa" doesn't resemble any Finnish word.

Natasha > Although "Minua" would be Finnish for "me."

Sally thought for a moment, then typed.

Portia > I think the person who used these words was from Wisconsin. Do a lot of people of Finnish heritage live in Wisconsin?

Clemens > There's a lot of Swedes, I can tell you that.

Well, that was something. Sally followed up the possibility.

Portia > Sweden is right next to Finland. Are their languages similar?

Natasha > No. They are completely different.

No luck.

Dante > Portia, did you met the person who spoke this language?

Portia > Yes. She is my big brother's girlfriend.

Dante > Does she have razor-sharp pointed teeth?

Sally did a double take.

Portia > No. Of course not.

Dante > Are you sure?

Esmerelda > Come on, Dante, give the kid a break.

Dante > I'm just trying to protect her. ^g^

Pierre > Knock it off, Dante. She's just a child. You shouldn't try to scare her.

The conversation had become incomprehensible. Sally wanted an explanation.

Portia > Will someone please tell me what you are talking about?

Natasha > Dante is making a joke. Your brother's girlfriend apparently speaks a language that resembles Finnish, but isn't.

Portia > So what's so funny about that?

Natasha > That would be true if she were a Minervan.

Sally stared at the letters on her computer screen in disbelief. But then the shock was relieved by another line from Dante.

Dante> So, about those pointed teeth?

Esmerelda > I think she has answered that one. No pointed teeth. You don't need to worry Portia. Your big brother is not dating a Minervan.

Pierre > I wouldn't be too sure. The report that Minervans file their teeth so they can drink children's blood could be propaganda. It sounds too extreme to be really true.

Clemens > What are you, some kind of atheist? They are satanic aliens, you know. I suppose you doubt they have horns as well.

Pierre > Actually, I heard that Minervan women were really quite beautiful.

Esmerelda > Keep fantasizing, Pierre. Beautiful alien women from outer space, indeed. What's your problem? Can't find a date on Earth?

Saki > If you want to find out if your brother's girlfriend is a Minervan, challenge her to a race. The one who murdered the two students at LaGuardia outran everybody at the airport. I was in a chatroom yesterday with someone who was there. According to him, they had her surrounded, but she moved so fast that no one could lay a hand on her.

Again Sally froze at the screen, but then she relaxed. The suggestion was powerful, but not decisive. Alice was certainly a good runner, but she was by no means superhuman. If Sally had not provided blocking, those two guys from Mahopac would have caught her short of the end zone. She typed.

Portia > In what other ways are Minervans different from normal people?

Natasha > Supposedly, they can read minds.

Could Alice be a Minervan? The idea was incredible. Certainly there were things about her that didn't add up. She appeared to be a nice All-American girl, but for a minute it had seemed that she didn't know what a turkey was. Then there were her initially weird table manners, and the fact that, despite her athletic nature, she had never played touch football before. That her views were non-conformist, Sally did not mind; after all, she was a radical herself. But how was it possible that anyone would not know what the Call to Prayer was? And then there were those mysterious words. Olekildi. Aladapa Minu.

Maybe with the information she had now she could find out what they meant. She called up the Finnish-English translator in her computer. Natasha had said that the Finnish phrase for "please" was Ole Kiltie. And "Minua" was "me." Close enough. "Aladapa" however, was not Finnish. But what if, in the dialect Alice spoke, "t" was shifted to "d." The two consonant sounds were pretty close, and that would explain the transition from "Ole Kiltie" to "Olekildi." So maybe the "d" in "Aladapa" should be "t" as well. That would make "Aladapa" into "Alatapa." She typed "Alatapa" into the translation line, but no meaning emerged. But what if, like "Olekildi," "Alatapa" was really two words run together.

She typed in the line; "Ole Kiltie Ala Tapa Minua," and hit the return.

This time an English language translation appeared on the line below. In large red letters it said:

"Please Don't Kill Me."

In the throes of her nightmare, Alice had been begging for her life. In Minervan.

But that still left the question open. Had she been pleading in Minervan because she was a Minervan, or because she was trying to convince Minervans not to kill her?

Sally had to find out. But how? She couldn't just ask. A Minervan in disguise would lie anyway. And if it were the case, as she had assumed last night, that Alice was actually a Kennewickian whose family had been murdered by the Minervans, accusing her falsely of being a Minervan would be the cruelest thing she could do. Sally thought long and hard on the issue. If Alice really was a Minervan, there had to be a way to make her give herself away. Finally, she had an idea.

That night, as they each lay down in their beds, Sally turned to Aurora.

"Alice," she said. "When you were a little girl, what was your favorite book?"

Aurora was alarmed. She could hardly answer truthfully with "Ariel, the Owl Rescuer." She had no knowledge of titles of Earthling books, let alone which might typically appeal to young girls. Of course, she could find out, simply by reading Sally's outer mind. Unfortunately she had given her word to Hamilton that she would not do so. But Hamilton had evinced rudimentary telepathic power during the hearing on the Weegee ship, and his sister had the stronger brain. Perhaps she could be tricked into emitting the correct answer.

Aurora moved her psychic position to just outside the periphery of Sally's outer mind. A favorite book from childhood should have powerful emotions attached to its title. If properly stimulated, even a feeble telepath might well inadvertently project its memory this far. She said to Sally, "What was yours?"

Sally smiled. "I asked you first." She peered intently at Aurora, awaiting her answer.

The thought of the title of a book did indeed emerge. Aurora seized it and fired it back at the girl.

"The Gulag Archipelago," she said. "It's such a wonderful book. I've always loved it."

"Really," said Sally. "That's just what I was thinking."

Chapter 29

"This is Kolta Bruna reporting for the GNS with the latest news from the primitive planet Earth."

The small TV in the kitchen was on, and the Hamilton family watched it as they finished their breakfast.

"Authorities here are blaming a rampaging Minervan priestess for a string of murders that now cover most of the provinces of the so-called United States of America, or USA. The murders began two days ago, when the owl-worshipping witch escaped from a Weegee transport and killed two theology students who attempted to apprehend her in the airport of New York City. Since then, there have been 34 additional murders accomplished using a variety of means marking a grisly, if apparently randomly directed, path across this stricken kingdom. The USA is the primary source of assistance to the Kennewickians seeking freedom from Minervan oppression, and most observers believe that the priestess's murder spree represents an attempt by the Minervans to frighten the Americans into abandoning their Kennewickian brothers, and to prepare them for their own enslavement. The government is warning all citizens to be on the lookout for the witch, who is considered armed, malevolent, and extremely dangerous. An award of one million American dollars— equivalent to only 2.42 blue backs but a princessly sum here—has been offered for her capture, dead or alive."

Harry Hamilton eyed his pump-action shotgun above the mantelpiece appreciatively. "If she comes around here, it'll be dead or dead," he said. He turned to his son. "What do you think, Andy. Would 'Old Blood and Air Betsey' be good enough to do the job?"

Andy nodded.

Sally explained to Alice. "He calls her 'Old Blood and Air Betsey' because after he fires her at the target, there is generally nothing left but blood and air." She studied Alice's face, hoping to detect a reaction, but there was none.

Kolta Bruna continued. "Meanwhile, in New York City, a group of devoted Christian theology students continue to hold the Northern Confederation priestess Urania in the basement of the Cathedral of Saint John the Divine. Today they released two of her fingers and promise to continue to amputate parts of her anatomy until all galactic powers terminate support for the ongoing Minervan persecution of this planet's native inhabitants. Despite pleas from the Northern Confederation and Central Union, the Western Galactic Empire has refused to accede to this reasonable request, thereby putting not only Urania, but the priceless Inca artifacts she was sent to protect, in the greatest of dangers."

"The Galactic News Service was invited into the Cathedral of Saint John the Divine, where my cameraman and I obtained this exclusive footage of the amputations. We warn that this footage may be too graphic for some viewers. However we feel that everyone in the galaxy needs to see it, in order to gain a fuller appreciation of the horror that the loveless owl-worshippers are inflicting on this planet."

The image shifted to the basement of a church, where a group of powerfully-built men was holding a tall redheaded woman down on the table. In the background, some other people were chanting prayers. As the woman screamed, one of the men started to saw off her pinky.

"Harry, please turn that off," Martha Hamilton said.

Sally's father complied.

"That's wrong, Harry," Sally's mother said. "They shouldn't be doing that."

"This is war, Martha," Harry grunted. "It's not always pretty. By capturing her, those men have at least forced some of the aliens to stop helping the Minervans. That's a major victory."

Andy said, "But Dad, if they kill her they'll lose all their leverage."

Harry nodded. "True. They are now going too far. They should just hold her hostage, and not cut her up, at least as long as the Norcs stay neutral. Of course, if we catch that Minervan, this will be a small sample of what she gets."

Sally stood up. "I need to take Blackie out for his morning walk. Andy, Alice, why don't the two of you come with me? There are some things I'd like to talk about with you."

Mother smiled. "So, its' a private meeting of the young folks, is it? Perhaps Sally wants to tell her big brother about her newest boyfriend?"

Sally blushed. She didn't really have a boyfriend, but Mom liked to tease her about every possibility.

Father smiled. "It's OK. You youngsters need to have some time on your own together. We understand. Have a good time."

Sally grabbed the leash. "Let's go."

When they reached the pond, Sally released Blackie so the dog could have some fun chasing the ducks. Then she sat down on a tree stump and called the other two over.

"So," she began. "Would either of you two mind telling me what this is about?"

Andy had a surprised expression. "What is what about?'

"This," Sally said with emphasis. She pointed at Alice. "Her."

Andy looked distressed. "I don't understand, Sal. I thought you liked Alice."

"Alice?" Sally said with a satiric edge in her voice. "Is that her real name? Are you sure it isn't Artemis, or Nendra, or Minaphera?"

"What are you getting at, Sal?" Andy said with attempted innocence.

The continued pretense got Sally mad. "Do you think I am stupid, or something? Just what are you trying to pull?"

Andy said, "I'm not trying to pull anything."

Alice cut in. "It's no use, Hamilton, she knows."

Sally turned to face the woman. "Who are you really? Tell me the truth. What is your name? Where are you from? What do you want?"

Alice returned Sally's accusing look with a level gaze that suddenly seemed much more sincere. "My name is Aurora. I am a priestess of the Goddess Minerva, 3rd Class. I was born on Pegasus 3, and now live in New Minervapolis. I am trying to get home."

Sally reeled. Up till now she had her suspicions, but she was mentally unprepared for their sudden absolute confirmation. A minute ago she had been on a pleasant walk with her brother and his nice, if rather weird, new girlfriend. Now she was face to face with a deadly Minervan.

She tried to be brave. "Are you the one who murdered those two students at LaGuardia Airport?"

"No," Aurora said.

"How can I believe you?"

"Because I killed them," Andy interjected.

Sally faced her brother in shock. "You killed them? Why?"

"Because if I hadn't, they would have killed her."

Sally was confused. "But she's a Minervan!" she finally exclaimed.

"Sal, she saved my life," Andy said.

"Twice," Aurora added.

Andy nodded acknowledgement. "OK, twice, if you count what happened during the battle."

'Three times," Aurora said, "if you include the incident on the space transport."

"Doesn't count," quipped Andy. "Your own life was equally at risk."

Aurora frowned a little and folded her arms as if upset about not getting adequate credit. "Very well. Twice."

Sally looked at the Minervan. "So, who is doing all the killing coast to coast? I know it's not you, because you've been here."

"I have no idea," Aurora said.

"It's probably just ordinary murders that have been linked together by press hysteria," Andy added.

Sally nodded. That explanation made sense.

Aurora said, "So Sally, how did you find me out?"

"Olekildi. Aladapa Minu," Sally said.

Both Aurora and Andy did double takes.

"You were talking in your sleep," Sally explained. "But that was only a clue. The thing that gave you away was your choice of favorite childhood book."

"The Gulag Archipelago was not a reasonable selection?" Aurora asked.

"The Gulag Archipelago?" Andy sputtered. "That's an absurd choice. What made you come up with that?"

"I thought it, so she said it," Sally said smugly.

Andy turned to Aurora. "Hey, you promised me no mind reading of my friends and family."

Aurora looked defensive. "I didn't enter her outer mind. If I had, she wouldn't have been able to fool me. She projected the title. I thought it was just mental leakage."

Sally snickered. "And you fell for it, hook, line, and sinker."

Aurora smiled. "You are a very remarkable Earthling, Sally."

That got Sally mad. "Earthling! Is that what you call us?"

Aurora looked puzzled. "What else should I call you? Isn't that what you are?"

Sally said, "Yes, I suppose. But it seems so demeaning. It has a negative connotation, like we're primitive beings from some little hick world in the Podunk part of the galaxy."

Aurora looked Sally in the eye. "Sally, the word 'Earthling' will mean whatever Earthlings make it mean."

They spent the most of rest of the day by the side of the pond. Sally listened wide-eyed as Andy and Aurora told her the tale of all of their fantastic adventures.

On their way back through town, they passed a telephone pole on which was stapled an advertisement for the Peekskill Community Theater's upcoming performance of "The Merchant of Venice."

Aurora looked at the poster, fascinated. "Is that a picture of Shakespeare?" she asked.

"Yes," Andy replied. "Although I can't vouch for its accuracy."

"And I take it from this placard that there is to be a public reading of his poems, by professional poem readers?"

"It'll be a performance of one of his plays, by talented amateurs," Andy said.

"Very talented amateurs," Sally corrected. "I'm in it."

"Really?" said Andy. "Why didn't you tell us before?"

Sally shrugged. "It's just a bit part. But I'm also Portia's understudy. So if Anna-Marie ever gets sick they'll see some real drama in this town." She held out her right arm and proclaimed theatrically, "The quality of mercy is not strained!"

Aurora's eyes brightened. "Is that poem part of this play?"

Sally nodded. "Yes. It's one of the most famous parts."

"When is the performance?"

"It opens tomorrow night."

"We must see it," Aurora said.

"By all means," Andy replied.

Sally smiled. It was about time someone saw that there was more to Earth than planet assassins and Inca artifacts.

The performance proved to be an amazing experience.

Aurora sat in the audience with Hamilton on one side, and his parents on the other. The auditorium of a building she was told was ordinarily used as a school for Sally and other adolescents was filled with

Earthlings. They were friends and neighbors of the Hamiltons, and most of them seemed well acquainted with the play. As the show went on, Aurora was able not only to enjoy the fine poetry pronounced by the actors, but also got some remarkable scientific work done exploring the interaction of the poetry with the outer minds of much of the audience. While none of them evinced anything like the conceptual abilities required to write such a play, many of them were able to resonate with it.

It was incredible, but the data was irrefutable. Under powerful and accurate stimulation in controlled conditions, significant numbers of ordinary Earthlings were able to think like actual humans. However, as soon as the performance ended, their enhanced powers of mentation rapidly began to dissipate.

There was no doubt that Shakespeare had been a human. A truly radical interpretation would be that he was a human Earthling. Aurora was not willing to go that far. Despite the Earthling's uncritical belief that the poet was one of them, a far more likely explanation that he was a stranded Minervan, or perhaps a Weegee or Norc. Nevertheless, the fact that they were able to embrace him proved that beneath their general insanity, large numbers of Earthlings harbored significant human impulses.

Could anything be done to elicit these impulses further? It was certainly food for thought. Perhaps when she returned to New Minervapolis, the wise women of the Minervan High Council could develop a plan.

If she could ever get back. And if she could convince them to try.

Chapter 30

The news of the disasters reached the Princess' court at Cepheus late in the afternoon. Five more heavily populated planets had been annihilated.

The Princess called a council of all of her top advisors to determine an appropriate response.

"The Earthlings are behind these atrocities, there is no doubt about it," Admiral Phillipus said. "We must deal with those tribes responsible harshly, and with finality. The safety of the Empire's subjects demands nothing less."

"It demands somewhat more," said Department of Public Safety Director Baranus. "We should pico-atomize their planet immediately and without warning and be done with the lot."

"But what of the Minervans," Commander Danatus said. "We are sworn to protect them. Surprise planetary pico-atomization would kill them all."

"That's irrelevant at this point," replied Baranus. "Three hundred billion more of Her Divine Majesty's subjects have been obliterated. Trillions more are at risk. Next to that the lives of a mere million Minervans matter not at all."

"But the word of my grandmother does," said the Princess.

Kalia said, "We could evacuate the Minervans first, and then blast the planet. But that would leave the Minervans without their promised homeland. However, if so ordered, the fleet can be selective in its targeting, as we were last time."

"And achieve the same results you did last time," said Baranus. "Eliminating an Earthling despotism or two is clearly insufficient. Planetary annihilation is the only safe answer."

Frondrippus said, "Your Divine Majesty to Be, this is insanity. For once I find myself in agreement with the Navy representatives. We must be selective in our action. Destroying the Earth would destroy the largest helicity reserves in the galaxy."

"And enrage the governments of the other Southern Sector planets that hold most of the rest," Junea added, "thereby perpetuating or even expanding the helicity embargo that is wrecking the galactic economy and turning our closest allies against us."

"Even so," said Baranus, "if that is what we must endure to protect our Empire against further planet assassinations, than that is the reality we must face."

"But it is not," Junea said. "There is a better way."

"Do you have an alternative plan to recommend, Reverend Ambassador?" the Princess said. "If so, please explain it. This court has no time for riddles."

"Divine Majesty to Be," Junea began. "DPS Director Baranus is obviously correct in his assessment that the Navy's plan of targeted retaliation is insufficient. We must have a more definitive and permanent solution to the Earthling problem. Planetary annihilation would serve to meet his objectives, but would destroy the galactic economy, betray the Empress's commitment to the Minervans, alienate our allies, and cause the death of Urania and the loss of the galaxy's storehouse of precious Inca artifacts."

"All true," the Princess said. "So what is your answer?"

"The solution, Divine Majesty to Be, is to make an agreement through which we recruit some of the savages to enforce peaceful behavior on the others."

"How can this be done?" the Princess asked.

"By combining the two fundamental tools of diplomacy, helicannon and sweetraffa, to enlist the active aid of the most powerful and most moderate of all the Earthling despotisms, the United States of America. You will recall the USA was our ally in the fight against the Peruvian planet assassins, providing us with the locations of all the assassin camps. Now we need to employ the combination of helicannon and sweetraffa to coerce the Americans to become our enforcers against all the more radical Earthlings."

Junea continued. "The helicannon in this case is Admiral Phillipus's fleet, through which we threaten devastating action unless they agree to our terms. The sweetraffa is some minor concession we have the Minervans throw them, so the American tribal despot can pretend to his subjects that he has obtained a victory. This will strengthen his hand internally, and by thus stabilizing his despotism, we will make it a more powerful enforcer against the other Earthlings."

"What minor Minervan concession did you have in mind?" the Princess asked.

"Only this," Junea answered. "That they give back a portion of the land they have occupied to give the displaced Earthlings of Kennewick an independent state of their own. This would pose no threat to the Minervans. After all, the entire United States of America was unable to defeat them militarily; an independent Kennewickian micro-despotism would be much less capable. Yet it would meet the needs of the American tribal despot, since it would secure some measure of justice for the oppressed Kennewickians, who are after all, his former subjects. In return for this trivial boon, the American leader would mobilize his Army to overrun and exterminate the neighboring despotism of Mexico, which, as Commercial Consul's Fedris' capable intelligence staff has just briefed us, was the country of origin of this most recent group of planet assassins."

"Even using primitive native technology, the Americans are the most powerful of all the Earthling despotisms. If we gave them a small amount of our most obsolete equipment, they would be invincible in battle against all other Earthlings. Then we would give them carte-blanch to invade and exterminate any other Earthling tribe that committed planet assassination. Peaceful and friendly relations between Earth and the civilized galaxy would thus be restored, and because local rule remained in indigenous hands, the other Southern Sector tyrants would approve of the arrangement as well. Helicity prices would be returned to normal, galactic trade would be restored, our allies would be grateful, and Urania and the Inca artifacts would be saved."

The Princess said, "that certainly would be a preferable outcome to any I've heard offered by other plans. But do you really believe the American despot could be made to accept such a servile role on our behalf?"

Junea nodded. "Yes, Your Divine Majesty to Be, I do. The export blockade which you wisely ordered has caused him serious problems, with many of his subjects rioting over the loss of their joycubes. He needs painprisms imports to enforce order, but without any bluebacks from helicity exports he can't afford them. And of course, there is no way he can resist our fleet. He is ready to give in to your will. All he needs, however, is the cover offered by a Minervan concession, so he can pretend to his subjects that through his leadership, they achieved victory. He can't give in to you without that, because were he to do so, his subjects would tear him to pieces. But throw him that bone, and he's yours."

The Princess smiled. "I like this plan. Reverend Ambassador Junea, I commend you for your incisive tactical thinking. I hereby appoint you to be my special representative charged with the responsibility of inducing the American government into accepting it. Admiral Phillipus will provide you with a squadron of sufficient force to make your diplomacy effective."

"That should more than adequate for the helicannon, Divine Princess, but as for the sweetraffa?"

"You may tell the American despot that cooperation will be rewarded. If he agrees to become our enforcer, the Kennewickians can have half, but only half, their land back. However you should also make it clear to him that if he does not choose to be agreeable..." The Princess pursed her lips and emitted a brief high-pitched whistle, imitating the whine of a psioray battery projecting shrinking radiation at full power.

Junea bowed. "Thank you, Your Divine Majesty to Be. I'm sure I can make him understand the situation. I shall leave for Earth immediately."

The Princess stood up, and everyone in the room jumped to their feet. "For Reason, Love, and Justice; Everywhere and Forever," they chanted in unison.

The Hamilton family viewed the news broadcast with horror. Five more planets had been destroyed, and the Weegees were reconcentrating their Cepheus Sector fleet for a "decisive" punitive expedition against the Earth. The President had issued a public statement condemning the actions of the Mexican extremists who apparently were behind the latest acts of interstellar terror, and calling upon the Universal League to intervene to resolve the true source of the problem, to wit the Minervan occupation of Kennewick. At the Universal League, the Central Union and the Northern Confederation had echoed this call. But while the speeches went on at the UL, thousands of Weegee battleships were on the move.

"Those crazy Mexicans," Harry Hamilton said. "There's going to be hell to pay for this."

"Thank goodness the President has made it clear that we are not to blame," said Martha Hamilton.

"I've got to get back to Kennewick," Aurora said.

There was a silence at the table.

"But I thought that..." Mrs. Hamilton began.

Aurora cut her off. "I'm sorry. I need to leave." She stood up and walked to the back door. For several seconds everyone was too shocked to move. Then Sally followed her out into the night.

The girl found the Minervan sitting on the fence in the backyard, staring at the starlit night sky.

"So that's it. You're leaving us just like that, now, tonight."

"No. I'll need your brother's help to cross the country. We should leave in the morning."

"But you won't be sticking with him afterwards."

Aurora turned to face her. "Sally, there would be no real life for your brother in New Minervapolis."

"So then why don't you stay here, with us."

Aurora smiled a sad smile. "You know I can't do that."

"Why not?" Sally asked forcefully. "He loves you, you know that, don't you?"

Aurora nodded. "Yes."

"Then you should stick with him. Look, I know my big brother may be a bit of a lunk, but he's the real deal. You've got to see that."

A tear dripped from Aurora's eye. "Sally, what you are asking is impossible."

"Why? Because he is an 'Earthling?'"

"No, I mean yes, kind of. It's not that I look down my nose at him. I did at first, of course, but I've come to realize that he really is a very noble being. And I like and admire you too, Sally, very much. But I can't live like this. You don't know what it is like for me here. Everything is so weird, and please don't take offense, crude. I mean the clothes, the customs, the food..."

"Oh, yeah, it must be rough. Turkey dinners and ice cream shakes. I don't know how you have been able to stand it."

Aurora shook her head. "I apologize for that comment. It was inappropriate. But Sally, there are bigger reasons why I must return. I'm not just a Minervan, Sally, I'm a priestess of the Goddess Minerva, of the Third Class. I have a calling. There are things that I need to do. A crisis is coming, and I have to go back to help my people."

Sally had no answer for that.

Aurora pointed up into the sky at a bright dot that stood at one corner of a large square of stars. "Do you see that, Sally, that's the star where I was born."

Sally stared at the incredibly distant point of light in amazement.

"Everyone needs a star to attach their life to, Sally," Aurora said.

Sally blinked away the tears that were beginning to form in her eyes. "You could find your star here," she said.

Aurora reached over and hugged her.

The next morning they loaded up the old family vehicle with food, extra clothing, and outdoor camping equipment. Hamilton told his parents that he wanted these things so he could save money on the trip, but of course the real reason was to minimize contact with Earthlings along the way. With reasonable luck, no one would suspect them.

As Hamilton went into the house for a last load of consumables, his father took Aurora aside.

"Alice, would you mind if we go for a little walk? There's something I want to tell you."

She agreed. When they had traveled only a just far enough from the house to be out of visual contact with the others, he turned to face her.

"It's me, isn't it?" he said.

Aurora was puzzled. "What?"

"I'm the reason you are leaving."

Aurora shook her head. "No, I just need to get back to Kennewick."

Harry smiled. "Ah, you want to fight the Minervans, very commendable."

Aurora couldn't lie. "No, I just want to help my friends."

Harry nodded. "Yes. Your friends. It's good for a person to stick by their friends. But you know, you don't need to do this."

"I don't understand."

Hamilton's father sighed. "Look, I'm an old-fashioned guy, and I'm not likely to change. But I understand that there is room on the sea for more than one type of sail."

Aurora said nothing.

Harry continued. "My son's a real straight-arrow, just like his dad. I'm real proud of him. But you take my daughter, Sally, she's a radical. I don't care, I'm proud of her too."

"As well you should be," Aurora said. "She's a wonderful girl."

Harry looked at her closely. "Right. Now you take yourself. You're a radical too. Don't ask me how I know, I can pick 'em out. But if you were part of my family, I wouldn't care. In my family, blood runs thicker than water. Why if you were Andy's girl, I wouldn't even care if you were a Minervan. You'd be family to me, and that would be that."

Aurora looked at the old man in amazement. "You wouldn't care if I were a Minervan? I thought you hated the Minervans."

"Well yes, as a group, I do. They're enemy invaders, and we have to defeat them. But you see that restaurant down the street?" Harry pointed at a storefront that was adorned with both American lettering and another kind of script. "The owner of that place is Vietnamese. Now I was in Vietnam, and if in Vietnam I had met that guy while he was running around in a rice paddy wearing black pajamas, I would have blown his brains out. But here he is a member of the Elks Club and his son is an honor student at Sally's school, and it's fine by me."

"So let's say there was a Minervan living right here in Peekskill, but instead of acting like the Minervans we see on the news she was just trying to live a normal life like a regular American. I wouldn't stand in her way. Especially not if she was important to the happiness of someone in my family."

Aurora could only stare at the man.

"Now, of course," he continued, "we both know that is not the case here. You're just a nice girl from Wisconsin who happens to have some really weird ideas about a few things. But it serves as a useful example to make clear where I stand. I'm a family values man."

Aurora reeled at the thought of the mental leap Harry must have forced upon himself to make these astounding statements. But she still couldn't give him the answer he wanted to hear. "Thank you, Mr. Hamilton. It's very kind of you to tell me this. But I still need to go home."

"Well think about it," Harry said. "In case you ever change your mind."

Chapter 31

The trip across the country proved fascinating. Everywhere Aurora saw scenes of unspeakable degradation, but everywhere she also met people who exhibited the same human-like and proto-rational tendencies she had observed among the Hamiltons. Mostly they slept in an outdoor fabric structure that Hamilton had brought from home. But when they reached the mountains the night was too cold, and they decided to stay indoors at a house that provided rooms and beds to sleepers in exchange for the green tree-flesh the Earthlings used as a form of currency.

In the sleeping room, Aurora found a book that had been left there, apparently on purpose, by an Earthling society that called itself the Gideons. Leafing through it, she discovered that it contained the Earthlings' sacred mythology. Interested, she spent much of the night examining its contents. In the morning she decided to speak to Hamilton about it.

"Hamilton, this Earthling holy book is a wild mass of contradictions. How could anyone base their life on it?"

"We try," Hamilton said.

"Yes, but it contains some writings that are directly opposite to others. Parts of it call for extermination of all of those who do not submit to the herd-mind. Those could have been written by Kolta Bruna's mother, or your own Aaron Vardt. But other parts, here, listen to this." She opened the volume and quickly turned to a passage she had marked. Then she read:

"Seek the truth. The truth will set you free."

She looked at Hamilton. "That line is lifted word-for-word from the writings of Penelope the Wise. It is the Second Commandment, given to her by Minerva herself. Anyone who embraces it must also embrace the Goddess of Reason."

Hamilton smiled. "So now you are telling me you think Christ was a Minervan."

"Apparently," Aurora said, ignoring the Earthling's misplaced irony. "Although a rather poorly trained one, I'm afraid. Or maybe he was feverish. In any case, his attempts to explicate the core ideas underlying our doctrine were certainly very confused."

"Maybe he thought he had more time to get his message out. He was executed at a young age."

"Really?" said Aurora. "That was very unfortunate."

"A lot of people seem to think so. Come on, let's hit the road."

Aurora followed Hamilton out of the sleeping room. But she kept the weird book for further examination.

At last they entered the river valley that led to Kennewick. The task now was to get past the large contingents of American soldiers that surrounded New Minervapolis. Fortunately, however, the primary orientation of the American army was to prevent Kennewickians from escaping to the United States, not to stop Americans from entering Kennewick. That, combined with Hamilton's knowledge of the customs of the US Army and Aurora's ability to read minds made penetrating the American battle lines surprisingly easy. Finally they were through the neutral ground and approached the zone of the camps.

"Halt, Earthlings," a voice called out in American, but with an unmistakable Minervan accent.

"We are not Earthlings," Aurora answered in Minervan.

Two Minervan men in militia robes emerged from behind some bushes. "Nice try, Earth-girl, but your smell gave you away. So, you've had some language lessons, have you?" He moved in front of Aurora, adopting a somewhat threatening position.

Aurora tried telepathy. "I am Priestess third class Aurora," she projected powerfully. "Please let us pass. I have business with the High Council."

In response the man struck her a powerful blow, knocking her to the ground. Hamilton leaped to her defense, and slammed the militiaman in the chest with a forceful kick, but was sent down as well by defensive helishock from the militiaman's clothing. Before Hamilton could get up, the other militiaman smashed him senseless with a savage kick to his head, and then jumped on Aurora, pinning her to the ground.

The first militiaman got to his feet. "Assassins!" he yelled. "Do you think you can fool us so easily? So you want to kill the High Council do you? You Earthlings are all alike."

"Not quite exactly alike, Tikander," the man sitting on Aurora said. "They made a special effort with this one to find an Earthling female whose horrid looks wouldn't give her away. Such efforts should not go entirely unrewarded, don't you think." He smiled a salacious smile.

"Right," said Tikander. "Let's have a little fun with her before we turn her in. You can go first, Flakander."

Flakander nodded, and holding his hand on her neck, started to remove the fastenings of her clothing. Horrified, Aurora was paralyzed for several seconds as she realized what they planned to do to her. Then she rallied all her mental resources and projected a huge and horrifying image of the Owl of Torment into Flakander's outer mind. "May you burn forever in Tartarus if you touch this woman," she had the holy owl say.

Flakander froze.

"What's wrong?" Tikander said.

"Let's just take these two in for questioning," Flakander muttered.

They threw Aurora and Hamilton in a windowless box, and locked it tight. It was completely dark inside, and the lack of ventilation was suffocating. But Aurora could feel the slight vibration as they moved the box rapidly overland on levitation skates. Then the vibration stopped, and the box opened, revealing they had been deposited in an empty holding pen in the militia base. The walls shimmered, immovable and impenetrable.

Hamilton began to wake up. "What happened ?" he muttered. "Where are we?"

"We've been taken prisoner by the militia. We're in New Minervapolis. Don't worry. They're certain to send for a senior priestess. We'll be out of here soon enough."

At that moment there was a sound outside the holding pen, and one of the walls disappeared. Backed by four militiamen and a militia senior officer, a woman stood outside, dressed in the robes of a Second Class Priestess. Aurora recognized her immediately. It was Phendra, Vice Chairman of the Minervan High Council.

"So," Phendra began. "It appears that the Earthlings have added a new level of sophistication to their tactics. I am told you can not only imitate human speech, but perform elementary projections as well."

"Your Eminence," Aurora replied in high Minervan. "Don't you recognize me? I am Priestess Third Class Aurora."

Phendra started, then peered closely at her. "Why, praise the Goddess. It is Aurora! My dear, we all thought you were dead. The Weegees told us you were murdered by the Earthlings who kidnapped Urania."

Aurora smiled. "No, I escaped."

"Indeed," Phendra said. "This is a day for rejoicing. Our dear Aurora is back from the dead."

Phendra then pointed to Hamilton. "But who then is this Earthling?"

"He is Hamilton, my study specimen."

Phendra laughed. "My dear, you are incredible. Not only do you escape and make your way here across an entire continent full of Earthling savages, but you keep your study specimen with you through the whole process, so you can continue your research without disruption. What a scientist you are going to make!"

Aurora shook her head. "Hamilton helped me a great deal. He should be released without further delay."

Phendra smiled. "Now, now, my dear, we can talk about that later. Why don't you go back to your home now, and take a few showers. You really need to, you know. " She wrinkled her nose to make sure Aurora got the message of just how rank she smelled. "Then change into some clean clothes and have a little raffa. We'll return Hamilton to his quarters where he'll be safe and comfortable until you feel ready to resume work."

"But Your Eminence," Aurora began.

Phendra cut her off. "That's all for now. We'll talk more tomorrow when you've had a little time to get back to your old self." She snapped her fingers at the militiamen. "Take the Earthling back to his former quarters."

As the men grabbed him, Hamilton shouted, "Aurora, this isn't right!"

"I know," Aurora said miserably, as she watched her friend robbed of his freedom.

When Hamilton was gone, Aurora turned back to Phendra.

"Eminence, the militiamen who captured us attempted to violate me. They need to be disciplined."

"They will be talked to. But really Aurora, they thought you were an Earthling. Try to show some understanding." Then Phendra smiled and added, "Welcome home."

Two days later, properly cleaned and wearing the dress robe and owl pendant of a Third Class Priestess, Aurora presented her full report to the Minervan High Council. Every Second Class Priestess in New Minervapolis was in attendance, as was the High Priestess, Her Divine Eminence, Priestess First Class Nendra herself. All listened spellbound as Aurora related the full narrative of her adventures among the Weegees and the Earthlings.

"And so, Your Eminences," Aurora concluded, "in view of his life-saving services to me, which were in no way necessary to his own survival or welfare, I must ask that the High Council honor my promise of safe conduct to the Earthling Hamilton, and set him free at once to return to his people."

There was silence in the room for many seconds. Then High Priestess Nendra began to speak.

"Dearest Aurora," Nendra said. "You have had some of the most remarkable sets of experiences of which I have ever heard. Imagine, a young human girl, living for more than a month among Earthlings. Yet you not only survived, you contrived to return home across a continent populated with hostile savages, and even managed to keep the key subject of your scientific work in your possession while you did it. This is an adventure so grand, it will the subject of epic poems written and sung by bards for ages to come. Through all your trials, you have acquitted yourself as a true daughter of Minerva, worthy in every way of your mother and grandmother. How proud they both would be if they could see you today. Sisters! Let us all rise and express our appreciation for Aurora and the honor she has brought to our people and our faith through her meritorious conduct."

All rose and chanted, "Child of Reason, we salute you!" Then they started to applaud in the Minervan style, slapping the backs of their hands into their palms, first right, then left.

Aurora waited for the applause to subside, then she pressed her case. "But Divine Eminence, what of my request for freedom for the Earthling Hamilton. My sacred word is at stake here."

"Dearest Aurora," Nendra said gentl., "You have kept your word through your passionate plea to the Council on the Earthling's behalf. No one can doubt your sincerity, or question the certainty that if you had your will, the Earthling would immediately be set free."

"But you will not grant my request?"

"No, I am sorry, we cannot. The Northern Confederation has request-ed that he be transferred to the Anthropo Institute for study, under your supervision if you desire. Given our need for allies at this critical junc-ture, we cannot very well snub them for the sake of an Earthling's con-venience."

"But it is unjust to treat a person who has done so much to help me in so cruel a fashion."

Nendra raised her eyebrow. "Unjust? Cruel? Those adjectives hardly apply. He is a murderer, after all. And at Anthropo he would have better living conditions than anything he could possibly find roaming among the Earthlings, or perhaps even here. You yourself are being invited to be the custodial investigator, so you can insure that he receives humane treat-ment. If you decide not to go, he will be placed in the custody of your own life-long friend Freya, who you know is one of the gentlest souls to be found in all the galaxy."

"But…"

"Aurora really. These are Norcs we are talking about giving him to. For all their diune heresies, we know them well as gentle, humane peo-ple. Everyone admires you for the stand you took denying the Earthling to the Eegees. They would have used him to commit sacrilege, and the sin would have been upon us for facilitating it. But this is not the case here. The Norcs honor the First Commandment. There will be no sacrilege."

Aurora gathered herself for a rebuttal, but no strong arguments came to mind. So she offered what she could. "Divine Eminence, all that you have said is true. Yet, irrational as it may be, I know that Hamilton would greatly prefer to retain his freedom living in coarse conditions among his fellow Earthlings than to be maintained in comfort as a study specimen at Anthropo."

Nendra smiled. "But we know better what is best for him. And should not rational beings decide what is best for irrational ones?"

To this there could be only one answer. "Yes, Divine Eminence."

Nendra nodded. "Very good. Then we are in agreement. I am very happy for you, Aurora. You clearly have great scientific talent and dedi-cation. The opportunity to continue your research with the superior facil-ities available at Anthropo will give you the chance to do work that will establish your reputation as one of the galaxy's leading scientists."

"But am I not needed here?"

"There is no doubt you could do many useful things if you remained here. But you can do more to help us by going to Anthropo. Much of the sympathy that we Minervans enjoy among sectors of the Weegee and Norc public is due to our many contributions to galactic science and culture. By enrolling yourself prominently among the current pantheon of well-known galactic scientists, you would do much to uphold our reputation as leaders in the divinely ordered search for truth."

It made sense. "May I have some time to prepare for the journey? I have only just returned home."

"The Norc starship will take two weeks to arrive."

Aurora stared at the floor mosaic in thought. "That interval should prove sufficient." She lifted her eyes and faced the High Priestess directly.

"Divine Eminence, before I go I need to say that, on the basis of my studies, I believe that our policies towards dealing with the Earthlings require alteration."

"Oh, in what way?"

"My studies, conducted not only under laboratory conditions here, but in-situ among relatively pristine populations of Earthlings themselves, show significant evidence of proto-rational potential and perhaps," here Aurora hesitated, for she knew she was crossing the line of scientific respectability. Then she nerved herself to continue. "Perhaps even human potential."

The room was filled with an uncomfortable silence. Then Tildra, one of the most orthodox of the Second Class Priestesses who composed the High Council rose to speak.

"My dear Priestess Third Class Aurora. I am told by some of my more scientifically-inclined sisters on the Council that your evidence for widespread proto-rationality among Earthlings in their embryonic and infantile phases, with such powers dissipating with age, while not conclusive, is strong enough to form the basis of a serious scientific publication. That may be. But it is quite another thing to claim that Earthlings are potentially human, actual carriers of the Goddess's true spark."

Aurora could sense the telepathic grunts of affirmation, as most members of the Council expressed agreement with Tildra's remark. Still she continued. "I am aware of the distinction, and how unlikely the claim must appear. Nevertheless, I believe that the available data supports such a hypothesis. For example, there is their affection for the work of the poet Shakespeare, whose compositions are clearly of human quality."

"Yet you yourself readily agree that this Shakespeare could not have been an Earthling."

"Yes" Aurora admitted. "That is obvious. Yet the fact that ordinary Earthlings find transcendent pleasure in his poetry shows a deep internal yearning on their part to reach towards that which is human."

Tildra said nothing.

Aurora continued. "Then there is their holy book. I have studied it."

"Yes, so have we," Tildra said. "It is a psychotic mass of contradictions."

"Indeed," Aurora agreed. "But mixed among those contradictions there are sections representing an attempt by someone to explain true thought, and some of the Earthlings like those sections."

"Are you claiming that the potential exists to convert the Earthlings to Minervism?" Tildra asked. "That would indeed be wonderful, but it hardly seems possible. In addition to being demented and savage, they are fanatical believers in their own anti-rational Christian faith."

"No, the Earthlings would clearly rebuke any open attempt to convert them. But perhaps we could create a syncretism, where we gather the fragments of divine and human thought that can be found in their religion or popular culture, infuse them with additional necessary Minervan concepts, and package the whole within the guise of Christian mythology. Such a faith, if propagated widely among the Earthlings, could liberate their human potential and lead them towards civilization."

Tildra was horrified. "So now you are suggesting, that we, the priestesses of the one true Goddess, should degrade ourselves by willfully composing and disseminating a false religion?"

Aurora did not back down. "Is that not exactly what our ancestors did in the great days of yore when they spread the ideas which became the basis of galactic civilization?"

"And look what it has brought us," Tildra said angrily. The Centrals reinterpreted Reason as Love, and then transformed Love from Rational Love into Erotic Love, the antithesis of Reason, with its own demonic Goddess committed to our destruction. Then there are the merciless Eegees, who have replaced Reason with the cult of Justice, and who barely tolerate us, despite all we have done for them."

"Yet," Aurora pointed out, "there are also the Weegees and Norcs, who still celebrate Reason, and without whose help we could not survive."

Tildra looked at Aurora angrily. "Priestess Aurora, are you an adherent of the doctrine of derived divinities?"

Aurora stiffened her back. "Yes, I hold with many of our race that Love and Justice are divine attributes, but derive their divinity from Reason, which as we know is the true form of the Goddess herself."

Tildra turned to Nendra. "So there you see it, Divine Eminence. This is what comes from allowing Weegee heresies to be preached within the priestesshood."

Nendra frowned. "Tildra, you go too far. The doctrine of derived divinities is not an orthodox part of our faith, and I myself do not uphold it. Yet it has never been condemned as a heresy."

"It should be," Tildra answered.

Nendra shook her head. "No, it should not be. There must be room within the Minervan Temple for those who dare to think unorthodox thoughts. Also, from a practical point of view, the doctrine of derived divinity has provided our faith with members, such as young Aurora here, who can present our creed to our non-believing friends in a form that they find most palatable. Despite her immaturity, I was glad when Aurora was selected by Princess Minaphera to speak for us among the Weegees. I am happy today that she will soon be representing our race among the Norcs. Her somewhat heterodox views endow her with precisely those characteristics that will show our kind in its most favorable light to the liberal polytheists."

Aurora spoke up. "But Divine Eminence, what is your view of my suggestion that we develop a pseudo-faith to lead the Earthlings towards humanity?"

Nendra smiled. "Dearest Aurora. I admire you greatly, as a scientist, a Minervan, and as a woman. You are as brave and truehearted as were the daughters of Penelope themselves. Yet you are no theologian. Pursue your science, Aurora. Win the Norcs to our side by showing them your truehearted nature. But leave theology to those who have made it their life work. Despite the anecdotal evidence you have discovered for phenomenon among Earthlings that mimic evidence for human potential, the countervailing evidence is far more massive. Humans do not stenchify themselves. Humans do not mutilate themselves. Humans do not commit mass sacrifice of their children. Only a psychotic religion could possibly appeal to such beings, and as Minervans, we have no interest in acting as the agents of propagation of psychotic beliefs."

There was a conclusiveness to Nendra's final remark that told Aurora in no uncertain terms that it was useless to pursue the topic further.

"Yes, Your Divine Eminence," Aurora said.

Nendra approached and put her hand on Aurora's shoulder.

"Do not feel rejected, young Aurora," the High Priestess said. "No one is right all the time. Despite your mistaken ideas about creating a faith that could lead Earthlings to humanity, we all still love you, and have the greatest of respect for you. To make matters perfectly clear as to where I and the majority of the High Council stand as regards our appreciation of your merits, know this: When you leave for Anthropo two weeks from now, you will leave as a Minervan Priestess of the Second

Class."

The entire High Council rose as one and burst into a joyous soaring hymn. The High Priestess joined in the song, and following her urging pat on the shoulder, Aurora did as well.

Standing side by side with the High Priestess, singing her Hymn of Ascension before the Minervan High Council; it was a moment Aurora had dreamed of since she was very young. It should have been one of the happiest moments of her life. But it felt like one of the saddest.

Chapter 32

Hamilton sat in his cell, listlessly watching the latest news on the holotheater screen. A Fleet of Weegee battleships had arrived in the solar system. There were more raging anti-Weegee and anti-Minervan mass demonstrations in the US and Mexico. The theology students who were holding Urania had run out of fingers and toes to amputate, and so were releasing videotapes showing her being tortured in various ways each day. They had also added a demand for an end to negative galactic media stereotypes of Earthlings to their list of requirements for the Norc priestess's release.

Meanwhile, there were more child-martyrs being killed or mutilated in New Minervapolis, and there were reports of traitors being caught and executed by Aaron Vardt's Faith Police in the refugee camps of outer Kennewick.

It was all so dismal, especially the last. He wondered who the so-called traitors were. Charlie the trucker? Nurse Susan Peterson? Melissa Berger? He wished there was something he could do to help.

How could Aurora do this to him? He had saved her life. His family had offered her the warmth and affection of their home. The two of them had been friends, comrades, sharing a grand adventure together. But now, it was as if none of that had ever happened. As soon as they had returned to New Minervapolis he had been sent back to his cell, and was being treated as nothing more than her study specimen once again.

There was a sound at the door. It was obviously Aurora, entering as she always had in the old days, without asking permission. He turned to face her, and was startled to see her wearing the formal robe and two-Owl insignia of a Second Class Priestess.

"I see you have been promoted," he said.

"Yes. The Minervan High Council thought very highly of my work."

Hamilton made little effort to conceal his disdain. "Well, allow me to be the first Earthling to congratulate you. It is such a privilege to have been of assistance in furthering your brilliant career."

Aurora cast her eyes down on the floor. "It's not what you think."

"Oh, no?"

She tried to meet his eyes. "I pled for you, Hamilton, I really did."

"Apparently not hard enough to make a difference. Or to offend the promotion committee."

"Hamilton, the High Council does not see you the way you see yourself. You think of yourself as a human being. But when they see you, they see one of those." She gestured to the holoscreen, where an image of thousands of Americans screaming "Death to the Western Galactic Empire" and defecating or urinating on effigies of Minaphera and the western galaxy were on display.

"And you, what do you see?"

Aurora looked at him sadly. "I see a loyal friend whose services are being improperly rewarded."

Hamilton noted that she had side-stepped the issue of whether she considered him to be human. However, at least she had conceded that he was not being treated squarely. He decided to go with that.

"So, then your High Council does not care whether what it does is just?"

Aurora shook her head. "Their first obligation is to Reason. They do not see any rational basis for reducing the community's chance for survival in order to please the irrational preferences of an Earthling."

The statement puzzled Hamilton. "I don't understand. Why not let me go? If they are afraid I would take up arms against them again, I'd be glad to give my parole. You can read my mind, so you could know with certainty that I would not be lying. How does keeping me captive here increase the community's chance for survival?"

"They do not intend to keep you here."

Hamilton felt a sinking feeling as the suspicion dawned on him that the situation could be even worse than he had thought. "What do they intend to do with me?"

Aurora walked over to the window and stared out at the sky.

Hamilton asked again. "Aurora. Tell me. What is to become of me?"

Aurora let out a deep breath. "The Northern Confederation would like the opportunity to study you at the Anthropo Institute. We need their good-will. Consequently, you are to be transferred."

Hamilton recoiled in horror. At least in New Minervapolis he would have the occasional companionship of other Americans trying to live their lives under Minervan rule. At Anthropo he would be a friendless freak, kept in a cage for the convenience of alien scientists.

"It won't be as bad as you think," Aurora said. "The Norcs are very gentle and humane people, and I'll be there as custodial investigator, to make sure that the work is productive and that you are treated properly." Obviously reading his mind, she added, "There will be no cage. You will live in a pleasant dwelling, and go for walks every day with me and diverse Norc scientists. We will converse about various matters of interest..."

Hamilton completed her sentence. "While you telepathically observe the thoughts you provoke as a result."

Aurora nodded. "Yes, that is the basic idea. We will use both the natural techniques I have employed up to now, as well as various enhanced methods enabled by Anthropo technology. But all observations will be conducted in the outer mind only. The First Commandment will be respected. You may be sure of that. And," she added, "you may also rest assured that the work we will do will be top-notch research, suitable for publication in the galaxy's leading peer-reviewed scientific journals."

"I'm so glad."

Aurora did not miss his stinging sarcasm. "Look," she said. "What's so bad about it really? You would be safe and comfortable, and we would be together, doing important work advancing the frontiers of scientific psychology and anthropology. Why can't you just accept it?"

"I want my freedom," Hamilton said.

"Why?" Aurora asked forcefully. "Why is that so important to you?"

"Because I am a human being."

"You haven't proven that."

Hamilton looked the priestess in the eye. "But you know that it is true."

Aurora said nothing.

Hamilton pressed the point. "You do, don't you?"

Aurora turned and left the cell.

Junea looked down at the ugly little Earthling known as the President.

"I don't think you understand," she explained. "I have not come this time in my usual capacity as a roving Imperial Ambassador. Princess Minaphera has made her special representative. The squadron currently investing this solar system is at my command."

"Good," said the President. "Then wipe out the Minervans and we'll all be friends."

"I'm afraid it is not so simple. The Princess has placed these warships at my disposal in order to help convince you to accept a diplomatic solution to the Earthling-Minervan conflict. She has accepted my recommendation for a partition of Kennewick. Now, so should you."

"Have the Minervans agreed?"

"I have spoken with the Minervan High Council. They are willing to cede ten percent of the land under their control in order to allow for the establishment of a Kennewickian state."

"Ninety percent for them, ten percent for us. Oh, that is very generous of them. Madame Ambassador, has it ever occurred to you that before the Minervan invasion, one hundred percent of Kennewick was American territory? We could never agree to such an unfair split."

"Why not? Accept it, and we'll help you take over Mexico." She gestured at the large map of the North American continent that adorned the meeting room wall. Mexico was one of the three largest tribal territories shown. Kennewick was too small to see. "That's much bigger than all of Kennewick."

"That is not the point. This is not about territory, it is about principles. The Minervan presence in Kennewick is a defilement. We cannot have pagans polluting sacred Christian land with their unholy presence. We have a God-given duty to exterminate them. Being a pagan yourself, no offense, I can't expect you to understand that. But that's the way we feel."

"So you are not willing to compromise at all?" Junea let some of her frustration with the little chieftain show.

"Did I say that? By no means." The President smiled genially, showing his disgusting mutilated teeth. "It's just that any compromise must be one that reduces Minervan territory to a small enough size where it becomes possible for us to wipe them out. So I tell you what. We'll agree to split Kennewick, but we get ninety percent, and they get ten percent."

Junea shook her head. "I'm sorry, but that is not good enough. Princess Minaphera has specifically said that the most you can be given is fifty percent. You will have to settle for that."

"No way. We want more."

Junea saw that it was time to apply some pressure. She looked at the map, where the President's domain, colored yellow, was divided by dotted lines into subdistricts. She indicated one of these with her finger. "What is that place called?"

The President looked where she was pointing. "Iowa," he said.

"Very well. If you do not accept our generous terms, I will order an immediate psioray reduction of the inhabitants of Iowa."

At this remark, a number of the President's advisors who had been hanging in the background appeared to grow concerned. They approached their chief and consulted with him in urgent whispers. However after a few moments of this, the President said loudly, "Don't worry, guys. She's bluffing." He turned and looked at Junea with as much dignity and threatening aspect as such a pathetic little creature could be expected to muster, then added, "She remembers what happened to them when they attacked Peru. I'm sure she knows that whatever Peru had, we've got one hundred times as much. So I'm sure she'll want to be a bit more careful before she takes us on."

Junea smiled grimly to herself. She had indeed remembered the battle with Peru, and had taken precautions accordingly. A special light cruiser had been fitted out with the Empire's most advanced cloaked-heledo detection gear and placed under the command of the Princess's own protégé, the daring young Commander Danatus. Moving quietly through subspace, Danatus had brought his own hyper-stealthed vessel into position directly above the American boss's little despotism. Interestingly, Danatus had reported a complete absence of Earthling cloaked-heledos or any other orbital defenses. Perhaps they were out of ammunition, or more likely, had withdrawn their limited space-defense assets into ground shelters to avoid Western Galactic Imperial Navy minesweepers. No matter. The Earthlings were under Danatus' guns right now. She opened a tele-psych channel to his bridge.

She spoke, as if to the air in the room. "Commander Danatus. Do you have targeting coordinates for the Earthling satrap known as Iowa?"

The room's air spoke with Danatus' voice. "Yes, Reverend Ambassador."

"On my order, please proceed with a three-second psioray bombardment." She turned to the President and smiled. "Last chance."

The President's advisors seemed alarmed, and tried to get his attention. But the President ignored them. Instead he looked her in the eye and said, "Go ahead. Make my day."

"Fire three," Junea said. A moment later the air in the room was shattered by an ear-splitting whine as the tele-psych link relayed the sound of a psioray battery firing at full power. Then the noise stopped.

The advisor the President called Fred ran to a console and picked up one of the hydrocarbon plastic-encased electromagnetic devices that the Earthlings used for voice communication. Junea waited patiently while he pushed various buttons and shouted into it. Finally he put it down and walked back to where the President was standing. Junea noted with satisfaction that most of the blood appeared to have been drawn from Fred's face.

"Mr. President," Fred said. "They've done it. Everyone in Iowa has been shrunk to the size of insects. They're being eaten by birds even as we speak."

"Are you ready to compromise now?" Junea asked.

"Don't make me laugh," the President said haughtily.

Junea walked over to the map and made a show of shopping for a second target.

"Mr. President," Fred said urgently. "I really think this may be a good time to negotiate."

"Keep your shirt on, Fred," the President replied. "So they reduced Iowa. Who cares? It's far away, and no one there ever voted for me anyway."

"What's this one?" Junea said, pointing to a curiously shaped province further to the east.

The short, fat Earthling with transparent solid lenses in front of his eyes and the worst smell of the lot spoke up. "Oh, that would be Virginia."

The President snapped at the fat humanoid. "Beasley, would you shut up."

"I was just trying to be helpful, sir," Beasley said apologetically.

Junea spoke to the air. "Commander Danatus, please lay in targeting coordinates for Virginia."

Danatus' voice spoke back. "With pleasure, Reverend Ambassador. However it's Captain Junior-Grade Danatus now. In recognition for our victory over Iowa, I've been promoted again."

"Congratulations, Captain Junior-Grade Danatus," Junea said. "Please prepare another three-second bombardment."

Fred said, "Mr. President, they are about to reduce Virginia. We need to do something."

"Relax Fred," the President said. "Even if they do, we still have 48 more states."

Junea said, "Captain Junior-Grade Danatus, are you ready?"

The voice replied, "Yes, Reverend Ambassador."

Junea licked her lips. "Very well. Let's do a little countdown. Fire in ten, nine, eight, seven…"

Fred interrupted, quite rudely, Junea thought. "Excuse me, Madame Ambassador. How accurate are your psioray bombardment systems?"

"Generally speaking, the beam-width variation can be kept to within one tenth of one percent of the range. Why?"

"Well," Fred said, "I was just wondering. How far away is your warship?"

"About two of your planet's diameters."

Fred turned to the fat Earthling. "Beasley, what would be one-tenth of one percent of that?"

"Well," said Beasely. "The Earth has a radius of about six-thousand four hundred kilometers, so two diameters would be around twenty-five thousand kilometers, making one-tenth of one percent of that twenty five kilometers."

"Madame Ambassador," Fred said. "Do you realize that Virginia is just across the river? If your beams have potential targeting errors of up to 25 kilometers, we could easily be hit here. You're putting yourself in the line of fire this time."

"Oh, don't worry," Junea said brightly. "The beams are tuned to only affect Earthlings. I'm in no danger at all. Now where were we? Oh yes, six, five, four..."

Fred turned to his leader and screamed. "Mr. President!"

"Okay, Okay, I get the point," the President said. "Stop the count."

Junea had just reached "two" and was vaguely disappointed. Still, if the savages were coming to heel, her purposes could be accomplished. "So," she said. "I take it you have decided to be reasonable."

"Sure," the President said. "If fifty percent is non-negotiable, we'll go along with that. But in view of how much we are giving up, you really ought to sweeten the deal a little bit."

"Well, as I said, if you agree to serve as enforcers of order on this planet, we are willing to give you some technology that will improve your military capabilities dramatically."

"But not as good as what you give the Minervans," the President frowned.

"No, of course not," Junea said. "The Princess has ruled out any technology transfers that would give you qualitative equality. However, given your superior numbers, and the increased vulnerability an appropriate border revision can create for the Minervan settlement, it may be enough to tip things in your favor."

"But it may not," the President sulked. "You know you're getting a lot out of this deal, Junea. We're not only conceding half of Kennewick, we're ending the helicity embargo, and giving you the full services of the United States of America in the war against planet assassins. We're going way out on a limb doing all this for you, risking the displeasure of religious Christians everywhere. You really shouldn't be short-changing us like this."

"You're getting Mexico," Junea said cheerfully.

The President made a rude sound, mimicking a rectal gas release by blowing air through his lips.

Junea looked at the map. She pointed to a large pink-colored territory located vertically above that of the President. "Very well," she said. "What if we throw in this one?"

Fred's eyes seemed to brighten. "Canada? You'll give us Canada too?"

Junea smiled. "Why not? As I said, cooperation will be rewarded." Then she hardened her expression. "But you have to settle now."

Fred looked sharply at the President, who shrugged in response. "Sure," the despot said. "What the hell." He advanced to Junea and held out his vermin-infested hand in the Earthling sign of agreement.

Junea took two hasty steps backward and made the sign of the Triune blessing.

It was a deal.

Chapter 33

Aurora sat in the café in the main plaza area of New Minervapolis, sipping raffa with Freya and Danae.

"So," Freya said cheerfully, looking at Aurora's bright new two-owl insignia with admiration. "I suppose we shall have to call you 'Your Eminence' now."

"Oh, that won't be necessary," Aurora said. "We're all old friends…"

Danae cut her off. "Would Your Eminence care for another cup of raffa?" She snatched a drink off the tray of an Earthling servant boy who was walking by.

"Please Danae!" Freya said. "Her Eminence requires raffa that is freshly squeezed! I'll take this one." She called out. "Boy, another cup of raffa here!"

The boy turned and set a drink down. Aurora reached for it, but before she could touch the cup, Danae's long arm got it first. "Let me taste this for Your Eminence," she said, then tossed it all down. She tilted her head thoughtfully. "Definitely not suitable for an Eminence. But I'll have another." She snapped her fingers to get the attention of a tray-boy.

Aurora fumed. "Will you two cut it out!"

"Certainly, Your Eminence," Danae and Freya said in unison, then burst out laughing.

Freya said, "This is all so wonderful, Aurora. Your promotion, and the two of us getting out of this dump to return to civilization together. And it can't be too much longer here for Danae, from what I hear."

Danae smiled. "I take it you are referring to the likely consequences of my little brother's rather spectacular career success. I can't say for sure, but…"

Freya cut her off. "Let me guess. You are being transferred to the

Princess's court in Cepheus."

Danae blushed.

"When?" Freya asked breathlessly.

"I expect in about two months," Danae admitted. But something in her tone suggested there was more to say.

Freya forced it out. "And?"

"I am informed that our family is to be ennobled," Danae said simply.

Freya's eyes lit up. "Goddesses alive! A countess!"

At this moment, the tray arrived with the second drink Danae had requested. But Freya grabbed it first and handed it to Aurora. "Here you go, Eminence. You better taste this for the countess-to-be."

Aurora tossed it down, then said, "Definitely not fit for a countess. But I'll have another."

All three women burst into laughter.

Freya turned to Aurora. "You must be so excited about finally being able to examine your study specimen with proper equipment. The mind-imaging facilities at the Anthropo Institute are the most advanced in the galaxy. And as the Institute's newly appointed Associate Director of the Primitive Subhuman Department, I intend to keep them that way."

"An Associate Director!" Danae and Aurora said in unison. They both eyed Freya's raffa cup, but before either of them could make a move, Freya snatched it up herself. "Don't even think of it," she said gaily.

Her announcement made, and her raffa safe, Freya turned her attention back to Aurora. "Yes, it is the opinion of the Northern Confederation authorities that the hard work that I've put in here as Acting Director of the local UL Humanitarian Commission merits a promotion. So it's off to Anthropo!" She smiled. "That poor little Earthling of yours will not be able to have a single thought without it being imaged, measured, scanned, and analyzed with absolute precision."

"All in the outer mind, of course," Aurora said, seeking reassurance.

"Of course," Freya said. "At Anthropo, we scrupulously observe all regulations for proper laboratory ethics. So there certainly will be no inner mind violations. However, our equipment is of such high quality that, given sufficient time and expertise, a group of researchers using it can draw almost as much information about a subject's mental construction in an outer mind survey as would be possible with a direct examination of the inner mind using traditional methods."

"Is that possible?" Aurora said, somewhat staggered by the thought.

"Certainly," Freya said. "Aurora, you've been living behind the times. Everyone is amazed at what you have been able to accomplish using old-fashioned natural telepathy techniques. But once we combine your scientific skill with our technology, believe me, there will be nothing significant about your specimen's mind that you won't know. Especially since, with our involvement, it will be possible to stimulate portions of his mental architecture that you have been reluctant to engage."

"What do you mean by that?" Aurora asked.

"Well," Freya explained, "as you know, those who embrace Minerva attain certain mental abilities denied to those who do not."

"Of course," Aurora said, somewhat puzzled by Freya's oblique method of explanation.

"Well, other unique skills are given to those who embrace Aphrodite."

Aurora looked at her old friend. "Are you suggesting that we actively stimulate his erotic emotions?"

"Sure," Freya smiled mischievously. "Don't worry. It'll be fun."

"But such stimulation could induce major psychic stress."

"That's the idea," Freya said. "The stronger the stimulus, the greater will be the resolution of the response. We're going for fine detail here, girl."

Aurora shook her head. "I don't think it would be proper."

Danae laughed. "Aurrie, you're such a prude. I thought you agreed that Love was a divine attribute."

"Yes," Aurora said. "But so is Justice. He wouldn't know he was being played with."

Freya smiled. "Aurora, really. He's just an Earthling."

"You must agree," Junea told the High Priestess.

"But you are asking us to risk collective extermination," High Priestess Nendra said.

"Not at all, not at all," Junea waved her hand dismissively. "We are simply asking you to return fifty percent of the occupied land to the Kennewickians, so they may have an independent tribal despotism."

"I don't see why that is necessary," Nendra replied. "The Kennewickians never had an independent tribal despotism before. They are in fact indistinguishable in language, race, and religion from other Americans. So they already have an independent despotism. It is called the United States of America, and it is thousands of times the area of New Minervapolis."

Junea nodded. "Yes, from a rational point of view, that would certainly appear to be the case. However the American tribal despot feels that it is necessary that they have their own state."

"So why doesn't he give them one then? His territories are vast, and much of it is unpopulated."

"He feels that since they are from Kennewick, they can only live here in Kennewick, on their sacred ancestral lands."

"Most of them don't want to live here. They want to be free to live and work in the many other American cities."

"Yes, but he wants them to live here."

Nendra shook her head. "But Reverend Ambassador, Can you not see that this is pure insanity?"

Junea shrugged. "Of course."

"Then why, in Minerva's name, are you accommodating it?"

"Well obviously, since the Earthlings are insane, it would be unrealistic to expect them to agree to rational ideas. Therefore, if we are to have a diplomatic solution, it must perforce contain large elements of insanity. Otherwise the Earthlings would never agree."

"But why do you seek their agreement at all? They are savages who have committed hideous crimes against your Empire. Why not just crush them?"

"That would look bad," Junea explained. "When you have an Empire like ours, galactic public opinion is very important. You don't want to look too bossy. Anyway, my job as a diplomat is to get everyone to agree. I've gotten the Earthlings to agree, and now you must agree too."

Nendra was curious. "How did you secure the Earthling's agreement?"

Junea curled her finger in her hair. "Oh, we offered them some of their neighbor's land, and some arms..."

"Arms? You're giving the savages arms?" Nendra's shock showed on her face.

Junea was unflappable. "Yes, but just ancient tenth-class rubbish, nowhere near as good as the eighth class material we have provided you."

"But still much better than anything they had before. Such weapons could greatly increase our vulnerability."

"Possibly. But I think you'll get by. Anyway, it wasn't enough to convince the savages, so I had a cruiser psioray one of their provinces. That brought them around."

Nendra's eyes went wide. "Are you proposing to do that to us too?

Bombard us with psiorays if we don't agree?"

Junea waved her hand dismissively. "No, no, don't be ridiculous. You Minervans are civilized rational people, and I'm sure you'll be much more agreeable. And even if you weren't, we would never consider using force against people who have been such long-term friends of the Western Galactic Empire."

Nendra was quiet as she waited for the other sandal to drop.

"Of course," continued Junea, "should you not agree to the peace plan, the Universal League has recommended that to minimize violence in this sector there be a complete embargo on all military technology, to all sides. This would include, of course, recharge units for reflective disarmers. Given the current state of galactic public opinion, we could hardly be expected to veto such a resolution."

Nendra could not contain her dismay. "But without recharges for our disarmers, we would be completely helpless against the savages. They would overrun New Minervapolis and kill us all!"

"Indeed?" said Junea. "Not being an expert in military strategy, I hardly feel qualified to evaluate what the new local balance of power might be in the event of a galactic arms embargo. However, if you really believe that it would be so severely to your disadvantage, I would suggest that you go along with our plan."

Nendra took two steps back and then collapsed into her chair, suddenly feeling like the very old woman she actually was. "So there is no choice," she mumbled.

"None," Junea pronounced.

Nendra gathered herself a bit. "Very well. We agree. I will send a messenger to the Mayor of Kennewick to arrange a meeting to draw up the actual boundaries."

"No," Junea said. "The Mayor of Kennewick is dead, or soon will be. You will conduct your negotiations with the Kennewickians' true representative, the Minister Aaron Vardt."

Nendra stared at Junea. "Aaron Vardt? But he is the leader of the Kennewickian assassins!"

"So?" said Junea. "What is your point?"

Chapter 34

Hamilton stood up as Aurora entered his cell. "Come," she said. "I have something to show you before we go." He followed her without a word.

Over the past ten days, Aurora had treated him coldly. It was as if she had hardened her heart to him, denying any reality to their past friendship, and dropping any pretense that she had seriously fought for his freedom before the Minervan High Council. Now their departure for Anthropo was imminent, and she was making it abundantly clear that his status there would be as her study specimen, and nothing more.

Hamilton had once felt real affection for Aurora, perhaps actually loved her. Her playful arrogance towards him during the early period of their acquaintance had been easy to forgive, and her tragic past and secret little-girl vulnerability had made her easy to love. But her current behavior towards him, her betrayal of him after all they had been through together, engendered the darkest anger, verging on sheer hate. She knew he was human, she had to know. But she chose to deny it so she could advance her career at the expense of his enslavement. She was a cheat, a liar, a fraud, and a traitor.

As they walked in silence up the hill that overlooked the zone of the refugee camps, Hamilton noticed that Aurora was carrying a cheap telescope. A three-foot long refractor, it must have been looted out of some defunct department store in inner Kennewick. It was an absurd accoutrement. With the ability to refocus her eyes that all advanced galactics seemed to have, Aurora needed no telescope, and if she wanted to show him something, a pair of binoculars would have been a much better choice. But telescope it was, and he was too disgusted with her to bother asking her the reason.

They reached the top of the hill. Looking down towards the camps,

Hamilton could see muzzle flashes and hear the popping sounds of gun-fire.

"Look at that," Aurora said. "As soon as they find out they are to have a state of their own, the first thing they do is start to kill each other. Each faction wants control for itself." She pointed at some tents adorned with red crosses. "You see that? Those are Melissa Berger's hospital tents. She and the other proto-rationals are holed up there, and are under assault by Aaron Vardt's men, who are going to wipe them out. Then they'll kill the child patients too, supposedly to complete their destined martyrdom. That's Earthlings for you, mindless murderers."

Hamilton peered down into the valley. Studying the gun flashes, he could make out the contours of the battle. What Aurora said was true. Melissa and the hospital volunteers were outnumbered and losing. Yet their defeat was not inevitable. Vardt's men were attacking without any proper tactical organization. They were strung out in a long line, and their left flank, on the end leading up his hill, was completely unprotected. If he were free, he could sneak up behind the far-left exposed man, break his neck, grab his gun, and then roll up the whole line from one end to the other.

"Aurora," he pleaded. "Let me go and help them. I can save them."

"No," Aurora said coldly. "You are needed for scientific study. I just brought you here so you could watch the murders and understand how disgusting you Earthlings really are. Then maybe you will stop whining about how you are being mistreated. Here, take the telescope and watch." She handed him the telescope and then turned to watch the battle.

Hamilton felt completely enraged. Had she no pity? She had once expressed admiration for the Bergers. Once it had seemed like she had some compassion for the wounded children. Now she was using their deaths as a show, just to rub in his face his own inferiority. Just to justify her stinking careerist betrayal.

Aurora's back was turned to him. The gun flashes were advancing towards the hospital. His friends were about to die. He could save them, but she would not allow it. The situation was absolutely intolerable. Hamilton's anger welled up like a torrent. Gripping the telescope he smashed it down hard on Aurora's head. The black-robed priestess went down like a pole-axed steer.

Hamilton looked at the ground. Aurora was unconscious, breathing shallow breaths. It would be best to finish her off. He knelt down and put his hands around her neck. He hesitated. She was still so beautiful. The arrogant expression was gone, and in its place was the cheerful girl-next-door smile that he had come to adore. Then she coughed a little blood and suddenly, instead of seeing the formidable alien priestess, he saw the little girl hiding in the barrel, fearing for her life.

He shook his head. Aurora wasn't evil, she was just…Aurora. Her leaders had told her it was necessary to the Minervans to ship him to Anthropo, and she had saluted. But they had been through a lot together, and she had done him a few good turns along the way. It pained him immensely that she refused to accept his humanity, but he couldn't kill her.

Hamilton dragged the priestess into the bushes so she would not be found by any Kennewickians. Then he kissed her softly on the forehead. "So long kid," he said. "I just wish…" He stopped, and brushed away a tear. Turning swiftly, he scrambled down the hill to do what he could for Melissa, Charlie and the rest.

Bullets ripped through the side of the hospital tent, setting off another wave of screaming among the terrified children. Melissa ducked and ran to the entrance to see what was going on outside.

The situation seemed hopeless. The medical volunteers and parents who were trying to defend the hospital were outnumbered, and armed only with hunting rifles and shotguns. Some of Vardt's men had M-16s. A few of the volunteers were hunters, and their superior marksmanship had inflicted some losses on the attackers. But the enemy's edge in firepower was considerable, and their advance was relentless.

The volunteers were falling back. Now the defensive skirmish line was just fifty yards in front of the hospital. As Melissa watched, Charlie Malone came running back through an alley to climb up the rear side of a house. Then, positioned on the roof, he drew a bead on a target with his rifle and fired one shot. A hail of automatic weapons fire in return sent him scurrying off the roof. He dashed towards the hospital entrance.

"We can't hold them much longer," he said panting breathlessly. "We've got to get the children out of here."

"But where can we go?" Melissa asked.

There was no place to go.

Hamilton moved quick and low from bush to bush down the slope of the hill. Ahead of him was one of Vardt's thugs, in a kneeling position, blasting away maniacally with an M-16 at a rooftop from which somebody had just fired a rifle shot.

"That's it, baby," Hamilton mumbled to himself. "Keep firing. That way you won't hear a thing." He made a final rush and hit the man from behind like a ton of bricks. The man tried to struggle, but Hamilton grabbed his hair and yanked back his head to break his neck. The man died without a sound.

Hamilton examined his victim. In addition to the M-16 and a lot of ammo, he had a long bayonet and two grenades. Excellent. Hamilton loaded a fresh clip into the M-16 and switched it to the semi-automatic setting. Then sighting down the line of Vardt's skirmishers, he fired three shots in rapid succession, putting bullets in the heads of three of Vardt's men.

The entire flank cleared of Vardts' men, Hamilton took off at a run for a house just to the rear of the center of the fanatics' advancing line. He quickly climbed a vine to gain a commanding position on the rooftop. Then, he pulled the pin on one of the grenades, counted to two, and lobbed it into the middle of the main group of the enemy.

The grenade went off about six feet above ground level, with terrific effect. Then Hamilton threw the other one at the last remaining organized group of thugs a bit further up the line.

Vardt's men panicked, and those that could took off in a mad dash towards the rear. Hamilton switched the M-16 to automatic, and opened up on the fleeing mob, with devastating results. Then he climbed off the rooftop and pulled the bayonet from its sheath. Moving silently among the wounded, he completed his work.

"Boy, are we glad to see you," Charlie said.

"I thought we were done for," Melissa added.

Hamilton lowered a handful of captured M-16s on to the hospital floor. "Distribute these to your best men, Charlie. They're going to need them. Vardt is certain to attack again."

A tall elderly man approached. "This is Deputy Mayor Bill Thomas," Melissa said. "Or I should say Acting Mayor Thomas. He's all that's left of the old city government now that Mayor Wagner is dead."

Thomas extended his hand. "I want to thank you, son, for everything you've done."

Hamilton nodded and shook Thomas' hand.

"How did you manage to get here?" Susan Peterson asked.

"Aurora took me to the hilltop to watch your deaths. She wanted to rub in my face how barbaric Earthlings were. But she turned her back on me, and I seized the chance to slam her on the head with a telescope, knocking her out cold. Then I ran down the hill to help you."

Melissa said, "She really took you up a hill just to view our deaths? That seems kind of odd."

Hamilton nodded. "Yes, I know. Aurora had sometimes acted oblivious to the pain she was causing, but I had never known her to be such an outright sadist before. I saved her life in New York, you know, and I had thought that she had finally developed real feelings of friendship for me. Then a week ago the Minervan High Council ordered her to ship me off to some alien planet for scientific study, and she suddenly became colder than ice. She made it real clear that when we went there together, I would be nothing but her lab specimen. I was very lucky to get this chance to escape. The transport arrives tomorrow."

Melissa exchanged an odd glance with Susan. Then she turned to Hamilton. "You say she turned her back on you, then you hit her with a telescope?"

"Yes."

"Where did you get the telescope?"

"She gave it to me."

Melissa and Susan exchanged another significant glance. Then she stared at Hamilton with an odd smile on her face.

"What?" Hamilton asked.

"She must have been very foolish to expose herself to attack like that." There was a touch of irony in Melissa's voice that Hamilton could not miss.

The Ranger did a double take. Melissa's statement made the whole sequence of events seem absurd. Aurora was anything but foolish. And she could read his mind. She had to know the attack was coming. Then there was the telescope, more useful as a club than an optical instrument. It was obvious.

Hamilton stared at Melissa in amazement. "You're saying Aurora set me up. She baited me, then turned her back to give me my chance. She wanted me to escape!"

Melissa and Susan looked at Hamilton with big knowing smiles on their faces. "And that means?" Melissa prompted.

"That means…she loves me!" Hamilton reeled at the emotional impact of the thought. "But I left her unconscious in the bushes. Come on, Charlie. We've got to get her to safety before any of Vardt's men find her."

Hamilton charged out of the tent, followed by the trucker. Moving behind terrain obstacles to avoid observation, it took them over half an hour to reach the hilltop where he had last left the priestess. It was dusk when they got there.

Hamilton entered the grove of bushes. In the dim evening light he could see three pairs of fresh boot tracks in the dirt. Aurora was gone.

Chapter 35

Aurora awoke in Tartarus. Or in a place that seemed as bad as Tartarus. It was cold, dark, and damp, and filled with hideous smells of feces, vomit, blood, and decayed food. There was an unbearable ache in the side of her head that throbbed with a pain that would not quit.

She rolled off of a hard surface and fell onto another that was even harder. Pain shot into her elbows as they took the fall. She moved her hands along the ground. It felt like concrete with a thin covering of wet filth. She opened her eyes and saw a grid of metal bars covered with flaking yellow paint. Crawling forward she touched them. They were very cold. She pushed at them, but they didn't move at all.

Gripping the bars, she hauled herself to her feet and then looked around. She was inside of an enclosure marked out by bars on three sides and a concrete wall on another. There were two short sides roughly two meters in length, and two longer ones about three meters in length. Inside the enclosure was a wooden platform raised about half a meter above the ground. Apparently she had been sleeping on this until she rolled over and fell. A meter away from the platform was a bowl of the general form that Earthlings used for defecation, except that it was made of steel, not ceramic, the usual toroidal hinged seat-edge cover was absent, and there was no tree-flesh available for self-cleaning. The dim light that filled the cell came from a bare incandescent electrical current bulb in the neighboring cage.

Aurora looked at herself. Her robe and owl were gone. In their place were dirty loose orange garments made of Earthling fabric of a quality very inferior to those which Sally had lent her. One of the garments was a short-sleeved pullover shirt and the other was a pair of trousers. Both the shirt and pants itched wherever they touched her, and there were no undergarments. Her feet were bare.

She sat down on the wooden platform and tried to collect her thoughts. This obviously could not be Tartarus. It was much too crude. Instead she was in some kind of Earthling holding pen.

How had she gotten here? She tried to remember. Where had she been last? The hill. She had taken Hamilton to the hill to try to provoke him to escape. Apparently he had done so. But then had he brought her here? That was unexpected.

Hamilton had to be freed. That thought had dominated her for the past week. After what he had done for her, after the trust he had placed in her, the High Council's order to reduce him back to study specimen status was immoral. She would not have been able to live with herself had she allowed it to be enforced. Yet, she could not defy them openly and simply release the man. To do so would have caused her to be branded a traitor, and disgraced her family name for all eternity. No, she had to set it up so it would seem like he escaped through his own effort.

Obviously Hamilton could not be told the plan, since anyone could read his mind either before his escape, or afterwards, should he ever be retaken. So she had kept him in the dark, and prepared him for his role by enraging him with cruel treatment. It had taken more effort than she had expected to trigger him into violence against her. But faced with the alternative of allowing the death of all his friends, he had been forced to choose action.

Hamilton was a soldier. He wanted to be human, and he defined his human essence through his commitment to his chosen role as defender of the good. His chances of survival in the combat with Vardt's lunatics were low, but that was a secondary matter. If he died fighting them in an effort to save Melissa Berger's children's hospital, he would at least die as a human. At Anthropo, he would have been denied that right.

Aurora imagined Hamilton in that first moment after he had achieved his freedom, the full dignity of his restored humanity filling his soul, charging down the hill to save the helpless and defend the right. He was one in spirit with the heroes of ancient lore, like the sons of Theseus, who had fought not from starships but from chariots, and sword in hand had rescued Ariel and the other fair daughters of Penelope from the evil owl hunters. What a man he was. If only he hadn't been born 20,000 years too late.

"Fare you well, noble warrior," Aurora whispered. "May Minerva guide you and protect you. May she reward your courage with victory over evildoers in this life, and a place with the blessed brave in the next."

The thought of the next world brought Aurora back to the present. What was she doing here? When she turned her back on Hamilton that last time, she had expected to awaken in the Elysian Fields. She had represented herself to him as an enemy, and as a trained soldier Hamilton certainly knew the folly of leaving disabled enemies to recover. Yet he had done so. After all the cruelty she had directed at him he had still decided to let her live. Not only that, but the feelings that had caused him to do so were so strong that they had been able to kick in within seconds of his first assault and overpower the strong violent instincts which she had willfully provoked.

There was only one emotion strong enough to do that; love. Infatuation wouldn't do, only real love could make a man act in such a way. Sally was right. Her brother was the real deal. Aurora brushed a tear from her eye. If only...

She looked at the cell bars. If love had stopped Hamilton from killing her, it certainly would also have prevented him from bringing her here. That meant someone else had.

A door to the side of the cell block opened and a large husky Earthling with a horrific smell entered and stared at her from outside her cage. He wore a mottled green military uniform similar to the one Hamilton had when he was captured, but instead of three stripes on the shoulder, this man had six silver stars, and was carrying a baton. Aurora tried to scan his mind to learn more about him, but it was futile. There was an antitelepathy device installed in his brain, making him completely unreadable.

"Well, good morning," the man said. "I see we are finally wide awake. I hope you found the accommodations suitable." The man snickered. "Your Eminence."

"Who are you?" Aurora asked.

"I am Field Marshall Douglas MacArthur, Supreme Commander of the Army, Navy, Air Force, and Space Force of the Empire of Kennewick."

Aurora rubbed the side of her head. "Huh? I thought Aaron Vardt was the boss of the Kennewickian assassins."

The Field Marshall became instantly enraged. He rapped his baton against the cell bars. "You will refer to our glorious leader by his proper title. He is the Premier Imperial Grand Magnificent Emperor, or PIGME for short. And we are not assassins. We are freedom fighters, pledged to liberate first Kennewick, and then the rest of the galaxy from pagan tyranny."

Aurora looked a the man. She recalled seeing a picture of an American military leader named Douglas MacArthur at the Hamiltons' house. This man bore no resemblance.

"You are not Douglas MacArthur," she said.

The man blushed. "No. Technically speaking, I am Herman Witherspoon. However when I became Field Marshall, I felt it would be appropriate to assume a more glorious appellation. I have also renamed all my top officers. Never before in the history of conflict has anyone commanded so many famous generals at the same time."

"So you work for the pig-mee?" Aurora inquired, trying to be polite.

The Field Marshall rapped his baton again. "It's pig-meh, NOT pigmy! Don't you dare ever call him the pigmy. He hates that."

Aurora scanned her mental archive of Hamilton's thoughts to find out what a pigmy was. She found a reference. Apparently the word pigmy referred to a small person of inferior civilization. "Why?" she said. "It seems like an appropriate designation."

Field Marshall MacArthur scowled. "I think Your Eminence will need to learn some respect. From now on, this will happen to you every time you are disobedient." He shouted towards the door. "General Patton, bring in the owl!"

Another man in uniform, this one with only four stars, entered the room carrying a tray on which there were some cooked bird parts. Aurora recoiled in horror. They were going to make her eat owl! She would be dammed forever.

The two men entered the cell. Aurora backed away, but there was nowhere to run. Then Field Marshall MacArthur grabbed her and forced her mouth open. "Give her a piece, General Patton. I'm sure she's hungry."

Aurora tried to struggle, but the two men were much too strong for her. The bird part went into her mouth, and she was forced to chew and swallow it to avoid choking. The men chuckled and exited her cell, slamming the door behind them.

Field Marshall MacArthur looked back at her. "So did you enjoy your owl?" He smiled.

Aurora, however, had recognized the taste. "I've had better turkey," she said. "But this will do." She picked up another piece and nibbled on it. "Do you have any sweet potatoes or cranberry sauce to go with it? I believe that is customary."

The Field Marshall's face turned black with disappointment. "You think you're very smart, don't you. Well, we'll show you."

But before he could do anything, another four-star soldier came running in and saluted. "What is it, General Pershing?" the Field Marshall said.

"Glorious Field Marshall," General Pershing began. "I bring bad tidings. The entire Fifth Division, sent to arrest the heretics at the hospital, has been martyred. Apparently a group of Berger's traitors got behind our men and took them by surprise."

Aurora's heart soared when she heard the news. "Having a little trouble with your doctors?" she said.

Field Marshall MacArthur frowned at her. "I shall return to deal with you later." He turned to his men. "Generals, defeat is unacceptable. The PIGME will want to know who is to blame. Come, let us look into this and assign responsibility."

The three men turned smartly on their heels and left the cell block. Aurora took another bite of the turkey, which suddenly tasted almost as good as that cooked by Mrs. Hamilton.

Junea said, "I'm so glad you could all spare time from your busy schedules to make it here today. I think this is a historic moment. At last we are all sitting down together to begin a peace process for Kennewick."

Nendra looked at the other occupants of the meeting room in horror. In addition to Junea, there was a hideous Earthling who she recognized as the assassin leader Aaron Vardt. However it was the fourth person whose presence most thoroughly shocked her.

Junea continued. "Allow me to do the necessary introductions. This is the Premier Imperial Grand Magnificent Emperor, or PIGME, of Kennewick, the most holy reverend Aaron Vardt. PIGME Vardt, meet Her Divine Eminence, High Priestess Nendra, chief executive of New Minervapolis."

Vardt said, "I understand that you meant no disrespect, Ambassador, but my title has changed. I am now to be refereed to as the 'Supreme PIGME.'"

Junea nodded. "My deepest apologies, Supreme PIGME. I will be certain to avoid inadvertently demeaning you through the use of an inadequate title in the future. Allow me now to introduce to both of you the person who will serve as mediator for these negotiations, Universal League Peace Commissioner, Countess Himla Petana."

Himla Petana's blonde hair and red robe with twined snake insignia marked her out as a high official of the Central Galactic Union. Not that Nendra needed such signs to recognize the woman, as she was well known to history. Fifteen years ago she had been the Governor of the

Andromeda Province of the Central Galactic Empire, and in that capacity had coordinated aphrodemonic anti-Minervan extermination programs in over a thousand star systems. She had been tried and convicted of war crimes, but had her sentence suspended because she was nobility. Now she had apparently been allowed to reenter political life, and was the Universal League's chosen representative to serve as Peace Commissioner for the Earthling/Minervan conflict. Nendra shuddered.

"Good afternoon, everyone," Himla Petana said. "I am so glad to be here to finally initiate the peace process for this poor benighted world, so full of historic and unique archeological treasures, yet until now, so full of despair. I'm sure we all share a common objective in seeking peace. There may be many obstacles in our path, but I'm sure we can transcend them if we keep in mind three simple truths: peace is love, love is peace, and love conquers all." She smiled at Nendra in a way that made the High Priestess positively sick.

Himla Petana continued. "Now, since we are all very busy people who have many other things we need to do, I suggest we get right down to business. The Supreme PIGME has put forward an excellent plan for the fair and equitable division of Kennewick. On behalf of the Universal League, its four major interstellar Empires or Confederations, its several thousand insignificant barbaric Queendoms, and its 120 quintillion inhabitants, I endorse his plan. I therefore request that the Minervans accept it as well."

"May I see the plan please?" Nendra said.

"I don't see why that is necessary," Himla Petana replied. "You're going to have to accept it, whether you like it or not."

"If I am not shown the plan, I will not agree to it," Nendra said with a determination that surprised even herself.

There was silence at the table for several seconds. Then Junea said, "I see no problem with that. The plan is quite fair. Please show her the plan, Countess."

Himla Petana shook her head. "Really, Ambassador. You indulge these Minervans far too much." But she handed Nendra a piece of osmopropylene, on which was inscribed a set of conditions comprising the draft agreement. The terms read:

1. The territory on the primitive planet Earth, Procyon District, Southern Sector, known variously as New Minervapolis and/or Kennewick is to be split on a 50/50 basis between the Minervan High Council (MHC) and the Imperial Grand Magnificent Empire of Kennewick (IGMEK).

2. The split will occur as follows: All odd-numbered addresses on

odd-numbered streets and even-numbered addresses on even-numbered streets will be assigned to the control of the MHC. All even-numbered addresses on odd-numbered streets and all odd-numbered addresses on even-numbered streets will be assigned to the control of the IGMEK.

3. For purposes of this agreement, all streets which are known by names, rather than numbers, shall be considered odd-numbered if the first letter of their name has a position in the alphabet which is odd-numbered when considered in the standard American Earthling sequence of letters beginning with "A" and ending with "Z." All other streets shall be considered even-numbered. Thus for example, "Broadway" whose name begins with "B," the second letter of the American Earthling alphabet, shall be considered an even-numbered street, while "Columbus Street," which begins with the third letter shall be considered an odd-numbered street. Certain streets, such as "Fourth Avenue," whose name refers to an even number but whose initial letter holds an odd-numbered position in the American Earthling alphabet, shall have their status determined later by a special arbitration commission to be appointed by the Universal League.

4. The MHC will be responsible for policing MHC territory, while the IGMEK will be responsible for policing IGMEK territory. Should one of the parties require police actions against individuals operating in the territory of the other, they will refer such complaints to the responsible authorities of the other party's government for appropriate enforcement action. In no case shall law enforcement activities by one party be permitted on the territory of the other party.

5. Both parties agree to immediately cease and desist from the practice of inflicting injury on children of the other party, including children who may be carrying traditional weapons.

6. In order to maintain symmetry of power between the two parties, each party will be provided with identical ninth-class weaponry for their law-enforcement agencies by the Universal League. Both parties agree not to seek or accept any military assistance beyond that outlined above.

7. Both parties agree not to damage Inca artifacts that may be in their possession. Furthermore, both parties agree to transfer custody of all such artifacts that may now, or at any time in the future, come to be in their possession to responsible authorities of the Universal League without any delay whatsoever.

Nendra looked up. "I can't sign this."

Himla Petana looked at Junea. "You see? What did I tell you? They are nothing but trouble."

"Have patience, Countess Commissioner," Junea urged. "I'm sure whatever minor problems the Minervans may have with the agreement can be worked out."

"Very well," Himla Petana said. "Let's deal with each point in the peace plan, starting with the most important. If the Minervans will not agree to that, I see no point in continuing these discussions at all." She turned to Nendra. "Your Eminence, do you, or do you not agree to point number seven?"

Nendra glanced at the contract, then faced Himla Petana. "The Minervan High Council has no difficulty accepting point number seven, provided it is in the context of an overall agreement whose other clauses are also acceptable."

Himla Petana scowled. "What is that supposed to mean? Either you accept point number seven, or you do not. Answer carefully, Minervan. The people of the galaxy will not look kindly upon those who willfully place priceless cultural treasures in danger."

Nendra shrugged. She had more important concerns to negotiate. "On behalf of the MHC, I agree unilaterally to point number seven. We have no Inca artifacts in our possession, but should we acquire any, we will hand them over to the UL at once."

Junea smiled. "There, Countess Commissioner. I told you they could be reasonable."

Himla Petana nodded. "Yes, perhaps they can, when they have a heli-cannon pointed at their heads." She turned to Vardt. "Supreme PIGME, will you also agree unconditionally to point number seven?"

Vardt cleared his throat, emitting a smell that caused Himla Petana to back away suddenly in thinly-disguised disgust. Apparently she was not used to Earthlings. "Well, Countess Commissioner," he said. "I certainly would like to. However, unlike the Minervans, we of the Imperial Grand Magnificent Empire of Kennewick are a democracy, and we must take the opinions and feelings of all of our people into account before making a decision of this magnitude. Inca artifacts represent a precious cultural heritage which is deeply valued by all Kennewickians, and while we were prepared to give them up in exchange for an equitable peace agreement, to do so in the absence of such represents a step that many of our people may be unwilling to take. Naturally, however, as a person who is sensitive to the aesthetic demands of galactic public opinion, I will do my best to obtain the agreement of my people to your request. Of course, it would be of great assistance to me in doing so if comparable major concessions could be extracted from the Minervans in return."

"Thank you, Supreme PIGME," Himla Petana said. "We'll see what we can do."

Nendra said, "That's good enough for you? You demand that we give an unconditional answer, but you let the Earthlings get away with mere equivocation?"

Before Himla Petana could answer, Vardt interrupted. "Countess Commissioner, I object. The Minervan has just referred to my people as 'Earthlings.' I demand that you instruct her to stop doing so, and to apologize immediately."

Nendra was puzzled. "Why do you object to being called 'Earthlings.' You are Earthlings. That is a fact."

"The term 'Earthling' has a demeaning connotation," Vardt explained. "It suggests negative stereotypes of irrational fanatics and planet assassins. I refuse to negotiate with someone who insists on insulting my people in this way."

"Would you prefer to be called 'Americans' or 'Christians?'"

"No. Those have the same negative stereotypes associated with them."

"Then what would you like to be called?" Nendra asked.

"I'm not sure," Vardt said. "It's pretty clear that whatever name we choose, it will be ruined for us by the Minervan-controlled galactic media."

"Perhaps we should move on to the other points in the peace plan," Junea said helpfully.

"Yes," Himla Petana said. "Since we have fundamental agreement on the most important point, I suggest that the Minervans yield on the rest and we conclude the deal immediately."

"No," said Nendra. "We cannot agree."

Junea said, "Your Eminence, you and I talked. You said you would agree to a 50/50 split of all disputed territory with the Kennewickians."

"Yes," Nendra admitted. "I agreed to point number one. But I did not agree to points two through six."

"I don't understand," Junea said. "Points two through six simply represent an equitable and peaceful means of implementing point number one."

"No," Nendra said. "They are insane."

Junea smiled. "I concede there may be insane elements in the plan, but as we discussed in our previous conversation, that is a requirement in this instance in order to reach agreement with the other party. But let us consider this as reasonable women. What exactly are your problems with points two through six?"

Nendra gestured at the draft. "Well, if we are to split the territory, we need to have defensible boundaries. Points two and three mix up the domains so thoroughly that there will always be Earthlings…"

"There she goes again!" Vardt said.

Nendra ignored him. "who are within effective range of our people with their projectile weapons. We won't be safe anywhere."

Junea nodded. "Yes, I can see how you might find that inconvenient. But we felt it was necessary in order to insure that each side received equal amounts of land of every quality within the territory. I'm sure you will agree that the homogenous distribution enabled by the odd-even patchwork split in the proposed plan assures the fairest possible division. So, do you have any problems with the remaining points, or are we done?"

"Yes, I have plenty of problems with it," Nendra said. "Point four places all responsibility for law enforcement within the Earthling territory on Aaron Vardt's own men…."

"I beg your pardon," Vardt said. "I am to be referred to as the Supreme PIGME."

"He's right," Himla Petana said. "It is a violation of diplomatic protocol to not refer to a negotiator by her, or in this case, his, proper official title. I'll have to censure you for that, Your Eminence."

"In that case, please refer to me as 'Your Divine Eminence,'" Nendra said. "I am a First Class Priestess, you know, not Second."

"Don't get huffy with me," Himla Petana said, "you ugly little owl worshipper."

Nendra glared at Himla Petana, who returned the look.

Junea interrupted. "Ladies, please. This is a peace conference. We are trying to end a war, not start another one. If you would be good enough to continue, Divine Eminence."

Nendra gathered herself. "Thank you. As I was saying, point four gives responsibility for law enforcement within the Earthling zone to the assassins themselves. That makes no sense."

"It may make no sense to you," Himla Petana said. "But it makes sense to us. An independent state for the Kennewickians requires honoring the basic UL principle of self-determination of savages."

"Excuse me?" Aaron Vardt said. "Savages?"

The women ignored him. Junea said, "That takes care of point four. Do you have any objections to points five and six?"

"Certainly," Nendra said. "Point five would prevent us from taking any action against the Earthling child-assassins."

"It also stops the Earthlings from inflicting any injury on Minervan children who are attempting to assassinate them," Junea pointed out.

"There are no Minervan children engaged in such activity," Nendra said.

"That may be," Junea answered, "but you must admit that the clause is entirely fair and symmetrical in its equal application to both parties."

"Indeed," Himla Petana said. "I have to add that I am horrified by your objection to this clause. The Minervan brutality in mutilating Kennewickian children is a shameful affront to the conscience of the entire galaxy. That you should demand the right to continue this activity, simply because the Earthlings do not engage in it, is an absolute disgrace. You must agree to point number five, and that is final."

"I find your deep concern over Earthling child-assassins rather odd," Nendra said to the UL Peace Commissioner, "given your own role in murdering millions of innocent Minervan children on over a thousand planets."

Himla Petana glared. "That comment was uncalled for. Those actions took place over fifteen years ago in a time that was very difficult for all of us. It is quite rude of you to bring them up in this context."

"Quite right. Let's please try to avoid personal attacks," Junea said. "Anything else?"

"Yes," Nendra answered. "Point six is absolutely intolerable. It would insure our extermination, and is not what we agreed to at all. You said that we would continue to be given eighth class weaponry, while the Earthlings would be limited to tenth class equipment. This represents a direct violation of our agreement."

Junea appeared shocked. "Give me that," she said, pointing to the osmopropylene draft.

Nendra passed the document to the Weegee ambassador, who examined it closely. Then she turned to Himla Petana.

"She's right," Junea said. "Point six has been altered. Countess Commissioner, what is the meaning of this? Point six was supposed to read tenth class arms for the Earthlings, eighth Class for the Minervans, not ninth class for each. On what basis did you make this alteration?"

"Well, as the representative of the Universal League in the peace process, I felt it was important to assure qualitative military equality between the two sides," the Countess said.

"However, as the representative of Princess Minaphera in this District, I do not. The Minervans must be given qualitative military superiority."

Vardt was very upset by this comment. "But I thought you told me that the peace plan would give us a chance to wipe out the Minervans. How does giving them better weapons than us fit in with that?"

"It doesn't, per se," Junea explained. "But many of the other points do. In any case, what I told you was that the peace plan would give you a chance to defeat the Minervans, I didn't say it would offer you a certainty. Indeed, that would be counterproductive. If the Minervans believed that the peace plan assured their annihilation, they would never agree to it, no matter how much pressure we applied. Given the Earthling superiority in numbers, some Minervan advantage in quality of arms is required if they are to believe they have any chance for survival at all. If a diplomatic solution is to be reached, they must believe that, just as you must believe that the plan gives you a reasonable chance to exterminate them. In my view, giving them eighth class weapons as compared to your tenth class provides just the right dynamic balance and lack of clarity needed to bring everyone together in a peace plan we all can support."

"Ambassador," Himla Petana said. "I object to the wild favoritism you are showing to the Minervans in this negotiation. As Universal League Peace Commissioner, I insist on maintaining the clause as written, with ninth-class arms for each party, thereby assuring qualitative equality."

Junea looked irritated. "Countess, it's getting late. I know what I'm doing here, and you don't. So please stop giving me a hard time and just change the document back to what I told you to write in the first place."

Himla Petana's eyes flashed dark in anger. "Ambassador, may I remind you that you are a commoner who is talking to a Countess? So I suggest you mind your manners."

Junea smiled. "Countess, may I remind you that you are a noblewoman who is talking to a commoner who has at her disposal a fleet of 1,000 battleships, a detachment of which is above our heads even as we speak? So I suggest you do what I tell you."

Himla Petana looked up at the ceiling and gulped. Then she said, "My apologies, Madame Ambassador. I see your point." She took out her scribing wand and with a series of swift motions changed the writing on the draft.

Junea said, "Thank you, Countess. So if there are no more questions, let's all sign the treaty and celebrate the coming of peace."

Aurora sat in her cell, reclining on the raised wooden platform that served as the bed. From the angle and color of the ruddy sunlight which entered the cell block from a small barred window at the far end of the row of cages she estimated that it was approaching evening.

There was a sound of a door opening and closing, and Field Marshall MacArthur entered the cell block outer walkway, followed by General Patton and General Pershing and another Earthling who Aurora recognized as Aaron Vardt. She gazed at the notorious assassin leader with interest.

The Generals stopped walking and drew themselves up in the Earthling military pose known as "attention." Field Marshall MacArthur spoke. "The prisoner will stand and kneel before the Supreme PIGME of the Imperial Grand Magnificent Empire of Kennewick."

Aurora did nothing.

The Field Marshall glared at her. "I said stand and kneel before the SPIGME of the IGMEK."

"I don't see how I can both stand and kneel," Aurora said coolly.

"First you stand, then you kneel," the Field Marshall explained. "Now do it!"

"Why?"

"Because I said so!"

"Insufficient reason."

Field Marshall MacArthur appeared flustered. He turned to Vardt. "Supreme PIGME. Allow me to have the prisoner raped, mutilated, tortured, and murdered. That will teach her not to show such disrespect."

Vardt appeared calm. "Please relax, Field Marshall. We are a civilized empire, a member of the Universal League. We don't do that sort of thing."

"We don't?" the Field Marshall asked, looking disappointed.

"No," said Vardt. "As Christians, we never abuse our prisoners."

Aurora was intrigued. "So then, what are you doing to Urania?"

Vardt shook his head. "There you go again, tarring us all with the same brush. The IGMEK has nothing to do with those people. They are fanatics, albeit well-meaning ones. We are reasonable people, and do not engage in such grotesque tactics."

"But you are willing to send thousands of children on suicide missions to be killed or mutilated."

"Of course. That activity is a legitimate part of the national liberation struggle."

Aurora could not follow Vardt's logic, or detect it for that matter. She decided to focus on his statement of greatest immediate interest. "So, if you are not going to abuse me, what are you going to do?"

"You will be kept in pristine condition and then burned at the stake as part of the entertainment at my official coronation."

Aurora nodded. She had studied Christian religious rituals and expected no less. However there was one detail about the proposed procedure which disappointed her. "You are not going to try me for witchcraft first? I believe I have a right to a trial." The point was worth pushing. Not that there was any chance of adjusting the predetermined verdict, but a witchcraft trial pitting her against these buffoons would have been fun.

"Certainly, Your Eminence," Vardt said. "You certainly do. In fact, as I understand it, it's already been done. Isn't that right, Field Marshall?"

Field Marshall MacArthur pulled a piece of tree-flesh out of his smelly green jacket. "Yes, Supreme PIGME. We took care of it this afternoon. We have the paperwork right here."

Vardt smiled. "Good, so we're ready to roll."

Aurora said, "So when will this happy event actually occur?"

"Next Sunday," Vardt replied. "One day after the treaty with the Minervans ceding half of Kennewick back to us goes into effect."

Aurora was shocked. She had known that an agreement in principle to allow the formation of a Kennewickian state had been reached, but she hadn't expected things to move this fast. She could tell by the grinning expression on the assassin leader's face that the treaty had to be a total disaster for the Minervans. Still, perhaps there were things she could do to puncture his bubble.

"You seem rather happy with the way things are developing," Aurora said.

"You bet I am," Vardt replied. "As soon as the treaty goes into force, we will wipe out the Minervans and then I will be Supreme PIGME of the entire IGMEK, stretching from the city line on the west side of town, all the way over to the city line on the east side of town."

"Today we rule Kennewick, tomorrow the universe," the Generals and Field Marshall chanted in unison.

"Why do you wish to be the SPIGME of the IGMEK?" Aurora asked.

Vardt appeared puzzled by the question. "Why? Well because as SPIGME of the IGMEK I'll be famous. I'll be able to reward my friends and punish my enemies. I'll be able to take whatever I want, and kill whoever I want. It'll be great."

"And how long do you expect these privileges to last?" Aurora inquired.

Once again Vardt seemed baffled. "Why for life. I'm going to be SPIGME of the IGMEK for life. It is a permanent position."

"Really?" Aurora said. "Do you really believe that the President of the United States will allow you to remain ruler of Kennewick?"

Vardt did a double take. "The President? What does the President have to do with this? I don't need to listen to him. I'm a much more important man than he is. Why, do you know that I have been invited to be a guest on the Kolta Bruna show?"

"Perhaps," Aurora said. "But his army is bigger than yours."

"Not so," Field Marshall MacArthur interjected. "We have more Generals and more Admirals than he does, and nearly twice as many divisions."

"Yes," Aurora said. "But my understanding is that his divisions are significantly larger than yours."

Vardt shook his head. "This discussion of comparative military strengths is irrelevant. The President is a Christian man, and all Christians are allies. Christians always help each other. We never harm each other."

"Those statements do not correspond to my observations," Aurora said.

"Well perhaps not, " Vardt huffed. "But as a pagan you cannot be expected to understand Christianity, now can you? In any case, we have been doing God's work, ridding Kennewick of pagans, and the President has supported our activity one hundred percent."

"Yes, but once we are gone, what further use will he have for you?"

Vardt stared at her. "The President is a Christian man, and will stand by his loyal Christian friends."

"Like he stood by the Peruvians? Like he is standing by the Mexicans? Like he stood by Lisa White?"

Vardt drew himself up in a dignified pose. "Lisa White was a traitor to Christians everywhere. She went in secret to the Weegee fleet and betrayed the positions of the Peruvian freedom fighters."

"No," Aurora said. "I was there when she appeared before the Princess. She did so as the official representative of the United States government, with the full approval and backing of the President of the United States. The images of the Peruvian assassin camps she gave to the Weegees were obtained by US military aircraft, acting under the President's orders. The President used her to deflect the anger of the Weegees from the US to Peru, and then placed the blame for the betrayal on her."

"That is the most preposterous thing I ever heard," Vardt sputtered. "In any case, Lisa White was not killed by official representatives of the US government, but by theology students who were acting entirely on their own."

"I understand that there are theology students here in Kennewick as well," Aurora said dryly.

"Yes, well we'll see about them." Vardt turned to his officers. "Come gentlemen. We have some work to do."

The three men strode out of the cell block.

Chapter 36

Sunday.

Gunfire rattled through every corner of New Minervapolis. Everywhere, different factions of Earthlings were firing on the Minervans and on each other.

Leading a small group of militiamen and junior priestesses, Colonel Iskander made a dash across the main square leading to the holy Temple of Minerva. Earthling bullets ricocheted off their tunics, pummeling them like fists. Iskander activated his disarmer, but the Earthlings had tenth class disarmer jammers, which delayed the disarmer's helibolt targeting system for several seconds. It was too long. Taking advantage of the extra time afforded them before their projectile weapons exploded, and the slow speed of their targets whose skates were jammed, the Earthlings scored two hits. A priestess and a militiaman went down, each shot in the head.

Then a high-velocity projectile ripped right through the robe of another of the priestesses, wounding her badly. "Change shielding frequency!" Iskander shouted. The Earthling's shield descramblers were obsolete, but sometimes they were fast enough to make the Minervan protective clothing penetrable. They had even been able to open transient gaps in the helidome covering the city and send several artillery rounds through. Fortunately most of the shells had fallen on their own people, but one had hit Minervans, and the carnage had been horrific.

Formerly the casualty ratio in battles between Earthlings and Minervans had been a hundred to one. Now it was a mere ten to one, and sensing the fact that they were finally inflicting appreciable casualties, the Earthlings were disregarding their own huge losses to keep coming, wave upon bloody wave. If it weren't for the fact that the different factions of Earthlings were spending almost as much effort slaughtering each other, the situation would already have become hopeless.

Iskander's company made it to the Temple steps and took cover behind the row of stone lions. The Colonel opened up a hypercom link to Major Pinander, commanding the Minervan heavy weapons unit. "Pinander," he said, panting to recover his breath. "Get some thumpers and squash the Earthlings in sectors 47, 84, and 102."

"But sir," Pinander replied. "Those sectors are Kennewickian territory. Under the treaty, we can't..."

Iskander cut him off. "Major, I don't give a pack of rotten raffa rinds what the treaty says. You squash those Earthlings and do it now. That's an order!"

"Yes sir!" Pinander said. Immediately several large areas across the plaza loaded with assassin snipers were smashed flat.

Iskander turned to the company's chaplain, Priestess Fourth Class Meliora. Since the company's captain was dead, she was its ranking officer.

"Meliora," he said. "I've got to go inside the Temple to report to Nendra. This company is to hold position here at all costs. If the Earthlings attempt a charge across the plaza you are to use the thumpers, is that clear?"

Meliora nodded. "Yes sir. We will not retreat from this spot."

An urgent hypercom call signaled from Captain Araster, commanding the sixth company, located near the Universal League compound.

"What is it, Araster?" Iskander answered. "Make it quick."

"Sir, there is a Weegee official here who is requesting we provide her military escort to the Temple."

"Who is it?"

"She says her name is Countess Danae."

Iskander thought for a few seconds. Weegee aid was their only hope. "See to it, Araster. Get her here as fast as you can. Use all necessary force to break through."

He turned to Meliora. The girl was obviously trying very hard to be brave. "Fear not," he said. "Minerva will stand by you."

"Yes sir," she said.

He gave her a quick hug and ran inside the building.

High Priestess Nendra was there in the central hall, praying together with all the Eminences of the High Council. Upon seeing Iskander, however, Nendra immediately descended from the altar.

"Colonel Iskander, your report."

Iskander activated a holomap, and quickly explained the situation. "Divine Eminence, we have withdrawn from all our nominal territory outside the old middle perimeter. I have companies stationed here, here, here, and here, with thumper backup units positioned in sectors 6 and 9. The IGMEK army divisions are located here, here, and here, and are advancing in force towards the Temple along these two vectors. They are being slowed down because they are also engaged in heavy fighting with two different groups of protorationals located here and here, as well as three mutually-opposed factions of Christian hyper-psychotics based here, here, and here. Also, an IGMEK General named Lee has split off from the main command and declared himself sovereign of the area south of 15th street. Generals Stuart and Jackson have gone over to his side. In addition, we've identified units of the US Army that have slipped into town and who seem to be raping and killing more or less at random."

"It sounds like pure chaos," Nendra said.

"It is. However Vardt seems sufficiently in control to press his advance against us and carry through with his coronation this afternoon. And as a result of the fact that his forces now have jammers and descramblers, however obsolete, our casualty rate is way up."

Nendra gulped. "How many have we lost?" she asked softly.

"I estimate over eight thousand. The Earthling losses have been ten times as great, but they just keep coming. The thumper batteries are now on their last reserves. We are being driven in towards less defensible positions, and our logistics will soon become untenable. If we try to hold on to the fish farms, we will lose the Temple."

Nendra's face blanched white. "Holy Minerva," she whispered. Then she seemed to gather herself and faced a woman Iskander hadn't noticed before who was sitting in the front row of the Temple pews. The woman wore the uniform of a Weegee Ambassador at Large.

"Ambassador Junea," Nendra said. "This peace treaty of your has turned into a total disaster."

"Only if you consider it from a purely local point of view," Junea answered. "In terms of the larger picture of galactic geopolitics, it has worked out quite well. In fact, I am informed that even as we speak the United States Army has invaded Mexico and is eliminating that entire nation of planet assassins. This is a huge step forward for incorporating the principle of self-determination of savages into an interstellar legal structure that will go far towards maintaining stability not only on this planet, but throughout the entire Southern Sector. You should really be proud to have been a participant in such an important accomplishment."

"But we are being wiped out!" Nendra exclaimed.

"Perhaps you should seek a non-military solution," Junea said. "I'm sure the Supreme PIGME will be generous if you agree to lay down your arms and accept his rule."

Nendra looked aghast. "If we lay down our arms, he'll have us all killed."

Junea waved her arms. "Now really, you have no proof of that. Give him a chance. He may well prove to be a wise and kind ruler."

Nendra drew herself up. "Ambassador Junea. The situation here has become untenable for us. As High Priestess of the People of Minerva, I hereby request that the Western Galactic Empire evacuate us from this planet without delay."

"I'm sorry," Junea said. "But I am not authorized to conduct an evacuation. You'll just have to make peace with the Earthlings on terms they are fully willing to accept. If you like, I would be happy to act as mediator."

Both Iskander and Nendra were speechless.

At that moment a contingent of Minervan militia entered the Temple central hall. It was Captain Araster and his company. With him was a striking young Weegee woman wearing the robe and tiara of a Countess.

Junea jumped to her feet. "Countess Danae," she said. "How nice of you to come."

"What's going on here, Junea?" the Countess snapped.

"The Minervans seem to be having difficulties using their old methods under the conditions of the new realities," Junea explained. "I have suggested to them that they consider using diplomacy rather than force, as the latter will no longer work for them now that the local military balance is more equal."

Nendra cut in. "Countess Danae, I beseech you. Please evacuate our people before the savages massacre us."

Danae turned to Junea. "You have refused their request for evacuation?"

Junea smiled. "I believe it would be better to give peace a chance first."

"Are you mad?" Danae said. "The Earthlings will exterminate them. If we stand by and let that happen, it will destroy WGE credibility forever."

"I'm sorry," Junea said. "But diplomacy needs to run its course."

Danae looked darkly at Junea. "As a Countess of the Realm, and as such ranking Imperial Subject on this planet, I order you to initiate evacuation operations immediately."

"No," said Junea. "I am Princess Minaphera's personal representative, and I have authority here."

Danae folded her arms. "Are you aware of the fact that the squadron of Battlecruisers orbiting this planet is under the command of my brother, Count Commodore Danatus?"

"That may be," Junea replied. "But he has been detailed to my command."

"We'll see about that," Danae said. She opened a telepsych link. "Give me Count Commodore Danatus."

There was a momentary pause. Then Danatus' voice echoed is the room. "Danatus here."

"Danatus, this is Danae. The Minervan defenses are collapsing. They need emergency evacuation. Initiate transport operations immediately."

Junea spoke up. "Belay that order, Commodore. We have no authorization to evacuate."

Danae said, "Danatus, we have to act now. If we don't the Minervans will all be killed."

"My authority comes from Princess Minaphera herself," Junea said, "and..."

Danae cut her off. "And you have betrayed her clear intent. Danatus, I am your sister. Listen to me. You know the Princess would not want the Minervans murdered."

"No, certainly not," Danatus answered. "What is the situation down there? Is Aurora safe?"

"No," Danae said. "The Earthlings captured her several days ago. She's probably already dead. It's up to us to save the rest."

"Why those dirty…" Danatus muttered. "OK, sis, what do we do? We need a large smooth area to land the transports. The closest one is Seattle."

Iskander broke in. "That's too far. But there are several hundred square kilometers of flat land nearby in this place called Hanford." He displayed his holomap to Danae. "Your battlecruisers could blast it smooth with their helicannon."

Danae looked at the map. "Right. That should work. You got that, Danatus?"

"No problem, sis. Will commence firing immediately. Transports will follow. I'll see you all on orbit tonight. Danatus out."

Seconds later there was the sensation of helicannon bursts followed by a huge thunderclap, as the massive batteries of the squadron's big guns rent the air only miles away from the Temple.

Danae turned to Iskander. "Colonel, I require more of your services."

"Anything Countess," Iskander said, unable to contain his gratitude. "I am yours to command."

"Good," said Danae. "Then place that woman under arrest." She pointed at Junea.

Aurora stood, hands bound behind her, on the flat platform in the back of an Earthling vehicle that slowly made its way through the jeering crowd. She was dressed again in her Minervan priestess robe and owl pendant, and the multitudes screamed in triumph as this representative of their hated enemy was displayed to them prior to her execution.

Earlier that day she had heard the helicannon blasts, and for a moment she had hoped that it signaled Weegee military intervention to save the city. But it was now clear that the helicannons had simply been used to clear a landing strip for evacuation transports. She could see them now, several miles in the distance, taking off and landing in an endless stream. The Minervans were leaving, and with them all hope of rescue.

The truck entered the plaza in front of the holy Temple. Aurora surveyed the area, which had once been the scene of happy Owl Festival dances. It was clear that there had been some serious fighting here. Several large areas were squashed flat with thumper impacts, and the bloody dead bodies of dozens of Minervans and hundreds of Earthlings littered the ground. But the delirious crowd took no notice of them. Instead they jumped up and down on the bodies of their enemies and fallen comrades alike screaming "Death to the Minervans! Death to the Minervans!"

The truck reached the center of the plaza, on which there was a raised platform. Aurora was lifted off the back of the truck and led onto the stage, in the center of which was a pole fixed in a vertical orientation. Aaron Vardt and Field Marshall MacArthur were on the platform, as were Generals Patton and Pershing. The three officers were all wearing elaborate uniforms with ceremonial swords and many glittering medals. The two Generals grabbed her and tied her to the pole. Then they started piling fragments of a murdered tree around her feet.

As Aurora watched in horror, a group of Earthlings passed a cage full of owls from the ground onto the platform, where it was hung on a pole above a pile of broken wood. They were the holy owls from the Temple! The Eminences must indeed have departed in a hurry to have left these behind. Now they were going to share her fate.

Aaron Vardt walked up to the input device of an electromagnetic voice amplifier and addressed the crowd. "Fellow Kennewickians, I give you the holy day of victory!"

The crowd roared its applause.

Vardt continued. "This is the greatest day in human history. On this day, the pagan invaders have been driven from our sacred city! On this day, the power of Jesus Christ has anointed us with the most glorious victory of all time! On this day, the Imperial Grand Magnificent Empire of Kennewick is officially established! And on this day, I, your divinely chosen leader, Vardt the First, shall be crowned the Supreme PIGME of the IGMEK!"

The cheering of the multitudes rose in mad triumphant waves.

"Death to the Minervans! Death to the Minervans! Death to the Minervans!" They chanted.

"Yes," Vardt smiled. "Death to the Minervans. They are fleeing, but our Empire will follow them throughout the galaxy and someday we will exact our full just revenge. However, through the mercy of Jesus, we have been provided today with one of the foremost pagan witches and all of their idolatrous owls through whose incineration we can celebrate the divine purification of our holy land!"

The crowd cheered wildly.

Vardt nodded to Field Marshall MacArthur, who turned to Patton and Pershing. "Generals," the Field Marshall said. "You may commence the ceremony."

Pershing and Patton each picked up a stick around whose end was wrapped a rag drenched in a smelly hydrocarbon fluid. They approached MacArthur, who withdrew a small metallic object from his pocket, which he manipulated with his thumb, causing a small exothermic chemical reaction flame to be initiated. The Generals placed their rag-sticks in contact with this flame, and immediately the reaction spread to the rags, growing an order of magnitude in size in the process. Pershing then turned and stood erect before her, holding his flaming torch, while Patton walked over to stand before the owls with his.

Field Marshall MacArthur said, "Gentlemen, you may commence the purification."

Each General knelt and solemnly placed his torch in the woodpile before him. Vardt placed his hands together in the pose the Earthlings regarded as representing piety, and the mob roared its approval.

Flames started to expand in the two woodpiles. The owls hooted in terror as smoke rose into their cage. Aurora felt the heat grow, and tried to will her body to resist the searing pain.

A siren wailed. It was the Call to Prayer. The transported multitudes of delirious Earthlings, from the humblest member of the mob to the Supreme PIGME himself, all fell to their knees and pressed their faces to the ground, praying in the direction of Washington. Aurora choked in the smoke as she tried to mutter her own prayer to Minerva.

Suddenly a truck roared into the plaza, approaching the platform at breakneck speed. Aurora gasped as she saw Hamilton leap from the back of the truck onto the platform, carrying in his hand one of the short swords the Earthling soldiers sometimes attached to the ends of their projectile weapons. Paying no heed to the leaping flames, Hamilton ran onto the blazing woodpile, and slashing with his short sword, cut her bonds with one stroke. Aurora fell onto the platform, and rolled clear of the flames.

Looking up from his prayer, Vardt saw what was going on. "She's getting away," he yelled. "Stop them!"

Patton, Pershing, and MacArthur leapt to their feet. Pershing rushed at Hamilton, who skewered him on his short sword, ripping it upwards to cover himself in a fountain of blood. Seeing the blood and homicidal expression on Hamilton's face, Patton took a step back. But MacArthur, who was huge for an Earthling, was made of sterner stuff. The Field Marshall drew his long ceremonial sword, and pointed it at Hamilton. "En garde, traitor," he said. Then Patton drew his long sword as well, and side by side with Macarthur, advanced upon the Ranger.

Aurora could not believe her eyes. Like a figure out of myth, Hamilton stood on the platform, using his short sword to parry the saber blows of the two large savage commanders. Thrust, parry, thrust, parry; the three combatants moved rapidly back and forth across the platform, the fury animating Hamilton making up for the fact that he was fighting two better-armed men at once. Then Vardt grabbed a large crossed staff, and moved towards a position from which he could strike Hamilton from behind.

Aurora launched herself at the Minister, knocking him to the ground. Then he rolled free and stood up, and lifting his cross back, prepared to bring it crashing down upon her.

Aurora had but an instant to act. Seizing the moment the assassin leader's center of gravity was farthest back, she stuck her feet behind his heels and pulled, sending him tumbling. Vardt landed on her blazing woodpile, which collapsed under the blow of his fall, engulfing him in flames. As the Supreme PIGME screamed, Aurora turned, just in time to see Hamilton knock MacArthur's long sword deeply into Patton, and then rip his own short sword back to sever the Field Marshall's neck.

Hamilton pointed at the rear of the truck in which he had arrived. "Come on, Aurora, jump for it! The prayer is about to end."

Aurora looked at the cage containing the terrified owls. "Just a second," she said. Picking up Vardt's cross, she knocked out the peg that was holding the side of the cage in place. The side fell away, and the owls, hooting gloriously, soared to freedom.

Aurora ran to the other side of the platform, grasped Hamilton's hand, and jumped with him into the back of the truck. Hamilton hit the rear of the driver's compartment. "Step on it Charlie!" he shouted. As the truck sprang into motion, Hamilton pulled a lever, causing a device on the rear of the vehicle to emit thick clouds of black smoke.

There was shouting all around them as the prayer concluded and the crazed Earthlings looked up to see their prey escaping. A few random shots ripped the air, but with the smoke blocking the assassins' view, all missed their target.

Aurora, however, was close enough to see what she wanted to see. She reached over and grabbed Hamilton, and ignoring the blood and the sweat, kissed him as no woman had ever kissed a man since Ariel expressed her love to Patroclus, the bravest and the noblest of the heroic sons of Theseus.

Freya stood by the landing strip, scanning the horizon for any late arrivals escaping from the city. As Acting Director of the Universal League Humanitarian Commission, it was her job to rescue all she could. In desperate hope she had kept one final transport waiting on the ground, pushing the time for departure to the last possible minute.

The commander of the detail of Weegee Space Marines who were protecting the landing area approached her. "Reverend Commissioner," he said. "It is time to go."

Freya looked at the Earth's star, which was now glowing red just above the western horizon. "No," she said. "We will go when the local star is hidden from view, not before."

The officer grunted. "That won't be long."

Suddenly, in the distance, Freya made out a machine. Her hope flared and then died, as it became apparent it was an Earthling truck. The officer saw that too. He spoke to his hyper com. "Sergeant Locratus, this is Lieutenant Critus. We have Earthlings approaching. Please be good enough to focus a thumper on that vehicle coming up the road."

Freya put her hand on the officer's sleeve. "No wait," she said. "I'm not picking up any hostile thoughts. Scan it for weapons before you squash it."

Critus seemed irritated by her interference in what was clearly his job, but he complied with her wish. Looking at his scanner, he shook his head. "No weapons." He reopened his hypercom. "Hold off on that thumper for now, Locratus," he said. "We'll let these approach. But stand prepared in case they try anything."

The truck pulled up to the landing strip, and a small Earthling woman descended from the side opposite the driver. She approached Freya.

"I am looking for Commissioner Freya," she said.

"I am Freya. Who are you?"

"My name is Melissa Berger. I have a message for you from someone you know."

Freya said, "All right. Give it to me."

"It is in my mind. She told me to tell you to look in the fourth quadrant of my outer mind."

Freya was surprised. This was certainly an unusual way for Earthlings to transmit messages. Curious however, she entered the Earthling's outer mind, and went to the indicated location, where she received an incredible surprise

Aurora was there, in the form of a psychic recording. "Speak," she told the mental simulacrum, initiating its sequencing.

The simulacrum of Aurora spoke. "Freya, my dearest friend. Please honor this, the last request I will ever make of you. The Earthling who stands in front of you is Melissa Berger, the Director of the Kennewick Children's Hospital. She has with her several other hospital personnel, including Nurse Susan Peterson and rescue vehicle driver Charlie Malone, as well as a group of thirty children who were injured in the course of the conflict in Kennewick. Please take them all to one of the Norc refugee planets. The adults are protorational, and while Earthlings, they have big hearts, and could do much good working for the Norc refugee agency. The children are insane, but with proper care, their minds and bodies could be healed. Please save them, heal them, and give them to kind Norc families for adoption. Thank you old soul mate, I know you will do this. With Reason and Love I embrace you. Your friend, Aurora."

Freya walked to the back of the truck and looked inside. She saw dozens of frightened Earthling children with big dark eyes, and an Earthling woman of middle years who was trying to comfort them. The woman wore a white uniform and had a kind face. Freya spoke to her. "Come," she said. "The transport awaits."

Freya turned and faced Melissa Berger, who had followed her to the rear of the truck. "Why did Aurora not come as well?" she asked.

"She says she has found a higher calling," Melissa answered.

Freya looked to the east, where the stars were beginning to come out. "Good luck, old friend," she whispered. "May Minerva protect you."

Epilogue

Aurora sat in the living room of the Hamiltons' house in Peekskill and looked at the odd piece of folded tree-flesh that had been handed to her by Mrs. Hamilton. It was a thing the Earthlings called an envelope, and used to contain messages that were meant to be transmitted very slowly. The front of it was addressed to "Alice Hamilton, 14 Pine Street, Peekskill, New York, USA." The rear contained what was known as a return address. This one read "P3C Urania, Inca Ruins, Peru." Could it be? She opened the envelope and examined its contents.

The letter read as follows:

"Dear Aurora;

I can't tell you how glad I was to find that you were still living here on Earth. Perhaps I could visit you sometime.

Allow me to tell you a little about my adventures since we last saw each other in LaGuardia Airport. I'm sure you heard about how I was taken prisoner by Earthling theology students, who cut off my fingers and toes and tortured me in the hope that they could thereby induce the galactic media to report on their cause in a more favorable light. I have to say that I did not enjoy this at all. However, fortunately, when the Weegees intervened to evacuate New Minervapolis they also sent a detail of Space Marines to New York to rescue me, turning much of northern Manhattan into a light-textured finely ground dust in the process. I saved some of this material, as I think it may have unique potential for use as an artistic medium.

Anyway, after I was rescued, your old friend Danae was very kind to me, and had the excellent Weegee fleet doctors restore all my amputated appendages. They offered me a ride back to the Northern Confederation, but I felt that someone needed to stay behind to protect the Inca artifacts, so I returned to Earth, this time traveling incognito.

I am now living in Peru, where I am taking advantage of the unique opportunity to study the Inca ruins in-situ. My data should prove invaluable in insuring accurate reconstruction when it comes time to relocate the ruins to a more accessible location at Anthropo.

You will be interested in knowing that despite being reduced by psio-ray bombardment over a year ago, many of the Peruvians are still alive. I protect the good ones from birds and lizards, and accordingly they worship me as a goddess. The bad ones, such as those who were members of the planet assassin groups formerly based here, I capture and torture at length in various ingenious ways. I do this not out of malice or desire for revenge, but to help instill proper values in the others and thereby discourage similar tragic misconduct in the future. This educational program may not work, since the savages are very stupid, but I do what I can, and anyway, it's fun.

If you get tired of living in Peekskill, perhaps you can move to Iowa. I understand they have an opening for a goddess there as well.

Please write me and tell me all about your new life among the Earthlings. Is it really true that you decided to marry your study specimen? You have to be the most dedicated scientist I have ever met. I deeply admire you.

So let's get together as soon as possible. It'll be great talking about old times.

Love,

Urania"

Aurora put down the letter and sighed to herself. Urania was such a flake. Still, it would be nice to have an old friend to correspond with.

Harry Hamilton walked into the living room and switched on the news.

"This is Kolta Bruna reporting from the primitive planet Earth. I am speaking to you live from Washington DC, the capital of the principal Earthling tribal despotism. The scene here today remains one of pure chaos, one week after an Earthling mob led by the so-called Radical Opposition seized control of the capital. The rampaging mob murdered all of the country's duly elected government leaders except for the President, who escaped by helicopter and whose whereabouts are currently unknown.

"According to the Radical Opposition leaders who led this coup, the revolution was motivated by the discovery that the many horrendous economic problems that beset this country were caused, not by the Minervan occupation of Kennewick, but by the corruption of the President and his cohorts in the ousted administration. The RO claims that this is proven by the fact that the nation's hyperinflation has continued, and in fact worsened, over the year since the Minervans abandoned their foothold here. Knowledgeable observers contacted by this news service dispute this view, however, pointing out that the Minervans, who have now reconstituted their settlement on the neighboring planet Mars, still have the capability to cause most of this planet's ills."

Aurora shook her head. Kolta Bruna would never give up.

The broadcast continued. "In other news, it was revealed today that former high-ranking Weegee officials Ambassador Junea and Commercial Counsel Fedris, after escaping custody on Cepheus, apparently sought refuge with the Eastern Galactic Empire. The Western Galactic Empire has demanded their prompt return for trial. However, according to Eegee Prison Commissioner, Her Eminence Gita, this will only be done after their brains have been dismembered for proper analysis. Inside sources tell the GNS that the Weegee government plans to accept this answer."

"Meanwhile, in the world of high society, everyone is buzzing about the upcoming marriage between Princess Minaphera and the Grand Duke Admiral Danatus…"

Aurora rose and excused herself from the room. It was time for the meeting.

She opened the door and walked down the steps to the basement. The girls were there, all twelve of them, Sally's brightest friends. They greeted her warmly. "Good morning, teacher."

"Good morning, girls" Aurora responded. "Now who here can tell me the true story of Mary, which you all were asked to study last night?"

Every hand went up. Aurora selected Karen, a pretty brunette of 16.

Karen began her narrative eagerly. "Mary was the mother of Jesus, of whom we read much in the New Testament. Mary was a goddess, and sent her son to Earth to teach us the path to wisdom. However, being male, Jesus' understanding was imperfect, and his teaching was confused. But fortunately, Mary also had a daughter, named Penelope, who wrote down her teachings exactly."

"Very good, Karen. And what," Aurora asked the class, "is the First Commandment of Mary as written down by Penelope?"

"Respect the Mind," the class answered all together.

"And what is her Second Commandment?"

"Seek the Truth, for the Truth will Set You Free," all the girls said.

"And the Third?"

"Accept the Truth."

"And the Fourth?"

"Reject the False."

"The Fifth?"

"Let Not the Herd-Mind Lead You."

"And the Sixth?"

"Think!" the girls shouted as one.

Aurora nodded. "Very good, girls. I can see you have all been doing your homework."

Karen raised her hand. "Yes, Karen?" Aurora said.

"Teacher," Karen said. "I have noticed that since I have started studying with you, that I can occasionally see what boys are thinking. Will I get better at this?"

Aurora nodded. "Yes, Karen, provided you study hard and discipline your mind to follow the teachings of Mary and Penelope, you will soon be able to read the thoughts of all boys all the time, as well as those of any girls who fail to embrace the faith."

The girls all looked at each other and smiled. The power a liberated mind gave to its user was a strong inducement to study. They would all work hard, and become not only believers, but missionaries, and innumerable other girls would want to join them. The new faith would spread. Eventually, even males would enlist in droves.

There was a loud crashing sound. Aurora recognized the noise as gunfire, three huge blasts. Alarmed, she ran upstairs to see what was going on. Sally ran right behind her.

Harry Hamilton stood on the back porch, his shotgun in his hand. The bloody corpse of the trespasser lay prone under the apple tree.

"That will be a warning to those crooks to stay out of my yard," Harry said.

His son walked over to the corpse and turned the body over. "Hey dad," he said. "It looks like you just nailed the former President."

"Yeah, I recognized him." Harry commented. "Serves him right. It's bad enough the way he raided the country's treasury. Now the bum thought he could come here and steal my apples. Well I guess Old Betsey and I showed him a thing or two." He kissed his gun tenderly.

"Good shooting, dad," Sally said.

Aurora turned and shooed the girl downstairs. It was all well and good for people like the Hamilton menfolk to go around shooting the President and others of his ilk, but she and Sally had serious work to do. If Earth was ever to be saved, its people would have to be taught to believe in Reason.

She resumed her place with the circle of young women. "Now girls," she said. "Who here can explain the meaning of these first six commandments?"

All the hands shot up.

Aurora smiled at her eager charges. With eyes as big and wide open as young owls preparing for their first flight, they were stretching the wings of their minds. They would make fine priestesses someday.

The young men of Peekskill would soon be in for some amusing surprises. While strictly speaking it was not the purpose of priestess training to enable such girlish pranks, the opportunity to indulge in them was a nice perk that encouraged recruitment, which was certainly in everyone's best long-term interests. In any case, Aurora knew it would be unrealistic to expect the acolytes to refrain entirely from using their newfound powers to rectify prior imbalances.

After all, they were only human.

THE END

About the Author

Dr. Robert Zubrin is an internationally-renowned astronautical engineer and the acclaimed author of *The Case for Mars*, which Arthur C. Clarke called "the most comprehensive account of the past and future of Mars that I have ever encountered." NASA has adopted many of the features of Zubrin's humans-to-Mars mission plan. A former senior engineer at Lockheed Martin, Zubrin is president and founder of Pioneer Astronautics, a successful space technology research and development firm. Zubrin is the author of over 100 technical and non-technical papers in the areas of space exploration and nuclear engineering, and holds two US patents. His other books include the non-fiction *Entering Space: Creating a Spacefaring Civilization*, *Mars on Earth*, and the hard science fiction novel *First Landing*. *The Holy Land* is his first work of satiric science fiction.

Commenting on *The Holy Land*, Zubrin said, "One of my favorite science fiction books has always been *War with the Newts*, the 1936 work by Czech humanist Karel Capek which ridiculed the appeasement policies of the great European powers. Looking around the world today, I think the charades associated with the current 'War on Terrorism' are ripe for similar treatment. Science fiction has an important role to play in such matters. Sometimes the truth needs to be made fantastical in order to be seen."

Dr. Zubrin lives with his family in Colorado.